The Blood of Roses
Volume 2
Jun, Eujasia, Mechailus

The Blood of Roses
Volume 2

Jun, Eujasia, Mechailus

Tanith Lee

IMMANION PRESS
Stafford England

The Blood of Roses Volume 2, by Tanith Lee © 2nd edition 2020. First published in hardback only, as one volume, by Legend, 1990, UK.

Cover Art John Kaiine
Interior layout by Storm Constantine
Cover Design and Interior Illustrations by Danielle Lainton

ISBN: 978–1–912815–08-1
IP0159

Author Site:
Daughter of the Night: An Annotated Tanith Lee Bibliography:
http://www.daughterofthenight.com/

Facebook Page for Tanith Lee's readers: Paradys Forum – Daughter of the Night – Tanith Lee

An Immanion Press Edition
www.immanion-press.com
info@immanion-press.com

Contents

un

Book Three

Chapter One

From the first seed, which fell like a burning moment of time into the hot soil of the beginning, the forest was. Long before it became shadow and substance, and covered over the land, it was a condition of the land. In the earliest days, when men made their way between the slender stalks of it, its bones no wider than sticks, they spoke of it as the great wood. It breathed with winds, wove like a spider a tangle of undergrowth, gave birth out of its loam, was a hive of hidden life.

And when the forest had grown tall, dense and constant, so that trees might fall and not be numbered, the soul of the forest was strong enough that what passed through it or took refuge in it made offering.

At first the offerings had been random. What died there left its decay, its skeleton, its cooling blood. Trees grew from the spines of foxes. Out of the dead cups of human skulls the pines went up.

It began to be that these gifts of building were anticipated.

As though the trees had whispered of a need.

There were those who lived from start to finish in the great wood, never saw another place and disbelieved what they heard. Was not the world one whole forest, perhaps split here and there by waters, and yet the trees grew in the waters too, and only mountains lifted, and the mountains were clothed in the forest.

The forest was mother and father, womb and grave, living and extinction. They worshipped the forest, for, being all things, the forest was also God.

In the spring evening, the Chosen, Jun, sat on the ground outside the Woodman's hut, playing with the hare. The hare was nearly white, a spirit like albino of the forest which came in the afternoon or at dusk to drink the milk put out for it. Sensing, it seemed, that the boy was also special, the hare allowed him to pet it, and would jump over twigs that he held out, or toy with a grass rope. Sometimes the Woodman would ask the hare questions, and the hare would demonstrate its replies by particular movements, or the shape of droppings left on the edge of the clearing. Now and then a spotted snake would also cross the clearing, and the Woodman took note of its track. Latterly, the Woodman too would ask Jun to do certain things, such as selecting from a scatter of objects in the hut or answering a riddle. By now Jun was empowered: as he had approached the God day by day, he had waxed more magical. To touch Jun brought a blessing, but very few came to the Woodman's clearing, which lay below the Tree. The Woodman was the intermediary between the supernatural and the people. The earth there was galvanised, wondrous and danger-filled.

Very soon, several hundred would come to the clearing, but that was different.

From the clearing, in winter, and in spring when the lesser trees were only starred with green, it was possible to behold the Tree, the Lord. It towered up, smooth and purely black. It looked eternal, and so it was. The first tree of the forest, it had spawned every other, of every kind. For the Tree was not of one kind only; even the child could see this for himself. From the huge trunk, the limbs lent out like a crown of snakes, and the leaves, though some were like needles, were fleshy and silken, while others were heavy flags with long veins and ribs in them. The Lord never lost foliage, even when the snow came. This the boy had seen for himself as well, for he had lived here in the Woodman's hut all winter, under the Tree.

The Choosing was in the late summer, after the garnering and harvest. Male children of nine or eight years were brought to the Woodman, from the hutments round about. Even from the Landholder's estate in the valley they were brought, unknown to the master. He was a convert to the religion of the Christus, the tree-god in other form. Misunderstanding the truth of sacrifice, the Landholder would not countenance what went on in the wood, turned a blind eye to it. His forefathers had come to witness, and at certain eras, when required, had themselves taken the Woodman's part – even once given a son. This was no longer conceivable.

The nearness of the Lord Tree to the estate, once the reason for the construction there of a landholder's house, was now awkward, and strange.

Perhaps prudence had caused the snake and the hare to make no choice of boys from the valley.

Of those picked out, a careful scrutiny and interrogation was performed, both by the elder men of the hutments and by the Woodman, their priest. The child must be virgin, must not even have set hand to himself. He must be perfect.

Jun was nine years. He had been worked hard, but never beaten with a rod. Sexual desire of any sort had not yet found him. He had no scars, no irregularity or deformity. He was a quiet boy, with an oval face and thin well-made body sheathed in white skin.

He wanted the honour and the bliss of the Chosen as much as any of the others, but he did not aim at it, did not brag or show off, or make anything of his beauty. There were three other sons in his household; he could be spared. The grace of his choice would see the family favoured. Only the woman wept a little. They usually did.

He did not mind going to live with the priest Woodman in the clearing. It was a wonder. It was the road to Heaven.

For half a year then he was between the God and the world, drawn ever nearer to immortality. He was treated gently, fed the very best, given nothing to do that was not pleasant, instructed in secret rhymes and spells whereby to prove himself at the instant when God took hold of him. Nor, obviously, did he fear that moment. He had been taught it was a commencement, not an end. He would be enhanced, changed, lifted up where the pine tops balanced sun, moon and stars. They were a brotherhood, all those that went before him. He would become the forest; he would become the God. Even the hutments knew that. No, Jun did not fear.

The hare ran across the glade and bowed once to a reed which grew there.

The Woodman stepped from the hut and asked Jun if the hare had bowed.

'Yes,' said Jun, and the Woodman, who had been kinder than Jun's father, smiled at him.

Jun had been in awe of the Woodman. He was perhaps more respectful now, for through the months Jun had watched his priest carry out sorceries both harmonious and unusual. He could call beasts and birds and seemed to know their speech. He had caused a hemlock tree to burn with a still blue flame that left it entire. In lesser ways, the Woodman entertained the child, making items disappear and reappear, or altering them to a semblance or actuality of life – an axe that chopped their wood, a bowl of beans which made patterns... The awe had been enriched by love and trust. A son among a crowd, Jun had never properly known how to love before. In this cocoon between two worlds, there was a margin to find out. The Woodman, now his father on earth, who would give him into the hand of Forever...

'And which animal do you think,' the Woodman said now, 'will you want to be the first?'

Jun knew that once he had become a part of God and the forest, he would be free to experience and to do all things.

'A hare,' said Jun. 'I'll be a hare and run here to show you.'

'Do that,' said the Woodman gravely. 'One who went before you, long ago, he came to me as a raven, and told me a word of the other life – but not much. He wasn't allowed to tell too much to me, I being mortal still.'

Jun was jealous of the raven. 'I'll tell you,' he said, *more.*'

'No, you'll think as the God does. Don't mind it. I'm glad for you, the joy and strength, the happiness you go to. Of them all, my best.'

The shadows lengthened, as they lingered there. The mighty umbra of the Tree came down and put its blackness upon them. They were silent in the midnight pool of the Tree. Neither had reason to disbelieve. It was only that the priest knew that the child might suffer, somewhat, before his transformation. Yet it was the price. He himself would have paid it, to be what the boy would be. He was sad to see Jun go. He would look for a black hare with beautiful eyes.

'Tonight,' he said, Jun's protector, 'we begin the last teaching. In seven more days, your day will be here.'

'Truly?' The boy was eager. He forgot the priest, reaching forward with sudden spiritual desire, for godhead, sanctity, *power.*

His death began at first light, when the Woodman roused him with a warm hand on his brow. There was a cup of holy stuff to drink, a wine manufactured from crimson and brown buds of the wood, the flowers of its floor. Jun did not know what the drink was, did not query. After he had taken it, the enormous half-sickening excitement in him quieted, and a marvellous new emotion, nameless, enveloped him.

The Woodman washed Jun in a tub in the hut. Blossoms were crushed in the water, which had been heated. Jun's body was rubbed with aromatics of the pines. He was clad in a goatskin, which had been dressed and was soft on his flesh. Jun felt joy, not knowing quite what joy was.

Outside, there was a mist brushed on the clearing. The sky had a high greenish light.

Two young women came across the glade, and between them, without speaking, set a garland on the boy's dark head. There were wild roses in it, he could smell their scent, and cones from the pines, ferns, asphodel.

The two women went away speechless, and the Woodman came, and led Jun over the clearing by hand. (Only once, Jun looked back, hoping to see the hare. But never mind, he should play with the hare as a brother soon enough.)

Outside the clearing, there were people packed between the trees, and as still as the trees, standing up straight like the trees. Jun had never seen this before, since no children but one attended, and no woman who had not born a child. Jun glanced about, for his mother and the man who had sired him, but he could not be sure. The mist veiled everything, and his eyes did not focus normally, and anyway, he did not care.

The Woodman led Jun lightly, steadily, up the slope. Towards the Lord of All.

Not once had Jun gone to the Tree. It was forbidden. Only the priest might go close, might *touch*. Sometimes he made simple offerings on behalf of his people – carved bone, fruits of the harvest, never, never blood.

They reached the tree.

It was like the whole world.

It was the meaning of the forest, and of being.

A pillar, dividing sky from ground.

The child looked up the length of it, fearless in joy, and saw eternity in the tower of its blackness, in the serpent boughs that flew from it, the wings of leaves and needles. Its colour was perhaps green, but then again it had no necessity of hue, or even texture. It rang and boomed with an immensity of silence and in its immobility was volition. An axis.

These matters the child understood without words. He gazed and was dazzled, felt the God already stretching out.

'Jun,' said the Woodman, tenderly, 'Jun, you must stand here, and let them put a hand or finger on you. Will you do that? For their sake?'

Jun nodded.

He waited in the whirling stasis of the God, and dimly was aware of the fingers and hands on his breast, forehead, arms. A procession passed him. Probably he had known some of them. He was already transfigured. No one expected anything else.

After a while, the procession dwindled, and then it had gone back into a circle, surrounding the Lord, and leaving the Woodman and the boy alone there.

The priest held the hand of Jun.

'My best, do you trust me?'

Jun nodded again. He smiled.

'Drink this,' said the priest. There was a tiny polished acorn which he put to Jun's mouth. Jun swallowed something that surprised him; it was bitter. He blinked, and the priest said swiftly, 'Now you may go and embrace the God. When you do that, you'll be gone from me, and from us all. There may be pain, but that will soon be over. Do you see?'

Jun smiled again. The priest turned him, and there was the pillar of God. It burned like the flame in the hemlock, but black as a winter river. Jun went slowly to the Tree, and lay against it, and put his arms about it. Then he felt its heart, he felt its *life*. It was as if he grasped the centre of all things, the pivot, the fountainhead. He loved the Tree. He gave himself to the Tree.

Far away, someone had torn the goatskin. A sharp thin stinging blow came on his shoulders and was repeated. It was repeated many times.

Jun felt but did not feel the smart of the briars striking him. He was absorbed by the Tree.

Even when there was another pain, twining his head, curious and startling – he half made to think of it, could not – for neither did this concern him. Only the Tree. Salt fire ran into his eyes, and tears welled out between the lids, so he closed them.

Fire was coursing down his arms, his feet burned wet.

Jun rubbed his cheek against the Tree, and pins of pain stabbed his temples. But then the Tree had gripped him. The Tree pulled him upward, incredibly, by his arms, up and up into itself, into the hub of the world…

Miles above the earth, the child hung, and tipped back his head. He did not bother to look. He was suspended in ecstasy, of which the pains of his body were becoming part.

Above them, the spectators at the sacrifice, whipped and crowned with his second wreath of thorns, the perfect boy swung from the cords of the pulley that bound his wrists. The veins there were already severed, as were those at his ankles. Blood trickled scarlet down the whiteness of the briar-blemished body, down the inebriate and sacred pallor of the face, and splashed the diverse structures of the leaves. His full weight was on the ropes. From the pressure of that, the innocent phallus had engorged. The sight was cruelly exquisite, not obscene or even shameful. It had nothing to do with human lust. Already he gasped, stifling on the ropes. The blood went out in bursts, rocking to his struggling heart. If he knew anything anymore was not obvious. The God hovered in the black canopy of the Tree like an eagle descending.

Gradually the worshippers fell to their knees, or full-length on their faces.

The agony in the Tree excluded them. They could only offer it. They were envious of Jun, they loved Jun.

The Woodman stood dreaming, proud of the accomplishment, the glory to which he had sent the best of all the fair and good.

An hour after the sun was up, a gold round in the sky, the wild hunt came over the hill and into the grove where the centre of the forest and the world of the forest had root.

Groups of the congregation were still present; some had paused to catch a trickle of blood from the leaves, which was allowed them, a terrible and divine undertaking. The Woodman was under the Tree, keeping vigil, his old eyes shut. He was an elderly man; this might have been his last officiation. So much was now certain.

The riders of the wild hunt were a storm of green and reddish brown, like levels of the wood itself. In the midst was a purple raven flapping on a square cloth. Immediately they were known, and the people separated from the Tree, flung off from its aura. No longer devout but screaming in fright, they tore down the slope into the pines, where some stumbled, or were chopped to the ground by the clubs of the pursuers.

The Landholder reared in his stirrups, roaring. He was calling them vile and profane things, in the name of the Christus. The grove of the Lord Tree seemed blasted, singed. And the Tree itself had gone to immeasurable distance, leaving merely its emblem, but the Landholder, under his Raven banner, mistook the emblem for the Tree and railed against it. There was a white-faced riding Christus priest too, frothing at the lips, shrieking of Hell, damnation, pits and traps.

Then the noise broke into pieces. They flew off and went to nothing. The elderly Woodman was staring up from beneath the Tree, staring up blind at the Landholder. One of the rough soldiers of the Landholder had driven a sword into the old man, directly through the heart. The Woodman died moment by moment on the blade, shaking his head, sighing.

The Landholder glared about from his horse. The whole grove seemed to have turned red with bleeding and cloaks and rage. So he shouted again.

'You see? I've put a stop to it – your bloody barbarism. I warned you! I told you. No more. Did you listen? You listen now. I'll bring you to the true God by my sword. I'll save you from Hell by steel and the rod. I'll have you, I'll have you, you filthy, godless excrement.'

Mailed men were dismounting. They stood attentive. As this happened, the Woodman was pushed off the sword and curled to the ground. The soldiers kicked at him, and laughed, and the Landholder bellowed: 'Shut your row. Do you see that child up there? Hung like a bit of butcher's meat – God's cross...'

And the priest shrieked awful curses, till his throat cracked.

Then the Landholder pointed out who should be striped with the rod, and he sent the soldiers through the women, hacking off great raping swaths of their hair.

'It's over,' said the Landholder. 'You'll give no more of your boys to that abomination.' He looked round, and there were his men, with axes ready. 'Cut down their Tree,' he said. 'Cut it down, make it into kindling. Fire it.'

There were no more cries. Now the silence was complete. It was the ending of the world. Pointless to resist.

But a sound came, impossibly, of the first axe upon the Tree.

The Landholder turned his horse abruptly and cantered along the slope. His priest sat there a minute longer, gnawing his mouth, then he too made off.

The soldiers, the dregs of twenty places, paid by the Raven Lord, loyal to the Christus, leered and hurled their axes at the Tree, while the red and white child depended above them.

The forest people free to do so escaped. They ran away. Those who could not averted their faces. They escaped as best they could.

The sun was going up the sky. The thudding of the axes went on like hurt in a wound. The trunk of the Tree was like iron. It would take hours to fell it. The soldiers blasphemed the Tree. They took intervals to drink, and to possess three of four of the comelier women left behind.

Conversion to the Christus had scoured the topsoil of the forest from the soldiers of the Raven garrison. In a stone house in the valley, they took the body and blood of the God, and forgot those similar rituals their progenitors had acted. The new God was more stern in some sort, yet also He could be fooled. You had only to confess, and to pay – in a fast, or a coin – and He forgave you. With the old God, so a part of them vaguely remembered, forgiveness was not anything to do with it. Wrong was wrong. There was no blame, the God did not sob at your sins. But if there was a punishment, you could not buy it off. It was like life itself. Like birth, like breath. Inevitable.

The giant, black and freakish Tree began to give way in the afternoon.

The grove was puddled by tawny lights, and the differing foliages of the tree shimmered with them.

The men had long ago stopped glancing up at the hung child. He was dead. They would have to get out of the path of him, when the tree came down. Then give the brat a proper burial – the Landholder had vowed it – up here, in pagan ground.

The men did not look forward to that. They had done a great deal of killing. Few of them had killed little boys, and never in the foul, disgusting manner of the sacrifice. (They had violated the women particularly viciously, for their wickedness in attending here. The men who had been beaten lay on the turf motionless. It served them right.)

Suddenly, as the sun started to dip into the western sea of the wood, shooting through every intervening bough in showers of chrysolite, the Tree twisted from the axes and turned around upon its riven base like a gargantuan wheel. It seemed to take the measure of the grove, deciding if to go towards the south or the west, the sun's death.

The soldiers leapt away, shouting.

The architecture of the Tree, like a beam of the sky, stroked slowly sidelong with a deceptive smoothness. It met the heads of the pines, a young oak, and smashed them into splinters. From the forest below, against the dying blaze of a sun now entirely visible, birds went up in breakers, calling and trilling. Every tree left standing seemed to give out its creatures like a cry. The undergrowth rushed, and a cold wind passed over.

The length of the Tree, the long beam of Heaven, struck the earth.

The ground shuddered. It *moved.* From a hundred hidden valves and vaults, a murmur rose, and faded in the air like smoke.

Then came nothingness. It was like the stopping of a heart. The whole landscape seemed hollow.

One of the soldiers stamped his feet noisily. 'That's done.

Where did the corpse go? We'll have to have it out.'

The boy had gone with the Tree and the pulley and the ropes away into the sunset, downhill. The spume of leaves and birds was sinking there. It had happened none of the captives lay where the Tree had fallen.

The lines of ebbing sunlight shone across the smashed grove. They lit the levelled stump, and one at a time, the soldiers turned to see it.

The hybrid Tree had had huge rings, the centuries of its liveness inscribed within it. They were uncountable, so many. Each ring bled. It was ichor, it was blood, in the dying light it was red.

The Landholder's men stared at this phenomenon, the bleeding of the Lord Tree. They found out, glimpse by glimpse, that the ruined grove had been splashed and dotted by blood. That they themselves were dappled. That their axes and their hands were crimson.

The blood bubbled up from the stump. It poured over and spilled into the ground. The countless rings of the Tree were no longer to be seen, the blood had obliterated them to a lake of ruby, gleaming back the sunset.

As the framework of a thousand victims had blended with the Tree, grown into it and become the Tree, so their blood, feeding it, had filled the Tree. It was vegetable, but also flesh. Tree, but also man. But also God.

A vessel deep inside the severed trunk erupted.

A fountain of blood sprang into the sky, high as (once), the great Tree, a pillar of fire by day… But the last sun shrank into wood and the sky was an opal, and the fire of the pillar of blood sprayed across Heaven and came down again, drenching the grove beneath.

The soldiers ran screaming, and the horses, tearing from their tethers, raced out with them, neighing and voiding themselves in fear.

The country about was another land. As if a wall of glass contained the grove.

Men and beasts vanished as a second wall of darkness ascended from the earth.

It rained in the night. There was a cloudburst. The forest flooded with sounds of water. Things washed away.

After the rain, the sky was clear, and the stars cracked with cold, shrill light.

When the Christus priest should come, quavering with his cross and faith, in the morning, nothing would speak of anything in the ancient grove but the debris and black stump of a fallen tree.

The punished peasants would have made off; that was to be expected. The corpse of the Woodman, and the child, too, they would be gone. Plainly the peasants had taken these bodies.

The Landholder would hunt the people of his woods for months. He would get slaves. He felt some onus on him yet, to make straight the way of his God. It would require two years of putrid luck, rotten harvests, disease and small terrors to cause another thought to enter him, like a thorn under the skin.

The child had not been dead, at the moment of the Tree's severance. Dying, adrift... As the life began to wash from the Tree, Jun lay at the brink. He was the Tree's possession, had been given to the Tree, had given of himself. When the Tree fell, Jun was smashed also, every bone of his body snapped, dislocated, and the skull fractured. Jun did not die then. Most of Jun died, and left him there. And the spirit of the Tree, its thunderous, endless power, which was the forest, and the world as forest, entered in.

To Godhead all is possible. Where the psychic dimensions overlap, a million angels might dance upon a pin: the teaching of the Church of the Christus.

As the steel rain sluiced the grove, the body of Jun mended itself carefully, piece by piece.

When the eyes of Jun opened, in the starry night, something looked out of them that was not boy and was not tree, having slight memory, having no specific aim or longing.

When the body of Jun arose, and walked away between the walls of the wood, there was only one last impulse, like the faint taste of wine left in an empty cup.

It was the impulse, therefore, which went down into the clearing.

The soldiers had also, on a brief sortie, knocked flat the Woodman's hut, meaning to return and burn it. Anything of worth they had looted, but there was not much. A charm or two the forest people had already taken to comfort them, as they had absorbed the cadaver of their priest. The rest of his dwelling sprawled under the injured trees: shorn logs and turf roof, a table in four parts, the tumbled stools and broken vessels.

The pale hare, which had come for its milk and not found it – only outcry above in the grove – came back in the starlight, as if searching. It glowed in its pallor, turning its head, its long forefeet raised, steepled ears listening. When the other hare appeared, the albino retreated nervously. The second hare was stronger. It was dark like the darkness, and propelled itself in a hesitant silky lope. The coat of it was rough as leaves or needles. It rustled as it moved, like the forest overhead. Its eyes were the eyes of a human child.

The white hare darted away.

The black hare went haltingly about the wreckage of the hut.

No one was there, no hint to allay the sunset of a memory.

The black hare lifted to its hind limbs, in the posture the albino had adopted, copying. Then it *shifted*. Like a cloud over a moon. The child stood up from the cloud. Jun who was not, now, Jun.

And the child who was not Jun, that went away into the night.

Chapter Two

The hostel kept for travellers by the religious women was a dismal affair, cheerless and cold. Godbrother Orro was sorry for it. The snows, which had vanished from the forest, lingered in the stone walls, the fireplace with its trickle of flame and few grudging, thin and unencouraging logs left by. The Church instructed that they should be hard upon themselves, but not, surely, on the poor benighted travellers who must seek this haven? For himself, Orro was used to the comforts of the brother house at Timuce. The family Esnias, that owned the land in the forest, had built the brother house and the chapel there on the forest's edge. The ground was full of Esnias graves. A pious and belligerent household. And busy. In return for its support, the priests must be prepared to obey the Esnias Tower, besides the Church, let alone God. Vre Esnias had decided that the Hermitages and Domas of his woods should come under scrutiny. He selected Orro for the work. Such tasks normally devolved from Khish, but Orro had not argued. Vre Esnias was suing for pardon from the Church Fathers at Khish, for a feud murder of an overly violent and publicised nature. Everyone must help. But uncomplaining Orro, in his fiftieth year, had found the spring journey difficult. He took this out on no one. Where he discovered laxness, he mildly upbraided, and where repairs were needed, he only prepared a report for his Vre. Perhaps the harsh Handmaidens here might be persuaded to more altruism by the gift of some slight luxuries.

A vicious scratch on the door announced that the Administress had arrived.

Orro bade her enter, and in she came, an ugly warty woman full of resentment and dislike. Though eschewing a mirror, she had cherished the image of her face in her mind. Hatred of God was what had driven her to worship Him. She was a Tower daughter and had refused a marriage; the man doubtless had looked askance at her.

Orro spoke gently.

'I've been writing here. Certain items should be sent you, for the upkeep of your charity.'

'Vre Esnias is godly,' she snapped. (Esnias was not her Tower.)

'Please sit,' offered Orro.

She took the unfriendly chair – he had been making do with the rheumatism-inducing stool. She folded her ugly hands and flashed a bitter, unconscious glare at them. She said, 'There's another matter. We want your help sorely. I wondered if you'd see for yourself, but of course, you are so *burdened*...' She bit her sarcasm off. Who more than she could be burdened, but who bothered with *her*? 'In your painstaking efforts for Lord Esnias...'

'Something's amiss?' said Orro. He was used to this. There always was something. 'Can you tell me what it is, sister?'

'I hesitate.'

He waited.

Presently, her hands opened a little like fly-eating flowers. 'Godbrother, our two novice sisters... You must believe me; I don't put any faith in demons. God is too strong. However, the weak and fallible...' She broke off again.

After several long pauses, and a pair of promptings, she informed him the two novices had come under demonic influence. They themselves had conjured it, but it grew palpable, they gave it life and vitality. The older women were afraid.

'What form does this influence take?' he asked. He had heard this tale before, indeed since his beginnings at Khish. As for the woods, the pagan ways were still prevalent, and the isolated villages rife with stories of ghosts, unusual creatures, changelings and sprites. Already, not far from this sisterhood, he had been regaled by fantasies of a werewolf in the vicinity. Obviously, with the winter, there would have been wolves about. But the villagers insisted that a beast had prowled the forest there for generations, part wolf, part man. They left it offerings in a glade, and the offerings were always taken. Orro's innocent comment on the gratitude of polecats and rats was not heeded. He blessed the village, but their charms against wolf-men were not removed. On an oak tree by the glade of offering, wolf skulls hung in rows, decorated with tarnished ribbons, mummified blossom.

'They say,' said the ugly woman, 'an angel appears to them, in the wood. At first they hid their foolishness, only giggled and wept over it. Next our sister Resa accused them of spying on some peasant youth who went bathing in a pool nearby. This they denied, and then came out with their notion.'

'An angel,' said Orro. 'How strange it is. We credit that the pure and holy often saw such things, but always in the past. What is immediate makes us suspicious. And yet we suppose, don't we, sister, that through the Christus the chance of miracles remains?'

'Yes, godbrother,' she said. He perceived that she did not suppose this.

'Then again,' he amended, 'caution is essential. Truth will prove itself despite our doubts. Did you wish me to talk to your novices?'

She said that she did. Really she did not know what she wished, except that someone be chastised for something.

He anticipated the two girls might be pretty, or else ugly and unwanted like the Administress – envy or frustration a contributory cause, something like that. But they were very ordinary young peasant girls, healthy, shoved into the order to please God, not because they could not have attracted husbands. Then again, it was the peasants who leaned fervently towards the supernatural. It turned out (they spoke freely), that this image of an angel was mostly a redepiction of the myths of childhood. The angel was the god of the wood, a being they reverenced and made sacrifice to, and who, represented by a virgin youth, had, a century ago, been sacrificed in turn, the forest over, to keep the bond of blood between the trees and the people.

'It was dusk,' said the younger girl, who was brown haired, an uncommon fairness that perhaps her village had not liked, 'and I'd been sent to fetch water. I was frightened. It's not good to be in the forest after dark. And I knew that I mustn't say the rhyme my mamma taught me, only trust in the Christus, so I prayed. Then, when I looked in the water, I saw something white and gleaming. I looked, and there was a naked man. He hadn't a stitch on him.' There was neither prurient interest nor disdain in her voice. 'But his hair was long and black as the wood in the dark, and he had black wings. So I kneeled down, as he was an angel. I shut my eyes and asked what I should do. But when I looked again, he was gone.'

The brown girl confided in her fellow novice. Next evening, they contrived both to be out. And for some evenings after, since he did not at once show himself again.

'Why did you think that he would? If it was an angel, surely once would be enough?'

The girls were puzzled. Orro beheld they reasoned to the peasant format; the forest was itself based on repetition.

And sure enough, the god of the forest returned, and each girl saw him. The second girl said she did not see any wings, only a sort of shadow that went up at his back. But he shone like the moon.

Thereafter they were granted their vision six or seven times, usually at dusk, or sunset. But once the darker girl, going out in the early morning, saw a whiteness passing through the pines beyond the chapel. That had been the angel, too.

A light-hearted, self-congratulatory hysteria grew up between the girls over the vision. When it broke the surface of their chapel, and Sister Resa put in her word, they were shocked and enraged. They had seen plenty of peasant youths, clothed and unclothed, enough to know them from an angel.

'And no other of the sisters has been privileged, as you have, to witness this?'

No one else, they said, was sent to and fro in the wood as they were.

He could believe that. They were young and hale, the rest of the women getting on.

'Tell me,' said Orro, to whom talking had been easy, 'why do you think, yourselves, a divine sight was vouchsafed you?'

They could not find the words. But from their faces he read an absolute: they were fresh and full of credulity and faith. If the Christus had hung before them on his Tree, with wounds of roses, they would not have questioned, only bowed down. The Administress would have demanded an explanation.

'Lord, I beseech you, deliver me from evil and from the sinful waste of my own unwisdom...'

Orro prayed, properly, on his knees, hurting and discounting it, in the chapel of the sisterhood. The plaster of the walls was chapped, like the skin of their hands. One should ignore the flesh, but surely, surely, if the flesh were ill-treated, it became clamorous. An iota of kindliness stayed the flesh in quietness. It would be good, if allowed. For he detected that the most devout and godly, of either gender, had been the well and happy. Lust might be put aside, but the headache, the chilblain – ah, they were the very Devil. God did not always require martyrdom. Sometimes He wanted, simply, love.

Orro examined his love of God at the altar in the forest. He thought, *I shall go out. Let us see. Will their demon manifest before a man?*

He did believe in demons – of the mind and of the earth, both. Anything was possible, the world being like damp clay, able yet to take an impress of all powerful things.

When he was done praying, he stood up, and rubbed his hurting knees. He had healing hands, even for himself, and soon walked to the door and looked out.

The sun was setting. The sky was like a lake of glimmering clouds, warm and cool, settling softly, unfearful of the night. Birds played, and the trees shook themselves. But the pines were already black at their hems.

As he crossed over the yard, he glimpsed the lighting of the candles, and heard the sisterhood arriving at the chapel for its devotions. The two novices would be with them. They had directed Orro, guilelessly, as if to oversee an assignation with an approved lover – but it was not actually like that.

Orro, leaving the buildings of the sisterhood, felt for a moment a predictable misgiving. He had felt it before, on the spirit-searches and werewolf investigations of the previous months. He hoped Vre Esnias enjoyed colourful reading...

The forest, where it took up its weave beyond the chapel and the wall, was now quite black. There were the ghosts of shapes, like mirages, not reassuring. The nights were cold, warning the waking leaves and buds of another winter of judgement to come. Yes, the forest was repetition.

He reached the pond, at the correct moment, as the dusk started to swell, a vast blue bulb. The pond was clear, fed by a streamlet which sprang down into it. Save for the ruffle of this entry, the water was a blue mirror.

Orro waited against the trees. He was not frightened, but apprehensive – yes. For all the mundane or imagined nature of prior events, he sensed this moment was not of that order; something had happened, did happen.

There was a glow at the corner of one eye. At first he took it for a trace of final light cast aslant. Then he realised, and moving his neck slowly, he turned and saw. An avenue opened between the trees. At the end of it, perhaps thirty paces away, a figure stood against the black curtain of the inner wood.

It was not like the ghost-shapes which the first twilight had formed. This shone, like ivory, and as solidly.

Orro looked, steadfast, blinking now and then, for his eyes had begun to water, from tension, or some other thing.

He determined gradually the body of a young man, unclothed. The hair of the head was long and black and burned out into the darkness of the trees. The hair at the loins was black. The eyes and brows were an impression of blackness. The face was shaven. The figure was totally couth. It could not be assumed to be anything average, explainable.

As Orro watched, the man moved, and was coming forward along the path, towards the pond.

Orro had an urge to be gone. It half surprised him, how forceful a hold the situation had got upon him.

There were no wings. That was an illusion, probably to do with the black mane of hair on the darkness... With a start, the priest saw that the wrists and ankles of the young man were circled by wounds, which still bled.

The god of the wood. There could be no doubt. The god of pagan belief, in his role as sacrifice. Each year they had slain him, and then, at harvest, he was born again, chosen, blessed, adored, given back to the trees and the earth in thanks, after the winter drew away... But these practices were no longer common. The Vre at Esnias had muttered about a neighbour, the Raven house of the Korhlens, saying spring sacrifice went on there, for all their parade of a new chapel, a priest, and offerings to the church at Khish. But again, Esnias did not care for the powerful Korhlens. One did not always do well to leap at such bait. Besides, the pagan rites were so often represented in small ways or wedded to the rituals of the Christus. Who did they see upon the cross of wood, the peasants of the forest, but their old god again, the perfect scapegoat, flawless and dying in consent, to set them free of sin and sadness? Orro suspected that at Korhlen the act, if done at all, was managed symbolically. It was not always practical or compassionate...

The young man, white and black, passed Orro.

From his body, which was indeed unblemished and beautiful, and that of a man about nineteen years, an odour came like the growing of the leaves, bruised grass. Pinecones were caught in his hair, tidily, a garland.

He was by the water, and on the water he reflected.

Orro felt a tightness in his chest, he was cold, and there were tears in his eyes. It was like a vision. He could not confuse it with anything sacred. It was profane, yet so completely pure neither could he resist it.

He found himself thinking that the being must evaporate. But that did not occur. The god of the wood went about the pond, and into the threaded loom of the trees on the far side. The light was going out, and only the night and the wood caused a vanishment.

It would be sensible therefore to say, *This is some questionable joke that the local people are perpetrating against us.* But Orro did not say this, inwardly, or aloud, on his return to the Doma.

The ugly woman came in and sat before him with her hands held tight one to the other. She was eager as a hound. He dashed her questioning at once: 'Your two novices are quite innocent of any blame. Some slight penance may be set them for wilfulness, but they're very young. There's no wrong been done. I'm sure you'll be glad to learn my verdict, sister.'

She was not and said she was, prim in disappointment.

He could guess she might write to the Vre at Esnias, complaining that Orro was a sentimental slacker, moved by youth when duty should be paramount. He doubted Esnias would pay much heed. 'As for this thing they have seen, yes, I attest to something, but I don't classify it as demoniac. It asks investigation, however, and some restriction here. Please send neither your sisters nor novices to get water in the early morning, at sunfall or after dark.'

She said she would abide by his ruling. Now curiosity had hold of her. She knew she must be meek and circumspect, but she tried vigorously hard to elicit from him the features and type of what he had beheld. Orro did not satisfy her. He left her wanting, and she was used to that. She accepted frustration as a familiar, poor wretch. He did not relax until she had gone.

'None of you should be afraid. God has us all in His hand.'

They looked at him dubiously. It was ridiculous to say such words, and yet there were no other means whereby to address them. They understood the idea of religious parlance. It consoled them even as they mistrusted its assurances.

'Bring your ordinary weapons,' said Orro. 'I believe you won't have to protect yourselves, except in the most routine sort.'

One said, after a long hiatus, 'But it's always been done, godbrother. And then it leaves us alone.'

'Since my great-grandda's time,' said another.

'Before that,' said a third.

Orro had already gleaned from their speeches and asides that the wolfman, and their offerings, had been indigenous in this area of the wood, and in other areas surrounding, for a hundred years. It was very likely. Pagan acts had been universal then, and the Christian ethic a force rushing in a narrow river through the trees.

'Because something has gone on for a long while,' said Orro, 'does not make it right. If you've been in error, let's correct the mistake.'

They grumbled, but he was there before them, the tangible aspect of the Christus. Had the wolf been there, speaking to them, it would have gone another way. What if the wolf did speak, then? No. It was doubtful the wolf would be able to do that.

Orro had put facts together in a fine mosaic. One heard stories of the woods. Children left to perish in the forest by parents who could not feed them, adopted by a family of wild creatures, growing without the human estate, into strange versions of the fox, the wolf.

The rumours of the wolfman, the sight of the naked boy, though they did not marry, yet they were a pair. It had come to Orro, through a mysterious and instinctive process which once or twice had assisted him in the past, that the god of the wood was in some form a symbol of the soul of that which ravened and raved about the villages of his previous visiting, the fleshly werewolf god, to whom the offerings were made.

The villagers were uneasy at Orro's reappearance, and his request. Before, his tampering had irked them. Now he wanted them to go out with him, to seek, to hunt the wolf. He insisted that it was not supernatural, save in the most finite manner. They could not argue. Orro represented the Christus, and the Esnias Tower.

They moved under the oak with the decorating wolf skulls. It was midday, the pine forest bright and dark green, slanted with sunlight, a warm and hopeful day. Alders at the stream were clung with beads of emerald, and the immature birches that had insinuated themselves bore feathers paler than apple skin.

The grove opened, the glade with the severed trunk, and the (new) offerings lying there, already scavenged by birds. A cloud of finches went up at their approach with scraps in their beaks.

The men stood about, with their primitive spears and knives, and Orro with his crucifix and his priest's habit, glancing this way and that. Did the wolf truly dine here, at the trunk of the tree? He went forward and examined the spot more thoroughly than he had done before. There were long scratches on the side of the offering table, he had taken them for marking and weathering of the bark... Across the glade from the trunk, something dully red showed up in the fern. Orro went to see, and found a rabbit's pelt, torn wide like a purse, and the money of the flesh devoured. These remains were left for him like a signal. With what would he have to deal? Orro did not allow his former nervousness to sweep through him. He had no choice. It was not a matter of feelings, but of conviction.

Orro beckoned one of the men. He was a hunter of the village, supposedly capable of tracking a beast to its lair – they had boasted of the wild pig he had got them. Now, he was shy, reluctant.

Not a word was exchanged. He knew what the godbrother wanted and pushed on through the bushes beyond the glade. He had not brought his two dogs.

Orro, not perfectly confident of the man, had already begun to search for symptoms in the fern and creeper. Suddenly a kind of track came visible to him, patent as if it had been carved against the trees and through the undergrowth. Of course, it was not quite animal.

The pines darkened and closed in, a night in day. Green twilight flickered with points of sun.

When the hunter started to prevaricate, Orro knew that they were now approximate to the wolf-place.

Orro was not afraid of wolves. It was spring, game plentiful. Winter was their murderous time, or when a madness came upon them, as with men.

Orro waved the hunter back. 'Stand there. I'll go on alone.'

'But godbrother, the signs are muddled here...'

'No. They're so clear even I can see them. You and the rest must remain. Be wary. You're not to run away. But I excuse you this.'

Muttering again, they fell back. They were like figures cut from wood, mossy, with the points of sun catching their eyes. They did not move.

Orro went between the trees. They shut behind him and the wooden figures were gone. The ground ascended to a ridge, where a stone outcropping pushed clear of the earth. It was thick with an ivy mantle undisturbed for years, save at one juncture. The entry into the rock was black. A coolness and stillness hung down, enclosing it. Somewhere a bird trilled, as if beyond a wall.

The priest climbed up towards the cave, and saw a bone lying in the tree roots. It was not human, a hare's from the look of it. There was a wolf stink about the cave, not very strong. There was no other smell, but that of the forest, its buds and liquors. Orro had been awaiting the stench of a man.

'God be with me, put over me His mighty shield. I am not alone. Even in the midst of foes, You are with me, Lord, if only I believe.'

The words of the prayer whispered, soft as the touches of the pines upon each other, and Orro stepped up, and looked in at the cave-mouth.

There were no wolves, had been none for several decades. Old relics of their occupancy, the continued practice of their kind, had kept their odour and their aura faintly attached.

The thing which slept on the floor of the cave was a twisted pattern of dark and pallor, snakelike, fearful.

Orro's comprehension hammered in his chest, with the shaken protest of an ageing heart.

As if the noise of it went out into the drum of the cave, the creature there stirred.

From the shambles of blackness, paleness, the snake neck turned. A mask was raised.

Through a black mass of hair and beard, like some showering out of the trees, the tangles of the fern and briar, the white face of a man rose on the air, as if disembodied, floating like a moon, and the black eyes met Orro's, directly now. They were not the eyes of a wolf, or a wolfman. An adamant intelligence informed them. It was this, and not the terror of the wolf, or the halfwolf, which caused Godbrother Orro to withdraw himself. He moved about ten feet down from the rock opening, and there, in a trance, he heard himself speaking softly, calmly, to sooth and charm: 'Come out, come out, now. I won't hurt you, and you mustn't harm me. God is with you, brother. Come out.' He had been so primed with what he must say, how he must not startle or incite, that now the words flowed from him. The will of Orro had made him still, had made him stop and attend the emergence of this thing from the wolf cave. But Orro himself was helpless. Inwardly he prayed to God for understanding, and his heart beat at him.

Then, perhaps in answer to his voice, or simply because it was the hour when it must be, what he had called came out of the cave.

At first, he came out as a wolf. On all fours. Orro had heard of this, and that the legs and arms in such a case were deformed, grown into unnatural shapes to accommodate walking and running as a beast. But next, the wolf stood up. It stood as a man. There was no deformity.

What Orro saw, though, was peculiar enough. As the ivy mantled the rock, the long hair mantled the man-thing; it was a cloak, and through the fabric of it Orro saw the naked slender whiteness of the body, the bones of the face. In the cloak of hair was the young god of the wood, the being he had watched at the Doma pond. Orro had known this would be so.

His prayer had been blind. It was sometimes inadvisable to theorise, to question, or to understand too much. Faith, not understanding, was frequently the key.

The young god of the wood poised on the slope, looking down at him.

Orro said to him, 'Will you speak to me? By the grace of God, are you capable of it?'

For several moments the face of the wolf came back, and then the hair of the face seemed to fall away, and Orro glimpsed the shaven face of the other twilight. This might have been a passage of shadows, for a little wind blew through the pines, all the motes of sun shifted, and returned.

'I speak,' said the wolf, or the god, or the young man of nineteen years on the slope. 'What shall I say?'

Orro was stone, like the rock. He could not have moved or shouted.

'Do you want me to tell how I hunt? How I catch the black hares and break their spines, and feast on the red meat? Or the ermine in the snow? On the streams where I drink, and the water like the jewels from the pedlars that the women wear in the villages? Or the mailed men I see who ride about here? Or the men who cut down the trees, and the trees where they hang the dolls and skulls? Or the ones like you are, who worship a tree crossed over with a single bough?'

'Dear merciful God,' said Orro. 'How long have you lived this way?'

The young man smiled. Orro could tell that he smiled because of the eyes, for the beard – which had come back with the wind's fall – obscured the mouth.

'Years to ten numberings of ten,' he said.

It was the way the peasants sometimes counted. Ten of ten – one hundred. One hundred years. The boy was crazed. He was twenty at the most. Besides, he could not have lived in this manner for more than two years. For he could speak, articulate, his voice came from him fluidly.

It was not a smile, more scornful than a smile.

For generations, the wolf-haunting, the offerings.

Faith – not theory. It was not wise, yet, to understand.

'You,' said the wood god, 'are like my other. He was a priest. You remind me.'

Orro shivered. And the wind blew again.

He said, 'We must take you from here. Do you remember your village?'

'Gone,' said the young man.

Villages of the forest died, as people died. In two years... possibly...

'Will you come down?' said the priest, courteously.

'Why?'

'I'd like to take you somewhere that you can be cared for.'

'I care for myself.' The wolf said (how had he thought the wolf could not speak?). 'I live on blood.'

'Come,' said Orro persuasively. The Devil was here, that he knew. The Devil, and the elder things. Now, in this instance, the elder things had not joined innocently with the Christus, they were apart, wicked and insuperable. Only through the Christus could this fallen creature be salvaged.

Orro found that the boy had begun to walk down the slope, lightly. His face was utterly expressionless. There was no ferocity.

I will take him to the men. Dear God, they mustn't run. There will come a moment, perhaps when he sees their village, or when I try to take him inside a hut – he'll panic and want to escape. The power of evil too will attempt to wrest him away. I shall need the men to help me.

The boy followed the priest along the uneven ground. Orro did not make physical contact with him, fearing that this might stimulate him to flight to violence. Orro walked a pace or so in front. The boy walking after him was like a burning flame at his right shoulder.

Through a gap in the pines, Orro saw the village men standing where he had left them. They beheld him at the same instant.

Orro moved into the open avenue, and let the boy come up with him. As Orro stopped, so did the boy.

He isn't a boy. What I saw by the water – his soul, some emanation of him – old as parts of the wood. Can it be? A hundred years?

It must be left to God.

Firmly Orro made a peaceful gesture to the wooden men below. To the creature from the cave he said, 'Now will you come down with me, go with us to the village?'

'They won't allow it.'

'Yes, if I ask it of them.'

'Why do you want me to go with you?'

'For your sake,' said Orro. He said it urgently, not meaning to. The boy laughed, but it was a wolf's growl. Something left over, he *had* lived with wolves, he had learned of wolves… 'Your name,' said Orro, 'do you remember?'

'Yes.'

'Will you tell it me, and let me use it?'

The men had not run off. They were watching the priest talking to the wolfman.

'Jun,' said the boy.

Orro thanked him gently and went on towards the men.

They stayed put, they only stared. They continued to stare over Orro's burning shoulder as Orro spoke to them.

'The Christus instructed us to shelter the homeless, to care for them. This is no demon, but a man. Do you see? Here in the daylight but bereft of everything. Now, you'll help me.'

Why did the beast from the cave have no smell but the smell of the wood? No scent of animal or man? No sweat, no foul breath from blood and marrow? Healthy and often in water, did that account for the absence? Even the flesh of women freshly bathed gave off aroma.

'He speaks,' said the hunter from the village.

They had seen it. It frightened them more than anything else. Were they right to be frightened, more clever than the priest?

The men were sidling, they were circling round, making the priest and the boy the centre of a ring – cornered.

'No,' said Orro. 'Don't…'

Just then the boy, unseen behind him, let out a snarling, slavering roar. Spit from his mouth struck the side of Orro's face. It repelled him; it was hot and fresh.

There was a whirlpool. Orro was knocked away from it. He staggered and turned and saw the boy on the ground, frothing and kicking, long jagged claws lashing out on hands and feet and the white teeth bared to bite. Wolf in a snare. The hunter had magicked the scene into life. He raised his spear to strike. Their placations and offerings were forgotten. They would no doubt decorate the skull...

Orro threw himself between the hunter and the boy, and flinging up one arm, cast off the spear. It was a passion like the ecstasies of joy and grief in childhood. Orro did not reason with it; he knelt over the horrid, foaming, Devil-possessed monster on the ground. The soul – the soul, beautiful and reasonable, shone from the black amber of the eyes.

Orro laid one hand, healing, on the matted hair, the low wide forehead, the second healing hand upon the plunging heart.

And the Devil went out of Jun.

His body uncoiled and melted flat among the ferns. He turned his head into the curving cupping hand of the priest and was asleep.

They remained at the village for only two days. The atmosphere of nervousness and wrong-being was highly charged. Gods, demons, should keep their place, like men.

The boy, however, all this while, was docile. He sat or lay quietly on the mattress in Orro's hut, eating the stews and gruels Orro brought him, as if he was accustomed to cooked meats from which the blood had been leached. He was not sick and did not need any nursing. Exercise he must have missed, but he was patient about that.

Orro told him, 'Tomorrow at sun-up, I'll take you to the chapel, the house where I and my brothers live.'

The boy looked at him. Orro had trimmed his hair and, using fat and a razor, had shaved him. A whole face emerged. To Orro's hands the boy responded with repose. There was no danger, it seemed. To Orro he seldom spoke, and then in fragments merely. The wolf was leaving him, though during the first night he had crouched by the hut door, staring up into the treetops and the moon. The ancient youth of the wood was leaving him too.

Perplexed, Orro beheld a man usurping the creature which had been surely more fascinating, yet terrible. It was the man who must be led forth, to God. For the extraordinary soul, what priest could doubt, having gained some inkling of the purposes of Heaven, that it had showed itself in such dark glory as a promise of sanctity. Within the frame of animal corruption, as in the past, there flamed a chance of something marvellous, greatness, saintliness, a warrior of God.

Jun loped beside Godbrother Orro's mule. Without escort they traversed the green paths of the forest. Spring was pungent. Now Orro was not troubled by any fear the beast would come to divide Jun from him. At dawn, midday, evening, Orro would kneel to pray. The young man would kneel by him, copying what Orro did.

'You learn swiftly,' said Orro, filled with rare rich happiness.

'I've prayed before,' said Jun.

Of course, the way back to the truth was always simple, if no resistance were made.

At Timuce, spring rain netted the stones of the brother-house, and beyond, the scrawl of village wavered in smoke and water.

The Administer sat in his chair with the cushion of red velvet, and Orro stood before him on his tired and aching legs, not bothering with them.

'The Vre should be entertained by these notes of your journey. You've been most thorough and written with some wit. But this, about the boy...'

Orro watched his Administer acquiescently. The rule of obedience was ingrained. One must not disagree, for in the end dissent was futile, and God moved all things as he would. Nothing was ever lost. Even the fall of the sparrow... 'I see, godbrother, you have some audacious notion of wrestling for his soul.'

'That's true, Administer. If I'm impertinent, I will step aside. But someone should do it.'

'My friend Orro, your modesty – no, you're to be commended. By all means. I give him into your charge. I'm much impressed by what you've already wrought. My only doubt – it seems the boy must be, perhaps, a little simple in the mind. His years as a beast in the woods tell against him. Oh, not in his demeanour, which, as I've seen myself in the past ten days, is exemplary – astonishing, under such circumstances – but this idea of longevity, to which you seem also to subscribe.'

'Administer, maybe Jun is speaking in other terms than mortal time.'

'Yes?'

'Of spiritual time. The years of darkness – how can he measure them? If he's in some way unhinged, that too is at the root of a strange holiness.'

The Administer regarded Orro. The Administer was very fond of the older man, his favourite among the brothers at Timuce. Orro's humble erudition and sweet, nearly naive, piety, delighted him. With another man, the Administer would have looked warily and long at this unison, the wolf boy and the priest. But Orro did not have the sins of the flesh. Or, if he had ever had them, they had become for him irrelevant as the hairs shaved from his face.

The boy, in himself, was remarkable.

Clothed now in the habit of the novice, going daily to tuition in the Scriptures, and to the devotions of the priests, he behaved for all the world like the son of some wellborn family at Khish (better than the barbaric boys of the forest Towers). It was scarcely credible that *this* had snarled and ravaged about in the trees, tearing rabbits with his nails.

'You believe, Orro, that God himself has selected this youth?'

'I daren't think I know so much of God, Administer. And yet, haven't we a score of saints who came from bizarre and awful beginnings, out of the sinks of the worst crime and depravity? As if the Devil himself had cauterised them in earthly fires. I think I do believe that Jun, who evidently was a pagan from the oldest heart of the forest, has been brought to the Christus, and that I, probably through chance, was made the instrument of it. I'm glad not to relinquish him.'

The bell of the Timuce chapel tolled. The Administer got up from his chair, and together he and Orro went to the glass window edged with blue crystal.

Looking out, they saw the courtyard in the rain, and through the rain, the brothers were passing to the chapel for midday prayers. Behind came the novices. Last of all, Jun walked in his dark habit. The hair was cut to the nape of his neck, shining like a raven's feather in the wet. He seemed to have walked across the court to the chapel a thousand times.

The other novices were frightened of Jun. He gave them no reason, and no attention. Orro had seen Jun in the chapel, before the ebony crucifix on which hung the Christus, crowned with the thorns of agony, his hands and feet pierced by the nails of death. Jun *knew* the Christus. Somewhere in the black of the emblematic hundred years of the wolf forest, Jun had become the possession of God.

'Forgive me, Administer. I must go down, or I'll be late.'

'Yes, go then, godbrother. For your report to the Lord Vre Esnias – it shall be sent today.'

The Administer at Timuce watched Orro's hastening figure appear in turn below on the court. His rheumatism was bad now, and he limped when hurrying. This would have been the last long journey he would make. For the report, the Administer would himself command alterations, without vexing Orro. Orro, anyway, as compliant as he was, would never object. He argued only in debate, but then so masterfully one was pleased to find him harmonious elsewhere.

It was only over the wolf boy that the Administer was to exercise caution. The rumours of a werewolf were to be left in to titillate the Vre; he was to learn too that a peasant lad named Jun, who had shown a vocation, had been accepted as a novice at the brother house. The lurid, intriguing and fervid passages concerning the "angel" at the Doma pond, and the speaking animal from the cave, these were to be excised. The Administer, who accepted that God moved all things, thought that men were also capable of a great deal of locomotion. The Vre at Esnias, a drunken rioter, on his knees before the priest one minute and out killing enemies in the woods the next, was not a fit vessel for the pouring in of such a tale. God knew what the Vre would do with it. God knew what upheaval such speculation and such dreams might set alight.

Orro himself would benefit from the omission, for the story suppressed would leave the brother house serene. Orro's orphan might then grow as best he could, to a nonentity or to a prodigy. As God willed.

In the evenings, after prayers and supper, the novice, Jun, would go up with Orro to his cell in the brother house. The cell was a room of some capacity, and full of books. It had a brazier too, in which hot charcoal sprinkled with herbs sent up a restful smell. Here, at a table, Orro taught Jun his letters. The boy's progress was like much else about him, his character, and apparent modes of thought. He could, by the fifteenth day of scholarship, read. Thus he read, forging on, seemingly privy to the ideas held inside the words. Then would come a sudden block to mental activity. The least taxing phrases became incomprehensible. When this mood fastened on Jun, he did not turn again into a wolf. Yet he became a *shadow*. Orro could see before him then a wooden man, like and unlike those the villagers had represented, below the wolf rock. Orro abided these breaks, these goings away. To reclaim, he must be a practical gardener. That his plant grew so fast at other times was a wonder.

Tonight, Jun read fluently for one hour. The text concerned the Commencement, the world unformed and forming, the paradise on earth, the Man and Woman, the Serpent and the Tree. Already Jun had been tutored in these portions of the Book. To Jun, maybe, the Garden of Eden was the forest; how else might he picture it? (In the same way the children of the wealthy in some city might visualise Eden as the walled garden of some well-to-do house, with paths and arbours, and the trees in pots.)

Sometimes, when Jun had read, Orro would talk with him, concerning the subject. It had appeared at first to Orro that Jun came to theosophy with a brain uncluttered by the trivia of life. And yet, Jun's brain was full, if not of the trivia then of the minutiae. Jun did not reveal that he had inhabited with men, save once, in childhood (when there had been the other, pagan, priest, of whom Orro reminded the boy, or so the boy had seemed to imply; he did not really refer to this era, merely it was occasionally to be glimpsed in a thicket of other things). But, living so long apart from humankind, yet Jun had seen them, watched them, knew their capers, and had kept within him their speech. Then again, he did not entirely have, beyond a phrase here and there, the idiom of the peasants, did not properly speak to any pattern. This alone would make it simple to form his expression, his syntax, in the mould of the brother house, which was to the good. It was the language of debate and prayer. Clarify outward communication, and inner meditation could only improve.

As for the knowledge of minutiae, it was, too, benign. If Jun had for ever and only come from wolfishness, what would the concepts of Man, Woman, God mean to him beyond flesh, *blood*, the elements, fate – those very forms which a priest must cleanse away.

The room was rosy from the brazier, and the books of old leather, some polished and one or two with glittering crusts of gilt, made it soothing to Orro. On the wall the wooden cross and the Christus were less stark, less tortured.

Jun's eyes (from a lifetime of acquaintance with dark eyes, the most general of colours, Orro saw in Jun's eyes a blackness that was different), Jun's eyes rested on the cross.

Orro had never inquired of Jun if he wanted anything other than to be a priest. The priesthood was to be Jun's salvation and release; you did not ask whether or not a starving man would choose to eat and drink.

'Will you tell me how you picture the Garden?' said Godbrother Orro.

'The world,' said Jun, 'before it was spoiled.'

'And there were many sorts of trees, were there not?

Jun smiled, just a little, without mockery. The child in him, still dimly there, answered a memory of the Woodman under the grove. But now, a man a hundred years of age, Jun did not respond in words.

Orro tried a second question, to see if the adult intellect could make its leap. It seemed to him the spring for this was inherent in Jun. 'You've been taught by the brothers about the life of the Christus. If I were to ask you how it is that the story of the Garden could become the story of the Christus, what would you say?'

'The Garden,' said Jun, 'is the Tree. Men are imperfect. One must be chosen who's perfect. He is God. The sin is the sin of loss, the separation from God. God becomes man to bring men back to Him. The Christus dies on the Tree. His blood rains on the ground from the wounds in His hands and feet. The blood's to be drunk. The power of God which can't die enters with the blood into man, and the separation is over.'

Two emotions, perhaps three, went through Orro. Each was sharp, almost stunning.

Initially it seemed to him that never before had he heard the truth of death and resurrection, the pity of the human Fall, its redemption, so adequately, so profoundly stated. But, at the same second a shock came over the priest. For he grasped that this was not the orthodoxy of the Christus which was being presented before him, but the ancient pagan religion of the wood. Orro had always acknowledged the inevitable association of the pagan rite of recurring sacrifice to the mystery of the death and rising of the Christus. Never before had he seen it conjured in this appalling image – for Jun, the Christus *was* the god of the wood. A fragment of the elder hierarchy, one of millions, a branch of a colossal Tree. The Christus was wondrous, but nothing new, or special, inviolate and unique. The Christus, for Jun, had always been, always worshipped, a festival of sacrifice and a gift of blood. For *this* reason, Jun came to the Church as though he had always known it. And it was wrong, was horrible, fiendish – for the seed was the wood, and the apogee, the sunrise, were the Christus – not, *not* the other way about.

'Jun…' said Orro.

And Jun gazed at him, the never-before-seen colour of black in his eyes, the face pale and lucid, nearly empty.

'The Tree,' said Jun.

The charcoals in the brazier settled, and the light fanned up the planes of the room, as light and shade fanned through the forest. The wood, walled outside, had got in.

The third emotion which had begun to well up in Orro took hold of him firmly. It was terror, nothing like fear, vaster than he was, seeming to push his soul up halfway from his body.

Vines grew over the plaster, webbed the ceiling, clusters of leaves hung down. The books were buried in the leaves, a spotted snake went rustling through… Behind the plaster stood the pines in upright rows. In the midst, in the air, the crucifix spread out its arms. It became a tree, tall, opening a multitude of boughs, like an oak, a pine, a tower. The white god hung from the tree and the scarlet jewellery of his blood rained on the ground.

'No,' said Orro, hearing himself from far off, 'the Devil is here.' He began to pray. His voice was so faint and dry. A stupendous silent roar was issuing from the wood.

The face of the god on the tree was not only Jun's, but a million faces, among which he could not find the forgiving beauty of the face of the Christus, the truth and the way.

When Orro regained consciousness, his room was vacant but for himself.

The reading book had been laid neatly aside, with its marker in it. Nothing was overturned. The brazier cracked rosily. No vines, or serpents. The wood had retreated.

Orro got up and went to his crucifix and kneeled down. He could not look at the crucifix. He shut his eyes.

'Lord, *what am I to do?*'

Chapter Three

It was at midsummer that, arrangements completed, a novice of the brother house at Timuce set out on a journey southward. Letters had been exchanged. The approval of the Esnias Tower had been sought and freely given. The novice, a scholar of unusual aptitude and expectations, was to join the novitiate of the Church at Khish.

On the morning of the departure, the Administer at Timuce received the novice, Jun, in his chamber above the chapel courtyard.

The Administer sat in the sunlight and watched the sun bloom in its turn on the young man.

Jun was quite marvellous. He would do them great credit, and if he rose high, no doubt he would remember their kindnesses to him. In the few months of his residence at the brother house, the Administer had found himself increasingly impressed, compelled. Observing Jun, and interviewing him from time to time, as was necessary, the Administer had come to believe – if not all Orro's flight of fancy, then very much of it. Strangely, as the novice progressed through victory on victory of learning, dedication, intellectual brilliance, it was Orro who had stepped aside. The Administer never asked why. This would be like Orro, to labour earnestly for such a pearl, and then humbly to leave it to the best ministrations of others.

'And today you start your journey,' said the Administer to Jun, who stood before him burning white and black in the sun's rays. 'A long ride, I regret. But you're prepared. At Khish, you'll be amply rewarded.' The Administer extolled the priestly library at Khish, the religious building and its ornaments, the clarity of its teachers, and its connections to the city of Chirkess, and to all the vaster arms of the Church Paternal.

Jun, at the appropriate instant, thanked the Administer.

'I shall be happy to learn of your successes. Perhaps,' said the Administer, 'you'll write to Godbrother Orro.'

Jun bowed his head, raised it. With such sparing, graceful mannerisms, the young man – who had been a wild beast – conveyed his intentions. His script was refined, also. There would be no problems in reading his letters.

The Administer prayed with Jun, blessed him, and sent him forth.

It was a shame Orro's health was so poor. The mission which had given up this astonishing treasure had otherwise not done the elder brother good.

When the star had gone away, the Administer went down in person to visit Orro in his cell. The godbrother had a summer fever, and had been excused all but the midday devotions, over which he fretted; they had only been able to keep him in his bed by the warning that his morning and evening cough disturbed the others at prayer.

'How are you doing?' said the Administer. In Orro's reddened eyes, he thought he saw the grief of Jun's going. 'He will do very well at Khish.'

'Yes,' said Orro, 'very well.'

For a while his hot dry coughing racked the room. Presently, he said, 'I should like to make confession to you.'

The Administer was surprised.

'There's surely no need – you'll have confessed at the normal times...'

'I have, but I left out, always, one item. I must confess it to you, because you won't believe me, Administer. Another confessor might have done. Besides, it's now too late. I alone will carry the sin of its secrecy.'

'My dear Orro,' said the Administer, 'you know quite well that you'll be well and hearty in a week or so.'

'Probably. But let me do this.'

'If you insist,' said the Administer. 'I can see it's troubling you.' He went to the bed and made over Orro the sign of the cross of the Christus. 'In the name of God, our Lord and Father, and of the Redeemer who upon Himself takes all our transgressions...'

'It is my fault,' said Orro, 'my grievous fault. I was afraid of being thought a liar, or a fool. Or else afraid of being taken seriously. Jun,' said Orro, 'is a demon.'

'Orro.'

'No, not the Devil. I think not the Devil. But out of that torrential army of Hell, an angel, a prince come on the earth.'

'Orro, your malady…'

'Excuse me, Administer. Not my malady. I'm powerless. I can't do anything. I was blinded. He blinds us all. What is so terrible, he reverences the Christus – he *worships* God, as I imagine the Devil also does, irresistibly, in some hidden room of his palace under the ground. How can the Devil not worship God? He, of all things, *knows* God. It's love makes the Devil fight with God.'

'Orro, lie back. Look at you. Now you must have a herbal. This is too bad.'

'I've spoken,' said Orro. 'It's over.'

He stared through the walls of his room into the forest, and saw Jun riding away on his mule, with the servant from Timuce who was afraid of him, and was fascinated by him. How green the wood, how high the trees. The figures of Jun and the servant were small and finely fashioned, like toys.

'It's over,' said Orro again, and went to sleep.

The journey to Khish was a long one, as the Administer had regretted. Coming from miles of greenness and darkness, out of the tunnel of the forest which was all he had ever seen, the young man emerged on the plains before the town of Khish, where the grain grew and the sky was a low roof: an alien landscape.

Under the roof of sky the town walls appeared.

The streets were narrow, and the houses hung together, and in the ravines below, pigs and sheep grazed on grasses rooted in mud and garbage. The town of Khish, whose sigil was a key, stank ripely, and the servant from the forest held his nose, but the young novice seemed not to mind the stench.

They rode to the church, which was of stone. A round window, set with glass like petals, fractured the sun.

At the church in Khish, the community of novices was thirty strong, and held within itself a well-educated, secretly arrogant, sometimes dissatisfied elite. These were the second or third sons of wealthy houses, given to the Church Paternal because they were superfluous to the genetic necessity of a family, and might turn out useful in the ranks of God. A few had believed themselves possessed of genuine vocation, a longing to serve the Christus. All had suppressed their anger at the rigours of religious discipline. It was either the refining process needful to bring them in to God, or the penalty of junior status which, with the coming of a better position – that of the priest – might be alleviated, avoided. Some of the novices had entered the Church from lowlier backgrounds, accepted as fodder; there would always be a job for slavish servants, the travelling priests, the messengers, those sent to the forest to counsel drunken Landholders, or into the villages to minister to the hopeless souls there. These lesser novices kept themselves apart from the aristocrats, in subtle and careful ways, for they were lessoned and worked and prayed communally. Occasionally, small, unobtrusive tests were set the inferior novices, tiny ordeals the priesthood overlooked. For although in the eyes of God all were equal, in the opinion of men this had remained a fallacy.

When Jun arrived at the Khishan novitiate house, word of him had gone in before. Jun was supposed to be a peasant, a clod. Some impertinent adroitness in learning and theosophy had brought the acceptance at Khish, and maybe some conniving also by a too-partial provincial Administer.

Jun was first seen at the evening meal. He had been travelling for almost a month, through the summer forest, to Khish. He appeared as quietly among them as any of their number long–established. He did not even attract undue comment by an effect of being travel-worn. He had no barest look of the peasantry, or even the rough and ready Tower nobility in the woods (a by-blow of which several had said he must be). He was slender, with long immaculate hands. His face, lightly tanned, had the carven symmetry and none of the lapses of an ascetic man two score years older. The eyes sought out no one, but here and there, where they seemed to pause in thought upon some object, they were already the eyes of the priest, the initiate – of one who *knew*.

They saw him generally once more at the late evening offices and reckoned to again during the offices at dawn. Between these times, Jun evolved in the novitiate dormitory.

This dormitory ran along the whole south and half the eastern arms of the cloister. A narrow corridor gave upon some forty partitioned cells, each with its narrow strip of window, its wooden pallet, chest and stool. Invariably, one candle in a pewter holder rested on every chest, along with such books as had been provided for study. Less frequently personal belongings, inappropriate and sparse, lay by the books, while in a dozen of the cells might be found a whole stand of candles, or a crucifix and beads of greater richness than the iron and enamel on the wall. Such interesting cells were located in the southern arm of the dormitory. Here it was the priestly aristocrats of Khish were given, without any word or acknowledgement, their quarters.

Twenty-three young men studied, prayed, slept, dreamed, applied penance, fretted, made vows to God and to self, in the southern dormitory.

As Jun entered, by the east door from the cloister, the other portion of this area, he must perceive at once that all the lights were extinguished here, but, at the turn of the corridor into the southern arm, candlelight flared brightly at plaster: all the candles *there*, it seemed, were still burning.

If he was aware of being watched, and Jun *was* watched, he gave no evidence. He entered his prescribed partition, laid down the bundle he had brought with him from Timuce, and without fumbling lit the single candle on the pewter holder.

Opening the bundle next, he removed two books, and placed them on the chest. It seemed he was not prepared to sleep as yet. Instead, he raised the topmost book's worn cover, and drew the stool up against the chest. Leaning his head upon one hand, Jun read over the life of the Christus, from the Scriptures the Administer had presented him.

After perhaps ten minutes, in which Jun moved only to turn one thick ochre page to reveal a drawing, crudely but determinedly done in red, white and brown, certain figures that had just now traversed the unlit east dormitory, blocked the doorless doorway into the cell.

Still, Jun did not look up. He might be unaware of them, but that was unlikely. They had come softly, but with a smoke about them of night beasts.

The man who stood directly in the doorway, just inside Jun's cell, was twenty-one years of age. He was handsome, and his body had been built by exercise with horses and with swords. He had known women too, in his father's house, and out of it. His father's eldest son had seemed set to die. Most of his life the novice Wedsek had known this. Then, in Wedsek's sixteenth year, the elder brother rallied, changed by some wonder into a glowing bull. Wedsek lost his position. A whim of his aunt's – the mother was dead – had Wedsek delivered to the Church to thank God for his brother's salvation. A fearsome rage had overcome Wedsek. He had absented himself, roved drunk and howling through the alleys of the town, made a drunk's plan for riding off to Chirkess, going for a soldier, a hired sword, anything better than *this*. In the middle of his outcry, one night he became sick, maybe from the drink, or from other abuses of the flesh. And as he writhed in a screaming delirium, a vision fell on Wedsek like a cool white rain. He did not afterwards properly remember it, and this enabled him to embroider for himself upon the theme whatever he desired. He gave himself up to his father's (his aunt's) will and went to God at the church. He stayed for himself however, as a soldier. That had been an element of his vision – in mail, he had hewn with a bright blade for the Christus. Heaven's choice, he had said no, until Heaven put him wise.

The warrior, Wedsek, stood now in the mouth of the cell of Jun, the bumpkin and upstart.

Wedsek ruled supreme among the novices. He was admired for his physical looks and prowess, covertly for the fierce and sinful life he had thrown away for God. He had been the talk of them all, and his pronouncements, in that little, airless, closed world, devoid of women, and offering only adventures of the spirit, were a sort of law.

Instinctively, Wedsek sensed the danger of Jun, the threat of him.

'Who's this?' said Wedsek.

Jun, even now, did not respond.

'The fellow from the woods,' said a novice at Wedsek's back. 'The one they think can make into a priest.'

'Ah. *Jun* is the name. I remember, it's so outlandish, a *woods* name. What you'd call your dog.'

'But you haven't a dog,' said the novice playfully.

'Perhaps Jun will be my dog. It's true. I miss the curs from the yard. Can Jun bark? Can he beg?'

'He *can't* hear,' said a second novice behind Wedsek in the dark of the east dormitory.

Wedsek entered the cell and planted his hands flat on the chest top. He lowered his head, and with the eyes a girl had once compared to brown mahogany, he glared smiling at the bowed head of Jun.

Jun looked up. The candle lifted its slim flame between them, lighting for each the face of the other.

Wedsek saw close to what he had witnessed in the refectory at the novices' table. It startled him a touch, maybe he had expected some change.

'I am Wedsek,' said Wedsek, 'formerly of House Crel. But that's all past. Now I belong to God. What do you say?'

Jun spoke. 'Each of us belongs to God, from the moment of his conception.'

Wedsek straightened up. He went on staring down into the composite face of Jun. There was everything in it, and nothing out of true there. There was no way in, for even the black eyes were impervious. This was a man of thirty who had passed for a youth of eighteen, being strangely without any marks of age.

Wedsek discovered he must fall back on a stupid sparring tone.

'Great things are mentioned of you, Jun. They think you'll beam and glitter.' Wedsek imagined to himself the listening row of black cells, the low-born novices, straining their ears. 'Do you say God summoned you to the priesthood?'

Jun nodded, slowly.

'That's presumptuous,' said Wedsek. It was his own credo; he would never have stipulated the fact at large.

Jun did not reply. He went on sitting at the chest, with one hand which, like the face, was not that of a peasant, on the book, and he did not move, did not blink or swallow or glance aside.

Wedsek caught himself sweating in the hot night.

'Let's hear you,' said Wedsek, dissatisfied, 'say a prayer.'

Jun rose, without hurry. He was as tall as Wedsek, and though far more slender, seemed purely hard, steel to brass. Jun's black eyes were yet fixed on Wedsek, and Wedsek felt a sudden weakness, a kind of fluttering as if something were trapped in his throat. *He now wished to look away, but could not, by God.*

Jun began to speak again, in his sombre and musical voice, already priest-trained to a standard rare even in the cities.

'O most mighty and compassionate God, Who like a gentle father regards the works of men, and hates no thing which He has made, revoke death from the sinner, let him only repent and resort him to Your service. Mercifully forgive us our trespasses. Spare us, for whom the Redeemer died, though we are vile, the mud and the dust upon the earth. Meekly we acknowledge our crimes, weeping for them. Send us then Your help that we may endure, and live through You, until the Final Judgement.'

There was silence. Thick as black snow it filled the air of the eastern dormitory.

Wedsek drew a breath.

'I commend your cleverness,' he said. 'You must have had good tutors at your wooden chapel in the forest.'

'Wedsek,' someone said anxiously behind him.

The accomplices, driven by feelings of unease, were withdrawing up the corridor.

The baiting of the newcomer was at odds with everything, even with the night. He was not food for them after all. They had started to believe that here at last was one unlike the rest. They would have no choice but to leave him alone. Tomorrow they might think differently, or not.

But Wedsek stood before Jun, unable to find a crevice, a crack, a flaw. And Wedsek blazed inwardly with an old nameless wrath he had reckoned was finished with him.

'Don't tire your eyes,' he said to Jun, 'you have to be in the church at dawn. No slacking here, we're diligent. I'll watch for you. I've taken an interest.'

Then Wedsek bolted, with leisurely swaggering steps.

Jun's candle filtered through his shadow along the corridor, until he reached the turn.

The novice Wedsek fermented the red emotions of anger and unappeasement inside his strapping and disciplined body. His flesh he could control, even the night-hungers of sexual appetite, but his brain and heart were prone to elude him. He took exercise, as was allowed him, in the cloister garden, wrestling with the fruit trees, hoeing, and repairing the paths. If he sometimes also snatched space to hurl stones at a mark, to weave and feint with a stick, fighter's moves, he confessed the truancy. Later, when a priest, he might regain his rights to ride, to train with sword and staff – it would depend where he was sent; he had longed for a city, the vast cathedrals like a lord's court. They had an inner guard, priests allowed the practices of a warrior, or so he had heard. They rode hunting too.

His mind did not exercise so skilfully. The esoteric labyrinth of religion did not lure him. He toiled at it as best he could. The plain thesis of God was enough, and the rest a trimming... Though he admired it vaguely, it was superfluous to him.

Two months of brown and arid town summer went by, the square and market, the houses, hovels, transmuted to a desert. The summer stinks increased, but there were the golden sunsets to alleviate them, and the blue-green dusks in tiaras of stars. Wedsek got some peace at sunset, going up to the walk below the church roof when able. He would tell his beads (rose quartz, jasper, the gift of his aunt), he would think of the blows he would one day smite for the Christus. Sometimes he recollected his debauch in the town: then he smiled. *That* Wedsek was another person.

Yet, when he thought of Jun, Wedsek was restless; he sensed the old Wedsek lying in wait for him. It was a test of faith. God had called him. He must resist the spearhead of rage he felt at Jun. An upstart, yes, a wretch who should be taught the lessons of Wedsek as well as the schooling of the church books...

Wedsek wasted time on his fury at Jun. It would not go. Each time he beheld Jun, the monster uncoiled its length within him. And when Jun was not visible, the red emotions bubbled in their vat.

Jun made no mistakes. He was exact. If any penances were set him, Wedsek surmised that Jun fulfilled them strictly, but in total privacy. No public punishment was ever the lot of Jun.

The other novices, even the resident godbrothers and the brother tutors, the Khishan Administer himself, probably, seemed to note Jun. And Jun did beam and glitter. When he read from the Book in the refectory at a meal, the quiet might be spooned up with the soup. The beautiful voice commanded. It brought the words out of their sleep and gave them freedom to order the reactions of men. Jun carried out all duties, the lowly, the holy.

Jun was valued. Respected, revered.

Very little was said of him. When he entered a room, the nave of the church itself, eyes went to him, and away, as if with the essential thought: *He is here.*

For himself, Jun was courteous and remote. He had no elected companions. One morning, as the novices paced the cloister with their books of study, a servant came running on some task from the kitchen. He knocked the volume from the hands of Jun. Jun stood quite still, and the servant plunged to his knees, scrabbling for the book, to hand it up to him. And it was a ludicrous scene, for there were three others also kneeling before Jun, novices, trying to fish up the book for him. One of these was a fellow of Wedsek's, a cousin from a noble house.

Wedsek took him aside later. 'What were you thinking of, you dolt? Some slave from the woods.'

'Jun isn't a slave.'

'What is he, then, that everyone bows down and crawls before him?'

'I don't know, Wedsek. I heard the brother librarian talking to his assistant. He said Jun was the clay from which the saints are formed.'

Wedsek laughed. 'God's heart. May the cretinous fool be forgiven.'

'I didn't hear your jibe, Wedsek.'

'You dare warn *me?*'

'Here, we are all one.'

'Jun is not.'

Wedsek's cousin hung his head. 'No.'

Beyond him, in the corner of the cloister up against the Confessional wall, the marble cross on its basalt plinth, nine feet in height, the outstretched Christus impaled by gold and crowned with golden thorns, looked away into the opposite corner, where the book had dropped and the novices and servant had scrabbled.

That evening, the duty came to Jun (a deed the Christus himself had once performed for his disciples) of washing the hands and the feet of his fellow novices, in the refectory before supper.

This act was never ridiculed by the aristocratic novices; their hauteur forbade their even speaking of it. They carried it out when it fell to them, frowning and careful. It was too apparent a trial to be flunked.

In the refectory, the candles were not yet lit. The day came down from the high windows, itself the colour of used wax. The shadows were long and syrupy, pooling from everything that did not move. The priests and the novices who took their places crossed this chiaroscuro in combing bars. Seated, they too cast heavy shadows, and if they should lift their hands, the light filled in the blood of them like garnet.

The Administer, the serving priesthood of the church, assumed their seats.

Through the door came Jun, preceded by the youngest (common) novice, a boy of thirteen, who held the bowl of water, the cloth and the towel.

The light of dying day painted the face of Jun to golden ivory.

He walked to the first of the novices, knelt, accepted the cloth, dipped it into the bowl and then wrung out the water on the waiting feet, murmuring as he did so the proper phrases of service, the prayer notes to God. The first novice stared at him, as if afraid. When Jun brought the towel to his feet and wiped them dry, the novice shook, his shaking visible. Jun clasped his feet within the towel. The shaking ended. The novice sighed, and Jun let him go.

To everyone the server went, and anointed him with the water, and clasped him in the drying towel.

Each man looked unsure, amazed, *altered.* The law of silence was on them. Only the one who read, or the Administer, might be heard in the refectory. It seemed they yearned to speak. Of what?

Jun came to the cousin of Wedsek, who sat by him on the bench. Wedsek watched from the corner of his eye. He braced his body, as if for the shock of pain.

Jun kneeled before Wedsek.

'As it was done, and in the sight of God...'

Wedsek did not understand these sentences he had listened to so often.

The water was tepid, pleasant. That was nothing. Then the towel came, dampened by the other feet, high-born and low, not to be winced at. It was not the towel – the clasp of the hands of Jun ran through the towel. Was it a heat, a laving of vibration that moved the fluid of his blood about? Like the fireside after snow, like wine.

Wedsek stiffened his frame, muscles, bones. He resisted.

And Jun drew away and, his ministry accomplished, was gone. Wedsek did not see into what or where. A dissembling of shadow.

Wedsek could not sleep in the scalding cauldron of the night. He might get up, go and draw water from the well in the garden, douse himself.

He rose from the hard bed and put on his habit, in the dark. He felt curiously ashamed.

At the doorway of his cell, Wedsek stopped, knowing why. He was not going to the well. Along the cloister lay the Confessional, where every night one of the godbrothers took his duty, sleeping on a pallet, ready to be waked by any who, in the dead hours, would creep to be heard.

What was it Wedsek would say? *I have a jealous hatred of him.* Was it that? *He has usurped what I wanted.* But what had Jun usurped – was it not there for all the men in this priestly bondage? No. For it was the mark of one chosen. It was the knighthood bestowed by Heaven – Wedsek writhed at the confusion and inadequacy of his words, and at the confrontation with his disappointment.

He would have to go to the elderly godbrother in the Confessional, he would have to blurt out that he wished to rob Jun of life. That he wished Jun had never lived.

As Wedsek emerged from the south dormitory door into the cloister, he saw Jun come out of the eastern door.

Perhaps Jun sought the well, as Wedsek had thought he himself meant to. Or the latrines. Oddly, Wedsek had never seen Jun visit them, in all these months, when every fellow novice had been encountered there at some hour of day or night. Well, did a saint *void* himself? Unthinkable.

Wedsek grinned, and as if he had detected the noise of Wedsek's lips in motion, Jun looked back at him.

Only three dim lights burned in the cloister, two beneath statues of Saint Eda and a nameless angel, and one above the plinth of the Christus on his marble cross.

Jun received a faint brushwork of this light; he seemed a figure of the darkness, something of basalt like the plinth, shining.

Well, Wedsek thought, *well…*

But Jun had turned away again. He was walking along the cloister, towards the statue of the Christus. Did Jun seek the Confessional?

Wedsek began to walk after Jun. An abrupt bravado was on him. If Jun had some sin that kept him sleepless, what was he but a man, an ordinary miserable thing of skin and hair and sludge, like the rest.

Wedsek had quickened his pace. Both men moved soundlessly. At the refectory turn, where the steps led down into the garden, Wedsek realised he could catch Jun up. Wedsek reached out and delivered a weightless blow to Jun's shoulder.

'God's serenity be with you, Jun. Where are you going?'

Jun had halted but did not turn, now.

Wedsek felt a pressure inside him that might be incipient triumph.

'Some miscreancy to confess?' said Wedsek. 'The poor old godbrother needs his sleep. Tell *me* first. Let's see if it's worth waking him.'

Jun did not turn.

Wedsek put his hand back on Jun's shoulder. It did not have the width of brawn, but it was shaped and flat, knit with lean muscle. Wedsek came around and gazed into Jun's face, which now had half the light from above the plinth washed along it. And Jun's, too, was a statue's face. The eyes seemed all burnished blackness, without white. There was a surge in Wedsek. He knew undeniably the instant had come, the contest between them. He, or the other.

'No, I won't let you go in and disturb the poor doddery priest. You must make your confession here, to me. I'll absolve you.' Wedsek pressed on the shoulder. 'Kneel down, Jun.' The shoulder did not give. It was like welded bronze.

Jun spoke to Wedsek. 'You misinterpret. It's the Christus that I go to. The beautiful image with the golden thorns, and the nails of gold through His hands and feet.'

Wedsek lifted his eyes, looked aside involuntarily towards the place, and Jun somehow had gone by him, was pacing up the cloister into the light.

Wedsek strode after him.

'You *wait*, you peasant, on my leave to go.'

Jun turned this time. Before Wedsek could predict, Jun's hand had flashed up and struck Wedsek across the cheek. It stung like icy water. Wedsek started back as if afraid. He was not. He was not anything. This went on too fast...

'Look at the statue,' said Jun.

Wedsek could not take his eyes from Jun's eyes. He seemed to see right through them, through two black gems, to where the Christus hung. The lamp above picked out the white features, the agonised crown. A shadowy moth was flying about the lamp, attracted to it. And suddenly the moth flew into the lamp. There was a spurt of pale flame. The Christus seemed to contort, rolling up His stare towards the sky. From under the thorn crown three scarlet threads unwound. They slipped down the marble forehead, the lids, across the eyeballs, out, like tears. They ran together on the lips, staining them red.

'In the name of God – God be with me...' Wedsek picked out his own muttering. He no longer saw through Jun, for Jun had left him again, without leave. Jun was standing under the statue, black under the whiteness.

Worms of blood were running from the wrists and feet of the statue under the golden nails.

'In the name of God...'

It was a miracle. He witnessed a miracle. Make it stop. He could not bear it...

Wedsek trembled from head to foot. His bowels were liquid. He tried, over and over, against the vocal expressions of prayer, to apply inner reason: *What is it? What is it?*

But it was that the Christus bled from His wounds. And Jun was there, looking up.

No. Jun was on the plinth. He had put up his arms and spread them out along the crucified arms of the Christus. Jun lay against the statue, three feet from the ground.

Wedsek did not know how Jun had ascended. It hardly mattered.

The instant had come. It was not the instant. It was all time, none.

Wedsek opened his eyes, and the statue was clean white under the dull sheen of the lamp.

Jun stood before Wedsek. Jun's wrists were red with blood, his palms full of blood like flowers. His lips were red and wet.

Wedsek kneeled down.

He did not know what to do. In terrible horror he floundered. And then he *did* know. It was so easy. A tide of thankfulness broke inside him. It was not battle. He was not unchosen. Jun was God's, and Jun chose Wedsek. Wedsek the warrior of God stretched himself out and kissed the feet of his redeemer.

Chapter Four

Late in spring, the grey church at Khish was dressed with asphodel, and lilies. An altar cloth of white and green, sewn with brilliants of glass but fringed with silver, replaced the darker cloth upon the high altar. The higher streets of Khish, too, dressed themselves with blossoms. A Factor had come from the city of Chirkess, to ordain the fledgling priests. The Factor, looking down his long nose, was entertained by the noble families of Khish. The beads he told were of sapphire, jade and pearl.

At the church, the Factor was inquisitive. He pried. If what he found was in order, an indifferent complacency bloomed from him. Where there was any fault, he smiled, and made a note on a parchment tablet.

But concerning the twenty-eight novices due to be remade by him, he was sanguine.

'An abundant and healthy harvest, Administer.'

The Factor observed, through a magnifying lens of crystal, from the gallery above the nave, the novices passing to their devotions. It was the Factor who undertook their final interrogation, who set them their final and most rigorous fasts, instructed them in the death of their male bodies, the birth from chrysalis of their spiritual being.

'There is one. The others attend him. In another situation this would be a bad thing, but I believe that here we see a special gift. This is the novice of whom you wrote to the Primentor at Chirkess?'

'Just so, Father Factor. That is Jun.'

'I'm impressed by him, Administer. I did not expect to be, despite, excuse me, your letter. Jun. He won't, I suppose, take ordination under such a name – of the peasantry, pagan most likely. It would never be correct.'

'The name of Saint Junion was recommended to Jun, as bearing some relation to his own.'

'Yes, yes.'

'But Jun declined use of this name.'

'Indeed? Do I detect after all a hint of disobedience?'

The Administer said, 'His rejection was made without any show of wilfulness. But the name Jun has chosen for himself as a priest may not please you, Father Factor.'

The Factor raised his long thin brows like quarter-moons of wire. 'I'm agog.' The Administer offered Jun's choice, and beheld the Factor's pallor tint itself. 'That's a lofty selection. I'm unsure I can approve it.'

'Jun told me very simply that he coveted the name of an angel in order to uphold constantly before himself an unattainable goal. He must strive towards it, could not turn from it, the name, like the flesh, being undetachable during life from the soul.'

'He theorises like one already in the Fraterium at Chirkess. Does he aim to get there?' The Factor put his crystal to his eye, and looked at a blister upon the chamber wall. 'Of course, this isn't an archangel. Nevertheless... to fix on an angel so closely in service on the Unsurpassable Sacrifice... I will have to question your Jun.'

The angels stood by the right hand of the Christus, who was seated amongst His disciples. Before them ran the table with its metal cups. The young men wore clothing like that of the priesthood, sombre and seemly; the Christus was clad in white, His head rimmed by the sunburst that swirled up into an arch of white roses overhead. Under the left hand of the Christus lay a crimson rose whose stem had emitted awful black and curving thorns. The first serving angel was fair, blue-robed, with wings of fleece. He carried on a silver salver the bread that was to be the Body. The second serving angel provided a note of fire to complement the rose. Black-haired and sable winged, he was attired in red. And in his hand was the chalice for which the Christus already reached: the chalice of the wine of Love, at the Last Supper on earth. The wine which was the rose-red ichor of the Christus: *Drink, this is my Blood.*

The mural had been vital thirty years before, but damp in the wall of the chapel had somewhat affected it. Despite that, the details were clear enough. And the name of the Angel of the Blood of the

Redeemer, who in a mystic story repaired after to the foot of the cross, catching the precious drops in his vessel that they might not sink and be lost in the ground, this name, though commonly obscure, was documented in the lists of the hosts of Heaven.

'And do you not think, Jun, that you aspire beyond your station?'

'Father, I aspire to be a priest. That's far beyond my station. I aspire to do the will of God. That is beyond the station, and the knack, of most men, even the best.'

'You argue very ably. This sophistry was taught you here?'

'Pardon me, Father. I only speak the truth as I judge the truth to be.'

The Father Factor leaned back in the chair which had been set for him. He regarded Jun with his narrow, too-clever eyes.

Jun was not ordinary clay. He had presence and enormous power, even so young. His voice could break and make the hearts of humanity. Already the novices, and half the priests here, were under his sway. He was a radiance that it would be idiotic to ignore.

'If I were to say to you, Jun, that this name is not to be yours, that you must put on with ordainment some other, how would you reply to me?'

'This is the name of what I am to be. Name me by some other name, I will abide by your command.'

'You're saying, then, that you'll obey outwardly, and inwardly rebel.'

'No. Now I go by the name *Jun*. That is not who I am. Yet I answer to the name *Jun*, without rebellion.'

'If Jun isn't your name,' snapped the Factor, wary, and bristling, 'what is your proper name?'

'Man,' said Jun. His eyes rested on the Factor, and the Factor grew still, measuring, weighing this paradox like the quality of peerless music. 'I am Man, the universal name we answer to, the race made by God in the image of the Most High.'

Inwardly the Factor preened himself, for peerless things delighted him always. He had never grasped that, save with God, this also was a sin and a snare.

'You must allow us time, Jun, to consider your request.'

Jun bowed to the Factor.

It was already decided. The Factor would permit this novice to have his way. Jun should garb himself in the name of the Angel of the Blood, which name was Anjelen.

After the fasts, the inquisition of faith, the day.

They rose four hours before the sun, two hours after they had lain down.

There was moonlight in the cloister and on the garden, powdering the apple trees and the vines on the wall. Each man bore a lighted taper. They entered the church.

The novices separated, like islands, and one by one knelt down. Kneeling, each man extinguished his taper, like an act of will. Then they were alone there together, in the cold spring night and the shining darkness of the moon.

Only on the altar, like a mountain, the lamp burned before the crucifix.

The Watching must last three hours.

It was the passage, in darkness, out of the dark.

In the final hour, before the sunrise, the golden wind would blow into the hall of stone, the dawn of rebirth. Candles, singing.

Before that, the meeting with self, utter and inescapable.

Only the star on the altar to be a guide.

How many men had kneeled here in this dark and cold, and in this form? Longing maybe for visions, or simply for the stamina to endure the Watch. How many minds had wandered from the vigil, slipped back into the past (the warmth or bitterness of childhood, the years of growth, before the going away into this), or forward, in greed, material dreams in the margin left for a meeting with the spirit?

Some fainted at the Watching. No one tended them. Some sobbed or prayed aloud. Some abandoned the taxing posture, taking up again the painful kneeling stance only when it could not be avoided. Once, or twice, not more, a candidate had fled the church, some inner demon having found him.

This Watch was unlike any other.

Separated in their islands of self, the waiting men had union. It was the power of the novice Jun, feeding them and upholding them. They felt it like a sea of soft lightning. It supported them, it refurbished.

And above them all, the lamp burned on the altar. And beyond the stones of the church, the morning trod slowly nearer to the east.

And in the mind of Jun, soon to be Anjelen, what was *there?*

The mind that had been a boy's mind once in the heart of the wood, and that had emptied, and that had filled again with the wild abbreviated eternity of the Tree. The mind which had lived as a wolf, and a god-thing, to which a decade was one hundred mortal years. The mind that came up from the shadow and stayed a shadow.

The mind of Jun was like a globe of glass. A million things were engraved on it. Lights and midnights played over and within it. It turned, and gave out, like silent chimes, all that it knew, had learned, had lived, and, too, it kept in, withheld, stored, and wasted nothing. Like a globe of glass, its clarity. And yet, like a forest also, dense and convoluted and *full.*

Not the mind of a man, or of anything supernatural in the spiritual sense.

Its intellect it employed as a beast of the field might use instinct.

Not human. No, it would regain humanness only gradually, and maybe solely through imitation.

Jun knelt straight as a post. He did not change his position. His breathing was barely visible. His eyes were open on the altar lamp.

He did not go back over memory, or forward into future.

He existed moment by moment. Each moment was new.

He was not accessible, scarcely alterable. He did not even know, Jun who was to be Anjelen, *what* he was, his purpose, his desire. He grew now as the Tree grows, blind and certain, upward into the sky.

In the hour before the dawn, the golden wind blew. The church doors opened, and they swept through the hall of stone, the boys singing in their white, and the priests with their candles. The Administer came in a robe of white, and the Factor in robes of red and white patterned with yellow brightness, and the utensils of yellow brightness were set on the altar, now like a green hill of flowers.

'Father, I present to you these, whom I believe, in the sight of God, to be worthy of the office of priest.'

'If there is any impediment, let it be spoken directly.'

And on the Factor's admonition, a minute was counted out by a sandglass, after which a bell was rung.

'Now, even as the Son of God ordained particular men, who through His will became the saints, so are we given to make for Him a priesthood.'

The service proceeded, and the heat of the candles drew up the scent of the lilies, and the incense clouded down.

Outside, inch by inch, the blackness lightened, and the stars went out. The moon was left, like mist, on the edge of a wall.

The Factor, the Shepherd and the Maker, stepped among the kneeling men, and laid his hands on their bowed heads.

'As it was done, receive now the spark of the fire that is God. Whose sins you shall forgive, they are forgiven them, who speaks to God though you, he shall be heeded.'

The dawn, despite everything, was overcast. No flame was in the east.

The Host was elevated, and the Wine of the Christus.

Silken grey light began to come in at the windows of the church. The light flickered like the candles. In the world, it rained.

The Bread of the Body was given to the priests who had kneeled as novices. The chalice was brought to them. They drank the Blood.

The rain reflected on the face of the Christus hanging on the crucifix above the altar.

Anjelen sipped from the chalice, the Wine of the Redeemer, and the cup continued to the mouth of Wedsek, like a kiss.

And the rain tears slid from the eyes of the Christus, reflecting the weeping of the sky.

'To Chirkess, these four or five; yes, I shall recommend it.'

Four, the sons of rich families, had been bought their places by charitable awards. The fifth priest, Jun (Anjelen), had won the prize for himself.

The Factor smiled upon the Administer.

'Impressive chances lie before them. You've done well here.'

Anjelen stood in the chapel, under the mural of the Supper.

Wedsek and three others, the new-minted priests, stood where the chapel opened to the church.

They waited on Anjelen.

At length, Anjelen turned and looked at them.

'Chirkess,' said Wedsek. 'It's sure.'

Anjelen said nothing, did nothing. He made no movement, was expressionless.

From his body, or so it seemed to them, the power of the fire of God flowed out.

They were rewarded.

Chapter Five

To those who had never seen a city, Chirkess gave a drab fulfilment to their assumptions. It was a sprawling town that had not checked itself. It spread along the shore of a narrow river, and up the hills to the east. A current wall was being built to contain it, since it had outstripped the other. Chirkess had an Overlord and was capable of making war. The towered building of her temporal power stood near the water, and the garrison was there, the wharves, and a few ships. The Cathedral of Chirkess, completed twenty years before, rose on a hill, surrounded by its own stout walls, and having its own military presence to defend it. It was the Cathedral that had the greater pretence to being a city. Ensconced within the battlements were the necessaries of life, granary, stables, candle-makers, forges, breweries and butchers' yards. There was a garden of beauty and harvest, an armoury that frustrated the lord below, a library that disconcerted him, since he could not read. Learning was yet the magic of the priesthood. And it was picky and canny whom it taught. There were ten clerical priests allocated to the court of the Overlord, aside from his confessor. He could not do without them.

For the priesthood of this place, save where they went about as tutors, advisors and spies, Chirkess was only the Cathedral.

The snow had been especially harsh that winter. The river froze completely. By-passing the lord's house, the citizens went up to the gates of the Cathedral and cried for help. They were chastised by hard words concerning their transgressions. Men kneeled praying and lamenting in the cold, dead snow. Then the Cathedral sent them bread, by the cartload.

The first wife of the Overlord had died two years before of a colic. He had had to attend to a year of penances, strictly watched by his confessor and religious counsellors, before the Church Fathers of his city awarded him permission to take another wife.

Now, the snow, the spring, the summer were gone, the lord's wife was with child, and early autumn blazed along the hills and fired the beautiful garden of the Cathedral.

In through the west gate of the Cathedral precinct rode a hunting party. They wore dull red and black, immediately recognisable, although they might have been lords from the city, as the priesthood.

They passed the forges on the slope of the yard and went up to the kitchens. Servants came out to collect carcasses, two deer from the plains; they had been grazing on the wheat, which the hunt had trampled in its career. The farmers would have to thank the Church for its kindness.

Above, over the grouping of walls and buildings, the Cathedral's great north tower arose, fluttering the banner of the black knot-cross on blank white, masonry capped with blue tile, and rimmed by gold, and with the vast eye of indigo, ruby and green beryl looking west and down into the city towards the river. The picture in the window was of the death of the Devil as a dragon, and the Christus ascendant. It was the colours which mattered. On clear nights, this was the jewellery moon of Chirkess.

Just visible too, across the roofs of the Cathedral behind a complex of small courtyards, a lower, squatter tower, round as a wheel, showed its grey shoulder to the garden.

This tower was older than the Cathedral. It had been an outlying garrison of the town a pair of centuries before.

As he rode up from the kitchen, Godbrother Wedsek, thinner, harder, pleased with his hunting and his prospects, oddly tense and bemusedly out of step with his life, glanced at this second, south tower. Almost he winked at it: an assignation.

Few servants entered the south tower. The trees that grew up against it from the garden walks below had partly rooted in the lower walls. Black moss and creeper licked out from the blocks of it. A series of window slits high up sometimes emitted faint light.

The lower room of the south tower, gained by a small warped door, put up the armoury of the Cathedral, weapons antique and edgeless, modern and harsh, hanging together. An inner stair led on to a further door, always kept locked.

There were gargoyles along the heights of the tower, having strange faces, their eyes masked by the visors of helms.

Sunset began in the river valley, and gradually the western gargoyle faces reddened.

Wedsek, having stabled his horse, had walked down into the garden. He should go to pray now, in the chapel. He was not ready to pray.

He stood beneath the south tower, looking for Anjelen.

Wedsek's first sight of Anjelen, every day, was sharp and accentuated, as if there had been long absences. Through their three years at Chirkess, this had never lessened. In fact it increased. Wedsek's feelings appeared to him a curious mixture of awe and envy, the subjugation of the self to another, the outcry of self to be acknowledged.

Anjelen had not failed Wedsek. Neither had Anjelen fulfilled Wedsek. There was a sort of tarrying. It seemed Anjelen could wait a hundred years. Wedsek understood that he himself could not.

The door moved surreptitiously in the ivy, and elderly Magister Egar emerged. Next came the three pupils who had today been with him in the under-rooms above the armoury. Wedsek beheld his fellows Behri and Kopis, and Anjelen alone in their midst and burning with a black motionless flame.

Egar paused on the step inside the trees. He waved Behri and Kopis on and leaned upon the shoulder of Anjelen. The Magister spoke to Anjelen, eagerly, intimately. The other two came down and found Wedsek. Their eyes were cloudy. Behri said to Wedsek, 'The peace of God. It's possible to make light in a lamp.'

'Yes?' said Wedsek.

'He showed us. Certain words…'

'Be quiet,' said Kopis. 'Those are secrets of the alchemist's chamber.'

'Rubbish. The trick of doing them's the secret. Neither you nor I, yet. Anjelen, however…'

'Then, when Anjelen gives you leave, you may talk of it.'

Wedsek said, 'Anjelen will tell me.'

'Yes,' said Kopis grudgingly. 'The *other* brotherhood.'

'And you,' said Wedsek, 'don't speak of *that.*'

They stood in triangle in the peace of God, lips formed to create blows. The pupils of the alchemist were in their habits, a red cord at the waist. Anjelen too was dressed in this fashion, and the aged Magister, whose lizardine crucifix of emerald and gold ignited on his breast at the sinking sun. Wedsek in his priestly hunting garb, short habit, breeches, boots, had put his right hand across his body. The hunting knife on his hip evidenced what was supposedly not discussed. There was the inner order at Chirkess, as on other heights of the Church, brothers who carried weapons, might exercise and hunt.

Egar and Anjelen were coming nearer.

Wedsek caught the quick soft gabble of the elder priest. 'The ignorant call such a man a magician. The bones of the word are apt enough. They imply learning, the follower of truth. But alchemy is science. It can be said to be as simple as the adding up of beads on a string. This *you* master.'

The Magister was a trifle deaf? His murmurs were audible and perhaps should not be. Already his eyes had a film on them. He hurried to pass on his knowledge.

But Anjelen. Wedsek had seen or guessed so much of what Anjelen could do, those prodigious things like dreams only half remembered.

'To give hope to the faithful among men, for this you learn to offer evidence of supernatural acts. In such a form, you must learn. Otherwise, the deed is unholy.'

'Do you say, your grace,' broke in Kopis, 'that we should mimic the miracles of the *Christus*?'

The Magister turned to look at him. He gave a sudden snakelike smile. 'If God grants you the talent so to do, my son, why not? If God does not grant the talent, well then.'

Kopis reddened like the gargoyle heads aloft in the setting sun.

Egar said to Anjelen, clearly, 'What you learned this afternoon required of me one year of my life. Go in God's peace.' He blessed them carelessly and ambled off towards the body of the Cathedral, with a wandering, somnambulist gait.

From the north tower of the window, the bell for prayer voiced its summons.

Wedsek repressed, as ever, his irritation. He must go in and wash himself and put on his priest's habit and rush to kneel in the

Cathedral with the rest.

Anjelen looked at him. Kopis and Behri had started off. They had gone into the courts beyond the garden.

'Don't you mean to pray?' said Wedsek abruptly.

'Life, for the priest, is a prayer,' said Anjelen.

'But the rituals must be observed.'

The darkness was coming to cover Anjelen, the bright-burning black flame of him.

Wedsek relaxed his body. 'I'm in no state to pray. Filthy from the chase. My mind elsewhere. I'll play truant and confess tomorrow. And you?'

But Anjelen was now moving towards the courtyards, the Cathedral. Wedsek got suddenly in his path.

Anjelen halted.

'I find it difficult,' said Wedsek, 'to be a slave of God. I'm God's warrior.'

'The two are one,' said Anjelen.

'Tell me what to do.'

'You know yourself what you're expected to do.'

Something rose through Wedsek, three years of waiting, like a tide. 'I was the son of the noble house of Crel, at Khish. They presented the Church with me.'

'Did they.'

'I had dreams of something. Of the might and glory of God – *you, you* were like the sign of it. That time – the blood on the lips of the statue...' Wedsek stopped. He pointed up to the south tower. 'Tonight. Is *that* only a ritual? Where does it go to, Anjelen? You know, I've served you. You aim at something. I *know* it. I'll follow you – to Hell.'

'Believe,' said Anjelen. He was a shadow, like the trees. 'What you worship is old as the world. Is the world. Believe in me.'

'I do,' Wedsek whispered.

'The rituals are not the passion,' said the shadow. 'But the passion has created the rituals. The rituals are games. As a child does, learn by them.'

A cold wind sped through the garden, smelling of the river and the dusty, dirty sprawl of Chirkess.

The evening star had risen.

Anjelen was going on towards the Cathedral, and Wedsek ran to his cell, to dress himself as a priest, to obeise himself before God. Subdued, convinced. Unsatisfied.

No servants at all entered the upper chamber of the south tower. It was large in scope, approximating the space of a lordly hall, in shape a seemingly exact round, like the wall without. There were, between that outer wall and the inner, both of stone, certain apartments and offices that complemented the round chamber. Four arched doors connected to them, east, south, west and north. Four crimson curtains on rods of gold obscured the doors. On the eastern curtain was a sun in gold and on the western curtain a crescent moon in gold. In gold upon the south and north curtains were a heron and an owl respectively. At the centre of the great circular floor, which was laid with a heavy paving of pale stone, lay a brazen disc, inset by a cross of black marble, its arms of equal length. From the disc a sort of web or tracery of gold ran out to all points over the floor, a pattern mathematical yet obscure, disturbing if regarded for too long. Twenty pillars of stone rose around the room, close to the circling wall. They were featureless to their tops; here they became stone trees, carved with branches and foliage. Three or four fruits of gold and silver hung in each, representations of the pomegranate, the pear, the quince and the peach. The roof of the chamber was painted blue and marked by golden stars in the form of constellations, perhaps, yet these too were uncomfortable to the eye if gazed at more than a few moments. The centre of the roof held a colossal depending lamp of brass on a chain of gilded iron. It displayed the beasts of the Apocalypse, an eagle, a lion with a serpent's tail, a bull with the lower part of a fish, an angel, all leaning out on wings of silver, with the lamps hanging from them in necklaces, ten bronze cups of oil to each figure and all alight.

Beyond the pillars, between them and the inner wall, a strip of chequered floor ran around. Above this, in the alcoves of the wall, lit by forty lamps of black iron, were forty carved stone faces, some of animals and monsters, some of men in torment and joy. As the lights shimmered on them, their expressions slightly altered or intensified, an audience compelled to watch for ever.

At midnight, the summons to prayer collected the priests of the Fraterium of Chirkess into the Cathedral. They went to their places and knelt down. Then, in at the door, there came a battalion of mailed men, armed, helmed and visored. Over the armour the tunic was white. No man in the Cathedral turned to look. Not the officiating priest, the Administer, the two Magisters, none of the higher or lower orders.

The Knights of God, of whom, at Chirkess, there were then sixteen, stood throughout the last ceremony of the evening. When it was done, they went out again, and their brothers remained, motionless, to let them go.

The warriors passed along under the wall in the silence, entered the garden, approached the south tower. All the doors stood open. They ascended through the armoury into the apartments of the alchemists and came up into the round chamber of the great lamp, via the south door of the heron, from which the curtain was drawn back.

The sixteen men assumed their stance around the wide central disc, the brazen plaque with the cross. The positions had been marked out, every one, with a little cross of jet set down there on the edge of the disc. Each man, arriving, knelt as he had not done in the church, touched his fingers to the small cross, and then to his lips. After that, he rose, and withdrew the helm from his head. In the auburn light, the faces recognised one another, without salute. They were not, here, as they had been.

The curtain on the south door dropped, and that to the north looped aside without visible agency. Through the owl door came a figure like that of a woman (no women were permitted here) cloaked in black. The figure advanced a few paces and began to sing to the glory of God, in a magnificent female and unreal voice. Raising her head and her hands, they might behold she was a skeleton, with palms of bone and skull of ivory. She sang of the fragility of man, lest they forget. An hour of time to live and to be. Only in God was life everlasting to be found.

When her song was done, her head and hands were lowered and put away, and she glided backwards from the chamber, out of the owl door, and the curtain sank.

At the centre of the central disc, where the greater cross had been inscribed, a mechanism operated. An inner panel parted from itself four ways, and out of the dark below came up a golden thing, like a vast coin. A black cup stood there, from which incense smoked, raw and sweet.

One of the Knights lifted his eyes, looking upwards; Wedsek.

Presently, from somewhere within the lamp of brass, a sword hurled itself down towards the cup, stopping suddenly three feet above it, quivering and ringing, on a metal thread. The blade of the sword appeared to burn.

The curtain on the west door of the room raised itself, and a figure in white entered. It had a white hood, a visor of silver, and in its hands a sword of steel. Though another doll, it spoke with a male voice.

'Say now, brethren, why is it that you gather here?'

Tonight Wedsek, who had not turned to glance at the west door, must speak the words of the vow. This fell to every man in turn, for two or three gatherings at a stretch.

Across from Wedsek, Anjelen.

Wedsek spoke loudly, with all his ability, to Anjelen, whose eyes seemed not to see anything that was in the chamber.

'We are here for our faith, to pledge service to our Lord, the Christus, by means of prayer and duty, and, with these, by force of arms and the sword. We alone, Knights of God, have committed ourselves to this, without blemish or stain of earthly wants, vainglory, or the jealousy of the world.'

Anjelen had spoken on the last occasions. The calendar of these rites was irregular, fixed by planetary conjunctions. It had been two months before.

And when Anjelen spoke, the stones had seemed to shift and shine, the sword to brace itself. A high honed singing note had whistled round the chamber. The lamps fluttered, reddened, sprang up more vividly. It was as if the roof would give way and a hand of light hover there, or a molten dove fly down. But these things had not happened. Wedsek did not suppose he was capable of creating them, if Anjelen had not done so. Nevertheless, his nostrils stung by the powerful incense, his nerves drawn like strings over the instrument of his heart, Wedsek tingled to unconceived possibilities, and stumbling on his words, had to collect himself.

Then, as the Knights responded in unison, he experienced a deflation of his soul.

Wedsek chafed against himself. These mysteries were romantic and proficient, but the marvels came from the alchemist's art practised below. Ignorance and paganism were the enemies of the Knights, and no battle was demanded save the spiritual fight asked of any priest. While the brushing wing of God must be taken on trust.

The responses were over, and the white-robed doll went backwards through the west door.

The eastern curtain of the sun lifted away, and a second white-clad priest-doll entered. Its face was masked in gold, and on a golden tray it bore the Chalice, which was of smoky green glass. The doll moved towards the disc and the circle of Knights, along a gold line in the patterned floor. Wedsek, over the sputter of the lamps, his own breathing, heard a vague sound of wheels.

When the doll reached him, it halted. It had not been given a voice. It was Wedsek who turned and took up the green Chalice, within which the liquid looked black as gall.

'And He gave them the wine,' announced Wedsek, 'saying, Drink, this is my blood. Hereafter do this always in my name. For He was the Sacrifice, dying for our sins, that we may be redeemed through Him.'

Wedsek moved about the disc, inside the rim of it, giving the Chalice one by one to each man.

And when he came to Anjelen, Anjelen only accepted the vessel, drank from it, and let it pass.

Last of the sixteen, Wedsek too sipped from the Chalice. He then replaced it on the tray of the automaton, that instantly backed across the floor and vanished inside the eastern curtain.

Children's games, by which to learn...

The Knights knelt in prayer.

'*Show me the path, Lord.*' Wedsek, in his brain: unsatisfied.

So in the henna smoke of autumn, Wedsek the unsatisfied went to his prayers, fasted at his penances, scourged himself, walked proudly as a Knight in mail once more to the room of symbols and crimsons, and rode in the chase on the plains below Chirkess. What he missed, and did not know, or must not know, was what his body hankered for – the fruit of the body, male life, the vaunting and lusting, the making of himself over in children, the responsibilities of which he would have been most capable – the management of a household, the ways of the world. But instead he had the bread of cold white love, the wine of sacred fire. From these exquisite ghosts he had tried to fashion for himself an alternative to that from which he had been sundered. These phantom foods must become, for Wedsek, savoury and devourable as the feasts of the flesh. But they had not, they were of another order.

Wedsek took the Christus as his Overlord, but the Christus would not come down from His cross.

Anjelen stood now between Heaven and earth. Anjelen was the only hope.

Out on the plain, the far side of the narrow river, the willows and the birch groves were full of the embers of leaves. The country passed down into red valleys of oak and poplar. Fir trees gripped boulders in their claws. This was woodland, but not forest. They hunted there, beyond the levelled grain where nothing fed now but the crows.

There were no great silences in these woods. The ending of the year would strip them bare, relining them in the white coat of the ermine.

They had hunted a wild pig. It had led them a dance. Firstly they were glad to get off such a distance from their fane. Then the sun went westerly and the day was running too.

Anjelen never rode at the forefront of any hunt. Its excitements did not touch him, apparently. Like the firs, he stood out black on the colours of the woodland, black hair and habit, and the black horse.

The six other men had gone rushing on. Wedsek said, 'No trace of it for an hour.'

Anjelen said nothing. He was looking about him slowly, deliberately, not for game, it would seem. At the foot of the trees, the scarlet leaves lay in dry pools.

Wedsek glanced here and there. Up on the naked bough of a

tawny ash, he saw, clear as surprise, something hanging from a bit of thread.

'Look – what is *that?*'

Anjelen did not look, he had already seen.

'The skull of a fox.'

The gaunt and broken thing reminded Wedsek – of what? A gargoyle from the church at Khish, or from the chamber of the Knights of Chirkess.

'An offering,' said Wedsek. He drew his knife and was about to slash the thread, to cut down this pagan atrocity.

'No,' said Anjelen.

'No? This godless frippery…'

'Not godless. What we do in church, they do here, under the trees.'

Anjelen had stopped the black horse.

Wedsek leaned about to see him.

'There's only one God,' said Wedsek. His voice sounded strained and anxious, unnerving him. 'This is worship of false gods. The Devil.'

'There is only God,' said Anjelen. The black eyes were there. Wedsek gave way to them. He felt a surge of alarm. He was glad. 'Don't you realise, Wedsek? Since there is only God, whatever is worshipped, must be God? They come to the ash and hang a skull on it, and spill blood at its foot like the red leaves lying there. The Tree must have blood, but it makes return. What dies for the Tree, who dies for it, becomes the Tree. Man and Tree. Both are one. Both Sacrifice and Lord, victim and master, together. And what else is the Christus?'

'I…' said Wedsek.

Anjelen had dismounted. He walked to the ash tree, and the skull began to move in the wind. Before Anjelen had reached it, the skull had become a wolf's head made of silver that swayed back and forth. It was a bell, it rang out. It was like the bells of the Cathedral, the little bells of the ceremonies.

Some sort of overcast had spoiled the sky. A vast cloud had come down on the tops of the wood. Everything grew veiled. A circle of darkness with a lid of shadow held them in.

Wedsek saw Anjelen under the ash tree, which towered now, into the grape-purple overcast, and was lost there, with the silver drop of its wolf bell ringing dimly.

Something fluttered. A huge moth, playing round the light of Anjelen, for only Anjelen gave light. He wore mail, as in the chamber of the Knights. His arms were outflung, so he seemed pinned by nails of black fire upon a cross...

Anjelen said, inside the brain of Wedsek, 'I will make you into what you are. Become mine.'

Wedsek moved towards Anjelen. As in certain dreams, he experienced nothing of the world, did not sense his footfalls on the grass or hear the leaves crushed under them.

Anjelen was the statue of the Christus, mailed. The moth flew away from it, but the burning nails pierced on, and from them ran the rubies of the blood. Not murky wine in a chalice, true ichor, so very red.

He did not hesitate, Wedsek, he set his lips to the wounds in hands and feet, in the side where the lance had torn the heart. Huge inner seas belaboured him, he hung like a lost leaf on the tree, until the gale shook him free into nothingness.

'And you will do this, in remembrance of me.'

They had found the wild pig. They cantered through the forest after it. The trees were much thicker here, fir and pine and spruce, hemlock and cedar mingled with the leavened autumn oaks. Branches cut at their faces like swords. They ducked and wove in the saddle and the horses ran on.

The boar was like a brown barrel rolled before them, hurtling through the undergrowth, breaking away.

Wedsek heard the other men shouting. He held up his left arm to defend his eyes.

He was not quite sure how he came to be where he was. He had paused with Anjelen, to discuss some token of theology – odd in itself, for Anjelen, knowing his preference, did not turn to Wedsek for such debates.

It was dark in the woods, dusk in day, though the sun itself must be near to going down, for frequently there came, ahead of them, a smouldering flare of red, as the wild pig raced towards the sunset.

Wedsek too shouted aloud, to try to start fervour or even agitation in himself.

And then, suddenly, in the manner of such a headlong advance, a glade burst out, flinging itself across and around them. It was enchained with red sunlights, thick with mast and fallen leaves, and there stood the barrel of the pig at bay.

The Chirkessian priests, who hunted like nobles not peasants, cast their spears. The boar, quilled with death, reared and plunged down. Two men were off and digging in their knives. They poised, action over, abruptly quite still, black on the flamey lights, and the forest settled round them.

The boar had not made any sound, as it died.

Wedsek swung off his horse and went to look. The other two drew aside, and behind him, Wedsek heard the soft trampling of the horses, reined in on leaves.

The pig was strange. It was not made of flesh, but rather it was like a nut from the trees, an acorn or walnut, a closed cone. Where the spears had penetrated, they had cracked its shell. The long fissures ran over its smooth carapace. Its snout was carved, its carved eyes shut. From the parted jaws stuck brown clean walnut teeth and a grained tongue like peeled bark. It was a vegetable of the wood, a pod, a seed.

The vegetable boar turned his stomach, but Wedsek was not afraid. He remembered he had tasted Anjelen's blood.

Wedsek woke, roasting under the single cover, which he thrust off impatiently.

He had been dreaming. He lay, trying to decipher what was dream, and what a memory of the afternoon's hunt.

'In the name of God...'

He threw himself upright. He stood. And the night's coolness sluiced down to tone the heat of his body.

There had been no curious, no lawless or blasphemous or wonderful thing. They had hunted in the woodland over the river, and come back with a pig...

There had been a skull tied in a tree and he had chopped it down.

No, Anjelen had prevented that.

God is God. Whatever is worshipped *is* God.

Anjelen flew up to the statue of the Christus, and kissed it, and wounds sprang out on Anjelen, and from these wounds Wedsek had drunk the Blood which was the Life.

Trembling and shivering, Wedsek dropped to his knees. He prayed, gripping the edge of his pallet, and beyond the partition (which at Chirkess, was of thin plaster), he heard the snores of Godbrother Kopis.

He is the Devil, Anjelen...

But how could the Devil copy the sacred stigmata of the Christus?

Anjelen, the Angel of the Blood.

A thrilling terror sang through Wedsek. He seized the scourge with its knots and beat his shoulders. He was possessed by great strength, both to inflict and to bear.

The Factor sat in his room high in the castle-Cathedral of Chirkess, and watched Magister Egar search about him for a chair.

There were one or two of these items, fine pieces of dark wood, with cushions of damask. The room towered with books, elaborate artefacts of religion in costly materials – ebony, marble – a painted panel of the Agony pointed up with gold leaf, and a sapphire in the aureole of the Christus.

Magister Egar could no longer pick out these things, as he could not, without difficulty, detect the alchemical splendours of his own cell. Chairs might be confused with cabinets.

'Allow me to assist you, Magister. This room, I'm afraid, becomes overcrowded.'

The Factor guided Egar. Egar allowed this without rancour. He accepted his plight, as God had averred all men must, meekly, without a single cry or kick.

'Some wine? My stairs are steep. The days are cold now.'

'Thank you, no.'

'Then how may I help your grace?'

Egar looked, or more precisely blindly stared, at his knobbed hands, deformed by rheumatism, agile only in pain. 'One of our number. A godbrother. We've spoken of this young man before.'

'Indeed, your grace.'

'Anjelen.'

'Ah yes... Anjelen.' The Factor added, 'I ordained him. He was Jun, then. Are you pleased with his progress in your science, your grace?'

'He has genius,' said the Magister. 'It seemed God had given to me the son I might never have. And for this audacity of mine, I'm punished.'

The Factor did not tense himself any more than he had already. The reflex was, in him, the coiling of the snake before it strikes. Anjelen, the Factor had always known, was a creature of lightning. He might be dangerous to fools, and half-blind old men.

'Can you explain yourself, your grace? I'm startled. Why are you punished in Anjelen? I hear nothing of him but excellence.'

'He's a Knight of God.'

'Of course. As were you yourself, formerly, until the prescribed age, Magister Egar.'

'And as you are yet, Factor.'

'I have, according to the tenets, nine further years in which to offer my service to God in such a form.'

'And Anjelen, favoured by you, was elected to the Knighthood.'

'Yes, Egar. While you selected him for tuition in your arts. Father Church, as we know, must encourage the flowers of his vine, not stifle them.'

Egar said, 'When last did you attend a gathering?'

'Of the Chirkess Knighthood? Well, Magister, not for some years. My task has been frequently to be abroad, on the work of God. Elsewhere I have attended, of course.'

'The ceremonies of the Knights here have passed by rote to Anjelen again. Now, he changes them.'

The Factor lifted his thin cruel brows.

'How is this known to your grace? You're no longer of the brotherhood of the Knights.'

'Alchemy plays its part in the ritual. I must oversee the procedure.'

Oversee? This blind man?

'Don't you, your grace, delegate younger brethren?'

'But they must report to me any oddity.'

'Reveal the oddity then, your grace. I'm most concerned.'

Egar looked up, peering at the Factor through the mists of his dying eyes. Egar spoke too loudly, out of deafness, and fear.

'The Chalice returned to me with dregs not of wine – but as I think, of blood.'

The Factor was as motionless as a viper under a rock.

'My eyes deteriorate daily, and my hearing is muffled,' said Egar. 'But I can smell and taste. The stink of blood gone cold was evident to me.'

'This accusation...' said the Factor.

'I accuse no one. I ask you, Father, in your role of Knight, to attend the next gathering in the south tower. They must admit you. Under the secrecy of the order, they may reveal what occurs. If not, you may demand it.'

When Magister Egar was gone, the Factor of Chirkess opened his calendar in its plates of ivory, and gazing through his crystal lens, deduced the proper night. Dullness had actually absented him from the rituals, though he kept up their privileges. The blaze of his living eyes the blind one had not seen.

Seventeen Knights had come in mail to the ritual in the tower, but behind the pillars with their dripping fruits, forty lit stone faces fleeted and blinked. There a man bitten by a cat, and there a sheep toothed like a wolf, a wolf with the horns of a ram, a child with three eyes... Perhaps not all the Knights of Chirkess had noted one extra was among them. But then they had grown dazed. Three conjunctions of stars and lunar orb had brought them in swift succession to the round room, which now changed itself. They had waxed and waned too, away from the room by day and night, doubting, questioning, yet held like flies in ice.

The crimson curtain of the heron door had sunk, the lamp of the apocalypse hung like a smoking planet.

There was a quiet, like winter on the land outside.

The curtain of the owl door raised. The lights in the lamp turned brown.

And in the brown light, Death rode out through the door.

Death on his pale horse of bones, in his mantle and hood, and crowned with a diadem of golden owls.

Death sang, in a boy's alabaster voice, of mortality. A raven of black bone perched on his left hand.

When Death was gone, the floor parted. And out of it there arose the kingdoms of the earth.

A plateau of waters and mountains, forest, and deserts of snow and dust. And golden cities shone there. It was the view from the height, the Temptation. And incense wafted from the censers of golden cities and the deserts of cinnamon.

Next the sword fell. But it was a hundred swords, which dashed like rain. Their blows smote the Knights of God beneath, insubstantial, potent.

And the seventeenth Knight, he endured also the swords of Heaven. *He has learned better alchemy. These are a mage's tricks.*

The swords were done, and through the door of the moon came the figure of the sword doll.

'Say now, brethren, why is it that you gather here?'

The Factor glanced, under his lids. It must be Anjelen to speak the first responses.

Anjelen, in his extraordinary voice, which thirty years of training would not have made, which only God could have articulated and tuned to construct this music, said: 'We are here for our faith.'

The Factor, once a seasoned campaigner of these rituals, at Chirkess and in more mediocre circumstances, and more illustrious, was used to the fluffing or forgetting of the lines, the stammers and inadequacies.

When Anjelen said nothing else, he was offended, deeply and horribly, thinking for a moment that Anjelen had fumbled, and failed.

Then, he saw, from the bearing of Anjelen, that nothing had been mishandled. It was Anjelen's formula to say no more. These words were all there were, now, to be.

And ordered up by them, out of the customary rhythm but obedient, the doll of the sword withdrew into its wall.

The Factor flicked his gaze now along the attending Knights.

They stood as they must according to writ, as if in the eye of battle, straight and speechless. Their eyes were glazed from the incense, as they willed themselves into a trance. He could remember that, the forcing wish for some rare thing, which had never come.

But now the curtain was rising up over the door of the sun.

The Factor let his eyes travel once more, and watching the door, saw then come out of it not the doll that bore the cup of the wine – no, nothing like that.

From the door of the sun slowly walked a figure, human, male, unmasked, naked white but for a linen loincloth, and on its head a garland if ivy and briar from the winter woods. Not a boy, but a young man. Black hair and eyes like black agate. And the whiteness not solely colour, but power.

The Factor, who was also God's warrior, directed his sight like a dagger through the circle of Knights. Anjelen was there, shorn and mailed. Yet, too, Anjelen came slowly over the golden tracery in the floor, mostly naked, a stream of hair like a mane across his shoulders.

Much better alchemy.

He found the evaluating words in his brain, and shook, the Factor in his ardour.

But the Chalice – where was that?

The hands of the figure, the second Anjelen, were empty. He was the sacrifice, equipped only for eternity.

Anjelen spoke again. The voice came as before from the mailed body in the circle, while the other approached across the paving.

'And he gave them the wine, saying, Drink, for this is my blood. Hereafter do this always in my name.'

The lids of the eyes of Anjelen the Knight were nearly lowered, and beneath was only blackness. There was no white to the eyeballs. Two slots like night in water.

The Factor trembled and held himself alert for any flaw. But the perfection of the almost naked man had moved into the circle. He had lifted up his palms, which were full of scarlet from the wounds of the nails. He went to each of the Knights in turn (missing only one, his double), and gave them to drink from the chalice of his hands.

And the Factor waited, shaking, but in control of himself, his intellect poised to receive or to rescind.

Each Knight drank the wine. The chalice was before the Factor. Like the rest, the Factor did nothing but lean forward to drink. As he did so, he scented the body of the creature, the holy odour of arboreal things, not mortal, not flesh. The blood lay like a jewel, and as his lips hung on the moisture of it, strange fire began. Abstemious, he did no more than touch to the fire his tongue. Not meaty or salt, not *blood.* Not blood or wine, but the spirit of God transmuted through the intermediary vessel. A red rose flowered behind the eyes. The petals unfolding and unfolding like waves or wings.

The ceremony was over. The creature that was of God, or was God, had gone away like the mechanisms. The Knights stood in their circle.

The Factor, having opened his eyes, beheld the rose of blood unfolding away into the face of Anjelen, and the eyes that had no whites were altered now, passing for human.

'What have you witnessed?' said Anjelen.

The Factor replied, 'You are more than I supposed.'

So, in some concealed sort of reverie, he had long planned that he would confront his Lord. Rational always, this man, for the Factor adored the logic and the intellectual soul of his religion. It was this he worshipped in the person of God, and took for God. The Christus of the Factor had, of necessity, been a prince, having for speech oratory and wit, having a weapon as a mind, beauty for a voice, an unblemished frame in which Godhead had poured itself – these were essentials of the God-in-man. God could not be shown forth in any other caste. Nor should God, returned to men, be greeted by rude outcry, exclamation, gross silliness. In calm reverence the Factor knelt to the lightning flash.

'I have given you the Blood of the Life,' said Anjelen. 'And in recompense, I ask the same.'

Each of the others, these spellbound warriors, they had offered back the gift, in this chamber, in some chapel, cell, some ruined tower, somewhere.

'Take what you will from me,' said the Factor, 'Lord.'

There was after all no one else in the chamber. It seemed not any longer a place of stone, but the vault of a tree, veined and ribbed, with beasts that looked with eyes of topaz and obsidian out of its galleries. Above were branches of stars in a neutral sky, not day or night.

Anjelen was with him, inside the tree. Anjelen struck the man's throat lightly and from it a fountain sprang. Painless, sure.

The Factor sat reasoning in his brain, savouring the ecstasy of the rite, praying deliberately and serenely to God. Thanking God for the salvation of mankind, for the promise fulfilled. And all around, the shadows watched as Anjelen drew the Factor upward, weightless like a child of two years, until the brim of the Factor's severed throat came to his lips. Anjelen drank the blood. And it was dark in the chamber, like the wood, black as the forest, under the trees.

The Magister, Egar, could only half recall, at the start of it, how he had prayed lovingly, earnestly to God, to melt away the frost from his eyes. But the methods of God were pitiless in their purity. The blindness came on, as the deafness did, gentle as breath in sleep. He must endure. Egar, by his own mathematics, measured his decline. A few months more, and they would have to lead him by the hand. A year, and only the highest notes of the singing, the twitter of the birds, the rasp of a file in the forge, would reach him. He was being walled up alive. Yet, still he trusted God. The teacher was stern, He beat and upbraided you, to bring you to the ultimate knowledge. As a tutor, Egar had modelled himself upon God. The side of his tongue was slicing as the whip, but he expended punishment only on those worthy of it, the bright pupil who had grown lazy or inept, the fanatic who was careless.

In Anjelen, when Anjelen had come to be, Egar had not perceived any kind of son. This cliché was wrung from him in the vicinity of the Factor, like a cry of hurt striving for speech. Anjelen was like the last light, before the night fell down. In him, Egar achieved a resurgence of faith, his trust shored up. For God had sent Anjelen to take up the torch of understanding. Egar showered the gold of his science upon Anjelen. *I don't matter. Truth matters.*

Here the vehicle is. I need not be afraid, for there is justice.

Egar crouched now, out of custom, over his bench, with a book open before him and the utensils scattered about. He could see them dimly, even the letters written on the page, though not their meaning anymore. He liked to touch these things, the alembics and pestles, the silken half-skull of a man which was the reminder of mortality, but also an object of miracle in its exact structure, one other proof of the genius of the Creator – as was the foetus of the dog inside its tube of crystal, the rock with the imprint of an animal old as the earth. He liked to touch, and now he must see by touch. He ran his fingers over contours, but he recollected the smell of blood in the cup.

The Factor had not spoken to him of the ceremony. As usual, the Factor stalked about the precincts, occupied by Church business. He had taken to wearing a high collar against the cold, a recent affectation among the Knights of God, as if to rival the red waist cord of the alchemists' school. Egar had not been able to discern the collar, but he had heard it remarked on.

Anjelen had charge of the mysteries of the alchemical ritual of the Knights' gathering. He alone would in future order them, conducting them from the chamber above, which Egar would have thought was not feasible. The Factor and the Administer had both condoned this new regime, Egar being disabled and doddery. Dismissed from his role, he would have no excuse to ascertain if the Chalice was again returned bloodied – or empty.

Thus, he knew it all. That evil had taken root, spread its leaves, grew up and pushed against the roof. The Cathedral was filling, day by day, with its spicy, pleasing perfume. Every pillar and brick was bound with tendrils. There was no defence.

No knock, loud for his deafness, drummed on the door. No step or rustle of a male robe could be audible to Egar. Nor had any shutter of light and dark teased at the remnant of his vision.

Yet he was aware at once, as in the corridors, in the dining hall, the cloister, alone or among others, that Anjelen was here and that the Devil, therefore, had come into his room with him.

Egar stayed still, one hand on the skull of man, the other over the emerald crucifix on his breast.

'You honour me,' said Egar. 'For what inconceivable reason do you need to visit me here?'

'You,' said Anjelen, 'are my tutor, Magister.'

The voice penetrated unhindered, as no other sound ever would again.

'No longer a tutor to any. Egar's found wanting. He has no work.'

Anjelen began to be visible, and for a second Egar wondered, in a corrupt hope, if he might see him fully and clearly, as he had heard him, the form, like the voice, of the Devil, burning through. But Anjelen was a shadow, only darkness, a pillar of smoke.

'I taught you the great science,' said Egar. 'But you didn't need my little lessons.'

'Yes,' said Anjelen, 'to give a name to what I do.'

Egar said, dismayed to be inflamed by this dialogue in Hell, 'Of course. If men can say, There is an alchemist, there is a magician, they miss the other name. But you were, for such a mighty one, curiously bungling over the blood.'

The shadow shifted; it drew nearer. It did not answer. Egar thought in sudden despair that after all, the cup had not been Anjelen's negligence. It was only that it did not concern Anjelen. He might do as he wished, suborn, destroy, hypnotise, anything, as he wanted. And even if he did not, where he hid himself and took trouble, as in the learning of alchemy, it was merely for convenience, a notion maybe, an alternative process of moving forward. Never, even in his meditations on God, had Egar glimpsed a supremacy like this. But then, he had never been this close, to God.

Then Anjelen pressed one hand on the forehead of the Magister.

The contact was momentary, cold and quick, and gone.

As it departed, it took all the rest. The room vanished. There was a greyness, but without colour, without even the vaguest blur of configuration, no depth, no brightness, no shade. In Egar's ears, two doors had swung shut.

He was within, closed inside the walls of his own head. Under his hand, the skull felt farther than a star. He could not believe in it. He let it go.

No fire of terror broke in Egar. He stayed. He searched for God, knowing that this ordeal was as random as anything Anjelen was prone to award, that he, Egar, had no special claim on the mercy of Heaven. Closed within the tower of blindness and unhearing, the sin of the seeing and listening Cathedral could not infect him. A blessing?

No terror, and yet, after an hour, a frightening childlike thing, which said, *How long? How long?*

'Deliver me,' said Egar, feeling the vibration of his voice.

Soon someone would come, after the prayers, or dinner, and see what had happened to him. He would say nothing of Anjelen, even supposing he could will himself to be intelligible with only the vibrations of his throat to guide him. And soon too this corpse body would dismiss him. That must now be certain.

Or would he live on, healthy for a decade or more, kindly led, impatiently spared, like a man with a boulder clasped on his head, his ears and his eyes changed to stone, sniffing about in the nothingness for the odour of the Wicked One? Egar gripped his hands together, held himself in the trap, and waited, waited, waited.

Chapter Six

Winter was Chirkess.

The alleys, hovels, houses, were made of snow, with black abrasions of mud before the doors. The smoke composed a cloud that seldom lifted. The river prepared to freeze.

On its terraces the Cathedral seemed bewitched. Was it possible to enter the gates? The gatherers of sticks and dung who wandered the streets glanced up without response at the mansion of God. It had not yet got to the stage of pleading for bread.

Unlike the city, the Cathedral garden had kept its cadences, paths freed of snow, laid in white squares, tented with white trees.

To Wedsek, it seemed he had walked in this way, a pace behind Anjelen, for miles, for weeks.

Anjelen appeared to tell his beads. Appeared? Doubtless he did so. About the garden elsewhere, the black figures perambulated. The pink winter sun shone on them, and slicked upon rounds of enamels, eyes.

They had reached the statue of a saint burdened by snow. Anjelen paused. He looked about him, and all the black figures in the garden stirred like reeds brushed by a current in water. So it was when he advanced through the building. None dropped to his knees, obeised himself; the Administer received Anjelen's bow. Yet, they were Anjelen's. His priesthood, his warriors, his disciples.

I have drunk his blood. He has had mine.

A shameful glory, like a blush, until the skeleton of Wedsek seemed to catch alight.

He might do anything.

Wedsek would follow Anjelen, to Hell or out of Hell. Whatever Anjelen was – Son of God, Son of Night. It had never come clear which.

Anjelen stood by the statue, and Wedsek murmured, 'Well, then.'

Anjelen's eyes moved over him.

'I mean,' said Wedsek, 'tell me, what would you have?'

Anjelen said, 'I have it.'

'What is your mission?' said Wedsek.

Anjelen told his beads. They slipped like a dark snake through his long fingers.

'What,' said Wedsek, 'is there for me to do?'

In various ciphers, this phrase had been now and then placed before Anjelen. Replies sometimes were elicited, but they had had no substance.

'It stands still,' said Wedsek. 'Like the winter. Is it just that? What are you waiting for, my lord?' And he said again, with iron passion, 'My *lord*.'

Anjelen did not speak.

'I ask only what you have in mind – the future – a month away, a year. But what is it?'

Magister Hyrus came through the garden on his route to the Cathedral offices. (Egar had become decrepit and was no longer seen.) The Magister did not acknowledge Anjelen, and yet the very garments on his body seemed to make deference. It was the will of Anjelen that nothing be overt.

Wedsek balanced on the edge of the unnameable and questioned it. The return must come, the whirlwind, the silent voice: Where, then, were you when I laid the foundations of time, gathered up the seas and lit the singing stars of the morning all together.

But Anjelen now gave nothing.

The snake of beads coiled through his hands, and behind him a slender tree, powdered white, made the same ebbing motion at a coil of wind.

'The lord in the city's churlish,' said Wedsek. 'Some bother over alms. Anjelen,' said Wedsek.

The Christus had drawn men to Him, from their work, their boats, their families, out of living into Life. *Do this, for me.* They wandered like young wolves over the land.

Even a reprimand might serve, to solace this inquiry.

'Anjelen, we're *brothers in blood*…'

A finger fell on Wedsek's wrist. He started at it. The bush at his elbow, clothed with snow and motivated too by the wind, it was this which had caught hold of him. And the white tree moved again. But Anjelen did nothing at all.

There was a moment of perceptiveness for Wedsek. He beheld, by means of some magic glass of basic human sense, the inner room of Anjelen's consciousness. Wedsek could not have said what he saw there. He recoiled at it. It was instinct which told him how and where to see, and instinct which blotted out every iota of the view. The tree grew, it ascended. It needed no more. It *was*. And the magnificent and blazing brain lay around it like a dragon to guard, to burnish, helpful and, finally, superfluous.

The white tree quivered, and the bush tapped Wedsek's arm. Anjelen was still, not even the beads sifting over his hand.

Wedsek knew himself orphaned and did not know why or from what. Nothing had happened.

Twelve white Knights rode through the city, after the bread carts. The provisions were sent unasked, on a freezing noon under sky like lead and swagged with new snow. The Overlord had been heard, in a peevish fit, to say it was his employment to supply viands; the Cathedral had its own work. The Cathedral, then, pre-empted him.

There was a different tone to this. It was militant. And the Knights in their mail, beings rumoured of and partly mythical, looking as if they had leapt down fully armed from the Cathedral's cornices and columns and the warlike window; they stoppered every protest. The Cathedral guard, with the red buttons on their helms, might have attended the carts, and indeed did so, sitting by on their horses in the slush and ice as the godbrothers and novices dealt out loaves. The Knights rode up and down, princely and obdurate.

Along by the river, the Overlord glared from a window, and saw it going on in the square below the Cathedral. He reportedly inquired who and what were the Knights. On being informed, he denied that this brotherhood, these priest-warriors, were ever seen; it was an act of faith with them to remain invisible, and to conceal their ceremonies.

But black and steel and white, the Knights were there, and behind the visors were the half-faces of remote and devout men encountered elsewhere in the capacity of religion, or of the priestly hunters who rode through the city too fast to gain recognition. The hunting had been blatant enough. The Overlord chafed, but his wife was giving birth in another room. She might die. Priests were always necessary.

The captain of the troop was Wedsek; he had been given this position five days before. Soon Anjelen was to be created a Magister. The winter went on and on, and the unloading of loaves was like the winter. But constantly Wedsek felt a vital spring within himself, at his own image in the mail, the way in which his men took his orders – inconsequential, of no importance, yet redolent of war for all that. Say, the city had been besieged, and they had come off the ramparts to feed it... *God give me battles.*

Wedsek rode back and forth along the carts. The people of the city had stared, and fresh ones arrived all the time and gawped in their turn. Wedsek absorbed their curiosity and slight fear; the faces meant nothing, their gender or sort. Until, in the tail of sight, Wedsek beheld Anjelen, on the snowy street, at an alley's corner, gazing with the rest.

Of course, it was not Anjelen. This Wedsek knew even as he glimpsed the apparition. Something in Wedsek knew a great deal, and tried continually to tell him the facts, but Wedsek, as most men grow to be, was fast at avoidance. He looked, and saw a young man, perhaps sixteen or seventeen years – Anjelen himself, though he must be past his twenty-first year, looked not much older (save in the eyes, the eyes). It was the eyes, oddly, of the boy on the street which were Anjelen. Not the core of them, not the expression or intensity, the (misleading) profundity of mind and thought. But the shape and line of the brows, perhaps the extreme blackness of the irises – that might only be a trick of the darkling day.

Wedsek did not consider. He saw the boy, who was Anjelen humanised and adjacent. Wedsek reacted.

'You,' he said. The boy froze like the river, and Wedsek rode over to him. 'Have you had your share of bread?'

The boy looked nearly frightened, yet he kept his dignity. He was some labourer, by his dress: a leather apron over rough and partly threadbare clothes.

'My mamma will have got it, sir. My dad's gone. She's collect for us.'

Wedsek disliked the boy's babyish use of *mamma*, frequent enough among the lower pockets of town and city, and in the back woods.

'Why then are you standing gaping?' said Wedsek.

'I never saw Knights before. Knights of God. My grandda said, was a lie. You never see them.'

'But now you have,' said Wedsek. He laughed suddenly, pleased and disgusted at the conversation. The likeness of Anjelen came and went like a ghost. When he could catch it, Wedsek was quick to disarm and unnerve it, and shocked as he did so – and then the mirage faded off like steam, and he thought, *What am I doing here with this?*

The boy lowered his eyes. When he did that, the resemblance to Anjelen was piercing. But it was an Anjelen fourteen years of age, before the massy power had set on him like stone.

Wedsek thought: *His family may starve. This one fellow to support them all, probably.*

'What work do you do, boy?'

'On the wall,' said the boy, proud of his trade, which would be that of apprentice still to some mason or block-layer.

'Don't they feed you?'

'Soup,' said the boy. 'Glad to get it.'

'And your house?' Wedsek did not know why he asked.

'Over by the wharf inn. I'm Larl.' Alert now, hoping for attention. It would do no harm to be neighbourly with a Knight of God.

'Get along,' said Wedsek. 'Don't neglect your work, or your mother. Remember God.'

The boy's face sank inward. He was not Anjelen.

Wedsek, sitting the horse, face of steel visor, steely lips and jaw, watched him go off.

For some while, Knights of God were seen about the city of Chirkess. They rode by on fine horses, as the hunting priests had done. Their arms were carried with authority.

The show had been made, the largess distributed. The Overlord had ceased his whining. His child, a boy, was delivered safely, and in his letters here and there he made no mention, that his priestly secretaries noted, of any annoyance or untoward matter.

Then, once or twice, God's Knights were seen after sunset, on the broader streets, the flash of mail under a torch, the snow-white tunic with its cross-cut of black. Faces masked by metal.

The Cathedral must have ordered it. It made the robbers and low-life uneasy, and if the whores slipped away like mice, you would find them in their usual underground haunts, the taverns and hovel alleys.

Let God's Knights patrol Chirkess if they liked. The winter was hard. On and on. Soon, there might be more bread.

Nights no longer made for sleep. For the priest, in any case, there never was much slumbering: the midnight praying, the prayers in the black early hours of morning, interruptions to nature that became habitual. Between midnight then and the first devotion of morning, the Knights of God rode about Chirkess. Not all; not all were inclined to it. The insubstantial order that had sent them out, attendant on the bread carts, had evaporated. Yet no further order came to draw them in again. They were like pale eagles, not easily mewed.

There had been a gathering of the Knights. Anjelen did not preside over it but was merely a player. The rite was bizarre in its meekness. Not one of them spoke of this, as they had never discussed the Rite of Blood, like a dream or vision, which occurred before.

Now three Knights were in the square below the Cathedral, riding lightly with a soft noise on the snow, and the faint jingle of harness and of three swords in sheaths of silver and hide, like the thin white wind that blew weightlessly along the ground. From the river came a weird hollow sound of emptiness, as if from a huge and unrung waiting bell.

Towards the mouth of this the Knights rode. They had drunk the Wine of the Sacrifice (bitter vinegar), and real wine they had brought with them from the refectory, for, along with their exercise and horses and hunts, red meat and strong liquor were permitted them.

'The Factor,' said one of the mailed men, low, under the windows of Chirkess, 'didn't vouchsafe his company, tonight.'

So, one of them had alluded to it after all.

'He has a chill,' said Wedsek. He had not heard any report of that; in some obscure way he was protecting the night from extraneous things.

'He'll return, our Factor, when Anjelen...'

Unstayed, the man did not finish. They halted beneath an archway, heavy with its cap of snow. Everywhere the city lay smothered. In parts a dull glow from some fire of rag-pickers under a wall, or the individual tinted smokes curled up from holes and chimneys, and from two taverns with an orange window apiece. In the house of the Overlord were tall lights, and a sentry walked along the roof, his own armament chinking. The wharves and the one ship moored there, ice-locked, with a greenish lamp at her prow. But mostly the scribbles of white darkness and the nullity of fools who slept.

'The wine tonight,' said Wedsek, 'it failed us.'

They sat the horses.

The man who had spoken before, Riazi, said, 'But it was the best the kitchen had.'

Wedsek said, 'The *wine.*'

In the slough of snow city and night, they had made a circle of three. Their faces under the visored helms were alien, each to each. It was in the manner of the south tower, after the curtain of the heron door fell down.

'What's your meaning?' said the third Knight. He was a man from a nowhere place, a town beyond Chirkess. He had been bought all his stations, would be a Factor in a brace of years, was a Knight almost by default. Yet, he too, he too under the visor and the dark, made up the circle.

'It's given to us,' said Wedsek, hearing himself, half amazed, and not able to stop, 'to act the rite to its utmost. We're beyond ordinary law. We're God's. And he instructed us.'

'Anjelen,' said Riazi, again.

'Do this in my name.'

'And after, in remembrance.'

An excitement, cold and hard, an icicle slanting upward from their circle of power, a white and glistening sword of urgent and willing *want*.

'He gives us his jurisdiction. It's the way of it.'

Wedsek felt the trembling in his body. It surprised him a little. He had not yet caught up with himself.

'Our blood,' said Riazi, 'is it capable of translation into the wine – without Anjelen?'

'Not our blood. To him, we give. To the king and lord. Without withholding. But for ourselves, as he does, we'll take.'

Their eyes glittered. The real meaningless wine of the kitchen had gone up into their skulls like sorcery. They trembled also, Wedsek saw. They were with him. Anjelen had united them, his disciples. The train of events opened here, the fabric of everyday life torn on a wild light. Go through, be proven in this war. For the enemy within had shown himself now. He was prudence, human edict, the codes of a priesthood outgrown, for a king might rearrange his kingdom how he chose. Perhaps Anjelen had waited on them, as they on him. *Do this in my name.*

Do this…

'I know one who's intended for us,' said Wedsek. A deep insensate thrill went through him, at the rightness of it, and because they were of a mind with him, these men. Not one, but a triple being, and he its head.

They rode into the bell of the shore, where there were the wharves and the ship. The garrison loomed downriver.

They came into a space between the houses, with one end open to the sheet of the river ice. A stooping inn, closed, unlit. A torch-pole smouldered in front of it, and a house leaned there, one room and some cranny above under a tumbling roof. Smoke from the chimney. Outside, a water butt, and a workman's mallet left by it, too battered and worthless for anyone to steal.

Wedsek halted, and the other men, Riazi and the bought Knight, did the same. They had not exchanged further words.

Wedsek dismounted and walked to the door of the hovel by the inn. Round about, nothing moved, nothing looked out, not even a rat from the winter refuse. But he was masked, what could any see? He knocked lightly on the door, a familiar note, not threatening. And a woman's voice called quietly, 'Is that you?'

'No,' said Wedsek. (Then she gasped.) 'Send out Larl.'

There was a nothing. Next a flurry. She said, 'Why? What do you...' and he said, 'Don't come to the door. Send Larl. Hasten.'

From the back of the room Larl said, 'What is it, mamma?'

Wedsek called quietly, 'Larl, come out.'

'It's the old fellow,' muttered Larl, meaning perhaps some overseer off the wall.

The boy drew the bolt and put his head round the door, and beheld the Knight of God, one of three, on his sill.

'You must come with us,' said Wedsek.

'I haven't done anything,' said Larl, frightened now and not dignified. 'I haven't – who's said I did? Didn't. I never.'

'Dress yourself, and come out,' said Wedsek, 'or we'll take you as you are, in your shirt.'

'I'm not guilty of it.'

'On God's business. Do you resist?'

'No,' said Larl. He came out, and he was already dressed in everything but the leather apron, a coarse blanket round his shoulders. He had been sleeping by the fire, for he was warm, and there was soot on his cheek. He looked not at all like Anjelen, and then, very like him.

The mother was flapping inside the door, trying to get out too and see. Wedsek said, 'Go in, woman. Do as you're told.'

Larl walked before Wedsek to his horse. The door had shut. Alone with the Knights on the snow, Larl withered. He began to cry. Probably he had blasphemed God at his wall-building, or else committed some theft or lechery. He reckoned he was to be punished, not honoured. Wedsek touched Larl on the shoulder. 'Calm yourself. You're chosen. Special to God. Get on the horse.'

When Wedsek had got Larl lumpenly on the beast's back, he led the horse away between the houses. The new wall (Larl's wall), was far from finished yet; there were a hundred ways out, through the alleys and along the riverbank, over the fields and into the groves of apple trees and the deathly vineyards.

The excitement was as cold as the night. It beat in the breast like a hammer.

They avoided areas of fire or activity. They passed one live and mobile thing, some wretch scurrying between the house-backs, who glanced, and went away the faster. There was no moon, only deep shadows and the patched whiteness of ice and snow and stars.

A ruined and deserted mill, a pool like a tear wept out of the river, and of varying thicknesses of ice, presumably having been broken for water on the previous day. Tall, blackened reeds standing like sticks of decayed sugar, like bars.

They gave the boy from the city some of the kitchen wine, and it cheered him up.

The Knights smiled and nodded, also drinking from the flagon. Wedsek laughed with Larl. But Wedsek felt no laughter. His whole body was primed and shining, sparks darted along his veins as he gestured, walked, breathed, sometimes startling him, but only with pleasure, like the first drunkenness he had ever known.

Riazi brought a wreath of ivy from the mill. He put it on Larl's head, and there before them, still laughing and cheered, they began to see the sacrifice, clad in a workman's clothes and blanket. The clothes did not matter. Only the final clothing, the skin, must be stripped to bring forth the naked blood.

Wedsek said to Larl, 'What we do now is sacred. Never speak of it. On pain of the severest penalty. Do you understand?'

Larl nodded. The garland had sobered him, cold from the snow.

'Swear,' said Riazi. 'On God's name.'

The boy swore. His eyes were like a child's. He was not Anjelen.

Yet, Anjelen was there. Wedsek felt the face of Anjelen covering his own like the visor.

They made the circle, not speaking the secret words. In the mind of each the phrases flowed by, and, ready, they turned to the garlanded youth at the circle's centre.

Wedsek took hold of the boy, and with the sharp knife, cut open his hand, between the palm and the wrist. Larl uttered an animal cry. Wedsek held him. 'You must keep faith. You swore.' Larl gave in, submitting to Wedsek as Wedsek had submitted.

And Wedsek took Larl to Riazi and lifted up the ruby hand that was jet in the starlight.

'Drink, for this is his blood.'

Riazi bent his head, and sucked blood out of the hand. Then Wedsek propelled Larl to the third Knight, the outdweller, who also lowered his helmed head, and swallowed the blood.

Wedsek pulled the boy around. The night was burning with a fierce pale flame. Wedsek strained Larl up his body, over the mail. He saw that Larl had fainted, from cold, shock, or strong drink. Wedsek grinned, but it was not a grin. He sank his teeth into the little wound, and bit the blood up from it, gulping, thirsty, and it was the Wine. He had made it so. The Wine of God.

When he could make himself stop, Wedsek found he was loaded with weakness, and putting down the boy on the ground, he shook violently. He wiped his mouth and cleaned his hands in the snow, and the cold ached through him, into the pit of his skull, his feet and loins.

They used the snow too to stop the bleeding. Bound up the hand with the boy's own rags.

They were like naughty urchins now, earnest to end the prank, cover up and be off.

The third Knight – Wedsek had forgotten his name – wanted to leave Larl by the mill.

'He'll live. He'll find his own road back.'

But they hauled him as far as the new wall, threw him flat, and spilled liquor on him there. He was reviving, whimpering.

'Recall your oath, or it's death,' said the third Knight.

Larl nodded.

They left him in the shelter of a hut and rode through Chirkess, wanting to get away from each other also. Near the Cathedral, Wedsek spoke. 'We too were bonded. Don't talk of this. Don't *regret* this.'

'You had his blood like a wolf,' said Riazi.

Wedsek stared him down, and the eyes of Riazi shrank back into the visor-slits. They would have to see each other again at the morning devotion.

'Blood is life,' said Wedsek. 'Only Anjelen can judge me.'

He thought: *Anjelen will know. No need to tell him. And God too. There's nothing to confess.*

Winter waited in Chirkess, lay there like a white beast, on its belly, brooding.

Men moved about like ants on a marble slab.

The snow turned gradually beige, and muddy, and nothing rebuilt it.

There was a bare blue sky, and the snow soaked into the earth, and there were white flowers, paler than the eyelids of the dead.

As the snow melted and the sky returned, on that day, almost spring, five old women going down for the fish beyond the garrison wharf found a body among the jumbled stones of the new wall.

The snow had kept it. Its eyes were open. Male brown hair straggled like weed where the asphodel was trying to come back. The boy was some fifteen years of age, clad as a rag-picker, in rags. There was a delicate gouge on his throat, and he had been let blood. Killed in some brawl, poor thing. The women clucked over him. There were fights and murders in any city. There had been two or three like this during the winter, all young men.

They left the body alone, only diverting to it a garrison soldier who came to ask their business with the fishermen.

It was the bought Knight who had begun the second phase. This man – nameless to Wedsek, who could never recall his name, had never heard him addressed by it only by the title of *Knight*, or *Godbrother*, while the man seemed to assume always Wedsek had memorised his name, and Wedsek did not correct him – he it was who, after the first time, had sought Wedsek in the cloister, both of them habited in the black of their order of humble brothers. 'When is it to be again?'

'When what?' said Wedsek, scared as a child, for once the fit had worn off, like all drunkenness, it left him compromised by self-doubt and reproaches. 'After the next gathering, do you want to do it then?'

'What happened with the boy...' started Wedsek.

The other broke in, 'It was you said *Blood is life*. And Anjelen has judged, hasn't he? When he keeps the rite it's a rite of blood, and otherwise milk and water, old men's mumblings. Do you see the Factor there?'

Wedsek said, 'What we did that night...'

'Was *good*. Was in the order of things,' said the bought Knight. He was hoarse with his purpose. He, plainly, had not believed any wrong done or danger enticed. He felt no shamed embarrassment at the memory of the labourer left against the wall. It was the bought Knight indeed who had declared Larl might be abandoned at the mill.

Wedsek resisted. But nights after, he rode by and saw the quiet uncomplaining smoke going up from the chimney of the house by the wharf inn. The mallet did not lean there, but neither was there any sign of distress. Everything was well. Larl had recovered, had not made an outcry. Perhaps he even boasted of the event in his heart, that he was chosen. Or else he had been terrified, as a man is who confronts a demon on the work of its master, the Devil. Which? That was the question for all of it.

But Wedsek's conscience grew slovenly. He calmed and thought of what had been done, not with the elation of the hour or the unease of the aftermath, but objectively.

The bought Knight did not nag on at him, pawing and whining. He treated Wedsek respectfully and distantly. Whereas Riazi avoided Wedsek, and Wedsek wondered for some weeks what had been confessed, there. For Riazi might have come to look on their act of blood as a crime, mistaking...

Mistaking, for it had not been a crime, a foul deed. It was an expression of worship, just as they kneeled, as they toiled, as they read from the Book, fasted and chastised themselves. Like that, but more.

When the gathering of the Knights came again, after some time, the proper conjunction delaying itself, it was the milk-and-water ritual the bought Knight mentioned.

The dolls were wheeled out, and the Chalice with the sooty drink.

Anjelen, far away as a dark star. Anjelen was away from them all now. Alone. At prayer, at table, in the cloister, mailed in the upper chamber of the south tower.

And Wedsek did not approach Anjelen.

When the dry gathering was over, he nodded curtly at the nameless bought Knight.

They rode into the city. And by a tavern they found a drunken man of about twenty, who thought they were the Overlord's soldiers arresting him, when they dragged him from the barrel where he rested in his sot's daze.

They went to the ruined mill again, but to a different part of it, where trees came thickly down towards the water. They did not need to give the man wine; he had had enough. For themselves they had taken no drink but the one sacred sip in the tower.

'Not the palm of the hand,' said the bought nameless Knight.

'Where else?'

'Where it was done with you, and with me. With the holy Factor, too.'

'The neck? It might kill him.'

'We lived. We have only the little scar. The mark of the fellowship Anjelen made. The blood from the throat – richer. Close to the heart.'

This did not move Wedsek. His desire was of some other sort, but evidently the nameless Knight of God was thirsty; a heat came off him like the smell of fire.

Anjelen had employed magic, when he took the blood. The power of what he was.

The idiot of a drunk leaned on a tree, swaying and murmuring to himself, not truly aware of them anymore.

Wedsek had dismounted. He drew his knife and crossed to the man. Wedsek felt, strangely, a savage sorrow. He longed to console the drunkard. He did not bother to say that this was sacred, or secret. The boy whom he had briefly believed resembled Anjelen had somehow demanded that, and if he could, Wedsek would have been faithful also to him, selecting him again for this, and maybe – how curious – paying him when it was over. But then again, he had not wanted the boy to be involved a second time, had not really wanted the boy at all.

'Get on, do it, do it,' said the nameless Knight.

'You take my orders,' said Wedsek. 'You *wait.*'

Silence then. Only black icy crackling, soundless awful night, and the river washing by below, and the trees growing under the whiteness.

Wedsek had cut the side of the man's neck, a shallow quick cut from which the blood spurted. The man did not cry out, but he shouldered himself up against Wedsek, shuddering, making stupid worried moans. 'Hush. Hold steady.' Wedsek soothed him like a nervous horse. He beckoned the other Knight over impatiently. Again, they had not vocalised the ritual words. Had not even thought them through. But they had spoken them in the tower. The nameless Knight approached in a hurry, grabbed and sucked for the blood. It had already run down across Wedsek's hands. It was not hot, only warm. It repulsed him. He did not think he would take it. This was not the Rite of the Blood...

'You, you,' said the other Knight. 'It's good.'

Wedsek's gorge rose, and as he did so he lowered his head and put his lips into the blood. They were like vegetables, flowers, fleshy curving borders to his need. The blood filled his mouth. It was the Wine. Just as before. Perfect. And he knew then it could not be wrong, or rather that it could not be a mistake. This was meant.

When he had had enough, he dropped the man on the snow. Disgusted, uninvolved, he watched the nameless Knight kneel down to drink again, gobbling.

Wedsek leaned and pulled him away.

'Leave it.'

The Knight sat back, accepting Wedsek's command.

The blood pushed from the neck vein, not easing. Despite some care, Wedsek had cut too deep.

He reached into his belt for the tinder. He struck flame.

'What are you doing – someone might see...' the nameless Knight, he was frightened now.

Wedsek stared into the face of his victim. The man was not unconscious, but horror had deprived him of everything else. Wedsek ran the yellow flame, which had given sudden white and red colours to all their faces, into the spout of the wound. The drunken man shut his eyes. He seemed to fall asleep. The wound turned black. It rusted down, and the blood stopped.

They ported him on Wedsek's horse back to the edge of the city. It was another freezing night, the snow packed down like rock. Probably he would not live, but they had not tried to take his life.

Two gatherings in the south tower fell close together in the space of a month.

Wedsek could not shake off his companion, the nameless Knight. This one's craving was obviously cannibalistic. He had performed extemporarily and taken to the deed. It surprised him, but then he accepted it. He was a man who liked to please himself, hold nothing back, or off. He had none of the normal human appetites for sex or wealth, food or power. Wedsek distrusted and hated him, but they were, as he himself had said, bonded. Riazi meanwhile had revealed nothing.

They hunted. They found. In each case, the man died. The third victim was another drunk, convenient. He bled violently, and by the moment Wedsek kneeled to cauterise the wound it was too late. This appalled him, but alarm had no room for itself in his goings on as now they were. The fourth victim was a boy – thirteen, fourteen. He pleaded with them, never consenting. He spoilt it all. His blood stank and burned and only the cannibal enjoyed it. Wedsek came from him all doubt again.

None of the victims were discovered, so far as Wedsek heard or knew. Save one at winter's end. There was a raw rumour in the city's lower sinks. Priests were called on to exorcise a graveyard from which spectres erupted to rape the soul and suck the blood.

Hearing that, Wedsek felt a whirling panic to explain. Should he confess at last? He did not confess to any of it.

Nor did Riazi. Let alone the cannibal Knight without a name.

Then the conjunction fell again for a gathering and Anjelen was to have charge of the ritual, out of turn, but this might be blamed on a casting of lots.

In a sweating anticipation, Wedsek sought the nameless Knight, as never had either really sought the other, only coming on each other after the gatherings and setting off without a word.

'This will change things,' said Wedsek.

'For tonight.' The other Knight had no look of anything except maybe glee, a man glancing forwards to his supper.

Wedsek yearned to strike him.

'No more will I go out and do what we did.'

The Knight smiled. Smiled. 'Where's the harm? Some louts. The city doesn't miss them.'

'We won't speak of it,' said Wedsek. 'But I'm done with it. You can do as you want.'

The bought Knight frowned. He relied on Wedsek's partnership, the physical edge it had given them to be two not one, and the comfortable kinship, where neither could let down the other.

'How abruptly,' he said, 'your liver blanches. Do you want to cause me trouble?'

'It's forgotten,' said Wedsek. His skin stiffened with allergy. *I could kill him. But what then?* The bought one was numbered, not a miscellaneous lout of no merit. 'It seems to me we misinterpret. I need the guidance of Anjelen.'

'And do I?'

'You'll do as you want. I've said so.'

'Another order.'

Wedsek left him. He was in turmoil. He longed to go to Anjelen and kneel at his feet, pleading. He wished to stand there and declare the act of blood to Anjelen, boldly.

Anjelen came across the cloister in the shadow of evening.

Wedsek stood speechless, and attempted to read Anjelen's face, but of course learned nothing. Then Anjelen spoke to him.

'The gathering tonight isn't for you. Absent yourself, Wedsek. If necessary, feign illness.'

'Why?' Wedsek blurted. He saw eyes. There was nothing else. 'Why? What have you heard of me? I didn't—' and Wedsek recalled the first boy, the one who had seemed to have an appearance of Anjelen. *I haven't done anything – who's said I did?*

Anjelen was already moving off. The decision was made, engraved in stone. Absent yourself.

Would it be admissible to disobey? What would happen – God

knew, and only God.

The ground, where the green spring grass was coming up black in the dark, seemed gurning and roiling, trying to pull Wedsek down into Hell.

The other one – had he received such a warning? Had Anjelen gone to him, gone up to him, too, and demanded this?

A sweat poured from Wedsek, and his bowels pressed and quaked. In a kind of mindlessness, he stumbled out of one court of madness, to a second.

That night a man went to a tavern down beyond the wharves. This was not unusual, for though it was long past midnight, the tavern kept open until sunrise, and then would dilate itself again for business if any knocked urgently enough. It lay at the confluence of five alleys, and there was mud several feet deep, a swamp at the door, from the melted snow and the fecund, thawed spring river. The man, who arrived about two hours after the midnight bell from the Cathedral of Chirkess, wore dark clothing of fine cloth and cut, but nothing about it to render much information. He might have been a clerk or officer of accounts from the better end of the city. But he was tall and well-built for a penman. They thought they could see why he was slumming: he would want a woman, with which species the inn was reasonably stocked.

The girl nicknamed 'Flowers', the best one, the favourite, went up to the man about two-thirds of an hour after his entry. He had been drinking heavily and quickly, as if he hungered for something else. A fair sign.

'Good evening, sir.'

The man glanced at her. He had eyes like shiny brown wood, but the whites were reddening. He was in need. It was most obvious.

'Can I bring you more ale? He never serves the good liquor to strangers. I'll tap the nice barrel for you.' Such a ploy, agreed long ago with the innkeeper, often worked wonders.

'This will do.'

The man spoke indifferently. It was not the street voice of Chirkess.

'Well,' said Flowers, 'but I can sit down with you? It'll save me my feet.'

'Sit,' said the stranger, 'if you want.'

After a long hiatus, Flowers said softly, 'Are you sad? Your eyes are tired. I'm not prying...'

'But you'd help. In what way? On your back?'

Flowers perceived she had one wise in the etiquette of tavern girls, and so she had, for Wedsek Crel had known plenty of that tribe before his family and his delusions sent him to God.

After a while, he shared his cup with her, and noticed she was ready to drink the less good liquor. She was pretty, the most attractive of that sort he had seen. And he thought about it, how he had come out dressed in his hunting garments devoid of any significant mark, like a man unordained, owing no one anything, and now sat slurping ale with a whore.

Next she offered food. Poor fare: soup, bread – the inn was not splendid. Wedsek said, 'I'm fasting. It's a penance.'

'But your priest didn't mention the drink, eh?' she said. She giggled, and they were in a conspiracy together against the legions of God. 'Those godbrothers, they get fat for all their fasts and sore trials. They don't know how it is to be a proper man.'

'No?' he said.

'Or a woman, either.'

'They want you to give up your sinful actions,' he said.

'Oh,' she said, 'and starve. That's very well.'

'Like the women who followed the Christus,' said Wedsek. 'They came to him in scarlet, but he robed them again in white.'

'White like cold snow,' said Flowers.

Wedsek the priest looked carefully, thoroughly, at the girl. A few years ago, he would not have dared to do so. His manhood would have engorged even to sit so near, to smell her, her youth and spice. But now, the rigours and the disciplines had trained him. He was drunk, a little, and full of anguishes and angers, but he did not want her. He was almost sure that, even if he had made a foray on her willing body, his own would not have answered – in the flesh perhaps, but not in actual lasciviousness. He would have been able to possess her, but just as nimbly to resist.

She had light fawn hair, a wild bush of it, and eyes like black berries. Her breasts were to be seen through the dress. Even the small cross she wore of carved cedar drew the eye to them. He looked at her breasts, at the buds of the nipples. He imagined putting his hands over them, and a twinge, no more than an itch, crept through his groin, and was gone.

He had taken control of himself. Wedsek ruled Wedsek. He was in every sense a full man and had formed himself to this calibre. And Anjelen thrust him off.

'The way you live,' said Wedsek to the girl called Flowers. 'How can it go on? Some disease, a childbirth, poverty inevitably when you lose your prettiness.'

'Am I pretty, then?'

'Have you no family? Couldn't you find other work?' He was recollecting, nostalgically, the girls of Khish, what befell them, and the old ones, unwanted, beggars at the age of twenty-five shedding their hair and teeth from ailments and malnutrition.

'But I like this work.'

He visualised, quite suddenly, changing her. He saw himself sent off from the brotherhood of the Knights, roaming like the wolf of God, bringing the lost lamb back into the fold, in his jaws. It was a joke, and he recognised it as such, and yet it got a hold on him. The ale was to blame. The only drink he had been granted.

'Do you say your prayers?' he said to her.

She smiled. 'Sometimes. Can you teach me how to pray so God will hear me?'

'Yes,' he said simply. He believed he could. He recalled the vision in his fever at Khish, and that God had selected him, and later Anjelen had done the same. It was essential to retain these facts. All was not over for Wedsek. Life had purpose and symmetry.

'You can teach me, then,' she said. 'To pray. But we'll have to go up to a room; he won't stand for it here. I must seem to go with you. He'll beat me blue otherwise.'

Symmetry, purpose...

The room was no more than a cubby, but it had a door, though no window.

Wedsek was exactly aware that the girl supposed him to be

playing some perverse game. That he wanted to humiliate her or pretend to pious magnanimity. She did not for an instant suspect that he was a priest, who might hear her confession, pardon her, advise her on the correct atonement, and put her forth like a new-born child, free into the world.

But she would starve, as she said, if she did not practise her trade, and the innkeeper below would beat her. No man would wed her now. Her other options were drudgeries as bad, though not profane.

'Have you never,' he said to her, 'seen me about the city?'

She looked sly a moment, wondering clearly if she had happened on a rich merchant, one of the Overlord's friends.

'I don't reckon that I have, sir. I'm sure I'd remember.'

'The Cathedral,' said Wedsek.

She appeared genuinely astounded. She did not think him to be lying. Before she could say he was a guardsman or servant of the church, Wedsek shook his head.

'A priest,' he said. 'I'm on God's errand. He sent me here.'

'Oh,' she said, 'is that how you'd like us to do it?'

She was brazen, but under that, afraid.

Afraid because omnipotent truth had found her out, he the hunter, the wolf of God... He detected his own bewilderment, a snagging of the symmetry, but before he could pick at it, she said: 'No priest would come here. Do they even let them out at night? But, if you like... godbrother.'

'I am a Knight of God,' said Wedsek.

All at once, her slight fear became an antipathetic fright.

He saw through it, as if to a book of written words, decipherable, having only one meaning.

She had heard some awful thing, in connection to the Knights of God. In a fashion the upper city had not, or did not care to, she had been privy to some incoherent garbled tale, of riders by night, and takings off, and blood – and blood.

Wedsek stood looking at the girl. Her skin was rosy from the hot, cramped room, the two fat candles burning, rosy with blood. The blood of women – it was unthinkable, unspeakable, and forbidden, that the lawless and unclean gore of women be associated with the flawless male blood of the Sacrifice.

'You don't want me,' said the girl.

'I'd like you to pray,' he said.

'No. I don't want to. You don't want me for what you ought to. He'll make a row downstairs. I have to go down to him…'

'You must not. Kneel here, and pray.'

'I have to go and see him.'

'You have to kneel with me here and ask God for His forgiveness.'

'You can't make me.'

She sprang towards the door, but she had secured it, snaring him, coming in. And as she fluttered at the bolt, Wedsek took her by the arms.

How extraordinary she smelled, of female skin and moistures, of long hair, and living sweet meat, and terror.

He had her. He pulled her against him. His arms were around her body. She was so heated she boiled against him like a cook pot. She struggled, and stopped, went limp.

'I'll do whatever you like,' she said, 'I won't tell. But be quick. He'll want me down…' She was lying desperately and not uncleverly. It might have fooled another man, but Wedsek did not want her for this, some corrupted and accursed coupling. He held her still in her boneless state, her hair over his lips.

'What prayers do you remember?'

She stammered, 'Forgive, forgive me, Lord, that I am fallen, fallen…'

He had his hand on her neck, did not know he had put it there, to feel the rush of her voice under his fingers.

'Don't don't,' she said.

He pressed her head back into his shoulder, and leaning over towards the vibration of her voice, a power gushed up in him, something he had forgotten, did not know, and that he altered, for the symmetry threaded into another mode. He had her flesh there by his mouth, and her hair, and then he tore through them, with the fangs of a wolf, to get at the red blood he had seen under her skin.

She attempted one scream. But her own life-fluid choked her

before she could release it – the noise was like a sexual one, and fetched nobody, even if they heard it.

When she died, Wedsek never saw. He no longer saw her at all. He ripped at her, with teeth and hands, crushed her open like the white and pink carcass of a flower. As he did this, he drank from her. It was not the Wine. It was the *truth*.

What finished him was what normally would have done so. Orgasm unlocked the valves, his penis ejected its spasms of agonised joy. Then, he came to himself, in the customary manner.

He found he was sinking down on remains, remnants, that were not now like anything human, brown leaves of dress and petals of skin, soiled in a sump of blood and semen, and he did not understand what he had done. It was as if a demon had claimed him in sleep and thrown him here. Wedsek slipped forward heavily into the mess of death and self-betrayal, fainting. What else was there left to do?

Near morning the man came up from downstairs to get back his best girl, the favourite, Flowers.

Unable to enter the room, he summoned assistance.

The door was broken down.

And there on view to all the occupants of the inn, lay unconscious Wedsek, and his deed, and the result of it.

Chapter Seven

Of the nature of the deed there were to be three versions. It was to be an act having the flesh of reality, but three souls, only one of which was spiritual.

After the rearrangement of the scene at the inn (the removal of bodies), during which the soldiers of the Overlord had presided, the priesthood came. There were seven black priests, including a legate sent by the Administer. Ten of the Cathedral guard sat their horses by the door.

Those at the inn – most of its present population – who had witnessed the upper room, were questioned. Having rendered their picture of the event, they were next told of what the event had actually been composed. This was not as they had thought. Yes, evidently an extreme butchery had taken place. A woman had been murdered. In the carnage lay a man from the Cathedral of Chirkess, already in the pandemonium identified. But perhaps not a priest; why had this conclusion been drawn? Nor could it be said that the man, lying senseless on a bed of ribboned skin and blood, was the author of the death. Why, also, should such a thing be deduced? Would the murderer not have fled at once? It was a fact there was no window to the room, but there were beings which could pass through walls. That was not to say, either, that the visitation of a demon should be presumed. However, the room was to be exorcised, just like the city graveyard.

Through the enactment of exorcism, a type of conclusion was laid down on the proceedings. All prior ideas and theories were unsettled, and gradually began to dislodge themselves.

After the exorcism, the room was boarded up, and sealed with the sigil of the Cathedral at Chirkess, a long-stemmed knot-cross guarded by a heron and an owl.

The body of a woman, shovelled in a box and covered over – not much else could be done with it – was not examined. The marks of what might have come to her were to be identified from description, apparently. Her employer at the inn must deal with the corpse. She was a whore, for all his avowal of her other tasks. Prayers would be said for her.

The unconscious body of the man, carted off by soldiers of the Overlord, was prised back from them.

It was made plain that this dish was not for any earthly table.

The man, whatever his rank in the Cathedral, was the Cathedral's own. No secular law could touch him. Be sure, the harshly righteous arm of Father Church would spare nothing. God's justice outstripped for ever the petty retribution of men. That, then, the popular soul of Wedsek's Deed.

For the Cathedral itself, the soul was this: breakage of vows, disgrace, a brawl, untidy, unclarified. Woman, the temptress, the apple of sex, the serpent of breasts and hair who twined the Tree, she had worked her mischief. If there was blood, it was immaterial. The act of horror was unchastity, by which the door had opened upon the galaxy of Hell. Demons rushed out. Demons lacerated and rent. And there lay the priest, ruined.

Within the inner mechanism of the Cathedral at Chirkess, the soul became the ethic, the unseen cluster of filaments, that knit up a stone chamber, lit by candles, having high slitted windows showing only darkness, almost square save for that outer windowed wall, which curved with the shape of the south tower.

Externally the gargoyles in their helms and visors had outstared the sinking sun. Inside the room, the men in their black habits sat their wooden benches, with gargoyle faces from a nightmare; for these were the faces of a foreign land whose language Wedsek did not know, whose customs he had not been lessoned in, and who hated him – worse, who cared nothing for him at all.

He was dead, but he stood there at the floor's centre, upright and aware, though not exactly of how he had arrived, who had conducted him. Even, for a moment, he had glanced about for the Administer – the Factor – could find neither. And for Anjelen. But how should Anjelen be in this gathering, this crowd of black crows masked in faces?

For himself, Wedsek did realise what he had done. He did not suppose himself possessed, or insane. He had fallen. From a huge height of self. It was so peculiar and unbelievable, so vividly obviously inescapable, that he was able to regard it all blankly. As if he had sheared off his right hand.

And he was dead.

He had accepted that too. Although he dreaded, childishly and irrationally, the instant when it would be spoken.

Magister Hyrus sat in a carved chair, across the floor. He did not look at Wedsek, but precisely through him, through his forehead.

'Among our brotherhood, there has been one. A man named Wedsek, absorbed into the benignity of God, living in the Fraterium at Chirkess, as our brother, in the holy and blessed ranks of the foremost servitors of the Lord.'

Wedsek stopped looking into the face of Magister Hyrus. Wedsek looked at the floor, where his own godbrother's habit, put on him an hour ago, met the booted feet of the mail he had had put on him a few minutes before the habit. This vaguely puzzled him, and his mind slipped off into some thicket of conjecture, before he drove it back to listen to the toneless voice of Hyrus.

'But the Devil will throw down any man. We must be always vigilant. There will come to us those that are wolves and vipers, clad like the gentle deer. From our hearts we must pluck out the poisoned root.'

The candlelight reflected in the floor, which had been laid with faded coloured tiles that did not matter.

'He is priest no longer,' said Hyrus. 'Strip him of that.'

And two men came at Wedsek from somewhere. He was unprepared for them, and though resistance was irrelevant, almost he did not object, but it was ineffectual anyway, the slight motions he made, the two or three half-expressed words.

They slashed the habit he wore, with little knives, trimly, and pulled it off him. He stood in the mail, then, yet disarmed, swordless, without the helm.

'Into the world he must go, but for him the world can be nothing. The world is God's. Fashioned by the Creator, like the Garden, for man. God is in all things. And for this one, who has been called Wedsek among us, there is no longer any God.'

Hyrus rose. Wedsek looked at him, not meaning to, into the bright flash of a sword. The sword was Wedsek's blade of Knighthood. Hyrus pointed it at him with the candles running gold along its steel.

'From this hour, there is no way for you to God. His eyes have closed to you, He does not see. His ears are stopped against your cries. Even the Christus, the Redeemer of men, cannot intercede. Though He grieves for you, though you are an agony sharper than the nails, the lance, the tearing of the thorns, yet He must let you depart into the desert of all-night.'

Wedsek flinched. The light of the sword flew off at him like drops of venom.

'Go out and roam the wild places like the beast. Avoid the houses of God. Enter no church, kneel at no altar; it can avail you nothing. Wander the earth, until death, and then travel down into the dark, where the worm and the maggot shall have all of you. For, at the last, there is no trumpet and no song that can raise up you, the accursed of God. You are excommunicate. Your soul is dead.'

Curiously, the sentence, spoken, like the acceptance of what he had done, did not pain, cripple, drive mad. It was more a colossal blow, which stuns.

Two – perhaps the two who had cut away his priest's robe – had Wedsek's arms. Their grasp was inexorable. Not rough, but like some mighty engine, which pushed him from the room of stone, through an aperture of stone, some foyer or passage, and in, in at a door of the round chamber of the south tower, but wrongly, for there was no door save only the four curtained entries, and this some crack in the wall that could not be. And then the hidden door was shut, had ceased once more to exist. All that existed was the chamber of the gathering.

The Knights of God were already there, without him. He had come late, yet they had attended on it. They had been shown too where he would enter, for they faced him in the form of a horseshoe, he in its open end.

Wedsek did not count the Knights. Anjelen must be here, among them. But he would never learn. For they were cloaked in white, every man, and every man leaning on a drawn sword, and over every helmed head a white hood that fell below the lips. No face, only the holes of the eyes, edged in silver, through which they stared at him. Or, maybe, they did not stare, having no care for him, the dead man.

Above, the massive lamp, brass and gilt and bronze, angel, lion, bull and eagle. The lights flamed on it. And in their niches behind the pillars of fruits, the stone faces leered and snarled and howled, and the floor had tessellations, and at the centre its brass disc was crossed by black marble.

The clockwork in the floor operated abruptly, and Wedsek was jolted; almost he shouted. Up came the golden thing from the floor, and on it, a broken sword. If it was not Wedsek's sword of Knighthood, it was the symbol of it.

A voice, Hyrus' voice, repeated out of the air:

'Go out now. There is no other way for you. Roam the wild places like the beast. Travel down into the dark. Your soul is dead.'

The horseshoe of Knights parted. Perhaps they were not men, but alchemical dolls, for they moved so exactly, smoothly.

Another door that did not exist had cracked open the further wall. It was between the crimson and gold curtains of the owl and the moon.

Wedsek did not move.

Conceivably, he did not move for more than the quarter of an hour. Time ceased. Nothing more was said to him. No gesture was made. The Knights of God stood in two white lines, white faceless faces of snow, silent.

There was nothing. No one to hear any cry. Not Hyrus, not Anjelen. Never, never God.

Wedsek finally began to walk across the chamber, skirting the broken sword, to the crack of door, into, and out of it.

Beyond, a faint glimmer of a lamp, a narrow twisted foul stair, like the course from a privy. Down this he went, for it was the only route.

At the bottom, a last door of wood, which gave at the mildest, most inadvertent contact.

Outside, astonishingly and inappositely, was only night, and the city. Was this Chirkess? It did not make much difference. It was a town of the earth that was God's as the ground was God's, the river and the trees, and all mankind. And he, Wedsek, a shadow that would wander there, unseen and immaterial. Dust.

The great pale ship, full-rigged as if with cloud, and every cloud striped with its black brand of the cross, clove down through the land. Where there was still ice, and here and there the wide river was rafted by it, the crew swarmed over, and made its way, with mallets, and with fires. By night, the cool spring moon shone through the sails. The dawn was stirred by oars, the mauve light in the water was broken. Birds rose, like prophets, announcing.

On either side of the river, islands of land, plains, valleys, hills, horizons of rock and mist, pushed at the sky. On the black, wet fields, the slaves and peasants stayed their work, to look. The overseers saluted the ship.

Women crossed themselves, and some kneeled down. Some brought their children to see. The ship was like a vision, lucky or fearful. It could be used as a date: that was the evening the Ship of God went sailing by.

There were villages, towns, cities. By night their rose-red windows, by day their markets and their quays, where all the craft teemed back, to let the great ship pass.

On the deck of the ship, the Factor stood, and the other, the one he had brought with him. The Factor pointed, but seldom spoke. He understood that he acted out the Devil's role, if with a difference, showing to his Lord all the cities and the kingdoms, demonstrating by such mighty, little things as the clasped children, the running fisher boats, and the power that the ship represented, the omniscience of the Church. All this can be yours, said the women as they crossed themselves, and the sailors staring on the quays.

The ship herself had come from nowhere, on to the river at Chirkess, summoned like a vast whale from the deep of the sea.

It would be possible to reach the sea. It would be possible to hem along the land for weeks, showing, demonstrating, the people bowing low, and the earth itself, spreading and waiting under Heaven's sway.

But the man, the Man, what did he think? Were the kingdoms

of the world of any use to him, this second time? He watched stilly. The Factor sensed the smallness of almighty power held up to view in the polish of those eyes.

'The Saviour was, and still may be, betrayed by one of the elect. On the perfect branch, one rotten purblind stem.'

The Factor was with Anjelen, standing in the well-furnished cabin.

'Nevertheless. I will go my own way, Factor.'

'Of course. How should I doubt it? I have shown you this, that you might see. But I'm yours to order as you wish.'

Anjelen had been made a Magister, at an age far junior to what was general, or recommended. In Anjelen's case, the general and the recommended were of no importance.

But the vileness of the dead priest, Wedsek, had besmirched them all, the beauty and sacred strength of the Rite of Blood. Anjelen had recoiled from it, not in any obvious or cited manner. It was visible through this declaration. Despite his station in the Church, he would take on himself a mission that fell to those godbrothers of the lowliest sort, that of the mobile priest, who toiled where he was sent, on the very road, ministering, admonishing, trackless and sometimes untraced.

'I can't gainsay your decision. However you must, thus will you accomplish your vocation. But I, and the Administer, as your officers, will see to it, my lord, that your path is swept and prepared for you. There'll be letters sent to the churches and religious communities. By any means you choose, you will be able to enter in, command, and receive every assistance. At the very least, there will be no chance that you yourself can be disobeyed. I don't imply by this,' the Factor added, 'that you would be incapable of such authority.' He smiled, displaying his logic and his jest to the Infinite. 'But there need be no stupid disruptions. No muddling of your purpose.'

'Yes,' said Anjelen. 'Then you'll see to it.'

The Factor looked briefly at a ripple of disappointment running the length of him. To the gift, such a casual return, as if Anjelen did not care, did not see its cost and value... But this was foolish. One could not judge him. One must look for nothing but to serve.

The Factor knelt, and Anjelen blessed him.

From the hand of Anjelen came a scorching cool energy like a drink of the eternal.

It would all be seen to. Couched in clever and tactical language, not offering too much that might be misread, cause scandal or doubt. Yet, through the inner method of a priesthood built upon assumptions of the Return, the Absolute, particular signals might be given. Not as a Baptist had given them, splashing noisily in the waters of wonder, but as the sophisticate and cunning modern man of letters might. Each missive a labour like that which facetted a jewel, heralding the promise, stating nothing. And Anjelen might pass through the land like an angel. Where he sought shelter, preference, military aid, such should be his. There was a daunting suspicion, already posited, that news of the third soul of Wedsek's crime had reached into the most potent bastions of the Church. That the Knights of God, who had been proud at Chirkess, were to be disbanded, pushed back into the cellars of ritual. Even, God forbid, if that could happen, Anjelen should work unscathed.

The purpose, the exact structure of this second attempt upon mankind's salvation, mooted in Anjelen, who could divine it?

One need not bother. Faith, not witless but pure of sight, was the token of the Factor's service. The brilliant mind did not question God. It knew it need not.

'All my life is yours. Until you come into your kingdom,' said the Factor, pledging himself.

Anjelen was only white and black, only eyes, only fires, only the dreams of men warped like wrecked stars from their parameters.

The Factor did not guess, kneeling there in his stupendous arrogance of humbleness, that Anjelen's kingdom, which was not as the Factor, anyway, thought it, would not occur for something in the region of a pair of centuries. That Anjelen, who could still be leisurely, would not do anything of much plan until this man was long, and by-the-way, dead and buried, lying in his grave for the last trumpet of Heaven. The Factor was spared that, both the foreknowledge and the awakening. He had not been the first to confuse the tree – the cross – with that which hung on it.

Chapter Eight

Once, among the Travelling People there had been a traditional necklace, worn by their girls until the day of marriage. It was a show of wealth on one side, a measure on another, but also flirtatious, since for any but a prospective father-in-law or bridegroom to make proper count on it was an offence liable to feuding. The necklace was made up of quartets of beads, each representing a season of the year, a white bead of enamel or alabaster for the winter, a green beryl or stained quartz for spring, for the summer a piece of brass, or nut of gold if it could be got, and for the autumn's freckled fall, jasper, garnet, amber, bloodstone or painted clay. Four beads comprised a year. By the age of six, there were usually enough to go about the neck, unless the necklace were very rich and the gems very tiny. By the age of eleven or twelve, most often the maiden was wed and the chain ended. The rare woman who achieved fifteen and still could add to her virgin necklace, did not. She was too old for marriage, and who would waste beads on her?

But the years themselves continued constructing their necklets of seasons, the winter white, the green spring and golden summer, the shattering leaf-fall of red and brown.

Like a broken mosaic, like curtains and clouds, waves, moods, they passed over the land, which, in its length of age, might perceive them more swiftly and flittingly. How fast they came and went, the lights and shades of time.

Snow descends, melts away, beryls stitch through and bloom into a golden rage that fruits and chars and drops and is done, and then the snow descends, and again, and again.

The trees, those that shed and those that appear changeless in their black-green spikes and furs, they stand fixed within the whirlpool, the coming and going, the flushing up and withering, clothing and unclothing, the colours. The trees grow. They drain the nurture from the soil and put down their claws into the arteries of the earth, levering up unnoticed as they do it, rocks, the foundations of houses, the flanks of mountainsides.

Sheep like grey boulders strewed the hills, under a white plain of sky. The baked grass cheeped in momentary winds.

These were days of the summer's golden rage.

Something else, too, raged on the hills. There had been talk of it, south and west, towards the town. Men went searching for a great wild cat, for it was not the white-bead time of the wolf. Snow killings, of that sort, were not uncommon.

On the hill structured like an axe head, grazing, the grey sheep clotted together under a thorn tree. Sometimes they rubbed their bodies on the trunk.

The shepherd was beneath the hill, sleeping by the stream where he had eaten his raisins and cheese.

The stillness was improbable. Something must penetrate its globe.

The sleeper felt nothing. He snored, with his cheek on the breast of the earth.

But the sheep, one by one, raised their flat-nosed heads.

They scented the predator, death, before hearing and sight discovered him. The stench of the meat-eater, always fearful, except in man, whom they trusted, and who cut their throats at times of festival and famine.

This was not man-scent. But nor was it like anything, not the cat or polecat, or the fox, the wolf, the dog.

The sheep began to move, restless. Thought stupid, instinctively they knew the trusted shepherd was also useless to them.

A wind, or something, slid through the high grass beyond the thorn, and the sheep ran.

They ran bunched together, a horde of dirty innocent rumps and small black feet.

The scent came after them, running them down. It had a sound now, heavy and yet vigorous, blundering but sure.

Where rocks came up from the hill, the sheep separated. They bleated shrilly, veering away in groups of three or four or five, and then one ran alone, and there came sudden confusion, a matted animal darkness that reared up and smashed down, and under it the sheep was slapped into the hillside. It lay pinned, and the dark smothered it up, and its baby-like bleating ceased. The blood oozed through the grass, and the dry hard ground refused it. Over the lip of the hill it trickled, from the mound of greyish and darkish life that died and fed together.

Blood did not rouse the shepherd; it had not made any sound, as the other thing had done, although the crickets in the bushes by the stream had dulled his ears to that.

Then the day began to ebb. The sun spread into an elongate and awful image, of a molten pupil-less eye. The shepherd drew himself out of the country of sleep and was back in the land.

Glancing up, he beheld his flock away to the east of the hill above him. They did not graze, but had posted themselves into the ground, staring westward from the sides of their heads. He knew the beacons of their fear, at least.

He took his staff, a young man not yet eighteen, and shook the shaggy black fleece of his hair out of his eyes.

When he came up, cautious, over the brow of the axe hill, he saw nothing at once, but then the sun itself tweaked a yellow ray into the heap of wool and blood. A carcass, partially devoured, that had been a live thing when he had seen it before. So quickly, death achieved his spell. The shepherd had never applied the formula of that to himself.

He looked hurriedly everywhere, recalling the tale of the giant wild cat. He was not afraid, only furious at his loss. Then the grass lurched upwards, and the shepherd gave a grunt, hefting his stick, ready.

Some devil of a Traveller, some homeless robber, dangerous, the leg bone of the sheep in his hand, but outmatched, worn and cragged and shaggy and unkempt, with patches and streamers of white in a blackish mane and beard – too old for the wandering, stealing life.

The shepherd did not issue his challenge in words, but he strode forward, hunching the staff, growling.

The old man was against the sun, but a twist of his head let the spread light into the beard, to reveal gobbets of blood and fat. He had been eating the repast as it lay, warm and raw.

Bestial, unlawful, preying on the flocks of others...

There were teeth too, some broken but all bared in the mouth.

And then the itinerant robber, the ageing man, was no longer anything of the sort.

The eyes in their gaunt hollows flared a coppery red. The red infused the whites, and they vanished: two furnace ovals slotted with black. The mouth had become a cave, fenced by the jagged fangs between which the red meat remained. The hair, the rags, were pelt. And the leg bone of the sheep, clamped close to him to gnaw, was not for a weapon, for now it was slung away. It was a wolf the shepherd saw, a summer wolf on its hind legs and tall as a tall man.

The shepherd plunged his stick across the body of the man-wolf. He felt no astonishment as the maimed gnarled paws in their thin gloves of grey old man's fur reached out and took the stick, and snapped it. And then the wolf weight leaned on the shepherd, the heat and roaring and the stinking breath and the pale scarlet eyes. One blow of a paw snapped the stick of his throat a second before the teeth shut fast in it.

In the village, where the stream went down in a fall of green water, and some trees grew, the women at the pool with their jars saw the man first, as he came along the track. They lifted their arms to shield their eyes from the sinking sun. Even on the blaze of sunset, they saw he was not like other men. Turning to each other, they exclaimed.

'She's in luck.'

'It's what her mamma prayed for.'

The man came into the village, and stopped by the women, looking at them. He was about twenty-four years, a young priest, his plain dark habit belted at a thin ascetic's waist with hemp. He rode a black mule that had on it no baggage at all, not even a gourd to store water. His eyes were marvellous, like a saint's in a picture. This village clove to the Christus, and even had a small stone box under a fir tree, where it had worshipped when the local godbrother was still alive. But he died at length, and unfortunately the religious fathers in the town had not been able as yet to replace him. The village did its best and married under the fir tree by the stone church, before the village's holder. But it was not the same. As for ancient ways, a girl might sleep with an acorn under her pillow, or tie a ribbon or a flower into the fir to mark betrothal, pregnancy. They did not otherwise do more than scorn such things as superstition. When the elderly women threw meal onto a fire at sunfall, they said Christus bless us.

So, it was good for Gisla that the priest had come by, the day before her wedding. The groom would not mind, but she would be glad, and the mother in her grave, doubtless.

The village holder's wife, who was at the well, went directly to the priest, and asked for his benediction. He gave it with a breathtaking elegance against the sinking sun. No peasant, this, but one on some journey from a town. 'You're right welcome, godbrother. Will you stay tomorrow and do a service of marriage?'

That night the young priest sat in the holder's hut, where the holder made stout conversation with him, intimidated, but anxious for stories of the town, from which it would seem the journeying man had come. The holder's wife waited on them. She was sorry that the priest ate so little of her cooking, but also pleased with such firm unworldliness. He had said the evening grace for them and would speak the morning grace for the entire village, sixty-five souls, at sun-up. His voice was so musical. He drank only water.

There were four other villages across the hills; he might go there too, but maybe not. Maybe only here. Then they could remember and boast of him. He did not seem to expect payment of any kind, no barter or tip. The low summer fire played on his face like melody. He had the beauty of all still things of vast, contained and secret power.

And that night, on the hills, the man-wolf lay low in secret grass, his belly full of meat and blood, watching the stars, and the curved anvil of the moon on which was hammered out the night.

Sometimes he recalled sufficiently he was a man to make a fire, but manlike tonight, he knew it would be unwise. Earlier, there had been a band of men on the hills, on the axe-shaped hill, with burning brands. They were looking for their shepherd, and they found him.

Far off, more than a mile away, in the quiet, he heard the uproar from that village, and dots of lights between the hovels there, but distant, removed. The sheep had been driven down. Warnings would circulate in the area.

A couple of times, after he had killed like this, a goatherd, a pair of woodcutters, the resultant wary searchers had come on him a day or two later, and he had been in the mode of a man, and having alerted him to the danger of a marauding slaughtering animal at large, they subsequently took him in, and he dwelled with them in their settlements. In the second village he even stayed a year, working in the forge, teaching them to fight – they thought him some strayed soldier. He had been trying perhaps to evade what was in him, but the phantom of his purpose was close at hand, two villages off. And when the eldritch dawning lamp moved on, he too went away, after it, as always.

He had had several interrupted man-lives. They were never properly real to him. Only what he followed, and which never beckoned, never looked back. Yet surely, his pursuit, the loyalty of it, and the obsession, these were known, and accepted. What he did, too, in the guise of a beast, wolf by winter, cat by summer, the white and red seasons, the gold and green. He had killed a Traveller girl once, with just such a necklace on her, unusual now, possibly not hers either, or accurate, for she was less than twelve years and the necklace, when he idly counted it after, in the blood, was fourteen seasons. He did not rape her. He did not experience any sexual thing. He had never gone with a woman, though here and there they offered. The one terrible time, that had purged him like the rupturing of a boil. That was how he saw it. Not crime, not fall, not anything but a sickness, from which he came forth.

Often, he was uncertain what he truly was – never who, since he had mostly forgotten – but whether man or beast.

Yet, one way or the other, he was a god's. No longer the Father, but the being who had proceeded from the Father. From the Creator, or from the Evil One. To this god, he belonged. And therefore, he was safe, the wolfman, the man-wolf. More than condoned, his acts were predestined and exact in the sight of the Lord.

As he shifted on the hillside, his joints ached. Sometimes in the heat, as in the cold, they hurt him. But he did not fret. When he was a man he limped, but discounted it, just as he discounted the name he gave those who asked, *Wedsek*.

He never entered a religious building. He did not want to. In the wilds, that was not so abnormal. In the woodland of the south, now and then he had been attracted to some bush or tree or grove where the skulls of animals were hung, bells and coins, pieces of hair, and wooden effigies of tiny men.

Only five occasions had he followed so close he had seen the god walking near before him. Twice this had happened in darkness. He always yearned for it. He yearned for the god to look back. To come to him. But how should the god see Wedsek? It was enough that he knew.

It had begun under the wall of Chirkess, the unfinished new wall, wrapping the city slower and slower, running down.

Now the memory was smeared and inchoate, bits of things, such as when he lay in the reeds beside the choked-up pond, in an agony beyond agony, agony of the soul, which died from a death wound inflicted only hours before. Strange recollections of a dawn coming up, a deadly and accusing glow, and panes of brilliance in the pockets of water. There was a visualisation of an exchange of clothes made – violent – some theft conducted upon him. Of other garments purloined in turn. Of a bank near a tavern down from the wall, above the river. Staying here some while, and they flung him scraps like a cur. Of the sense that all men knew him, but no one did. Paranoia of fear replaced by horror of personal dissolution. Invisible, mistaken for other things, wandering, days and nights, reeds and water, stone and wood and thatch, and trees. Silences without number that were loud with frogs and birds, the calls of men, or women with a catch of fish, and then the road that washed out of the city, straight down under the wall like yards of blotted rope. And the figure on a mule, the priest like a prayer coming on. And scrambling to the roadside, among the debris, and seeing it was the god, on the mule, with palms of sunlight and shadow cast before its feet.

And thus, Wedsek followed. There was nowhere else to go. Like the door, the stair... like life itself. No method but progression, after some goal, actual or ephemeral or false.

And then, this composite of time, the jumble of the beads, white and gold, green and red. Day and dark, cold and warmth, pain and momentary alleviation of pain, and food. And the wolf. Where the wolf began, how should Wedsek tell? In Chirkess, probably, those months at the very start. Or earlier, with the boy. Or in the round chamber. Or under the tree, in the drink of Everlasting Wine, from the vessel of Anjelen.

Anjelen.

Anjelen.

Everything and all things – were Anjelen's.

Anjelen was the world. To follow him was to follow the cycle of the world, to follow the circle of death to birth, through existence, to death again.

I am the truth. And the Life.

Not lost.

For thirty-one years it had gone on. The wolfman on the hill, sated by his murders and their blood, staring at the stars, he could not calculate and did not want to. It had blurred together and grown tough, like the layers of a plant. Thirty-one years he had followed Anjelen. Now an Anjelen riding a mule. Now walking. Now in a town, a village, some city outskirt. Anjelen entering a church. Anjelen changeless. A few years older. Only a few years. That was all the time it had taken. Four years or five. Or thirty-one.

Wedsek lay back deep in the summer grass.

A half dream moved on him, like the moon upon the ground, so for a moment he was elsewhere, young and laughing, in an inn, in his father's house. But then sleep came, and Wedsek was a wolf. He chased the sheep on the hill and took them in his jaws. But overhead were the black sky and the white stars, like the eyes of Anjelen his Maker, who loved him.

That morning, he blessed the village and said for it the grace. At midday there was the wedding. The bride, Gisla, came from her parents' hut, in a coloured apron, and with flowers in her hair. She was laughing and happy. The groom was bashful and aggressive by turns, but he bowed to the priest and looked in awe at him. The priest was only maybe a handful of years the bridegroom's senior, but educated, born obviously in a town, travelled and learned, and besides in league with God.

They went to the stone building that had been the church. The floor was scrubbed, and before the oblong unglassed window, a spray of the green wheat was in a jug, and long-lashed daisies. The statue of the Christus on his cross rose on a stone table beneath, a wooden rough-chiselled object. There were a few utensils of pottery. A wooden goblet, smooth from the handling of observance, stood for the wine.

The priest spoke, simply and mildly, all the correct words of the ceremony, much better than the holder's gabble.

The bride blushed and paled before him, drinking up his presence, the omen of it, on her day of days. The shuffling bridegroom mumbled when he must.

The Host was elevated, into the light of the window.

Everyone partook of the Body and Blood of the Redeemer.

After the wedding, they went over to another table set up in the street, piled with cakes and loaves and syrups, beer and ale, and a sheep which, roasting since sunrise and lancing the air with human hungers, was rushed at with carving knives.

'You'll stay and sup, godbrother? Brighten our feast?'

The holder's wife was still anxious he should eat of her cooking.

Their first cups were lifting when three men prowled on to the track above, along the hill.

'Look, who's there, wanting to feed off our table?'

The women called out, mocking these late and uninvited arrivals, but the men on the hill did not respond, and their faces, as they came nearer, were grim.

Getting to his feet, the holder called two of his own men. It was the worst manners, to spoil a marriage.

The bride and groom were busy eyeing each other. Birds sang in the trees and the gold sun was over the highest roof.

The priest sat calmly, looking on, as the holder marched up the track and met the visitors there. A dialogue ensued between them. One of the fellows from the other village pointed away across the hills. Every man glanced in that direction. Then the holder brought all of them to the table.

'Give these a drink, wife. Listen here. It's not the hour for it, but they've come out of kindness. To warn us.'

One of the newcomers said, 'There's a beast, perhaps a sick wolf, killed sheep up to pasture.'

'And the shepherd with them,' added a second man. 'A terrible killing. Man and animal part eaten, and the blood all ways.'

'I've seen the work of wolves,' said the third, the oldest. 'Never like this, not even a pack starved crazy.'

'Our goats are down today,' said the holder. 'We've this to tend to.' He indicated the table and the bridal couple. 'Happy for us.'

'Who did you lose? Your young man?' asked the holder's wife.

'That's so. Poor wretch. He tried to fight it off, broke his stick somehow, on a rock, maybe. Then it was at him. The throat,' said the neighbouring villager. All at the table sighed, but the priest, where he sat by the whey-white bride. (Omen less sweet.) He did not seem provoked or uneasy, not even consoling. Of course, it was the way of things, such deaths, on the hills, in the woods.

They would have to get the men from all the villages, search for the animal and put it down. It might have the children. If it found the pickings choice, it would stay. They could not know, although their priest, he knew, that this devilish carnivore would soon be gone, as soon as the priest was gone, in fact. The beast, following, would prey elsewhere.

Over the wedding meal then, preparations were made. The wan Gisla was cheered up, and affectionately cursed by her husband when she begged him not to go on the hunting. 'What? You're not changing me into a ninny. I'm a man.'

The priest sat still as darkness through it all, not eating, having only sipped from his cup or perhaps not even that, his hands folded on the table. Once, he too looked at the hills, flint, madder under the tawny base of the sky.

'Not tonight. First light tomorrow. It'll rest itself then, or go to drink along the stream. We can catch it then.'

'*He* won't want to be stirring early.'

But the bridegroom declared that he would, wedding night or no.

The stars wheeled. In altered time, he seemed to have learned how to watch them, so he saw their motion, and the long silver snail-trails they left behind, which slowly dried to blackness.

He did not want to devour again. He had had an abrupt hankering for brown bread and broth, and curds, and picked apples, and ale. It was a man-space come on him. Maybe tomorrow he could go down to one of the villages, play the forager, the orphan soldier. Anjelen was in the lowest village, to the north. During the day there had been a festival there, and Anjelen had sat out in the street with them, and later he retired into the largest hut.

Perhaps Anjelen would consent to stay and be their priest for a pair of seasons, the red and white. This had happened before. Then Wedsek certainly could revert to humanness. He might make a place for himself in a close community, and one day, as they hauled logs or tilled some field, Anjelen might pass by on his mule. Anjelen might raise his hand in blessing, a special moment between them, half a jest. Or one day Anjelen might summon him. *Do thus and so, for me.*

A black hare darted over the hillside. At first Wedsek was not sure of it, but then it went by again. Fearless, it paused, upright, its horned ears erect, with the stars embroidered about them. Then it was gone.

Wedsek lay down. He dreamed a few seconds: the hare was Anjelen and had come to call him to some meeting of angels on the plain below.

Something woke Wedsek. He sat up at once, attained his knees. He could not recall if recently he had kept a jhcxzknife or not. But he had. Uncleaned and rusty, it came loose and he got up with it.

It had killed the occasional wolf, in the winters, when they had come on him alone and would not leave him be. One time he had climbed a tree when a pack of seven or eight encircled him. He lay along the boughs three days, eating the snow and a piece of a kill of his own – perhaps its smell had attracted them. Finally they had given up and gone away.

But this was a summer wolf. He saw its shape now on the rim of the hill. It was whole and sound, not crippled nor favouring any part. Its eyes flashed. It trotted to within three yards of him, and halted.

Then, he saw the stars begin to point out through its flank. It went to a sort of smoke, and flowed off, and Anjelen stood up out of it, but he was the wolf still, black on the sky.

Wedsek was too amazed to feel joy. But he dropped back to his knees.

Anjelen spoke to Wedsek, and Wedsek learned he had forgotten the meaning of Anjelen's voice.

'How you stick to me. Here and there I shook you off, but you returned. Constancy such as this, Wedsek – or do you not recollect your given name? – asks some reward. What do you want from me?'

'Whatever – whatever you say.' And Wedsek's voice, out of practice, gravelly and strangled, made him ashamed. It was good enough for the rabble of the villages, but not for Anjelen. 'You tell me, Lord. Is it time?'

'Time for what, Wedsek?'

'For me – to serve you? The hour. The day.'

Anjelen said, 'Do you know where I'm going?'

'No, lord.'

'To my beginning,' said Anjelen. 'A long journey, doubling back on itself. Acres of earth and time. Too many years, Wedsek, for you. Though for myself, little enough. I have my own road. And on it, always, I hear this intruding step, which is yours. How frequently in some village street have I seen the outcry over the wolf or the cat or the wild man who's killed the flock and the shepherd. It irks me, Wedsek. You, always in my way. You've forgotten Chirkess. Your gross buffoonery, your acts of mindless inaccuracy. What's God to you? You can grasp nothing. What am I to do with you?'

Wedsek wept. Berated, he did not properly understand. Human speech had been reduced for him to the simplest phrases. Concepts, sentences, this tirade, had now no real relevance.

'Don't let me go,' he said. 'Don't leave me, lord.'

'What is it you want?'

'You,' said Wedsek, in a broken, embarrassed humiliated croak, 'the truth, the path. You. To follow you.'

'You want the Blood,' said Anjelen. 'Blood which is life as you came to believe it to be. You and all of you. In the roots of the world, they knew; but now there is a race of blind worms. Blood.

That's what you ask me for.'

And Wedsek, who had fantasised bread and ale, tingled at the mystery of the devouring, of the vase of the throat, and the Wine.

'Come, then,' said Anjelen. 'Follow me. I'll give you what you crave. I'll give you all and more, till the cup runs over.'

Gisla had gone to her husband a virgin. The union had been hearty and determined. He was no ninny. He hurt her and was glad, for her loud cry proved him a man.

When he slept, she lay and solaced herself with the hut, now hers, the cookpots and spinning wheel, her apron, the priest-wedding.

Tomorrow, she thought, *tomorrow I shall...*

And heard a noise out in the street.

Just before sun-up, the men planned to be off hunting the marauding cat, those whose heads were not too thick – she was gratified to note how many cups her husband had swilled. Could this be some early riser? Or had the holder put men to patrol the village?

The footfalls were odd. Shuffling, limping and loping. Was it the beast, which the women had whispered might be more than natural, out there, moving down towards her house?

The shutter of the small window hung wide on the summer night.

Gisla slipped from her bridal bed, wincing at the bride's pain, and went to the window. She was half afraid and half fascinated. She had always been the first to crowd to the ghost stories at the fire – and always the one that shrieked in her sleep afterwards.

A skinny waif of moon shone on the street.

Something roved along the track, unsteady and uneven, as if deformed. It was of great size – and then she saw it was a man, a kind of man, but in some way so ghastly that she would have cried out again. But next she saw another thing. A blackness unrolled before the uncanny man. It was like a black light on a black taper, and as it came, the ground under it turned also black, a stain spreading both in front of it and behind.

Gisla found she could not cry aloud, could not make any sound.

She tried the name of her husband, but it would not come out. Like the sheep on the hill, she also knew intuitively that her helpmeet was useless to her.

The dark in the street had stopped, and just beyond it, the other, the man-beast.

Gisla held her breath. Every pore of her body was aware that she was seen. And she thought of the shut door, and the bar down across it. She was safe, for she had not the strength to shift that bar alone. She must walk away from the window, shake her husband, or crawl in beside him under the sheet.

The thing that was a man was crossing over the moonlight towards her. His eyes were filled by Gisla. She seemed to see herself staring back from two sightless panes. The darkness on the track had spread everywhere. It made pools and puddles; she wondered hopelessly if it were only water. The black light that had rolled before the beast man seemed gone. She stared about for it. She must leave the window. The man was stalking, stumbling near. *Get away, get away.* As in the nightmare after the story, it was not conceivable her feet could move, her arms or body. She tried to draw back, and in that instant, the man-beast-thing was at the window. He smiled on her and reached out his hand, so gently she scarcely saw it, and then he had her, by the face. His grip was clasped around her forehead, cheekbones, his fingers in her hair, and he pulled her forward, forward, until her head was out of the window, her neck braced on the sill with the breath pressed out of it. She kicked, and coughed, and the husband in the bed muttered she must be quiet, he had to be up early, and Gisla coughed up her breath and the man leaned to her and tore the flesh of her cheek out with his teeth.

The stool by the window was kicked over.

'Gisla, shut your noise, you bitch...'

Gisla had shut her noise. But there was another noise now.

The bridegroom surged up on his elbow and swore at his reeling head.

'What are you at in the window, eh? Come here. Get me some water, for God's sake.'

There was Gisla, in her wedding shift, her head vanished into night, and in from the night came a feeding sound, and something smeared in down the wall, glittering.

As the drunken groom tore from the hut, Wedsek, still holding up his first prize with one fist, caught the second, and banged its brains out on the doorpost. Then Wedsek drank and fed from two dishes.

To the racket this had made, he was oblivious. Under the aegis of his protector and god, he might do anything. Anjelen had given him this, and to do this. And Anjelen had been there at his side.

But then the darkness of Anjelen furled away, like a black leaf blown along the earth, and fetched up in the doorway of the largest hut, the holder's house, and there it was Anjelen again, the priest, who seemed to have come out to greet it...

Wedsek saw the village running at him from twelve directions, all the huts and hovels there were in it. Men came with axes and knives, and women ran out behind them, children muddled in their skirts, while dogs leapt through the air. The sound was a madness. Like a festival.

The man-wolf let go both the dish-vessels of his kill, and stood at bay a moment, as he gathered himself to fly.

But a voice began to speak to Wedsek in his head, whose marvelousness he had again, incredibly, overlooked.

'Stay, Wedsek. This I give you.'

Wedsek glanced up. A dog was coming down, launched for his neck, glaring and slavering. And as it hung there, a knife slewed through it, nearly taking the skull from the body. The dog fell on Wedsek and the hot blood splashed his lips, tinctured with honey, for the knife had come uncleaned from the wedding breakfast, from the slicing up of cakes.

After the dog, a man's full weight struck Wedsek. The man screamed between wrath and terror. His throat gaped like a ruby.

'Drink,' said Anjelen from the high tower in Wedsek's brain, 'take your fill.'

Wedsek too had fallen. The earth was black and slippery and red. Somehow the red was visible in the moonlight, the only colour.

Blood jetted over Wedsek's face.

He tried to push it off, the heap of bodies, the fountain of blood.

A woman had collapsed on his chest. She made sounds. She too tasted of the wrong elements, herbs and bread.

The knives had turned in their hands, or flown after them from the hearths, or else the veins of their necks burst spontaneously like glass at great pressure, and out the crimson fire like juices sprayed. And they crashed and sank on Wedsek.

The taste of all the blood was wrong. It was only blood. It was not holy. Not Wine.

'Drink,' said the voice.

The scalding salty vileness poured in Wedsek's mouth; he could not avoid it. He tried to gulp his way free and, as he did so, spew it forth again. Burning hot, the blood gushed down his nose, and laved his eyes.

'Drink,' said Anjelen.

Wedsek struggled and floundered. All their weight was on him, the weight of mankind, the sins of the world.

The holder's wife sped last from her hut. She clutched at the priest where he stood, impassive as a stone in her doorway. 'Brother – in the name of God help us…'

She looked at the heaving mass, like erupting mud.

She rushed forward with her ladle, and as she met the wall of flesh, felt the vein in her neck give way so terribly she barely believed it. Her ladle skidded across the track. She lay on a spasming dead child, disorientated, dying.

Buried in skin and meat and bone, drowning in blood, Wedsek heard the voice say from the mountaintop of consciousness, 'Drink.'

And the cup ran over.

He had been dreaming of blood and heaped bodies, in some form the Day of Judgement. Black shadow coiled along the ground, and all that place was changed to blackness, a black season, a black bead upon a chain. He supposed, waking himself, sipping from the cup of milk left by his bed, that he was an old man and his kind had such dreams. The ending of the world was, for him, close at hand in a personal way. Yet, he had nothing to fear. Though he had been disappointed, mentally and intellectually, he had been enabled to contend with and subdue the vice of impatience. In his seventies now, the snatched peace of a painful physical age deterred him from much complaint.

Only he regretted, he could not help it, that he had never seen during his years as a man, the advent, the coming of the Second Kingdom on earth.

The boy rapped at his door.

'I'm ready. Come in and clothe me.'

The boy, clumsy and nervous, entered, and the Factor yearned for certain other men who had waited on him with skill and charm. But he had outlived them all, for their duties and advancements took them elsewhere, and now he had fetched up in this city, in the Cathedral apartments, with this lending.

'Today, I shall go upriver.'

'Yes, Father Factor.'

'To see how the building progresses.'

'Yes, Father Factor.'

There it was. Not a glim of interest or enthusiasm. Did this pudding of a novice understand anything of what went on? Ah, to adore excellence and end in the care of a moron: God's lessons. But anyway, Anjelen had spoiled the Factor for the value of any man.

My life has gone in his service. He knows it. The marks are everywhere. And in my last letter, which surely will find him at some hour in Chirkess, I reported upon this latest thing. My gift at the feet of God.

He must not be proud. That was a misdemeanour. But to cherish the work would be allowed.

The Factor was rich, and into his project his riches had flowed like blood (blood – that dream – no, the Devil soured the sleep of the just; don't think of the Devil, for old men thought of him too often).

Robed and gowned, and with his gold crucifix and beads of jade, sapphire and pearl, the Factor was carried out in his chair, to the room above the marble hall, where he breakfasted with the Cathedral's Administer.

'You're visiting the new church, Father Factor?'

'Not a church, my lord. Much more than a church. The palace

of God upon the ground. Heaven in the everyday.'

The Administer frowned. The tiresome dotard came nearer to blasphemy with every phrase he uttered. But there, his presents to the Cathedral here had been lavish. And it was said he had himself been one of the Knights of God, before the order fell to disrepute – a dangerous old gentleman.

The voyage upriver, in the huge white-winged ship, took some days. There were sand bars to be avoided. Flat miles of unkept land wavered in the heat on either side the ship. The rowers strained.

The Factor took the notion, as he sometimes did now, that all this was one continuous dream, which included waking and sleeping. Might he not at any moment see Anjelen himself coming across the deck in the sunshine, as on that other journey? The Factor had tempted Anjelen with earthly power, and Anjelen had rejected it. How beautiful that seemed now. How perfect. But who had built for the Christus a temple of gold and crystal and white stone, in the days of his years?

Where the river entered the sea, a range of mountains soared aloft. The breakers of the estuary flailed about each other peevishly. It was a calm summer day.

They came to an area where an arm of rock struck out into the ocean across a waste of white sand.

Twice a day, the sea drew off from this promontory, and it was possible to gain access to the building whose foundations now showed above the rock, balusted with scaffolding, and strange detritus, like the leavings of giant molluscs.

They had to wait for the tides.

When the elderly man was carried up the steep, lethal ascent in his chair, the workmen on the walls above wondered at it, but he was a priest: only the extravagant best would do for him.

The enormous seaward window was already sketched in.

The Factor sat some while, gazing at it.

He doubted he would see it finished, any of this, as he would not see the completion of the other, non-corporeal, edifice.

The overseer stood before the Factor, giving good account. The Factor listened, wandered, listened again.

'And there, down the cliff, a Doma for women, to house the

sisters of the order.'

The Factor was not interested in that. Women had never interested him. It was sensible that they should be allowed to kiss the hem of the garment of the Christus, perform their little adjunctive duties. They had their part, as did the animals, and women had souls too, for the Christus had said so, but not souls as men had them. That was not reasonable.

'The Christerium,' he said aloud. '*His* house, when he's ready.'

The overseer waited out this rambling politely. He was not positive whether or not to remark to this ancient father what had happened with the sand, if it was worthwhile even, for probably the elderly priest would not take it in. The legate and the factor minor from the city had both assessed the phenomenon as springing from the dead shells of crabs and other sea creatures turfed up by preliminary excavation. This did not entirely explain it. Some of the labourers, the artisans even, had been perturbed. A divine service was held under the promontory at low tide, to ease their minds. For the white sand was going to black, a curious soft bruise that spread away from the cliff towards the sea, like a shadow poured out there.

They had heard the buildings were for a special purpose, not Cathedral or Fraterium, something more. Those ideas of a palace of God on earth, common to all churches, had here some extra resonance. Why then the blackening of the sand?

The old Factor was shivering now in the bright day, and the anxiety-ridden attendant asking if they should heat some wine for him. But the Factor only said, '*His* house,' again, and stared up at the tower of the seaward nave and the etched window and the sky. And the overseer decided he would not bother with the story of the sand, which after all might indicate nothing of any significance.

Chapter Nine

The journey had meandered: acres of earth and time. It had been the journey of growth, of the coming to estate, and to such purpose as he could recognise, Anjelen. Wedsek's intrusions were not of such great moment. He sloughed them when it seemed to him they had become so. His judgements were just, and blind. To kill brought Anjelen no delight. Even power did not delight Anjelen. But the vitality of what he was, maybe that sparkled within him, the passion of pure strength that must know itself in every move it makes.

The years that elapsed before he reached his objective – the return, the point of starting – were their own device. He delayed, and as he did so, matters sorted themselves, coming also to their own fruition.

Other elements, too, fitted themselves home in their places during this period. The churches Anjelen might enter as a godbrother, as a nonentity, and as a Magister, and more as a prince – ranged far and wide. The Factor had seen to his work well, along with others who had impressed themselves into Anjelen's service. Anjelen might be anything in the name of God now. That he had not gone up into the highest spheres, to the purse of an Administer, the throne of a Primentor, displayed only that he felt no need to, that his requirements did not encompass that. Between him and the outer world of littleness there were the white and magenta screens of higher Church Authority. It was convenient. But for himself, he did as he liked.

The forest, as he finally came back into it, was altered. The cores of that fervid terrain were denser, deeper and darker; like sinking wells. But elsewhere the brand of man was on everything. Roads thrust through; clearings made bald. Not a taming of the wild, but a witless living with it, a going about under the shadow of black and mighty things too large to be seen. They did not know what they did, nor would they be forgiven.

He rode into Raven lands, where the best road was, and went towards the Landholder's house. It was the Raven tribe that had set themselves to root out the old worship, more than twenty-six decades ago, when Anjelen had been Jun, the Chosen, nine years of age, under the Tree.

There were no outriders, no servants from Khish. Anjelen rode a mule, the mount of a godbrother, with two or three suitable pieces of baggage, and a gourd to store water, for it was a dry spring and many streams had run to their gravel.

The house of the Korhlens was unimpressive, seen from above. The stonework of the defensive central Tower, the barns and outbuildings. The women's apartments, segregated, were of wood, bright with darts of paint. Orchards wound round it all, and fields went to the door. They had not yet thought to make an inn, although traffic might swell on the road in these parts, and push them to do it.

The priest met with the Vre before he had quite got down to the house.

The Landholder and ten of his men came pelting along the incline from the wood, with carcasses of deer snarled among the horses.

'What's up?' said Vre Korhlen, riding headlong at the priest. He eyed the priest as a dog might eye a beetle, deciding whether or not to squash this inane interloper.

The priest reined in his animal, sat and waited. Most men in his circumstance would show some emotion on their faces, annoyance, nervousness, a desire to placate or chastise. The priest showed Korhlen nothing.

The Vre's tunic was diagonally coloured purple, rust and green, and from a collar of gilded bronze hung the raven of his house in heavy silver. He was well dressed for his hunting, and the wristlets and boots of leather were chased with gold. His left leg stuck out from the side of the horse uncouthly. It was braced with three rings and two stems of iron. No ornament that, but a malformation coped with as best he could. It had not, apparently, stopped him in much.

'What's up?' said Korhlen again, beside the priest.

'I am on the business of the Church,' said the priest. 'Will you afford me shelter at your Tower?'

'If I must, I must, I suppose. We have our religious, Godbrother Vezion.'

The priest said he had heard so.

'And heard he's weak, too soft on us, no doubt. That's why you honour us with a visit?'

Out here in the forest, tough, feuding (Korhlen feuded now; the priest would have heard that too), they had small need of the Church. It pursued them as best it might. But even the Vre's wife was hale. She had borne him a healthy son five months before and was good for several others. The Vre was not desperate for any holy favours.

A mill was being built, up from the house and the Tower. On the half-sown fields, in the broad light outside the wood, the peasants of Korhlen toiled; and clearly immediate, there came the rap of a rod on a man's back.

Over the valley, above them now, the undulations of the pines, the immovable vista of darkness.

They rode into the yard. A stone flight led up to the door of the Hall, which stood wide. The Vre dismounted with a clash of his leg-iron, and a sort of roar to match it. 'Come in, priest, and take a cup.' Vre Korhlen gestured to a man, some steward. 'Fetch Vezion! He'll tell you what we're up to, our heinous badness, all that. You can set what penances you think we want, godbrother. We'll do our best with them, but we're busy, at Korhlen.'

The Vre's contempt was jovial. Plainly, he thought the Church nothing to be afraid of. It had its uses. In fact he was quite pious at the proper moments – talk at Khish had led the priest to believe so.

Nevertheless, the Vre did cast at the priest an occasional searching glance. This one was not like the other ones, the grumblers and mouthers, the stragglers of God who wandered about the forest. Nor was he to be jollied with drink. He would accept only water. Well, let him have it then, and be damned to him.

Godbrother Vezion, when he got there, was unhappy. His rumpled face tried to straighten itself out, he tried to sing the praises of the household, the perfect wife and mother, the abstemious nobles, the brave soldiers, the wise and patient Vre... while close by ravened the wretched, drunken, godless Esnias Tower, constant source of fighting, their boundaries running down the Raven's in so many spots...

'I've been given the apartment by the west barn,' said the visiting priest. It was not a shining area, a former storeroom, damp in winter, broiled in summer, always tumbledown. 'Perhaps you would spend an hour with me before the Tower dines.'

'Yes, yes, or course.'

When Anjelen was gone to the awful apartment, the Korhlen priest plucked his lord's attention. 'I think – we should be wary, sir.'

'Why? Don't puddle your drawers. I'll save you from him.'

'I think – he is more than he says or seems. I've heard, my lord, of a travelling priest, like this one, ascetic, with compelling eyes...'

'Were they? Looked half mad to me.'

'He's rumoured to be a Magister of the Cathedral at Chirkess.'

'Then what's he doing here?'

'God knows,' said Godbrother Vezion with simple faith.

When he went to the west barn apartment, Godbrother Vezion had reached the stage of tremor. He had some cause to be distressed. He was alert for the visitor to be cognisant of this and ready with traps. What could Vezion say? *Here I'm at the mercy of my master.* Your master can only be God – that was the correct reply to his mewling.

The dark priest from Khish, or Chirkess, had given as his name Godbrother Jun – an unlikely title. Jun was no name of any recognisable sort, the kind of phonetic the lowliest peasant might fashion in the depth of the wood.

But Godbrother Jun, anyway, was sitting waiting. He had somehow contrived for there to be a table. On it were spread only three things, but these surprising. To the left of Jun, a vitreous globe, polished, to the right a dagger with a bronze hilt. These were the accessories of a mage, the Magister, and recollections of what Jun might really be a false name? – drew near. Before Jun, opened, was the most alarming evidence of all. It was a book, quite small, but beautifully coloured and illuminated, of the Scriptures, or part of them. One of Jun's pale hands lay on it. Vezion noticed for the first time that, along with plain wood beads, the other priest had a cross of bare black lacquer on his breast.

'Here I am, brother,' said Vezion, with tremulous heartiness, the latter learnt off from the Lord Vre, the former all his own.

'Here you are. Do seat yourself. The stools are not of the best, but we must make shift as we can.'

Vezion sat. He looked at the Book dubiously. His copy was poor, with passages omitted or inaccurate.

'Is that fair thing from Khish?' he ventured.

'From somewhere.' There was to be no doubt; Vezion faced an interrogator. It therefore startled him afresh when Jun went on: 'With the recent birth of the Vre's son in mind, I've been reading this section. *Blessed be God, that He gave to me a son in my old age.*' Jun looked at Godbrother Vezion.

Who smiled timorously and addended, 'Although of course our Abraham here, the Lord Vre, is hardly old...'

'But,' said Anjelen, 'we may take for his age the length of the family line. The Ravens have held this land for some centuries.'

'Just so,' said Vezion, wondering what would come next.

What came next was that the immaculate black-haired head was lowered again, and the exquisitely trained voice – a city, a city – read on: '*And it came to be, God prompted Abraham, saying, Go you into godless country and there make a sacrifice to me of your son.*'

Vezion waited, alight with fears, expecting now theosophical debate. What did Jun want of him? The usual argument that God had required immolation of His precious gift in thought, not deed, in order to be sure of the fidelity of His servant?

'Sacrifice,' Jun repeated, coolly, and lifting his head, looked at Vezion again in that manner from which it was not possible to turn, and which it was such a horrible discomfort to behold.

While the word gave the key to it all. And Vezion quailed. Was it better to be honest at once? Obviously. Events had been discovered.

'Please understand,' said Godbrother Vezion in a shaking bleat, 'that it's very difficult for me, alone here in the forest, to deal with such – aberrations. The Vre's a godly man, I insist that he is. But these old rites loom large. One day I may bring him…'

'What are you saying to me?' asked Jun.

Vezion, up to his throat in the mire, stumbled and went down. He stared at Jun, through obscuring mud.

'Why, that – that what the Vre has done – that the sacrifice…'

'Can you be telling me,' said Jun, most gently, 'that Vre Korhlen plans to offer the blood of his firstborn to appease God?'

Vezion said, 'I'd assumed from your inference, Brother Jun, that the sacrifice at Korhlen' – emboldened of necessity, Vezion's tone was firmer – 'was to have the attention of the Church Fathers.'

Jun said, 'Of course.' He said it without any threat at all, and so appalled Vezion.

'Indeed, how could it be otherwise,' said Vezion. 'There's secrecy, but some account always gets out. They've done it since they first took the land. An offering to the god of the wood, a token in payment. The worship of the Christus stopped it. Then, some bad luck sent them running again to the ancient gambits. Not, as you'll be aware, human blood– letting – no, no. An animal, a sheep or pig, sometimes a horse. Every spring.'

Godbrother Vezion broke off because he got no response.

Godbrother Jun sat like a pale and dark stone, and regarded him, and at last Vezion could only lie there in the mud, suffocated and will-less, for what would follow.

'The eye of the Church,' said Jun, 'sees everything. It is the earthly minister of God.'

'Is he to be punished?' said Vezion. In his eyes was a vision of Vre Korhlen stripped of his possessions, land, wile, child, worst of all burnt alive as a pagan disbeliever, a practitioner of obscene rituals. In Vezion's heart was fright for himself. His own stripping, and maybe worse. He meant, *Am* I to be *punished?*

Jun answered him. 'You yourself are held quite blameless. I stress this, since I see you suppose you've condoned a crime. Vre Korhlen has acted ignorantly, but through his ignorance has yet approached a virtue. I am going to place in your keeping now, Vezion, a hidden truth. You must cherish and guard it.'

'Yes…' faltered Vezion.

'What,' said Jun, 'but the ultimate sacrifice, was the Christus?

Through his death he accomplished two things: the payment for earthly sin, and the assurance of eternal life.'

Vezion went on staring. His face was quite smooth now, childish, fascinated. Choked in mud, he had reached the moment of soporific ecstasy. The vitreous globe glimmered; the dagger pointed at him.

'You must understand,' said Jun, 'that blood sacrifice is neither alien to nor outlawed by the Church. You will find the Book threaded with it. To the unlessoned, naturally, the practice is never revealed, for it must not be profaned by the unlearned and vulgar. For the man here, he performs in unruly and impious rashness a very profound and sacred mystery. He needs only to be tutored, and shown how, by God's grace, he may acquit himself of the action better.'

'But,' said Vezion, 'it's a pagan thing...' He was so becalmed, he did not know what he said, or he would, definitely, never have quibbled.

Jun answered patiently and rationally, 'Go you into godless country. This was the word of God Himself. This deed must be done on pagan ground. Try to comprehend, Vezion, for as with all complete truths, the matter is both dauntingly complex and utterly plain. All is God. It is therefore impossible, when at worship, to worship anything but God. The rituals of the wood are also God's rituals. Their form is unlike, yet also entirely apposite. The tree, the flesh, the blood. The thorns and the roses. Put away the little, infantile things, Vezion, and accept the great Truth. The secret of the rose of the Blood.'

'Yes...' Vezion whispered now. 'The Wine, and the Tree...'

'What's been done is very well,' said Jun, 'but it lacks. It falls behind.'

Vezion felt as if he slept. Yet his brain was clear as the magician's globe, his hands were firm with excitement, gripping as if they clenched the dagger.

'The Vre has feuded for a month, and taken, I believe, certain prisoners.'

'Yes,' said Vezion. 'Thirteen Esnias soldiers. Only five can fetch ransom.'

'Long ago,' said Jun, 'slaves died by the score. But then, it came to be one man, a Chosen. And then a Chosen boy. Boy or man. The youngest of them. Tell your master the Vre. Before he dines.'

Vezion got up unsteadily. He said, 'There are other families in the woods, who sacrifice men.'

'I know it, Vezion. You reveal nothing astounding. But they're special here. The ground is special, here.'

Dinner in the Cup Hall had been strange and strained. Vre Korhlen had seen, in the orb of torchlight, the new priest down at his out-of-the-way and ill-served table. Vre Korhlen had seen his raven-haired wife too, in her saffron dress trimmed with green and scarlet, the child brought in for show, and given a lick of wine on a knife handle. He had seen his twisted leg, as ever, stuck out to trip unwary servers, the slaves, the rowdy Tower court. And when the women went and the drinking began in earnest, the first fisticuffs started, the first beer and bones rolled, and the dogs went dashing, and five men were kicking and pummelling among the trenchers. A bears' cave by firelight it was, constant as life. But he got up and left it, and went out into the scented spring night, down among the peach trees to where the chapel was.

There, in the stone vault as cold as winter still, he stood rubbing his wrists in anger, glaring at the new priest who had dared come here and know the secret and give it up to him in a fresh and fearsome way. Agitated, he did not simmer his words. He flung them raw.

'What bloody trick is this? What do you want, you crawling black-skirt?'

And the new priest, Jun, he said to Vezion, 'Stay here and pray to God,' And to Vre Korhlen he said, 'We'll go up the hill now, to the place.'

'What place is that?'

'The place of the sacrifice.'

'It's a pitfall. God rot him, that numbskull, what's he told you? You take on his lies? I won't be caught. Up there, at night? The stone – God knows, its bloody roots go down as far as Hell.'

'No more protests,' said Jun. 'You'll be silent now.'

Vre Korhlen opened his mouth wide to describe how no man gave orders to him, but a peculiar and vast murmur, not physical, neither imagined, quivered through the chapel. It was like the breath of God. And Vre Korhlen stepped off from it, caught despite his avowal, because he believed in things unworldly.

Jun was at the door. He went out of it, not looking back, and took the track up towards the mill, as if he knew the path well. He did not pause to invite or command the Vre again. But the Vre walked after him. And Vezion, as instructed, kneeled down on the paving to pray.

Birches grew about the grove. They had come up like white maidens in the mornings and the afternoons, the dusks and midnights, to coronet the ground. Inside, the grass was rank, strewn with mushrooms, cones, thick as horse-tails, with a ferny compost odour and a sweet fragrance in the dark. And there, at the centre, as at the centre of all things, was the Tree. It leaned now. It had lost bark, branches and foliage, every bough, every inch of height and vestige of wood. *But nothing else.* A black stone stood crooked in the ancient glade. Chopped down, eviscerated and petrified. And it was the Tree.

Above was a hole of night sky, limpid and bluish, with salt-grain stars.

Jun moved about the stone. He stood the far side of it and bowed his head.

'Well,' said the Vre, angry and afraid, the bravado of food and drink leaving him as if in the gusts of the night breeze, remembering eventually maybe the strength of the Church Paternal. Confused. For what did this one want, this renegade, who had apparently wed the cross of the Christus to the old dark shore of the wood? 'Well. What is it, damn you?'

'Be still,' said Jun.

His voice came like silver through the night. Now, here, rather than exacerbate, it soothed. Like a bell, softly it rang between the silent spaces.

Then, out of the black stone which the Tree had become, the Tree began again to grow.

It rose up, dim and ghostlike, hardly black, like a column of smoke that was also water. It put out limbs, and these put forth branches. Leaves like phantasmal metals, and needles that were smoky crystal. And in the belly of the Tree there were to be seen, like the skeletons of things in black amber, the spines and ribcages and skulls of men. Thousands of them there were, all folded, each behind the other, and away, to interminable distances where they grew slender as twists of ivory. All the young men who had died and become the Tree. The Sacrifice, over and over.

Jun raised his arm. He struck the Tree. From its side a stream of blood erupted, the colour of blood even in the dark, and elsewhere eyelets gave, and arcs of whitest water poured out. The Tree was the source of everything, of tears and the rivers, of the blood of death and birth.

There were eyes in the skulls inside the Tree. They looked on calmly, glowing.

High above, a man's white body hung between earth and Heaven. Stars were the three blazing nails which pinned him there, his arms outflung. His head was crowned with the bitter thorns, in which the blood had gathered like roses.

'Here,' said the voice of silver, 'is the kind Father who feeds you. In return, feed him. It is God. God is only One. It never finished and must go on. To the end of the world, it is with you.'

If Vre Korhlen made a noise now, it was not audible. If he thought of wife or child, land or goods, the priest or himself, was in doubt.

The Tree gleamed and flickered and was and was not. All the forest was there, the miles without number, the teeming of life within it, its centuries past, and to be.

'Father, forgive me,' said Vre Korhlen. He knelt down. '*Yet, if I walk through the Valley of Night, be with me, Lord, O be with me, Lord.*'

The man was dragged screaming. He had fought bravely in the battle with Korhlen's men and reckoned to be got home to Esnias before the summer. When they fed him and washed him, he felt lucky. But then they took him out and soon he guessed, for he had heard of such rites, and that perhaps Korhlen subscribed to them.

It was no easement to him that he had been better prepared than hordes of former captives meant for the Tree, and other captives due in future for the black stone.

They tied him to a rock.

It had not yet come to include a rite of manhood, the proving of the Landholder's heirs as their people's shepherd and priest. It was the Vre who took the knife. Nor did he cut the throat or neck veins, as he had thought fit to do with the animals butchered there.

He drove the knife in and upward, to sever the stomach and carve the heart. The ghastly scream, gouts, fountains of gore. As it should be.

The forest gave, and must have back, in some measure. It had always been so.

And as the summer swelled, the fields fattened yolk-yellow, the streams ran clear, the beasts proliferatively dropped their young, and his own wife hung heavy as a grape on the vine with his second child, the Vre beheld that what he had done was good. If he recalled its connection to the Christus – who could say?

Three years later that second son was to die, of a childish ailment not unknown in the forest. At the next spring sacrifice, Vre Korhlen took his firstborn, then almost four years of age, with him to the stone. He let the boy witness the sacrifice, and going to him after, anointed his forehead with the hot red blood. The small child, Kolris Korhlen, did not flinch or cry. He had already learned, at the hand of his bluff iron-legged sire, better than to do that.

Chapter Ten

At thirteen, when Catra became a woman, they had decided that her wits were not quite sound, but that did not matter so much as the other thing, over which they had worried. Ten was a normal age for puberty, and there were fears her lagging brain had slowed her body. But then she woke crying and the nurse ran down to the mother with the red-splotched bed linen. They were pleased with Catra and made a fuss of her. Now she was a worthy maiden. Now she might marry. So Catra was pleased also and smiled. She was a winsome child, after her own manner. If not too much was asked of her, she could pass as adequately as another girl, being only more docile, more tractable, which was to the credit. Otherwise, she was something of a beauty.

Her hair was unusually fair, like bleached cloth, fine and soft, and her eyes very pale blue. Where these pearly looks came from no one deduced. Perhaps fortunately for her mother, no man of this description was among the Hill Tower kindred, or servants, and none had ever been noted in those parts. Catra's father was the fourth brother to the Landholder, low in the crowded ranks of aristocrats, and his wife had already equipped him with two sons, black-haired and brown-eyed like all the rest.

It happened they had been waiting on Catra's coming to bud. An alliance with another Tower was thought suitable, following a slight disagreement. No daughters were legally available, but Catra, and another girl of twelve – fully a woman, but of even less vital birth, thought too removed from the Hill Tower's Vre to be an acceptable offering.

The union was to be with the Raven Tower of Korhlen. Her nursemaid told Catra all this, as Catra sat plaiting flowers for a chaplet, under the jagged stones of the wall. Below lay the forest, as it lay everywhere, a ruffled blackish carpet from which peaks of emerald, ash, grey and slaty blue expressed their heads. Catra was afraid of the forest, and in her infancy had had terrible dreams she could never explain concerning it.

'And he's a wonderful man, the Vre, a Landholder like lord uncle. And young. Not twenty-five, they say. His first and most precious bride you'll be. Won't you like that?'

Catra said she would. Already she had been given a gown embroidered with lilies, a necklace and bangles, earrings of blue enamel.

'And you shan't mind going away from your mamma, shall you?' queried the nurse.

Catra shook her flaxen head, a little doubtfully, but "mamma" did not represent very much, if rather more than "father", both of them stern and judgemental, spoilers and punishers. 'As for me, I'm too old to go. But you'll have the girl with you, flimsy bit though she is...' The nurse left off, seeing Catra had jumped, and that her dilute eyes filled with tears. In her hands the flowers were crushed. 'Won't you come with me, Nursey?'

'No child,' said the nurse, gratified to have caused pain, for who else valued her?

An hour later she was less gratified, for Catra had wept herself into a sodden state, and there was the lady, Catra's mother – for the nurse, too, a punisher and spoiler.

'What did you mean by telling her?'

'I thought no harm, lady. I'm not to go. It's better she grows accustomed. Once she's a husband, she'll forget me...'

'Yes, so she will, and sooner than that. From this day on, you won't see my daughter.'

After the nurse, snivelling reflexively in turn, had departed, Catra's mother paced her small stone chamber, which, situated above the stable court, was summer-doused with smells unwanted. Catra's mother did not herself feel comfortable or used to her daughter. Thank God this offspring had not been a boy; she would never have heard the last of it. To this hour, she remembered Catra's getting. A sudden frightful gurning and moving in her womb, so that she knew it had received a child. That night had been full of phantoms. She had heard mutters from the servants, of a ghostly figure seen at the edge of the forest, a robed man... And there were dolls hanging in the trees that the Vre had had taken down, for he did not like pagan ways on his Hill.

By suppertime, Catra was appeased. Her poor, limited mind generally could not keep anything for very long, even grief, though her instantaneous reactions were often febrile.

Calmed with sweets, she fell asleep, drifts of unbound, light-washed hair on the pillow. For what was needed, she would do.

Catra went to Korhlen, to the second stone Tower like, and not like, her childhood home. She was thirteen, childish, but not flamboyantly missing any element of herself. She took some boxes and chests amongst which were apparel, combs, beads, and a cithra she had almost learned to play, whereon she would pluck innocent tunes, and sing softly to herself.

Her bridegroom came out at her in the yard. He was black-haired, with a warm colouring, quite young, and surely young enough. But he frightened her, and she squealed, and that seemed to amuse him.

There was only the "bit" of a girl to sustain Catra now. The girl was one year older than Catra, and mentally old enough to be her mother. For that reason she had been picked. The girl served Catra in all particulars, was her advisor: she had even instructed Catra in the duties of the wedding night and been met with a sheer disbelief that did not augur well. Catra had seen, to be sure, goats and pigs at such activities. But a man with a woman? It was not kindness that had protected Catra from these sights, only decorum and, mostly, naivety. Perhaps Catra had seen them and misunderstood.

'He'll hurt you,' said her maid. 'You can cry out, but not too much. Let him do everything he wants. You must on *no account* deny him anything. It's the law of God.'

Catra went to her bridal in terror. She kept glancing at the red-lipped groom, whose eyes shone and who to her seemed aged as her father and her uncles. Alone in their bedroom he was due to turn into a monster.

Sensing her fear, knowing himself fear-inspiring, and thus not noticing her oddity, Kolris Vre Korhlen attempted to reassure. He reckoned the Hill Tower had lied, the girl was not much more than eleven, but he had had a girl younger than that, and was not put out. It showed the Hill Vre's desire to ally with him. And she would be all the better for children, the heirs he must achieve. For Kolris had had no children, for all his romps, though he had consented to acknowledge a pair of boys as his own, down in the Korhlen village, for the look of it. Could it be God would hold off from allowing Kolris the rights of fatherhood? He dared not even think of this. Blame his women all he would, fifty years before, the lack of an heir would have been enough to oust him, and at this date he would have to fight day and night to retain leadership. Catra had been examined and was a virgin. He would see to it she was true to him. He would sow her until God gave back an affirmative.

After the wedding, the feast. Catra was improved, she enjoyed the food, especially the pastry people, and the pastry ring Kolris cut and gave her to eat – it had sugar on it. Oh, after all what could be going to happen save they would ascend to bed in the Tower and sleep there? Though it was a disturbing thought, this great man wallowing by her, yet certainly she could endure it. She would not say no, and flout God's law.

When they had been lighted to Kolris' chamber, left there, and the servants had gone, Catra's maid with them, the Landholder sat down on the bed, and pulled Catra to him. He was rough in his handling of her, but that did not particularly upset her; all her uncles, when they dandled the pretty simpleton, handled her the same.

'Do you know what comes now?'

Catra lowered her eyes. She said she did not.

He said, 'Come, someone told you. Your mother.'

No, her mother had not told.

Kolris, in his twenties, strong and already erect from her proximity, said, 'Then I must show you, mustn't I? You don't want to stay a maiden. You want to be my wife.'

Then he began to undo her dress, which the clever maid had already made an easy task for him. He was therefore able to do it quite gently, not to make her start, for she was so youthful and tender. There would be enough bruising.

At first Catra was meek, then she was scandalised. The cloth slipped off her breasts before she was moved to squeak (an uncle had once done this; there were reprimands all round).

'No, no,' said Kolris, young enough to be mild, all his life before him. Anxious enough also to want to plough the furrow straight.

But Catra struggled, and then he grasped her firmly, and not bothering to kiss her mouth, rubbed his face against the small and lovely breasts, rocking her on his knee. He had had a great many girls, all willing to go with a Vre, but they had taught him a few of the things they liked.

Catra wriggled, but then, she relaxed. Body-pleasure, which she could never have associated with the flat instructions of the "bit" of a maid, began to move inside her, her veins and loins. She snuggled herself into Kolris, her husband, and allowed him to find out what any man might, who had dared lay all his hand on her, that she was at high temperature, a woods girl after all, glad and hot and willing.

When Kolris rolled her down and tried her, having to force to get in, she, with yelps of pain and amazement, thrust up to meet him. She opened herself wide and kicked his back with her bare pink feet, scratching his ribs and buttocks with her fingernails. She reached orgasm in a few moments, and only then did she cry out as it had been permitted her to do. Kolris crashed upon her, gasping.

Later, if not by much, when he wanted her again, she was more than ready. Later again, when the candles had burned to stubs, and the roars from the Cup Hall were dull with ale and exhaustion, she put out a leaf of hand upon his private parts and tickled him into a blaze. She had learned swiftly. He even wondered what she had been at, this sprite. If he had not had such positive proof of her sealment, the new red blotches on the bed, Kolris might have doubted her. But no, she was true, and if she was a minx it was for him, only for him.

As for Catra, she fell asleep at last, curled like a blissful sea-thing in a cocoon of warm bedclothes. She had neither remorse nor shame. Her simplicity provided her with the talent of acceptance. There had been sugar on all the night.

Hung in a balance of bright spring sunlight, the Christerium had leaned on its forepaws above the sea, its head raised, its one seaward eye staring. So he saw it for the first time. (Anjelen, for whom it had been made.) But what he thought of it, what he felt for it – useless to apply such notions to him. He felt nothing but a sort of oblivious rightness, as at a detail in its proper place. And he thought? Some abstract thing to do with architecture, contours, the play of shade and sun. The diamond brain made its assessment. The tree that was the man discounted all, aware only of the benign weather change, the correct season, something like that.

But for the Christerium...

You will know him by certain signs.

He himself was the sign. From coded and mystic precursors, they would discover him, from some clue of description physical and spiritual. The Factor had performed his labour well.

The porter at the gate did not question Anjelen. The porter's face went sallow. He took one look and let in the dark priest, who was on foot, carrying nothing.

All the gates, and the doors, opened.

The higher brotherhood came out to meet him. Some of them kneeled. In the church of the Christerium the bells began to ring, but the mass of priests did not crowd the walks and terraces, the upper towers and windows, to see. It was forbidden. They understood how they must greet him. Under a consecrated terror of joy they took him in, as it must be, like the awaited guest he was.

High in the south wall of the Christerium, an apartment had been made for Anjelen. As yet it had few furnishings. He would perhaps send for the objects that had accrued on his travels, from the storage in which he had left them... for alchemy had become his device, his foliage, like books and learning, like the priesthood itself. He bade them take the silk from the bed. The coloured windows were facts: the horned wolf ridden by the angel – the Manifestation, the snake with breasts and cat's cunning face, who roped the Tree of Fruit. How aptly the ignorant read him, while the wise fell at the wayside.

He summoned the high priest, the Primentor, who arrived with some pomp. In the first chamber, alone together, the Primentor knelt to Anjelen.

'Get up, my lord,' said Anjelen.

'You are my lord,' said the Primentor, whose robes flamed with jewels.

'But it should not seem so. I don't ask it. This isn't the time.'

This admonition would one day be passed on to a successor. The Primentor did not guess. Like the Factor, he was to be spared foreknowledge of lethargy, the test of faith that must endure not trial but, worse, a long, long wait. Anjelen was dressed for the Primentor as a Knight of God, for the order, which had been censored in the outer world, was succoured, and flourished, here. From such Knights, disciples would be drawn. It was expected.

A dove-blue choir chanted in the galleries below, like the sound of the sea that, in its way, was the noise the forest made, the hush and swell of waters, leaves.

His title, at the Christerium, was Magister. Not much was seen of him. He was not discussed. He came and went as he chose, through the days, the months, the years, the decades. Sometimes he was absent, although present. At others he was reckoned to be there but was away in the body. He led particular ceremonies of the Knighthood. The Christerium was, at his advent, close to three hundred strong, aside from its servants and slaves. (The adjunct women of the Doma did not count in any sense.) The numbers grew. The sanctum had an ambience of its own, although in general parlance it was supposed a seat of high learning, a remote kernel of piety and devotion, in another way, something which knit the fabric of the earth. Anjelen had imbued the Christerium. He was in every stone, every pane of glass. The gargoyles were aspects of his darkness and his piercing fire. The pictures of the windows and the walls reflected his soul, his intellect, his mythical nature, his actuality, and his demonic unsubstance that would never make sense. All unawares. It was as if his blood – the sacred and profane and dreadful blood which he used to feed those he took to himself – that blood ran through all the secret arteries of the building, and down into the very sand, that now was entirely black to the edge of the craving, pouring sea. There was a drop of blood also in the crucifix over his heart. Heart's blood, perhaps. A tear of blood let fall, crystallised, and turned into a flower that in turn turned to a ruby. He must have created, or garnered, the gem himself. It had not been left for him; they would not have presumed.

Thus Anjelen, at the hub of the edifice that had been formed to enclose him, to magnify and make straight his way. The palace on earth.

It was his study. His chamber of science. There he worked on what he willed, which had nothing to do with the religious or miraculous reveries of the Christerium priesthood. It was the business of a tree. That was what he toiled at, in the exquisite rooms of tinted lights and hanging swords inside the shell of stone. On the spore spreading mindless brainless bloody and insensate propagation of the wood.

And it was there, and in this way, that he formed the blonde girl Catra out of the mere genes, the semen, and the ovum, of a male and female.

That she must wed into Korhlen was his purpose. Korhlen, the area of the Tree. For that he made her, without great effort. Free of his body, in various guises, wolf, hare, man even, he moved about the forest's edges. He observed the boy child, once carried into the Raven Cup Hall, grow, as it might have seemed in a few days, to the youth of manhood. Kolris. Who was beaten by his father of the twisted leg, into a shape. These psychological semantics did not concern Anjelen. He noticed only that the Landholder of the Korhlen Tower must pick a bride away from his own kindred, and that he would be likely to make an alliance here with this Tower, or here, with this. That light hair was unusual and might entice. Anjelen constructed Catra to fulfil such essentials. He constructed her in the womb by introducing into her composition at the moment of conception (the man and woman thrashing on the mattress), the etheric splinter of himself. He melded with her, and through his will and his invisible physical presence, she was conceived. She was conceived also female, and after his design.

Catra had two fathers. Not the semen of Anjelen, kept close as treasure, but the psycho-fleshly matter of him. It was that which fused with sperm and ovum, and which made her. He fashioned her like a pattern, next concentrating and perfecting a little at a time. He did it unfeelingly, seeing her from a great way off, through alchemic and biological knowledge, and via a godlike callousness

that experimented, almost frivolously. He expected only success.
And from that high view, he did not jib when coincidental fate itself
removed her possible rivals to Kolris' marrying hand. Sickness
came, and carried them off, or other suitors. He, if needful, would
have seen to it, one way or another. Luring by omens of the forest,
through dreams, into disgrace, killing through hallucination,
whatever was necessary. He might accomplish so much, this
magician-priest, looking in his glass of quartz, manipulating, just as
he had structured the embryo of Catra.

Catra came to term and was born. Anjelen saw this. He was in
the room, somehow, unnoticed, a germ of flame upon a wall, in the
corner of an eye, a mirror...

Catra was his, but he had been careless. It was all done so
blithely. He had not made her, after all, quite right. The first
experiment in genesis was a failure.

The Tree, spreading seed, reproducing its life, did so blindly.

One failure did not spell so very dire a dismay. Yet also Anjelen
was becoming human, he had a mortal brain, transcended though
it had been.

Add then to the inconsequence, the barb of intellectual
irritation. Longevity had begun to impress upon him a man's
occasional mental symptoms. Partial pleasures, almost angers. The
hint of wormwood.

Catra was simple. His play with her had addled her wits. Yet,
that might not interfere. Korhlen took her, wedded, bedded. Her
use was to bear a single fruit. It was now feasible.

And in a near impatience, the Tree waited in its grove of marble
and shadow and painted saints. For a burgeoning of the Korhlens
out of the vessel of Catra: Anjelen's son.

'Don't cry now. You're my good girl, my clever little wife.' Kolris
Vre Korhlen embraced his shivering woman, and her flaxy hair
skeined over him, smelling of wood herbs and night. 'I'm pleased
with you. It's a shame you must go over to the women's rooms
once you're in the third month. But I'll visit you.'

She clung. Kolris fondled her breast, put down his head to suck
at the candy star of the nipple. Could she make him a boy, this

fragile lily? Why not? Who would have thought her so lusty a lover, so hot. She would bear well for him. He had hung her with necklets and put a comb of gold into her tresses, but the comb made her hair look more grey than fair.

'You'll like to give me a boy,' he said.

'No,' she said, and struggled, and he took it for teasing and pushed her back, but she was frightened, as if doing this again might make another baby in her, astride the first.

She had heard the tales, the birthing in agony, the woman shrieking and split. Did not the whole belly come apart, and the surgeon have to sew the mother together again?

Catra did not confide in Kolris. The accurate explanations of the Hill Tower maid had only caused more fear. The child did indeed come out of the belly, through the passage whereby it had entered. It emerged between the legs. There was blood.

Catra fought off her husband. She did not want to be penetrated. She wanted to forget that thing in there. Her belly was growing round and hard, and in the mornings she retched and vomited, and one of her teeth had begun to ache, and the maid had said she would lose it because of the baby, which ate her strength, the man must pull out the tooth with pincers. And maybe the baby would be pulled from her and she would tear in two.

Kolris hit his wife, to quiet her. He would not force, not wanting her to miscarry, but he was sorry his hour of relief and exaltation had been spoiled. The girl was backward; he had been stupid to ignore it. He must have her watched, in case she harmed herself and the child.

The Christerium was in darkness, but only that which holds a wood, for here and there the minutest lights were burning: the candles of some, late reading, the bakery ovens, the lamps at the latrines, and under the niches of prescribed statues, in the corners of walks where the gargoyles stared, and over the supreme altar of the church.

The church tower stood higher than any height of the Christerium. In its ruffle of embroidered stone, the door appeared shut, but was not secured. Any might open it, enter. None would do so, now.

Within, the church did not long stay in darkness. An undersea radiance bloomed out. It did not quite touch the landward windows that showed the battle of Good with Evil, the fallen Devil in his pit of garnet and chrysoprase. But the altar opened like a flower about the core of the lamp, the white and scarlet stamen of the Christus on his cross. The altar drape was red. It was embroidered in gold and picked out with large drops of fire opal. Before the altar, on the polished floor, there lay a vast crown of thorns, woven for the head of a giant. It was fixed there, in the island of light, sparkling faintly where it had been splashed with some fluid.

Under the altar stood twelve white Knights of God, in mail, tunics, cloaks, helmed and plumed, with swords at their sides. Twelve male faces, capped with metal, alike in the stillness as twelve pillars. Eyes beaded from veiled, smoking wax.

Directly by the altar, Anjelen, a Knight, the angel, god-in-man.

Soon after sunfall, Catra's labour pains started. She had been ill and restless all afternoon, and her women had looked for it.

The midwife came to the women's quarters.

Catra shrieked.

'If the lady screams now, what will she do when it really comes on her?' joked the midwife, a burly woman who had borne thrice with considerable ease and assisted at every difficulty with a contemptuous matter-of-factness. Trouble was for others. Perhaps they had deserved it.

Catra shrieked.

'She's very slight, very small,' whispered the maid from the Hill Tower.

'Slight she may be, but that's a great one she's got in her bag. Now, push, lady. You can't leave all the toil to he and me.'

Catra shrieked till her voice broke. Her eyes were insane with horror. She bit and struck the women who tried to help her, and only the bullying midwife got the better of her.

'We are here for our faith.'

The novice had come from the side door to the north of the nave, seeming to emerge from nowhere. He had thrown off the robe and was naked but for a loincloth of linen. On his head was a garland of autumn flowers. He entered the aureole of the candles, approaching gently, half-timorously, like a ghost. His face sightlessly adored Anjelen.

'They hung Him on a tree. He was perfect. For the errors of the earth He suffered. He said, Do this in my name hereafter. And He gave them the Wine.'

The midwife slapped Catra's back. The girl lay on her side. She had been in labour for ten hours, and it was almost dawn. 'Heave, girl. Get him out.'

Catra whimpered. She had let her maid come and hold her hands. Catra had no more strength left to her to fight anymore, her maid, the child, or the pain.

Blood, water, wine soaked across the sheets and into the straw laid under them.

Catra tried to scream. She had no voice.

The maid stood up.

'Call the surgeon. He must help.'

The midwife, red from her exertions and in her butcher's apron, laughed in the girl's face.

'He'll only want to cut her up. Best to leave it to me.'

The boy put back his head to gaze at Anjelen. From the silver wristlet on his left arm Anjelen drew the knife. He put his left hand behind the boy's head. With one glancing stroke he sliced open the throat. Blood jetted…

…It gushed out black and crimson, and in the centre of the blood the leaping thing rose white as a fish under the muck.

'A boy!' called the midwife. She seized the child as though in hatred, severed from it the link of birth, shook and swung the baby, scraping out the three holes of its face with her finger. The child voided its lips and nostrils, and wailed in the tone of a nightmare mouse, so thin and reedy, so *unhuman* was its noise.

The midwife glared at Catra, lying almost but not quite sunken as a sack, her eyes like colourless pools in hollows of dust from the moon.

'She's big still.' The midwife pressed on Catra's belly.

Catra managed to scream. Her cry was exactly like the child's.

'There's another to come out, God have mercy.'

'And this one is no boy,' added the maid with venom, holding the thing over the basin of water, a little white fish-rat with invert loins.

The Knights of God drank from the chalice one by one. They were moved, but decorous.

At last, the last of all, Anjelen raised the novice boy to his lips, kissing his forehead in a kiss of peace. The boy could not die, unless Anjelen willed it. The boy only need to believe, to give of himself, and so he did.

Anjelen drank from the brim of the well of blood, as the Tree had done so many countless times from the blood of men.

Catra was unconscious when the second girl was squeezed from her body. This girl was like the first, perhaps more flaccid, tinier, an even poorer specimen.

They supposed Catra could not survive. But she did.

Her husband was kind to her, the Landholder's lady in the Raven Tower. He said she was not to fret. She would give him a son next time.

Catra knew she would never let Kolris, for all the delight of it, into her body again, for she had learned what resulted from such unions. Anyway, she could not think that her rent flesh would ever be fit again to receive him. He had ruined her.

She lay in pain all day in her bed in the women's house. When at length they coaxed her out into the garden he had had made for her from the orchard, she sat passively. She did, so far, what she was told, even to nursing the two white, boneless, rat like daughters. But her milk was thin, and a nurse was got for them. The nurse did not like them either. They had strange eyes, too pale. Presently their eyes changed to a pink colour, quite pretty, like rose glass in a window. A white down appeared on the heads of the creatures. They were albinos. They would be odd, like their dam.

Even then, Kolris was kind. Catra had proved he was capable of generation. Unluckily, she herself was faulty. He had begun to ponder if an annulment of the marriage was procurable, and his words of sons were offered only to cheer the ailing wretch.

A letter to the Church Fathers at Khish, however, had gone unanswered five or six months. Which, even allowing for the onset of winter, was a long while. Winter, after all, was now over and the roads clear. He would not dare write again so soon. Wait and see. She was unhealthy and might die. Why make her miserable? There was still time.

Kolris Vre Korhlen did not know that his disappointment had been, in an oblique and unlike way, shared. That something, like the form of a black eagle perched upon a crag, looked down and watched his world through a globe of glassy stuff. That something walked his woods, went over his fields, and left the print of a wolf.

This unguessed participant was close in every way but the physical.

The slaves of Korhlen murmured, and threaded the trees with effigies, and now and then cut the throat of something at the forest's brink. The sacrifice to the stone in spring was looked for in a parched desire. And Catra sensed a sound of footfalls drawing near. She began to have the bad dreams she had endured in infancy and childhood. (There had been a child, then, gone astray, as sometimes happened, in the forest, the daughter of a good family. Word spread, and the nurse had blamed Catra's dreams on that, having herself recounted the gossip in her vicinity.) Surely, however, the infantile legend bore no relation to Catra's adult terrors? A tree of ebony grasped her, turned her round and round, plucked at her. Her hair was tangled in the boughs. The tree had hands like those of some monstrous man, jet-black and gleaming, articulate, hard, and inescapable.

Time moved, as the sea moved on the sand under the building by the ocean. It crossed the forest, stripping and returning leafage. The pines remained, and the granite trees of the Towers, though villages that might last two hundred years might also slip into the ground, vanishing in a week. For the forest jumped, as did the wolf, upon the back of anything fallen, and there devoured it.

Not much time. Enough to heal the silken lining of the thin pale girl, so she could walk through the orchards, and up the stairs of the Tower, and along the wooden galleries of the women's house. Enough to unfold the budded daughters into little white vegetables that skipped and meandered, holding to her skirts, for rarely would she grant them her hands.

These two things had hurt her. They were to blame, as Kolris was, who had put them inside her. She did not regard them as hers. They were two tumours that had been wrenched out of her, and external now, still kept a grip.

Having walked through the orchard garden, where the twin females had, at the persuasion of a serving girl, tried to pat a ball, mother and children were going back to the women's quarters. Catra, the Vre's lady, lived there now, as was quite proper, although several had thought he would discard the custom, he was once so keen to get at her.

Charina and Chirda made heavy weather of the ascent among the wooden buildings. Their legs were small for the climb. In keeping with their freakishness, they had begun to speak very clearly, if in malformed and often senseless phrases. 'Mamma,' said Chirda, repeatedly attempting her mother's cold and bony hand. 'Want Mamma.'

'Your mamma's there,' said the serving girl, coming up behind them. She was embarrassed by Catra's unnaturalness; it offended her on some deep and unreasoning level. 'Lady, won't you take your daughter's hand?'

'No,' said Catra, and brushed both her children off.

The little girls had quaint matching dresses of pale blue, with sewn eyelets to show blue and green checkered petticoats and strawberry stockings. But the clothes were infrequently changed and dirty.

In the long rooms, of which there were four, befitting the legal wife, Charina, and Chirda (the younger by seven minutes), recovered themselves and began to play more earnestly than in the garden, apparently consoled by the icon of their mother.

Charina took the cithra and commenced plucking the strings,

her fingers unable as yet to make more than a vague scratching. Chirda draped herself in a long scarf of her mother's and strutted about. They were like two dolls from the trees, almost without contours, so white, their hair fine as smoke.

Catra lay down on her bed and pulled over the hanging.

She lay staring up at the carved ceiling, where apples were painted a flaming dulled red. But there were leaves too, indigo and brown and green. Catra did not like the leaves. She started a dream, evaded it, sank back and was caught again.

The dim scratchings and patterings of her daughters had become an emission of the forest. Unseen animals patrolling, the scrape of needles against each other. What was in the woods?

Another child had been lured away, abducted by a tree spirit or demon. But Catra had avoided this. She lived on and was older now, a woman now. But no, she was only the age of Charina and of Chirda. She was tiny, and how high the trees towered up, and there was a tree blacker than the others, and like all the others together twisted into one shape…

Catra ran, but the tree reached out and grasped her. It pinched and worried at her, and Catra opened her eyes and found the punier twin, Chirda (though she did not like them, she alone could tell one from the other), had hold of her wrist. 'Mamma, Mamma…'

Catra absently stroked her daughter's head. Chirda had rescued her from the dream of the tree. Charina looked on with pink pebble eyes.

The curtain at the door was pushed aside and in came the servant with food.

The little girls ran to the repast, more curious about it than hungry. They had been weaned haphazardly, and still went to their mother, or the nurse, attempting to suck the breast.

'Now, lady, you must eat. Eat this bread and the whey with honey. See the fruit.'

Catra's maid from the Hill was nowhere near. She had entered into a romance with one of the soldiers in the Vre's garrison. Catra did not miss her, engrossed with depression. She missed her husband far more, although now she was afraid of him again. Catra ate some of the barley bread dipped into milk and honey. Chirda copied her mother. Charina had lost interest and gone to play with a toy of rags one of the women had made her.

Catra looked round the room, and round again, wanting something to happen. It was true the light changed places, going about and over objects, altering them, while the dark also reversed its shapes and positions. Catra watched the motion of the afternoon sunlight. She had not the capacity to envisage an eternity of boredom, and so did not totally despair. She had no suspicion that Kolris might try to cast her off. Left to herself long enough, probably she would have reverted to her basic needs, would have seduced the boy in him, and so won round the man, at least until pregnancy once more hunted her down.

But the light changed in a new way. A strange shadow stood up in the corner.

Catra was at once afraid and did not look exactly at it. Something of this kind had occurred before. She could not have said under what circumstances, maybe only in the thickets of her dreams.

(Detecting their mother's fear, the two children also reacted, each in her own way. Charina slipped off into the adjoining room, casually, as if eluding one who might, if properly convinced, forget her presence. This gambit was not directed at her mother; there was no cause for it to be so. And yet simultaneously, Charina did not seem to be aware of any motive for deception or flight. A moment later she was playing again in the sunny shadows under a window, plaiting the doll's tow hair. Chirda, however, recoiled, without looking, exactly as her mother had done. Chirda did not remove herself. She bit her nails with her head tucked in, looking nowhere and making no sound.)

The darkness in the corner was like a man, tall and etiolate. There was the suggestion of a face, a pallor, that might only have been a coin of light intruding through the shadow. A reddish beam was concentrated high up, as if on some jewel below the throat, but again an orphaned ray from the sun might have accounted for it.

Catra dropped her bread onto the plate. The red burnished apples in their dish were burning up like round fires.

A tension of terror had fastened on the room. It seemed lifted to another dimension, beyond all help.

Catra put her hands together childishly. She muttered a prayer, and the nearer child, without the formula of words, once more mimicked her.

'Lord, Who is above us, enthroned over the world, we praise Your name and entreat that Your power encompass us and all the earth as it does Your kingdom of Heaven.'

One of the apples dislodged from the bowl. It rolled and lay against Catra's plate.

Suddenly the clutch upon the room slackened. A wave of light throbbed, expanded, ebbed away.

Catra reached out and took the apple. She could not have told why. Perhaps it was the withdrawing of fear at her prayer, as the priests assured you fear would do. Or perhaps some item to hold that was warm from the sun, round like the breast, sweet for the mouth to suck in comfort...

Catra bit into the apple. She recalled biting the hand of a servant in her labour. The flesh had parted and Catra had tasted blood. She tasted blood now. The apple tasted of it. The apple bled. The blood trickled over her fingers from the wound in the apple, and out of the wound came something, bitten open at its centre, still weaving and wriggling – a scaled worm, a serpent. It raised its head, writhing, and it spoke aloud: 'Give us today our food and drink and forgive our sins that we may forgive those others that sin against us.'

In Catra's mouth, the piece of snake she had bitten out also wriggled. It went into her throat before she could stop it.

Catra screamed and jumped to her feet. The plates crashed, the fruit and milk were spilled.

Chirda screamed too, more thinly, and jumped up. And in the other room, Charina jumped up, stuffing her lips with the rag doll to keep sound in and the world out.

The maid from the Hill Tower, who had brought herself back to Catra's service, hearing the outcry, hurried to the apartments. She imagined Catra or her children were in a pet and coming in saw nothing at odds with that – save the face of her mistress, which was congested and scarlet, a volume of colour never before achieved.

In Catra's hand was an apple, with a bite taken from it, the crisp greenish flesh gaping like a wound.

Although she did not let go, Catra had forgotten the apple. She was jerking, half springing, her body in a wild dance. The noise she made was no longer to be confused with a tantrum. Then her face went dark and her eyes bulged in their sockets. She curled over and sprawled along the floor and kicked the broken plates with her pink feet. Froth exploded from her mouth and fragments of apple. Chirda shrieked and Charina stood in the distance with her doll over her face but not her eyes.

Catra's maid fought with Catra, trying to expel the fruit from her throat. But the spasms were already involuntary. There was no longer sight in Catra's eyes.

In the blazing of the awful sun, which now entered all the windows on that side of the house, no mistake could be made.

The servant got up. She sobbed and called for assistance. Who would come? This Vre would be glad to be rid of his sickly wife.

It was such a terrible thing. And the girl thought how her soldier would comfort her, when he learned of the dreadful accident she had witnessed.

Chapter Eleven

Under her checkered shawl, in the bouncing carriage, Anillia was sleeping. Outside was whiteness, stemmed and variegated with powder green and black. Someone sang to her sometimes, or told her stories in simple words... 'And then the wicked god sent his white bear to lean upon the humble cot, and its walls caved in. That was their reward, for having tempted his anger. The snow bear ate them up...' The man rode on a horse beyond the window with his servants; and the man-boy, who was indifferently cruel, he had been left behind in the town house. It was therefore safe and comfortable here, with only the mother, and the hot coals in their box, and the travelling rhythm, and sleep. Arrival had no form or allurement for Anillia. She was two years old.

The woman though, the mother, Lady Crel, was looking forward to their journey's end. She was anyway not so comfortable as her daughter, nor so warm, and certainly not so redundant from care. Her duties as a wife she found distasteful, but she bore with them, having no choice. Her spirit had survived despite bondage. Although she had produced two children, and carried another in her womb, she had her good looks still, was voluptuous, her condition evidenced only in the globular four-month stomach hidden in her velvet skirts. Her skin was lucent, her hair abundant, coiled and looped through tortoiseshell about her neat and bird-like head. She pretended often to be ill to stay her husband's appetite. She had never inclined to men either in a bed or out of it. Her natural desire might have been for women, if she had been permitted to discover as much. The first son, who had won for her praise and presents, she had loathed to touch him intimately. The second child, this daughter, Lady Crel loved.

Nor did she fear the forest. There was a legend in the Crel family of a noble of their lineage who had become a madman of the woods. But there was also a legend of a priest of the Crels who had gone astray, found with a whore in a tavern. Lady Crel preferred priests who were abstinent. She had always managed to fall well of them, by her respect, her chasteness.

It was her husband's business that had brought him to the forest. A tract of Crel woodland, a foolish steward. Lady Crel had not paid much attention. The husband had brought her with him, thinking the trek would revive her health – she had generally enjoyed travelling – but she was careful to pretend on with her vapours, keeping him away as successfully on the road, at the inns and in his woodhouse, as at home. The business with the steward sorted (there had been whippings), they returned to Khish through the forest. But then the winter snow came early. Crel was determined they should get back to the town. For herself, his wife had mixed thoughts. If they were caught tonight and could proceed no further, she might not mind it. They were due to stay at one of the larger Domas of the forest, a sisterhood with whom she had had dealings in her youth, for her own family had connections with a forest Tower, and she had received schooling with these sisters. The very old ones she had known in girlhood, and the younger were contemporaries who must revere her. She almost envied them, save she could never have brought herself to like the austerity of their life.

As evening wrapped the woods and the road grew worse and new snow began to descend, Lady Crel imagined their detainment there, at the Doma, among the women, and desired it less. She did not fancy carrying to term and giving birth out here in the wilderness. If only he had not saddled her with another baby.

The child slept. Lady Crel looked at her, wanting to wake her, to have the full consciousness of her daughter's eyes fastened on her face. But Anillia was two years of age and must be allowed to sleep. Indeed, her talent for peaceful sleeping was a useful one.

Lady Crel could not deny that she was half excited, approaching this female place of her girlhood.

It was the dinner hour when they reached the chapel of the Handmaidens of Saint Hrolowice, pitch black but for the snow glare, the men wet through, pounding into the courtyard with their habitual bombast of impatience, demands and cursing.

Presently Lord and Lady Crel were in a stony chamber, their belongings on the floor, and behind them, to her chagrin, the wooden box of bed thought correct for their married state.

'Well, madam, make yourself as comfortable as you can. I must go and see to my fellows, shoved in the stable.'

'Yes, sir,' she replied, and drew to the fire, holding her side as if it ached.

'They'll bring you supper, no doubt,' he said. He ignored her hand. He pointed to Anillia, who was sleepily awake now, seated on a cushion at the fireside and playing with her wooden doll. 'The child must nap in the cot there.'

'Thank you, my lord.'

'And you and I on the same couch.'

She bowed her head to him. There was a red light in his eyes that was not the firelight but the angry lust she abhorred.

'Tarosar,' she said, 'may I go to speak with Sister Virina? You remember she taught me to read and sew?'

'Remember? No. But I suppose you'll please yourself if you visit her, madam. Eat first. You must take care of your belly.' (He meant of his next son.)

'She's very skilled in herbal medicine. Maybe she can suggest some restorative.'

'And you'll take none of her recipes. Don't you recall you nearly lost the boy, spooning simples into yourself?'

Lady Crel bowed again obediently. 'As you say, Tarosar.' He had had the boy named after him, and the boy seemed fair set to become a replica, if rather lacking in his father's brutal good sense.

'I won't be abed till midnight. I shall hope to see you here before me.'

As he slammed the door, the child, used to his noise, looked up. Her eyes were dark as her hair, both burnished, her face a small perfection of paleness.

Lady Crel held out her hand.

'Should you like to visit Sister Virina with mother? Mother was in the care of Sister Virina when she was only ten years older than you.' The child considered, mentally striving to go this impossible distance of age which, in any case, she was not destined physically to accomplish. 'Can Dolly come?'

'Of course.'

Consenting, Anillia rose, and went to her mother. Lady Crel felt for a sour cold moment the sweetness of her child's freedom. The boy would never ask, he merely did. Only his father had jurisdiction over him. And she also, Lady Crel, must ask.

Suppose the thing within her now was another boy? She did not like to dwell on that, this absolute closeness of a male. She had prayed for a second daughter. Then the hardship and the agony she had to look forward to at its end would be worthwhile.

She knew the way down from the guest apartments, the circling stone stair, and the bare corridor with its rushes strewn for winter insulation. After twists and turns, the narrow door. Lady Crel knocked.

The door was opened to its widest. Inside was a scene that made her, despite herself, utter a brief cry of pleasure.

She had written to them a month ago, that she hoped her husband would break the journey at Saint Hrolowice Chapel. They might have gathered in this room and been waiting since the day that letter came. They were all there, all the old ones she recollected so vividly, those she had feared and loved, and the younger ones she had half admired, half scorned. And in her chair was Sister Virina, thin as a winter branch, ancient as a white snake, and beautiful, clad in her gauze of skin and sculpted bones, with the great greyed black eyes burning through. Ten women, all in all, to welcome the lady in her crimson velvet.

'And here's the child,' said Sister Virina, when Anillia was led to her. 'Will she be sent to us, to school her?'

'Lord Crel may not allow it.'

Between the two women, the tense unspoken censure, durance in chains. Without these men, *we*...

There had been such teachings, too, with the sewing and reading. The Scriptures themselves pointed them up, for only the male saints were flawless men, and only the Christus, who was not a man, but God.

They said no more of the child's tuition. Anillia sat at the old woman's feet, with her doll, and two of the younger women in turn played with Anillia. A chair was brought for Lady Crel. They asked her how she fared, and the stricter sisters asked after her religious observance, but Lady Crel was pious, and they were glad at her.

Supper was served for Lady Crel and the Administress, Sister Virina, in that familiar room, and one by one the other women melted away to their duties. The little girl might have been taken too, but Lady Crel would not hear of it. Anillia therefore played on with the near-mindless absorption of her two years, making now for the doll a necklace of ribbons, as one of the sisters had taught her.

'Then you're easy in your life, have pleased your husband, are not at odds with your Maker.' Sister Virina paused and supped her wine. Age had given her back certain comforts. 'What then, girl, is troubling you?'

Lady Crel lowered her eyes. 'I don't want this child that's in me. It's a burden.'

'That is a sin. You must cast out the notion. Where would we be on God's earth if no woman ever wanted to bear?'

'I've borne him a son. He should be satisfied.'

'Your daughter you don't mention.'

'He cares nothing for her. She'll cost him a dowry or may be plain. To me she's very dear.'

'So I've seen.'

'But the boy... He's already a man. Like his sire.'

'You must do your duty by your husband, whatever you feel for him. God has given you to him. You have only to obey.'

'I do. Look where it's taken me!' And with a spare, sharp violence Lady Crel tapped her belly.

The old sister raised her brows. Very little could shock her. And though she spoke of marital obedience, there was between them still the unvoiced other creed of womankind.

'The problem has no solution, my girl. To rid yourself of what's in you would be a crime against your husband and against God. Besides very dangerous, now. I trust you had no such idea in your head.'

'No sister. I have the hope that this is another girl.'

'God allots the gender of babies.'

'I've prayed to Him.'

'And perhaps He hears.'

'But sister – sister…' Lady Crel faltered. Her mind was back in the past, and yet she did not quite assay the memory, for the ways of the chapel might have altered.

There was silence, then a sigh from Anillia, who had once more fallen softly down into sleep.

'You must open your heart to me,' said Sister Virina. 'How else do I advise you?'

'Perhaps I'm at fault, sister. But I recall that when I was fourteen years old, in the month that I left you here, I made an offering to God, in a manner before unknown to me. My father wished to give me to a particular man. I won't name him, but I was afraid. I made the offering, asking to be spared that marriage.' Lady Crel stopped. She looked long at her hands, on which three rich rings fluttered the candlelight. 'I can't falsely say to you that I love Lord Crel. But he isn't a fiend. That other one – I might have died at his treatment. And when I ran to you and told you, you sent me with two other sisters to make an offering to the Christus. And I was spared. The creature was killed at his hunting. I'll never forget.'

'What offering then was this?' inquired Sister Virina. Her eyes were blacker than before, unblinking. The room was still. 'Come, now. I must be at late prayers very soon. Speak out.'

'It was years ago… We went into the wood. I remember nothing else exactly…'

'See that you continue to forget,' rasped Sister Virina.

Lady Crel looked up. 'Pardon me for mentioning the subject, sister.'

'See that you forget, and forget once more, if it happens that again you go into the wood.'

Lady Crel loosed the grip her hands had obtained on each other. Through her brain went the faded bright images of fourteen, the summer of the wood, the towering shadow of the pines beyond, some deep place where a spring bled out like silver from the ground. Sunset had come, and then the night. They had taken off their garments and washed, shy and startled at each other, in the water. Naked, crowned with leaves, they went among the trees. No, she did not remember all the words, the gestures of reverence, the garlands they had hung up, or the turgid wine with its smell of a recent pig-killing, poured along the ferns and grasses. The name used was the true name, that of the Christus. They exhorted Him as a young man standing overhead in the boughs. After, she had been frightened, but not so much as at her wedding prospects. At home in Khish, when they told her that her betrothed was dead, she had gone to the church to pray, she said, for his soul. She had thanked God with passion, that he had answered her invocation in the forest.

For what she wanted now, it was a jumbled thing. It was freedom, it was a condition she could not even picture to herself – Crel's death, some miraculous liberty – but in the prefiguring of a second female child, that was how she gave it shape. *Let me only be freed somewhat from men.*

At fourteen she had sent an offering also to the Hrolowice chapel. If her boon was granted now, she could send them something much worthier. She could say it was in token of a safe delivery.

Virina clicked her tongue against her fanglike teeth, all of which, though blackened, she had kept.

'You must slip out. If you're able. Go down to the back court, to the door. You must be no later than the second hour of morning. Someone will be there.'

They worship often in the wood, even in the snow, she thought, and was curiously calmed to think so.

'He may wake,' she said. 'Is there something I might give him...?'

'Certainly not,' rapped Virina. 'Am I to have you practise against your husband? If he wakes, you must desist. Accept it for God's will.' *Caution.* They must not be blamed.

Of course, she had wanted to drug him against his molestation of her in the bed. But there, if he were to work against her that act he so greatly liked and she so completely hated, coupled to the travelling and the chapel beer – what means were more sure to make him sleep?

Only, the child might wake up and cry for her.

The child must go with her. Into the wood.

That had its rightness. Let the god in the wood take heed of Anillia too, protect and bless her. One day she also would be a woman, and then there would be no help for her but God.

Crel entered the guest apartment a little before midnight. His wife, contrary to his anticipations, lay in the bed in her shift, her hair spread on the pillow.

After he had divested himself of boots and clothing and drunk the mug of ale warming at the hearth, he came to the bed.

'And how is your health tonight, madam? I must tell you, I'm anxious for your consent. Before long you'll be too hefty for the purpose.'

'I'm quite well, sir,' said Lady Crel

'That's good,' he said, and got in beside her.

With a taut body and some acute discomfort, she endured her husband's attention. She made herself give unresistingly, even when the thrusting of his member seemed to unseat her inner parts and she became partly frightened she would be damaged. She had never evinced wanting love, so he gave her none. The ale had slowed him, he took a time, and when he was done an awful relief made her weep.

'There,' he said sullenly. 'I'll leave you be.' He slewed over and slept instantly.

Lady Crel bit her fingers to end her tears.

Soon she was able to slink from the bed, shedding his wetness as she did so. She put on another shift and two cloaks from the journey. It was no method whereby to venture out into the frozen wood, but she had no option, she could not, as she now was, manage her dress without assistance.

How cold the chapel Doma seemed when she stepped from the red-fired room. Her child, shawled closely, she held in her arms and only stirring like a kitten accustomed to her, unquestioning.

The passages were blued with frost. At the courtyard door a flame burned in a clay dish. No one was there, despite Virina's promise.

'Damnation,' whispered Lady Crel, and cast about her in

annoyance, but before she could do any other thing two slight forms came from the passage's farther end.

They were two of the youngest sisters, glimpsed at arrival. She had never known them. Both made her a small obeisance. They wore the chapel's grey robe, their hair bound and hidden in black linen.

'Well?' she said.

'Lady, hush. Only follow and say nothing.'

The other had undone the door. They crept out into the snow like thieves and glided one by one across the black court. In their pens the wintered pigs grunted at their straw and mush. From the larger yard, over the fence, came the rufflings of horses, sleepless, and snores of Orel's men bedded in the byres and stable. There was a full moon; it stayed yet on the cones of the pines.

The women went through shadows.

At the outer gate there was a hesitation. Then the gate moved, seemingly of itself. Outside, an older sister, one Crel's Lady had known in her adolescence, beckoned them through, and on.

They went towards the forest, over the wide white space of snow. They stepped defiantly now, although the surface was treacherous, and the moon shone on them for any to see. But the chapel was mute at their backs and all the men slept. The first wave of trees accepted them.

Lady Crel was very chilled. She was uneasy now, for herself, and for her child. This was not wise. What had she been thinking of?

An abrupt colour flitted in the trees, bewildering her. Was there a torch ahead? They came between two hemlocks of enormous size, and she recollected them as if from a dream. Beyond lay the open place with the watercourse – through a palisade of slender young trees she saw the glade. It was not the glade of summer. The stream had vanished under the snow, and in a dark-running hollow near to the surrounding pines a fire blazed like a spotted lion in a tapestry. There were other sisters there, warming themselves. Not Virina, not at this hour, but two more at least that were known.

Without any deference to her rank, and now she was glad of it, they came forward and embraced her, like the girl she had been, then.

She was drawn to the spotted fire. One of the older women lilted the sleeping Anillia from her mother's arms. 'I'll see to her. We'll sit here by the fire and keep ourselves cosy.'

It was dreamlike still, not only the memory, but the changes. An owl went over the clearing with a stark and evil cry, and all the women lifted their heads, seeing only the white sail of a wing, a veil from the moon.

Lady Crel was shivering. From the hot ashes at the fire's edge one of the young women drew up a vessel. She wound it in a cloth and they passed it between them. It was indecorous beer, the man's drink. How invigorating it tasted, and all at once the dull pressure and gnawing of the cold went off. In her boots the woman felt her feet come back, and her fingers in their fine gloves. Her entire body stopped its quaking – had that begun in the open air, or when Crel left her?

It seemed unbelievable that they might go naked under the trees; until this moment she had dismissed such a theory as absurd.

But then she learned that the winter nakedness was of a different sort.

The Sisters of Hrolowice were unbinding their kerchiefs, letting down their hair. One of the younger women Lady Crel had known from girlhood came to her with a wonderful garland. It was of ivy mingled with white ribbons – just such as they had given her child to toy with.

The sister gently put back the two hoods of the cloaks and set the garland in the hair of Lady Crel.

'Do you remember?'

'Yes. No, I…'

'We must walk in the pines, there. It's there we do it. I'll touch your arm when you're to speak. Say what you want aloud. We must know, to raise the power of prayer before God.'

'Will you…?' she wavered, said more quietly, 'Do we offer blood, as was done last time?'

'A little blood, from the chickens your husband dined on, mixed in wine. Blood's sacred to God. Look how He colours the berries.'

They began to move towards the blackest stand of pines in all the forest.

The mother glanced back. The older sister sat by the fire, cloaked and scarfed, with Anillia quiescent on her lap. The vessel of beer lay again to roast in the ashes. It was a strangely domestic peasant sight. No beast would confront the fire. Yet, something quivered under her heart. 'Will my child be safe?'

'Come, Lady. We'll only be a tree or two away.'

Crowned with ivy, something in Lady Crel thirsted for the black immersion of the pines. At this moment she was free. No man to lord, no child to hold. Even her womb was light.

As if it were a state that must be passed from one human thing to another, the sister slept, the child awoke.

The woman was drowsy from beer, of which she had consumed a drop too much. The child had slumbered a great while, and the unbalance of cold and heat revived her.

Nearby, she caught a murmur. It was soothing, resembling the sounds she had heard in the chapel earlier. Like her mother, Anillia did not fear the forest. She widened her eyes, and, lying on the broad grey lap, looked off at it through the lick of flames.

Where the wood seemed darkest, a shadow of paleness came and went. The child could not decipher this. Soon she turned away, and found where the moon speared into the trees, parting them.

There, in the lighting of the moon's fire, a black hare sat upright, gazing back at her.

Anillia watched. Animals intrigued her.

The hare kept so still it might have been made of basalt. Then it darted out across the clearing. It ran as if towards the women's fire, and the child shifted and held out one hand. But the hare veered off, and was gone again.

It was after the hare had run away that Anillia began to pick up the other sound, which was very faint and clear, and which she knew from entertainments in her father's house. The dainty singing of tiny bells.

Again the child shifted, sitting up, feeling herself to be like the hare, alert and attentive. The sister eased her arm about Anillia. 'Softly,' the woman muttered, but she was asleep, and in her country, Anillia slept too.

The notes of the bells sprinkled the air like figments of the cold. Now they were near, and now farther off. The child looked round and round for them, and the sleeper became accustomed in sleep to her fidgeting.

Anillia's mother was perhaps thirty paces away, inside the wall of the wood. In another fashion, Anillia's mother was a world's length out of sight, lost.

The child looked over her shoulder, and there, not six feet from her, was a fascinating figure, all black, but sparkled over with gleams and glitters. It was a man, like the men in the travelling entertainers' plays who leapt and performed tricks. And it rang and chimed from all the little bells that hung on it, and were tinselly shaken as it moved.

The child reached out her hand again, to finger and ring the bells.

The figure slid back, out of her way.

Anillia laughed. She had slept enough and wanted diversion. She liked this game, and got down from the grey lap to continue it.

The sleeping woman (in sleep), felt after the warmth and weight of the child. And something lay down on her lap, shapeless and motionless, but of the proper weight, and warm. And the woman's arm rested around it protectively, while the child took three more quick steps to catch the retreating bells.

The women circled, their arms about each other's waists, breathing the burning air from each other's mouths. The pivot of their motion, half dance, half run, was a young pine, only a few feet in height. A briar had twined it and grown up with it, perhaps slowing its advance. The snow had been cast from it, and in the needles were knots of ribbons rusty and torn from weather, and some skulls of mice and birds, a chain of bones all sewn together by a crimson thread. It was not to this tree they had brought her formerly. Maybe its youth had significance, or the other had died. How did they explain its ornaments when the priests came to examine them at Hrolowice? Did they undress the tree – or blame superstition on the village half a mile off?

Lady Crel was exhilarated by the running dancing motion. When they stopped she would fall. But the circling ended and she did not. The other women held and supported her. She was dizzy, near to laughing. They sank to their knees, in the comfortable, glowing snow. It would be easy now to ask for anything.

One of the women, one she had never known before, began to sing in a high thin voice:

His crown is made of leaves,
His sword is made of wood,
He hangs upon the tree,
To save us with His blood.

And one sprang forward and spilled the blood of the chickens mixed with wine from a clay jug at the base of the tree. The liquid went into the ground at once, as if drunk down.

Lady Crel felt the touch on her arm.

She had forgotten what it was she must plead for. It did not seem to be of any importance anymore.

'My daughter,' she said, and broke out wildly laughing. The women stroked her. Lady Crel thought, *It already gives, and will give nothing else. It only asks. It wants, and will have. And then, I am a noblewoman of Khish.* She drew away from the sisters and said, 'Give me a girl child. I ask for the blessing of the Christus on my condition,' and crossed herself over in the snow under the tree.

Like the vast cathedral that it was, the forest unfolded a gigantic nave, between its pillars of ebony and ice. The Hour was ribbed with glass. The windows stood in their webs of branches, paned with stars. The child had burned her hand once on the moon-white snow, but her tears dried. She did not know the cold as yet, pottering on her booted feet, swathed in her furs and shawls, after the jet-black player of the bells.

And as he went, other things had been drawn to follow him, and this also enchanted the child. A mouse in its white winter hair, a white ermine with gemstone eyes, a tree rat with a plume of tail that skittered and pounced from bough to bough, dislodging soft snow that showered like sugar. These items were like pieces of a story her mother had told her. They were accustomed marvels for which the child had merely been waiting.

But the nave of the cathedral of forest night spread on and on. The child stumbled over roots. She tripped, twice falling, dazed a little more than hurt, but the mouse and the ermine ran away. The squirrel had ceased to scamper above her. She had been allowed no nearer to the magical bells.

And the wind started to ride up the forest, in his armour, with the spikes on his cloak and helm and on the hooves of his horse, just as her mother had said. Such spikes struck at Anillia. Pains woke in her body. Her hands and face ached, and her feet in their boots had given up their feeling, which scared her, for now she seemed to walk on her ankles.

Ahead, the man in gleaming blackness, black-clad in bone-tight flesh, black flesh of jet, black hair of coal, with black, jet-coal face and hands and throat, with eyes lacking any white, teeth black as iron, glittering all over as though strung with stars, ringing with the tiny bells that hung on him. The child waned. She stood in the nave of the cathedral, and her priest halted, and glanced at her, and beckoned her, and the bells sang from his wrist. A hundred tiny skulls they were, of mice and ermines, rats and squirrels.

The child cried. She took a step and stopped again, afraid at her dead feet.

The blackness of the figure of the man had seeped into the snow, a pond of shadow lay all round him.

She did not know, Anillia, two years of age, that she was now in truth all of a world away from her mother.

'Mamma,' she said, and put her shawl into her mouth.

But from the blackness at the rim of the blackness, something was pushing, shouldering up out of the ground. One thing, then another, and another.

Anillia took the wool from her mouth. She let out a banal, inconsequent, useless scream. It had no strength. She did not pin upon it any prayer. She knew, as only a child could, that the nightmare had her, and was unavoidable.

Black wolves pulled themselves out of the ground, and the snow skimmed off their backs... like sugar.

They rose up and grouped on the floor of the cathedral and looked at Anillia with eyes like stars.

She knew wolves. They were in the stories, too.

She knew what wolves did, and that she had no chance.

With a deadness and a dragging tiredness, Lady Crel, who had remembered herself, came from the sacred place, and saw the fire burning and the woman asleep with a bundle on her lap. Lady Crel looked at the shapes of these beings, and did not want them, or anything. Not the child she loved, not the life she disliked, her station, her rings, her sodden cloaks, her shivering body, the dreaded mound of the pregnancy, nothing. Only, perhaps, sleep.

Then walking briskly to the fire, she cursed her silliness in risking *his* anger for a pagan ritual, and was revolted by that old woman, Virina, probably senile, a witch and her mysteries. Yes, Lady Crel longed for her bed, packed as it was, and for the house at Khish, though not hers, and for morning, which was no one's. And she looked down at the dozing sister by the fire, who looked back smiling and patted what lay on her lap pridefully.

'My daughter,' repeated Lady Crel. Her voice was low and controlled. 'Where's my daughter?'

'Why, here.' In the woman's lap lay a dead and bloody hare. She peered down and saw it, shrieked.

The other women ran forward. They formed a clot of hair and skin and cloth and breath beside the fire.

Lady Crel poised in their midst, straight as steel.

She... stared into the forest. Ignorant of everything as she always would be, for those instants she knew it all.

Before her she saw also what would come after. The man's fury, his blows, her fever, sickness and shame, his lies to cover her lapse, lies believed in the passage of time. Time itself.

The forest had devoured Lady Crel's girl child. She was gone.

One single image, in that prophetic second, Lady Crel did not receive. That of a young dark priest and his counsel, of the strange rumour and the girl who would walk back out of the wood, Crel's daughter, no longer wanted, or recognised, no longer the symbol of anything, returned to her: Anillia.

Chapter Twelve

And it came to pass that Anjelen, who had been Jun, made Hell on earth for some through the mechanics of his will. But only in the way of creation, with only, here or there, a wink of malice. He was not a man, yet the emotions of men had grown in him a little, moss upon the tree.

When Catra was born, Catra that he had fashioned in the womb, he saw his work and it was not good. He waited on her growing, to see if even so she might fulfil his purpose. But it had happened that, even before her birth, he had foreseen a second means, and moved among those other lives, tearing them in bits, to make potentially another bride for the Korhlen house.

All offerings in the wood he was aware of, as of the rain which fell there, the snows, and the summer sun. He felt the blood poured at the foot of every pine and oak, every bush and shrub. It fed his soul, or what passed for a soul in Anjelen. So, he knew, in some unthinking, unconsidered annexe of his consciousness, when the Sisters of Hrolowice went out to worship. Then, too, there was the reminder of Wedsek Crel, for the woman had been taken into that house of Crel. She bore the name, and an invisible glint of malignity had prompted Anjelen to work on and against her, for Wedsek's sake, towards that end he envisaged.

To the brain of Anjelen, those crystals and razor edges, what was more simple than to prepare a slot, dug in the soil of history, wherein at a later time, if appropriate, might be dropped the unspoiled seed. For if Catra failed him, he would make a second Catra. He would make her out of himself, and from no other thing. The etheric rib, the flesh made of the flesh. And he would call her Anillia and send her back out of the slot in history and the ground which he had emptied for her occupancy when he removed the daughter of Lady Crel.

And Catra failed Anjelen; by her tenth or her eleventh year he knew it and began to move elsewhere again on the waters of lives.

He created the second Anillia, and brought her into Crel as a woman, by means uncanny and psychological, by advice given plainly as a sober priest, by subtle descants on the confused song of the human heart. And then, while she was at Crel, growing in the mould he had formed for her, he let Catra proceed into the Raven Tower of the Korhlens. And there, when she failed fundamentally, producing her two albinos, her unclean female fruit, Anjelen shifted events in a similar unperceived manner as before, killed and cleared, and brought Anillia from the Crel cupboard to become the perfect vessel for the Korhlen blood. And at last Anillia conceived, and bore, for Anjelen, Anjelen's son, Mechail.

But Mechail in his turn attempted to ruin himself. Sensing what was in him, what power, what root, he made to rip it out, and crippled himself, body and mind.

Anjelen watched now his son growing crookedly aslant. Anjelen watched Anillia, her determined and astonishing strength, the blowing and decay of the rose, and the claws of her life sunk firmly in the rock. He knew soon enough she would not die, for death was not able to stay her. She was as strong in her way as Anjelen. Maybe that surprised him (surprise, the emotion of the man, of Jun, if Jun had been all he was). He stole her bones easily from Korhlen and took them with him, to him (discarding like pips the necklace of Crel) about the time he garnered back Mechail, a wild harvest, from the wolf-wood. She had earned that.

The dwarf, Anjelen took also, Mechail's own random creation – product of Mechail's own power, and his bitterness. And the woods girl, the lizardine Jasha, with her low wide brow and green eyes and brown river of hair. For Jasha was Anillia's Catra, as the dwarf was Mechail's. And maybe Jasha was Mechail's also – Mechail, Anillia, they had made more obliquely, less astutely, yet rather better than Anjelen the mage and master craftsman.

This gathering, then, he had about him for a moment, it the Christerium, which men, in their order, had created for Anjelen as a god. The Christerium, which had no trees, which lay by the ocean, the restless liquid land that offered no spot for a wood to grow.

But the Christerium was itself a sort of forest, with the great Tree being the seaward tower, the branched openwork of the window, the trunk of its stone almost all-endurable. The Tree itself had gone to stone.

Anjelen sat high in the south wall of the forest of the Christerium, in the jewellery rooms decorated by the makes of his mortal part. Like a tree he was stationary, rooted in body. Now at last he too felt a fixing of himself into the ground of that place.

From the petrification of the Christerium he sent out the tendrils of visions and hallucinations and things formed of spiritual flesh that were not flesh. Within, he walked, and gazed outward, and therein he practised the rite which brought him the feeding blood of holy sacrifice potent with its willingness, the Last Supper of Love.

For his priests, they were the undergrowth of the wood, the lesser trees, which both concealed and led the way to him. For his Knights of God, they were the grove, the briar hedge which ringed him round. Should it be needful, they would die for him. As his priesthood, mostly, should be capable of doing.

His disciples, the Knights, the apprentices of his magicianry, attended him at certain times. He let them run in the shape of wolves, or think themselves so to run, and others so to think, also. He loaned his genius to them, as now and then he nurtured them in turn on the human-inhuman ichor of his veins.

And with his blood, he had fed Mechail.

Of all that Anjelen had wrought, or which had been wrought indirectly through him, Mechail was that being he had sought to create. As might have been guessed (that is, a man might have guessed it), Mechail was the very least of them, the saplings strewn about. Anillia, with her survival of carnal death, and Jasha who Anjelen had tested, sprung from the witch fire; the hunched and crumpled dwarf Mechi, who was also Mechail fathered of himself, risen from the deadly cold, a survivor of that most rigorous of trials, existence itself. Mechail, who had been the flawless flowering, it was Mechail who foundered. The others came to the door of the Palace-on-Earth as tyrants, wolflike, serpentine, vengeful and questing, *tenacious*. But Mechail would not cling, would not grasp even the extended hand.

He had run away, with the girl Jasha. Struggled over the treeless mountains, and down into a valley by a stream. He had wept, he had cursed God, unable to die, unwilling to live.

It was Anillia who had stood on the high tower and challenged Anjelen, and the dwarf who had scuttled with teeming courage over the boulders of the days with Krau, and Jasha who did not ask but took and held with talons of the psyche.

A painted stroke of violent light seared out and entered, without breaking it, the globe of quartz.

Anjelen, who had lived more than three hundred years, lifted his head, by which any would have told him to be thirty-five, a modicum more, or less, and retraced the passage of colour to its fount, the fruit on the Tree of Knowledge in the window of the outer room.

This, the first physical movement he had made for seven days, did not discommode him. The altered body which he wore was not like that, not human enough yet even for that. In the inner room the water-clock in the shape of a tower lowered its golden moon slowly down the day. The days were long still. Time was stretching itself out more and more. For ever lay in front of the Tree, dappled by metamorphosis only.

Anjelen lowered his head again and looked on his work, Anillia and Mechail, Mechi, Jasha. (Far off, he did not consider the albino daughters of Catra, rambling about in their bright madnesses. They were very nearly all human. He had let them be. Each blossomed as it would.) The clock made a sound. Another hour had passed, time so swift, and so slow. Was it winter or summer in the changeless wood?

Early in the morning of the dark tomorrow, the man named Mechail opened his eyes from sleep and saw a strangeness in the world. It was everywhere. In the shelter of the hut, which during the night had cracked and crumbled, and now let in a view of snows and trees. In the lack of sounds and smells, even so soon familiar, from the village by the stream. In some indefinable thing which hovered there. And in the girl too. Mostly in her. As though all of it seemed focused through her. For she sat by the hearth with a piece of stone in her mouth, chewing on it, as if she ate.

'In God's name,' he said. 'What are you doing?'

She removed the stone. She looked as he recalled, and he thought of how he had tried to have her, had done so, but incompletely, writhing with her before the fire. The fire was low and smoky now in the vapid light, and burned behind her. It showed a halo round her head, coppery and supernatural, until he realised this was her hair, growing back after the other fire on the beach, the witch-burning that he had got her from. Her hair came quickly. Already there were two or three inches of it. He had not noticed yesterday. Had it grown in one night?

Other events had gone on, evidently.

She said, 'I do it now and then, to file the broken part.' And he understood she meant she filed her broken tooth with a stone.

He did not know how this tooth had been snapped in the first place, for all her teeth otherwise were healthy. He had not asked; she had told him nothing.

He got up and pushed away the blanket – surely there had been others, the lending of the village? Now there was only the one he had brought with him from Anjelen's Christerium. Mechail stood on the floor of the hut, through which pushed the roots of trees that had not pushed there last night. He thought of his other wakenings, in the body of a wolf, next under ice, next in the cell of the Christerium. Of his humped shoulder, which was now whole and straight. Of his dead brother Krau. Of killing Krau. Of Anjelen. Of blood.

But Mechail's mind raced back again at once to the curious, leaning, tottering hut, and to Jasha, who he had tried to have, unable to expel his lust.

In the nothing light her green eyes were pale, like acorns. There was something frightful about her. She was all part of a weirdness that went on and on and which had no answers.

'Jasha,' he said.

She watched him attentively, uncaringly. He remembered her hands on him on the journey to the coast, in a dream, washing him. Her hands last night. Her whore's reassurance. She cared no jot for him, as why should she. In this place, worse than an enemy, she was a being without a reference.

Outside, the village had gone away. There was no solitary trace of it. Trees clustered near, black-green pines, ledged with whiteness from the snow, and over there the gleam of the cold, cold water in its bed of ice.

Anjelen could construct illusions. Anjelen had warned him, by inference if not by words. And *she* had said: *You're to go to him. He fetched you once. That was enough.* Or had she said exactly that? In some way she must be the agent of Anjelen, too. All things were. Even Mechail, after all, for Anjelen had fed Mechail with his blood, promised him power, given him life. A spiritual father. *Magister.*

'Jasha,' said Mechail, 'everything here was his sorcery. Did you know?'

She shrugged. She had done that before.

Beyond the first ascent, the mountains had been all one to her; she took very little notice of them, or of how they were negotiated. She had things of her own to think of. Even so, it was borne in on her fairly soon, the circling motion, the absence of new landmarks. She had nothing to say on this. It was not her affair, even though she was caught up in it. And Mechail did not ask her opinion. But the descent, the water, the forest, these she beheld with a sort of interest. Thereafter the village, with its huts, helpful, reticent women, the holder who made off with Mechail's saddle. She saw through them, not literally, but in other ways. And despite the fact that, of course, she went along with them, with everything, it did not surprise her, the morning after Mechail had lain with her (or attempted to do so), to wake and find that everything, or very nearly, was gone. Only the trees and the shallow stream remained, with the mountains scowling black and white on the snow sky. The bothy was ruinous, and single. There was no village, and there were no people. She went to look into their supper cauldron, out of curiosity, and there was soup enough for a pair of meals, and bread standing by the hearth, where a few logs still smoked. Not surprised, then, Jasha, but she pondered how he would react, her companion, who in the face of a score of contrary clues, had taken their circular rambling for a journey, and the wood for a village of men. He would now question (she surmised), what they had been led on, how they had been – he had been – fooled so completely.

He would ask questions of her impossible to answer, the more so in her more perfect understanding, for how could you explain an object you had seen to a blind man? Had Mechail never heard tales of places, persons, extant but vanishing in a night? Or of the complex illogic of mutated time? Yes, heard but not credited. He would swear and shy beneath this witchcraft, unable to accept. He could accept nothing, for he had accepted it all, swallowed it whole, and it had stuck in his throat, unable to digest itself and become a part of what he was.

Jasha was not like this. She was porous.

In the village the pain of her broken tooth had altered. It occurred to her the tooth was pushing up under the snapped crown. She found a slate and began to file, a little now and then, in the same way she worked on her nails. That she had come back out of fire was a fact.

There was nothing else to say of Jasha, at this hour, upon this or any day. Her action with the slate symbolised her as she currently was. There was not even now the instinct for subterfuge.

Mechail stood in the ruinous bothy, and said, 'I shan't go back to his God-house. He plays games with me, even here. God knows, maybe this is a hollow tree.' He stared on the inadequate walls.

Jasha sat composed before the hearth, where the logs still burned and there was a pair of meals in the cauldron. (There was also a lean-to on the hut, where the horse remained, saddleless, eating from a mound of hay.)

Outside, the snow was not so deep as yet. She had heard no cries of wolves or winds, nothing threatening. All wildlife had vanished with the phantom village. How far off to east was the Christerium? Since Mechail had gone mostly in a circle, she did not think it could be far at all.

Jasha did not tell Mechail she had had a dream.

If she had looked at him speculatively, it was probably an accident. She pitied him, respected his maleness, his therefore potential danger to her, that was all. The beauty of his body did not enthral her any more than the fine aspect of a tree.

'He sits there in that upper room of his. I can see him. Perhaps he lets me see.' Mechail paced about the hut. It trembled slightly, and next door the horse blew and stepped. 'I'm in the net. He hauls me in. But Jasha, I won't go.' And then, as if someone had responded, queried, 'Where else? Nowhere else. Sedentary. He let me get so far and here is where I'll stay the winter out. In spring...' He did not bother with spring. It was alien to him. Useless, the world. Jasha perceived in Mechail all that she was not. She did not condemn him or despise him for his differences either from herself or other men. To live was to live.

He did not ask her what she would do, presumably expecting her decisions depended on his. From the innate courtesy of caution, Jasha felt obliged to placate him.

'I won't hamper you,' said Jasha. 'I'll tend the house. How best can I help you?'

'But you can't. Not even in the sexual way.' He was white, he would soon hate her for showing up to him his own lack. 'However, I can't tell you to get gone. Where can you go?'

She sat meekly. They were trapped, she and he, by the season. And Mechail was under a doom, a shadow, or under some dark, dark blessing. Whatever it was, as he had said, he had rooted to that spot.

She thought of her father Carg Vrost. He had rooted in the forest. When he died, it was as if the time had come for it. She had known, days before, she would be leaving that place, and had been preparing. His death fit exactly the lines of her destiny. But she would not need to bury Mechail decently.

She heated the stew, and served him with it, and ate a little.

They lay down for sleep in the early night, separately, which would be good in the future time for her to creep away. She wondered if she would dream again, and slipped into sleep quickly, looking for the meeting.

The woman sat as before, on the mound of her grave. She wore Jasha's second green dress, and her hair in three thick plaits, as Jasha had done. The woman's eyes were black as wet stones.

Tonight Jasha went nearer, and felt the summer soil under her feet. A short way off was the hut, not the bothy she had shared with Mechail, but the wooden box of her birth. Until the dreams, Jasha's mother had only been the grave mound.

'Yes, you know me,' said Jasha's mother. 'My name is Anillia.'

Jasha watched her mother, excited by the dream contact as she had never been by anything else. Alluringly new, it had too a completion formerly always missed.

'Are you in the wood?' said Jasha.

'Which wood is that, Jasha? Or, are all the woods of the world one, and all Anjelen's?'

Jasha thought of the very few times she had heard Anjelen speak, and that her mother sounded like Anjelen. Intuitively Jasha believed she might fathom the relationship, Anjelen to Anillia, as Anillia to herself. Jasha looked at Anillia's silver ring, and wanting to vocalise her name, said it in the forest way, once, 'Nilya.'

Then, the dream shifted, and her mother Nilya-Anillia was riding a horse, astride as a man rode, and clad in a mantle from the priests' place against the cold.

The mountains were all about her, motionless, noiseless, and slowly but too fast day and night fled over them. The landscape also flowed swiftly. There were none of the tremendous geographical difficulties in view that Jasha recalled from her journey with Mechail. The mountains through which Anillia rode were changed, or had reverted to their original condition.

'Where are you going?' said Jasha.

Anillia did not answer: it was apparent, she rode towards the wood beyond the mountains, towards the hut where Jasha slept.

Jasha opened her eyes. The hut was silent. Mechail lay sleeping with his head on his arm like a child.

Jasha got up quietly, and went by him, to stand in the hut's doorway.

It was black as any night, normal, save for the peculiar half seen gleam on the edges of vision – the mountain– tops in their snow. Then there came a whisper along the icy ground, like the tingle of blood along a vein. Out of the substance of the dark, a woman came, leading by its reins a horse just now ridden in the dream.

A pale sunset had burned on the walls of the chamber, less red by far than the scarlet band that encircled the brow of the

Administress of the Doma of the Christerium. Less red by far than the blood she must beat out from her body. Inferior, weak woman's blood. It was the only manner in which, now, she could offer it, for her female courses had ended years ago.

The woman, fat with the blubber of frustrations, thickened by depression, by a world ruled with the words: *You shall not*, contemplated the rod, her terrible old ally, with fear. For tonight she must make fifteen inroads upon herself, she had pledged it, and she was half-terrified. She must not cry out, must not groan. And afterwards, bandaged, she must walk firmly to the Doma chapel. On a chest stood a stoop of rough wine. She would need it, when she was done.

Slowly, she unwound her poor gross body from its wrappings. How she had once longed to be fair – vanity, sin… In the fading of the light, her own scent came to her, stifled, and acid. She readied the rod. She must strike there, on the healed flesh, her belly and her calves – for her thighs were a mass of purpled wounds.

The Devil – he was everywhere. She did not dare to fail. The weight of them all, these women's souls clustered in this hive, depended on her.

She struck and gasped in agony.

Why, why did this become more demanding, harder, this act of her faith, each time that she gave herself to perform it? Of course, she had learned pain, what there was to dread. But more than that, surely. The Evil One was muttering, dissuading her.

She struck again, and her throat uttered a sharp, shrill cry. She could not control it. She paused, to discipline herself. Should she drink a mouthful of the wine? No, this pain must be borne to the full.

Her hand shook.

She stared at it, shaking, with the thorned rod protruding from it. She thought suddenly of a dragon, a snake. Then she remembered an image from a book once impiously shown her, in her youth, before she had taken her vows. It had been a picture of Eve and the Serpent, but unlike any image of them she had ever seen before. For the snake was a scaled man, and bare-breasted Eve, in a shower of golden hair, had hold of the Serpent's member. She held it like a flowering stem, and just so the fat woman held now the rod of her correction, like a ghastly flower, like the barbed penis of a snake…

'You know nothing at all of the method of a man with a woman, yet you know enough to damn yourself,' said someone, a girl, musical and disembodied, in a corner of the locked and empty room.

The Administress laboured her body about. Last bars of sun lay on the wall, and in them poised the demon girl, the witch they had burned, and who rose up from the fire. All her hair was down her back, and it was black now, and her eyes were black, and her face was not the same…

'Go you behind me,' hissed the Administress. 'Go left of me, to your lord, the Devil.'

'Stupid bitch,' said the Jasha-girl of another face, the music of her voice playing with the coarse language of men, idly, smilingly. 'What's the Devil to me? Or do you mean your devil, your Magister in his high place – Anjelen.'

The Primentor had warned of the Devil. That their holy actions outraged him. The virtuous could only expect further obstacles, more suffering.

The Administress turned again, lightly as a girl, and struck herself unflinchingly across the stomach.

She felt the blood flow, wetness and heat. No pain. In astonishment, she gazed down, and saw the wound with the marks of the barb in it.

Behind her, the Devil now was silent.

Renewed, the Administress struck herself, repeatedly. She felt the power of God assisting her. The blood leapt from her body and in her hand the rod murmured with a life of its own. The blows landed and she felt their impact – like the slap of a velvet ribbon, no more.

'God be praised!' she cried out, unable to help herself. 'He is with me! I shall fear nothing!'

The joy of the miracle filled the room as all light left it.

Then there was only the sound of the phallus of correction beating on against the thick white flesh that turned now in dark stripes and arcs, towards the colour of the night.

'Come here,' said Jasha's mother, 'let me look at you.' As a mother would have done. Still unsure if this were a reality, Jasha could yet tell, as she had before suspected, that Nilya was not a woman from the woods villages. She was a lady. Her hands, her fingers, felt perfectly real, and smooth from a lady's lack of use, when she traced over Jasha's face, stroked the thickly growing hair. Her breath was real and fresh, and touched Jasha's forehead, cheek. Nilya's eyes were lit and alive. Jasha was pleased. She was awake. She gave herself to the scrutiny and the caresses as does a young cat to its mother's attention and grooming. When Nilya had had her fill, she merely ceased. Her hands were removed and, ladylike, laid themselves graciously back on the reins of her horse.

'Our first meeting,' said Anillia. 'Do you think,' she said, 'that he's watching us?'

'Maybe,' said Jasha.

'I believe Anjelen means to do nothing. Or perhaps something so opaque it amounts to nothing. I've begun to feel that too, suddenly. A quiescence. An immobility in him that is itself a sort of motion. He made me for a purpose, and I made you, Jasha, for a purpose. But now I think we have no purpose but to be, and to continue to be.'

Jasha smiled. Her instinct – like that of any fox or wolf, lizard, cat, flower, tree, stone – had always known as much.

For some while neither woman spoke. The night spoke, as n had never left off doing, in its unique and hushed voices.

Then, from its makeshift stable, Mechail's horse whickered. and the beast of the dream, the reality of Anillia's horse, tried a soft answer.

Anillia nodded. She was gentle and potent, a storm held in exquisite glass.

'Is he asleep, Mechail?'

Jasha did not question. 'Yes, lady.'

All at once Anillia's hands again let go the reins; they darted up to her breast, her lips. 'I can't wait to see him – and I can't bring myself to see him. And yet,' she said, 'I saw him, through Anjelen's mind, like the globe he used to spy on you. Anjelen's mind formed my brain, and I read his mind, there in the roof of his palace, like a book. Can you read me, Jasha, since I made you?'

Jasha shook her head. She felt a low note of jealousy, primal as the ground, go through her. Anillia, her ghost-mother came back to life, had passed her, moving to the door of the bothy. She stood there now, looking in, with Jasha left behind in the snow.

It was not often that the sisters of the Doma came to disturb the evening meditations of their Administress, after the supper and before the first late office. But one of these women, emerging from a duty in the chapel, had had a feeling of great uneasiness. This centred on the court of unchaste women. The witch had dwelt there, the witch who, burnt to cinders, had sent up a demon to plague the Doma. Was the demon in the courtyard? Something was there, whispering and murmuring. The woman felt rather than heard some illicit monologue of the darkness. She treasured them, these links to the surreal, and having brooded in her cell, presently she sought the Mother of her order.

The sunset was long over, and the winter night had closed on the rock, the shore, the mountains. Soon the bell would sound the summons to prayers, tiny in the silence. The woman hurried up the corridor, full of an eager distress. Everything was blurred in a kind of black light, caused by the single candle burning in its alcove before a small stone saint. A hint of the lighted dark fell out on the door, which, as the sister approached it, groaned.

She caught her breath. She waited. She knocked vehemently on the door.

From inside came a curious noise, like that of a large animal rustling and coiling through leaves.

'Lady!' cried out the sister. 'Is everything well with you?'

Then the voice came. It was recognisable as that of the Administress, but only to one who had heard it frequently.

'Help me,' it said, 'for – the love of God... for His mercy. Help me.'

'What is it?' said the sister, stupidly, pressed at the door, afraid.

'Get me help,' said the voice, with an unsuitable random trace of anger in it now.

The woman meant to back away, and to run at once for assistance. Instead she lifted the latch and pushed open the door.

The blur of light and darkness mixed, slanted into the room. It divulged there a host of images that seemed without form though curiously cohered – whiteness and black, and a reddish substance that lay in the troughs, and shone. Abruptly there was the scarlet band that bound the face of the Administress, and two wide eyes that glared out beneath, and then some other features, a nose, part of a mouth... And with the movement of a snake striking, a firm white hand flared up clutching the stem of a rod but the hand had no strength left, it fell away cheated.

'Cut off my hand if you must,' said the Administress in her curious voice, altered by loss of blood and weakness, and by the mutilation of the lower lip and chin. 'Make it stop. No more. Help me. You must pray – for my soul.'

And there was a shift of perception, as might come in finding a hidden pattern in a game of some sort played with tiles.

The sister saw, brightly and clearly, that the Administress of the Doma lay on the floor of the room. She was naked, but not any longer with a female nakedness, for her body was a swamp of fleshy slush. In her hand, the rod of correction, which she had used until blood loss and faintness took all strength from her arm. They were on the floor now, the hand unscathed, quivering slightly, as if only resting. And in it the rod pulsed, its barbs catching each a white point from the candle. And from its upper end a fluid trickled, or appeared to, that was not bloody, milky rather, and already drying.

Hysteria of the same order and attached to the same root as that attendant on the witch-burning spilled the sisters and other women of the Doma round and about, like grey mice running in a maze by night. A distance off, the windowed towers of the Christerium looked on and did not see. Above and below the sky, mountains and ocean made no response. A bitter cold had pierced the lower world of the shore with hooks of platinum and steel.

It had become evident to the Doma sisters there was a demon in their midst.

To enter the Primentor's apartments was a progress, like that of the soul through halls of unknowing, confusion and wisdom, ascending to the Throne of God. Sufficient twists and winds of the passages were involved that all awareness of direction might be lost. Like a labyrinth that rose finally upwards, through a stone anteroom hung with tapestries of red and ethereal blue, and through a second anteroom clad with panels painted in the trials and eventual spiritual aggrandisement of the saints. A screen of figured ivory hid the door into the presence. It too was hung with masks of saints, with eyes of nacre and jet. Long seats padded by crimson velvet were set below the screen for those who must wait, and at the centre an ebony stand in the form of a bull, on which the Book lay open between the horns, for any to peruse, today, at a page which began: *God is in Heaven, and we in the world, therefore let your words be few.*

The priest, who had lived and served since late childhood in the Christerium, had, as it turned out, only passed this way once before. Whatever passage had then been highlighted in the Book, certainly he had dutifully read it, but his awe and trembling had kept from him its message. His mission that day had been slight, merely to summon the Primentor to a preordained office of the Church. But the priest had felt it keenly. Now, fifty years of age, with a mission more onerous, he was both duller and more fearful, for, even through the vestments of faith, he had learned something of this 'world' wherein he was.

After a pause of half an hour, the door behind the screen was heard to be opening. Out and around came the Factor Major, who had gone in before him. Grimly upright, he beckoned the lowlier priest with a thin, uncharitable hand. 'You may enter.'

The priest hastened into the sanctum of his earthly lord.

Over a sea of velvet carpet laid in one long spill of red, and hammered into the floor at each corner with a huge nail surmounted by a golden crucifix, over that, and between two high-windowed walls tapering with perspective but clothed with silk of heavenly blue embroidered by briaries of silver, there, was the great chair of white marble, with its cherry-red footstool, and above an arch of gilded wood from which hung fruits of gold, rising to an angelic host painted on the ceiling. In the chair, the Primentor, in his black crossed by white and scarlet. He wore only the jewellery of one vast cross set with two emeralds of remarkable size and lustre, his kingly hand ringed just twice.

The priest went forward along the burning carpet, and kneeled some fifteen feet from the footstool, bowing.

When he raised his head again, he looked at the emeralds in the cross. In any event, to look at the Primentor's hue was as barren as to have to read the Book on his previous visit. Study this face as you might, it never came clearly to the view. For the Primentor had been made featureless by his regalia. He was his station. He was every Primentor, and the faceless function of God.

The Factor Major, standing to one side now, spoke again. 'You may tell the magnanimous High Father what you have told me.'

The priest faltered a moment. Then he said, 'My lord, there's been a disturbance in the women's house, something fearsome...'

The Primentor's non-face awarded nothing.

The priest said, 'There was an outcry in the Doma. A servant approached our gate – a woman – then some of the sisters. We learned that the Administress was stricken.' The priest was at a loss how to relate again what he had already gifted the Factor Major.

The Factor bent to the Primentor's ear.

The Primentor said, 'The woman abused herself, misinterpreting the ideal of contrition. Or perhaps was attacked by some animal.'

'Those... may be the facts, my lord. But the women are shouting about a demon. They say the slaves have carried rumours that a demon also infested the Christerium, defiling the sacred Bread, approaching the brothers in order – to delude them.'

'There has been the tale of a vampire, currently,' said the Factor Major. 'Such stories blow about the villages. One cannot always be protected from these contaminations.'

'My lord,' said the messenger, 'the women insist some emanation or unholy spirit – perhaps a girl recently chastised there – haunts the by-ways.'

The Factor Major waited for the Primentor to intervene. There could be no laxity in his failure to do so. The Factor Major resumed, 'The women must put all such notions from them. They must fast and pray. The High Father will send them guidance, in the correct way, by a letter.'

Seeds of doubt scattered from the air like dry rain.

The priests of the Christerium were restless. They discussed, nearly blatantly, sudden deaths, vampires, Brother Mordin, who had died in the porter's lodge... Worse than the women, these men, for the women might be controlled.

When the priest had been shooed out, the Primentor said, 'The Administress, when recovered, shall be questioned.'

'She may not survive.'

'Can that be so?'

The Factor Major did not comment by his looks on the naivety of the Primentor's reply, since it could not be naive. 'She was desperately hurt.'

'This seems an infection,' said the Primentor, 'in the very form of the reported demons of the Christerium.'

'A fancy of unclean minds, my lord.'

'Yet there were deaths here. And marks upon the corpses.'

The Factor Major drew his brows together, as though to close a curtain against something feared.

The Primentor did not expect anything from his Factor Major beyond obedience, and a certain subservient simplification of events. The Factor Major was his translator, for the environ of the Primentor was rarefied, not of this or any earthly world. And his words were not few, merely of another language. Chosen to succeed the previous High Father of the Christerium, he had been swaddled, since the age of seven, in a cloud of what was to be. In time, he must choose his own successor, among the promising boys of the river city. Or perhaps, by then, the Kingdom would have come to pass upon the earth, and it would not be necessary. It was true that the Primentor was faceless. It was his soul which had no face. He had been created as a cipher, not a king but a slave. His master was close at hand and asked nothing and gave nothing. Yet to his master, to Anjelen, in any perplexity, he must have cerebral resort.

To Anjelen, therefore, like the slave he was, the Primentor had gone, a visitation which could not be accomplished without a progress. Off the godly throne, and through the complexes of the Christerium, with a train of attendants, to the alchemical rooms of

Anjelen. And to the Christerium in its knowing unknowing, there was no argument that he, the lordly Father, went suing to a Magister.

Inside the rooms, Anjelen had sat, amid shards of bright-coloured winter light smiting up and through objects of stained glass.

The Primentor, in his own language, which employed the phrases and phonetics of men, yet through its usage and symbols was quite alien to them, attempted to acquaint Anjelen, the expression of God's renewal, with this latest problem of the Devil, the vampire-demon. And Anjelen had sat in a rainbow, as if colours pierced through him, like the Nails, and he did not answer. Previously, when witchcraft had been detected in the Doma, his participation was exact, and blasting. But on this second visit he had sat like the dead, yet alive. If he heard what was said to him, it lacked evidence. At length the emblem of the king-slave had had no recourse but to say, 'Your wish and your will shall be done.' And to depart. There was in the Primentor then the most slurred and transparent tinge of trouble. Not much, for in a world where God had revealed Himself, undeniably, to exist, slavery was the only option for one enlightened, and took away all rebellion, all individual thought – and thus every insecurity and misgiving.

'You will,' said the Primentor to his Factor Major, 'suppress the wild imaginings of our order. As you say, unclean fancies. Do everything in your power to instil calm. For the Doma, one of the lowlier sisters must have charge of them for now.'

The Factor Major acknowledged his task and went out at once to commence on it. In the chain of incipients he too was a slave, and the inner glim of the Christerium, where he had resided only ten years, was but half understood, its whiff of Godhead. So, he was more free to feel impinge on him the essence of unease. As he left it, he noted that the great chamber was altered. A storm had begun to brew over the sea, and the high clear casements with their topaz, turquoise and ruby decorations, had changed to lead. A shadow descended.

Bujasía

Book Four

Chapter One

As they approached, the ruined mass was not quite as they had heard or told it, but that did not alter an inflexible tradition. The yellow sky of a dying summer's afternoon, the brown shadows that mobbed the broken walls and the blond cuts of light between, the bars of young trees that sprang now out of the avenues in shawls of brassy green, these things disguised but did not deceive. The Travelling People searched out and came across other signals. How the dark reflection of mountains crept quickly to this spot. How the shrill screeches of ferocious birds tore the air, as they wheeled above their nests in the huge cliff of a tower. It had been sacred once, this wreck, and was now profane.

The Travellers set up their camp in the first courtyard, where the collapsed gate gave swift access to outer regions. The premature mountain-shadowed oncoming of evening had already filled this yard. There was still supposed to be some esoteric, nescient life in the ruin, but that went on at its eastern end, where the edifice had been better kept up. Others of the Traveller tribe who had passed this way going along the coast, by the city there, to avoid the plains, had recommended a well down the rock, but warned that only the women might go to it; anything else incurred bad luck.

They lit their evening fires, and erected their totems, the skulls of horses and dogs on painted poles, and turned their wagon sides, thick with black crosses, towards the main area of the ruin. Their flock of cream-coloured goats nibbled at the grasses and tilted paving began to appear. In their shaggy breeches and high boots, plaited beards, orange jackets, the men swaggered before a knot of leering stone faces that bulged in an outcrop from one wall. All the men then urinated here, under these gargoyles, to demonstrate their determined territory for a few days and nights. Then one scattered a little sugar, a placatory offering.

Fifteen women went together out of the gate and down the rock, carrying their pitchers for the water. The site of the well was a smaller lower building, which had dropped headlong in the decay of total abandonment. Much of the structure had been wood and plaster. This had crumbled, warped, worn and torn awry in heats and gales. The stonework too had generally come down and littered the shore with the larger pebbles. Beyond, the sea was drawing out, bronze and pearl under the hollow of sky.

The women shook their scarves and hair and wigs of crow-curls. As the men had urinated, so each woman spat as she went over the threshold.

The mountains had already taken the sun. The sheltered courts soaked up the shade. The women scattered wildflowers by the well and drew their water, singing thin and cruel as the gulls that circled overhead.

None of the Traveller men would kill these gulls, which might house lost souls. The villages the other side of the mountain pass, where the forest lay, they had their own stories of the ruin.

The women hurried back into the camp and offered meal to the vanished sun, that he might escape the mountains and return in the morning.

Darkness came, and the Traveller hearths were red.

'Come ye the fire, godd'er,' the leader of the band suggested, standing over the young boy who had sat down under the wall. They had come across him on the lower pass. He was walking on the black bare rock in the after-dawn, under the crawled lichens and cliffs clotted by the builderly excrement of the gulls. He could not be more than fifteen, but to their people that was old enough for a man. Besides, he wore the habit of a priest, very much mended. His hair reached his shoulders, flat and drab with dirt, save where there were long streaks in it of old man's white. A journeying godbrother he must be, or novice out on penance. Since he had inadvertently attached himself to the Travellers, they liked to keep him close, for they trusted none but their own, and preferred to behold at all times what he did. Only for the sheddings of nature did they give him privacy. They had not asked a blessing of him, for evidently he was not worth much to men, or to his Father in Heaven.

'If you wish,' said the boy priest now.

He got up and went threadbare with the Traveller leader in his splendour of orange and gold-kinked beard. The women sat together on the west side of the fire, their flame-dotted eyes going up to him and away. The men paid no heed or seemed not to.

'Ye drink, eat.'

A piece of bread and goat's cheese was given to the godbrother boy, which he took and mouthed a little before setting it aside. Tomorrow, the leader said, they might catch fish in the sea and the women cook a stew with it. The godbrother drank from the cup they handed round.

The night was soundless but for the insistence of the sea, the crack and shuffle of the fires, that tossed iridescence over the disjointed ramparts.

The boy glanced up, and it seemed he saw, high in the standing stone of the south-easterly wall (above the gapes and crevices and holes like caves), two petals of light like stars, coloured mauve and emerald, cochineal and sapphire. He did not, the boy, point, exclaim. No person otherwise of the camp looked at the south wall.

And when a different sound, perhaps music, drifted out from somewhere like a cobweb, the Travelling women sung, and rose and danced, even the old women with half-covered faces, flouncing their skirts and stamping down the paving.

In the head of the ruined tower was a vague shining, like the firelight, but paler and colder, not comfortable. Some gulls lifted like unseated grains of the night sky, then dropped back into the shell.

'Of all the fish in this water, no fish ye catch that is black.' The Traveller who spoke drank from the circling cup and let it go on. 'Black fishes feed them on the wood in the sea.'

The young godbrother sat under their eye, listening, not looking now at the lit tower head, the two stars that were windows.

The Travellers told over, in the way one who is much alone may come to talk to himself, that a petrified forest lay under the ocean. It was black as the sand here, black as the water by night. The trees were ancient as the land, and once had grown and thrived from the mountains to the edge of the east, until the sea was born and covered them up. Then they altered to basalt, and fish swam between their branches of stone.

In the body of the wrecked building the living trees stirred softly at the breath of a wind.

The chant had ended in the tower. The Traveller women sat down again on the west side of the fire.

Later when the men and women slept in their wagons, the godbrother got up again under the eye of four or five Travellers who were the watchmen.

'Make water?' one said. 'Go wary here. Bushes for ye far enough.'

Above, the two windows were out and might have been sucked away into the wall.

The boy priest came back from his bush, lay on his striped hair, and observed through open eyes that seemed lidless as a snake's, the night urges of the camp, its indistinct flutterings to and fro, and away.

In the morning, a man was missing from the camp. He was not one of the watchmen, but a young husband from the wagons. His wife ran to the leader, fell and grasped his knees. The missing Traveller had gone out in the night, mumbling that he had been called to by his friend.

But the friend denied this, and all made signs of aversion, or fingered the skull poles.

The leader selected six or seven of his men. They would penetrate the building a short distance. Others should search outside.

The godbrother boy joined himself to the inner search. They did not thank him or send him off. Two of the men kept a constant watch on him, even as they pushed through an archway and entered the inner courts.

By day, the ruin remained mysterious, and indeed showed its physical dangers more boldly. There were everywhere strange subsidences, as if the earth itself had quaked and the foundations given way. Elsewhere steps went up to floors that had gone down in rubble. The sockets of windows gaped. Whole walls had parted company with each other. And between everything the grass and the green trees with their autumn roan beginning on them.

The men kept to the open ways. Entries to the inner storeys of the edifice they spurned. They would not even look at them. Sometimes they called out the name of the missing man.

Emerging through a brake of immature oaks, fey and slender and innocent of their age to come, they confronted a broken wall that exposed a heart of red plaster, blackened perhaps by fire, and with something painted on it. It was a man with a saint's haloed face. The Travellers squirrelled off from it, violently leaping the sundered stones.

The south side especially they avoided. They appeared to know the ruin well by hearsay. It had been mapped for them in tales.

The sun was not very high, less than an hour had gone in hunting, when they gave up their man for dead. This was an oddity among their kind. They were normally incestuously fond and protective of their own, and perhaps the ragged godbrother had been told of that, for he expressed puzzlement. Going up to the leader, he said, 'Won't you look for him inside?'

'No. Unsafe.'

The godbrother did not further protest, the leader tried no more elaborate excuse. The men turned back towards the western outer court. The two Travellers who had watched the godbrother marched menacingly at him.

'Come, ye.'

'I'll look about a little longer,' said the godbrother. 'What do I fear? God is with me, and with all men.' There was something sly and amused in his face when he said this, and under the low wide brow, from which the thick, filthy badger hair erupted, his eyes, that these people had called blue, might be unlucky.

The men drew back. 'Let be,' said one.

Westward a sharp keening cry arose. Not a gull – it was the woman who had lost her husband, judging almost to the second the search's abandonment, and that she must now count him dead.

'She'll need comforting,' said the boy, the godbrother.

He turned and walked off, slanting back towards the painting on the old smashed wall. They did not go after him.

There should have been, by day, several offices, but this priesthood no longer properly recognised daylight. Like a colony of beasts in the dark, it had gone underground, and was usually active only after sunset. Sometime during the night, it constructed a single play of worship before God. Occasionally there was another rite, ceremonious and powerful, for which they rang the bell, the great-throated brazen being in the tower, if only as best they could.

Beyond their daylight hibernation, the meagre priesthood of the ruined fane left ample spoor – they were hidden but not in hiding. It was to be found by any who chanced and glanced on the south and eastern areas.

The godbrother travelled across the masonry, through the half-arches, up or down tottering stairs. He saw a large hall full of benches and chairs hacked into kindling to feed its fireplace, where a few ashes stayed faintly warm. He almost entered, beyond a garden of ivy and weeds waist high, an endless domain so choked with the grinding down of velum, the erosion of parchments and books, that he shied from it and slammed home the unhinged door. But there had been candles set on the floor in dishes, pooled with cold wax that mice had nibbled. Overhead, through tunnels of omission, might be glimpsed corroded weathervanes from which no wink of silver caught the sun. Cracked and splintered glass flashed stains of red and blue. But on a terrace there lay a crust of bread, fresh yesterday. In the weedy garden was a crucifix not yet consumed by grass.

The godbrother came on gargoyles often, and always suddenly. They did not make him start, though they seemed to pounce out from alcoves and overhangs, and here and there they lay underfoot, fallen, disfigured, but still grinning in malicious pain and joy.

High up, by a well which stank from glaucous mud at its bottom, the godbrother looked over, and the sea was visible in a gap beyond, blue-black, on the black beach.

Time had dealt quickly with this place. As if the stones, cemented by false dreams and faith, abetted their own destruction. As though it had been built merely of faults.

The wind blew through and the tough young trees bowed mockingly before it, and the motionless stones came ceaselessly undone, minute by minute.

A little rattling at the boy's back might have been only one such stone, coming away. But he turned, the godbrother, to see. The light came at him from one side and the dark from the other. It became obvious that he was not, after all, a boy, but a young man. His eyes were not "blue" but the green of acid fruits. He gazed with them at what he saw, which had materialised not far away. It was like, at first, a swart toad, standing up monstrously on its hind limbs, so it was too tall for what it must be.

The godbrother's gaze had grown into a cool soulless stare It held an interest, once more a slyness, but sheathed in pale green like the sea that maybe could think and feel, aspire and want, but invisibly.

'Yes?' said the godbrother, in his low soft voice that brought to mind a woman's.

The toad was a dwarf, but the dwarf was tall – something bizarre and contrasting, that defied vision. The cramped body appeared stretched, like a bend of iron uncurling – yet stuck. This flowered into a pair of lean hands, with long strong fingers, and into a big unwieldy magnificent head, shaggy with black hair. The eyes were black and elder, as they had always been. Both creatures stared at each other. Metamorphosis became obvious, lingering, and cunning, and a composition like bodies made from branches, driftwood, shells, feathers, the moon – then altered into skin and bone, hair and eyes.

'Show you,' said the dwarf. His voice, now he could speak, had learned presumably some use for speech, had stayed mewing, a pawing plaintive sound. He had not learned also to smile or threaten.

'Show what? I've seen,' said the godbrother. 'The Doma's gone to shale. Does the sea dare to come nearer? Will it dare to sweep in over the Christerium itself? Or will the Christerium only fall down in a heap, and the gulls go homeless, poor crying things?'

'Show,' said the dwarf. 'Follow me.'

How novel for this animal, this dwarf, to bring out such a command. Even in the role of servant, he could now deliver an instruction, himself be in charge of an event.

The godbrother with the woman's voice, white-streaked hair,

green eyes, nodded, tilted his head anomalously, maybe in acquiescence. And at that, the dwarf turned and made off, trotting as he had done before, doglike, and the godbrother moved after him.

Almost instantly, the route went into shadow. That was where the dwarf led, the godbrother was obliged to follow if he meant to.

They climbed down behind and under the walls, into a vault of stairways that did not rock but that stank of wet, and where poisonous mosses grew. And then came a gargoyle on the wall, and next another, both with garlands of ivy. Then there was a twisting corridor, and in the corridor, whose walls were painted by warrior angels, swords and wings, a lamp hung, burning sick light, from the beam of the ceiling.

The dwarf motioned, holding up his articulate hand for stillness. He padded ahead to where the corridor angled, investigated, beckoned. The godbrother followed once more. They turned into a chamber which gave on a staircase. This sloped into darkness, although another ill lamp burned at its foot. A curtain of mildew decorated the wall, and all the shadows were there. The dwarf went to the curtain, became a shadow, beckoned again. Together guide and guided withdrew without distaste, above such nonsense, into the curtain's folds.

'Half-blind,' said the dwarf, and then: 'Listen, here comes.'

A pathetic tread was audible from the far side of the room where a doorless space gave on, perhaps, infinity. From its vagueness slid a man in a black robe, tied at the waist with hemp, a priest with rusty eyes, gliding forward as if on runners which themselves knew the way. In his shrivelled hands there was a silver dish, a chalice, blazing. He held it out, carrying it or drawn by it. He went like a pendulum across the room, seeing nothing, and coming to the stair slipped mindlessly onto it and up into sheer blackness.

The dwarf and the young godbrother stepped from the curtain.

'Where does he go, then, Mechi?'

The dwarf said, 'To Anjelen.'

'With the solace of wine.'

'I show you the wine cask.'

And now their dubious path was lit at intervals. They entered, in this quarter-light, a space. Here the dwarf darted forward, picked up a candle, roused it with a tinder and displayed – the wine cask.

The Traveller man lay on a mattress, a loudly tinted bundle from which his face had been thrown up, as if rejected out of hair and clothes, as white as flour. From his left wrist the leather armlet had been cut, and a bandage of black stuff wound tightly on.

'Drained but not yet dry,' said the godbrother. He licked his lips as if in parody. 'How salt, salt as the sea, salt as a fish, the blood of men.'

The dwarf stood off. He idled the candle, making the room weave and shake.

The godbrother ambled through the spurting light and leaned under a wall that made pretend it was about to fall direct. He gripped the shoulder of the senseless man. 'Wake yourself. Wake up.' And when the Traveller did not stir, the godbrother bent down and bit the lobe of the man's ear, and out of a depth of nothingness he woke screaming of knives and the dark. 'Be quiet. Get up. You'll be better soon. I'll help you.'

Day entered the mountains, was leached out, faded. Besides, the sky grew overcast. Abnormal colours floated in the sea. The hot wind exhaled greenish rags of cloud that mirrored over the floors of the Christerium and caused the lids and lips of the gargoyles to twitch.

The Travellers had remained in the outer courtyard. On the poles of skulls they had hung flowers, and marked the black crosses with liquor. Within the wagons, on the ground, ran a circle of fires, which the women tended carefully, and where nothing was cooked. The wife who had been deprived lay in her cart, with at her side a small rudimentary doll of cloth and twigs, hastily formed to represent her husband. To the doll she whispered on and on, speaking of their time together, ventures mundane and intimate, secrets of their loins and hearts. She addressed the doll by his name.

The storm sky infused like the sea, in which the flint blood of the petrified forest looked to have been released.

The Travellers ate their raw sparse meal. Coming together inside the ring of fires, they started to perform feats of the sort with which they would waylay the caravans of others or draw the money of the crowd in a town market. Their acrobatic tricks, like their magic, were to them, as was not always understood outside their tribe, an aspect of religion. By such means they joked with their gods, with God, wheedling, jesting, demonstrating both foolishness and skill, wantonness and self-control. Here, in the ruin, they used an athletic sorcery to protect, to shield, and to drive off elementals of the dark and of the stones. At midnight, a propitious hour, they would be away, and did not desire pursuit.

So they danced between the buffets of staves, turned cartwheels and strode on their hands. So too an oval of willow was brought forth and set alight, and through this final fire the older children, the boys of nine and ten, came diving, somersaulting down in showers of sparks to cries of fear and triumph.

When the very last child had tumbled for the very last time, they held the hoop up and waved it at the sky that was now black and starless. And another child came hurtling through the willow and landed there inside the fires.

The final child was a dwarf man. He had sprung off a walk some ten feet above, over the wagon tops and through the willow hoop, and come down like rain on the ground.

No one moved. Those who had shouted closed their mouths. They were in two minds. For he also was of a people that they revered, the japes of God, and must be treated with fairly. But too he had burst from the very sinews of the ruin. Tall he was, the dwarf, almost the height of a man, but crouching, with a savage head like a wolf's.

Then, in the entrance of her wagon, appeared the woman whose husband had been lost, clutching together her hands.

And at her, like one of the gargoyles, the dwarf winked. As if they might all, if they wanted, be in with him on *this* joke.

But probably she did not see what the dwarf did. She was riveted by the hoop of willow.

Framed by its limping running flame, standing in the night air, was a ghost. Nothing else could be sure about it save its vast gush of hair, in which it seemed to have clothed itself, brownish red as virgin malt in the firelight, yet woven with hanks of white.

A handful of seconds the apparition was suspended over them. Then the empty hoop dropped with a hiss. And from the blackness beyond – where nothing was, not even now the bright tears of windows, and where no sounds emitted but sea and wind – a man came staggering.

They let him get to them, the Travellers, this one who had been lost. They gave neither assistance – nor greeting. But when he was near enough, they brought him in through the fires. He stood there then in their midst, but not wholly present. He did not crane about to find his wagon or his wife. She did not come down to him, she did not call.

The leader said, flatly, 'Search him for any marks.'

And they laid the lost man gently down. He did not struggle. And they, they did not need to do more than unknot the black binding from his wrist.

The lost man rested there, on his back, and murmured something only his tribe could recognise, but this they did, and drew around him. He shut his eyes. The leader came to close the inner circle of bodies. He knelt by the man and got out rapidly some strings of words that were just identifiable as a forgiveness of sins. Silence again, and the fires spitting like cats. The leader of the Travellers leaned forward and wrenched at the man with his right arm, holding firm with his left hand. There was a crack. The leader rose up and walked away. On the paving where the goats had fed, the lost man had turned his neck right over. His dead features were pressed into the grass.

The woman in the wagon entrance did not keen. She had done that earlier. She went back inside, to snap the neck of her doll.

And like a human wheel, all the eyes in the faces with their coverings of gauze and beard and fleshy tissue rotated towards the dwarf. Might it be they had come on a question to ask him?

Chapter Two

Together in their claustrophobic webby world, dim sighted as moles, four aged priests were at a twilight baking.

There had been slaves and servants once, to fulfil such chores. The kitchen had been intact, the ovens less obstinate... They had forgotten. Their bread was unleavened, but that might be piety. The stores of flour were often full of maggots; they put the substance through a sieve, lamenting. When last was there fresh flour, cheese or milk? Meat was a dream, but it was holy to abstain – fish sometimes were spewed out on the beach and might be gathered up. Now and then offerings of food were left, amorphously threatening, in the westernmost parts of the Palace on Earth. The offerings were almost idolatrous, and there had been none for a great while. The priesthood knew itself beyond the mortal country. One foot in Heaven and one in the grave.

They bickered over the burning bread and the oven smouldered, but the stormy darkening sky would hide the smoke, if any had cared.

Only the gulls, who shared the ruin with them, screamed and came to see.

Once when younger, they had killed gulls with stones and devoured the flesh, fishy, and which they had made out was fish, losing observance of fasts and frugality.

Day had become night with them. Centuries of dereliction might have gone over, changing everything, melting it into an eternal dusk. Amnesia of the mind, inertia of the soul. A Fall. Yet all this, these acres and spans of time and falling were only years. Among the chittering at the bread oven, or creeping about the stairs and halls, might some have been vigorous and upright with black hoods of hair, a decade before? It was a spell, this that had come to them, as it was a kind of curse worked upon the building. Apple with worm. Canker in the wood.

Across from the kitchen and the dining hall, a slipstream of pacing went on about the tumbledown cloister, some further phantoms of priests with their beads. In a garden the priestly spiders froze on their looms and sipped the dew. A mile high, or in the sky, a star or a window lit, and another.

The paving before the tower of the church had all come up, depressed like molars out of black gums. That had a look of tombs lifting, Judgement Day.

The base of the tower had become ivy, and the stone bastion rose out of it like a tree. Storms had hammered the two apocalyptic windows; neither the Christus nor the Devil had kept purchase.

A priest crept hurriedly out into the tomb yard, entered the tower of the church at a gap where the ivy was not. Behind him night came, but in the tower there was night already. The glassless seaward window hung in black space. Beneath, just visible, was the tracery of a stair and the huge slab of the altar. The altar was not dressed. The horror of the altar was its nakedness. Gone, the crucifix, gold, alabaster, diamond. All the treasures had away. The priest (old like the others), contemplated in desolation, and far above he heard the gulls muttering in their nests. They had spotted the floor, the carvings, the gallery, the altar itself. But it was carts that had swallowed up the riches of the Christerium, one autumn afternoon. The happening was nightmarishly vague, he could hardly recall how or why, only a mighty glittering removal, the toiling of horses, and men in the livery of Cathedral guard, and one soldier with a sword, barring the way like an angel.

Standing so, with nothing in his hands for the altar, the old priest became aware of another immobile beside him, a brother in a religious habit.

The bread's burnt,' said the priest to this other.

'Yes?'

'Isn't it always. Uneatable. But we are not made for luxury.' They stood as a pair, but unmatched. In the dark the old one had not seen the other was young. The old one added, in the same voice that spoke of bread, 'There won't be any ritual tonight. We fail him. God pardon us.'

'The man ran away, did he?' said the second priest, the young one. 'I'd have thought him too weak and afraid to manage it. Who was meant to guard him?'

'Brother Ragis, but he was nowhere near. So long since there was strong wine for us. But the Magister had his. The first cup, as always. Will he be angry now?'

'Have you seen him angry?' said the other one.

The old priest, dislocated by an unusual turn of inquiry, knew suddenly that the priest beside him was not of the brotherhood. The voice was untainted, firm; it disturbed him, it was young.

'Who is it, there?' said the old priest.

'Brother Eujasius,' said the voice. Then it laughed.

The old priest crossed himself. The laugh – its quality had made him do that. But even as the second stroke of the cross went over his breast, he mislaid the potence of it. For they had begun obliquely to realise, growing up as they grew fossilised and senile, that their webbed world contained the Devil. It was the Devil in the Christus, some awful power conjured, that had cast them down into the Fall whose symbols were all about them.

'Brother Eujas…'

'Eujasius.'

'The name of an angel,' said the old priest wonderingly, like a child. 'Such a high name to be granted you. Where have you come from?'

'Out of the air' said the voice.

The old priest stepped back. He moved to where he knew some candles stood on the floor in clay dishes, and lighted one, and all the time the other stayed there, in the dark. The candleflame curled up, and the old priest beheld the young priest. Who was not like the Angel Eujasius, shown always with yellow hair, holding the salver of the Bread of the Body – *I told him of the bread being burnt* – from the same coarse unleavened dough they made do for the Host. It was a blasphemous quip, maybe, this naming for the Angel of the Bread of the Body of the Redeemer…

The young one went on standing on the floor, smiling a little. The old priest was reminded of a snake, of something female and debasing.

'Well, brother,' said Eujasius. But then he only looked all about at the church tower, as if he feasted on its shame.

'You're from the city,' said the old priest. 'You came along the river to the sea, or walked the plains, begging. Or from a village. A town.'

'Or over the mountains,' said Eujasius, still drinking up the ruin, stretching himself and basking in it. 'Stories are related.' he said, in his low, girl's voice, 'about this shambles. That there was a Knighthood here, insulting to God, and which called up demons. Wicked acts. Rites of blood. And there were suicides, murders, vampires. So then the arm of the Church Paternal reached out and snuffed the evil lamp, disbanded the order, burned papers and tapestries, smashed windows, looted and made off with the goods. And now all that go about here are ghosts and ghouls.'

The old priest watched as if enticed. He had seen something else, blocking out the torture of this recital. The turning neck was young and smooth, the pallid eyes were clear.

So that when the youth finished his gloating perusal and returned his gaze to the old godbrother's face, the priest said, 'You must be hungry and footsore. We have charity. We'll share with you what we have.'

'Will you?' said Eujasius. His eyes gave off a vivid flash, some trick of the candle. 'What about your master, the Magister?'

'He is above such things. We serve God as best we can.'

'And who is God,' said the boy, 'to you?'

The old priest attempted to cross himself again but could not discipline the tremor in his arm.

'Hush,' he said.

And the boy smiled widely and put one finger over his serpent's mouth.

It was breakfast or dinner in the Common Hall. (The Hall of the Novitiate had caved in beneath the snow winters before, the Hall of the Ordinate was flooded by the sea, and barnacles clambered about its figured walls.) The trickle of priests ebbed in through the courtyard door, sullen and loitering. There were so many limits upon where they might go, and here too there was no choice. A single table of planks had been spared and left up against the fireplace. The night was cool, and a chair burned on the hearth unwillingly, tended by one of the brotherhood, who fed in carved legs, and wretched knots of rubbish he and his fellows had found about the building and not wanted.

The table, rather than lit, was shadowed by seven candles. The priests affixed themselves and picked like angry old birds at the burnt cakes of bread, a mush of weeds, the brackish water in tin cups.

They had never been encouraged to conversation at the board, and now maintained a silence that was itself fraught and levered, these voiceless skinny rats and carrion crows upon the unnourishing carcass of vocation and of life itself.

Then, unsuitably, one spoke. 'Pass me the cellar of salt.'

'It's empty.'

'That's a lie. I gathered salt myself yesterday.'

'No, you didn't. You're neglectful, brother.'

'Brother Ragis is neglectful.'

The scavenging heads went up, and through the jolting fuse of the candles, discovered Ragis gnawing at his bread. He looked back in turn, frightened and fierce. 'I took the drink. I took him the wine.'

'But the man,' grated out the chiding brother, 'what of the man?'

'He must have run off. Who was there to watch but me? And the lord's servant came to me. Take him the wine, he said.'

The brotherhood crepitated to itself, clawing with parchment hands at the table and plates, crumbs and robes.

'The dwarf,' said another one, 'like an imp of Hell.'

Ragis said. 'It must be as the Magister wills it. The Magister sent for me.'

'You cut the vein,' said the chider. 'You cut too deep or more than once or didn't bind him tight enough. He crawled away and died.'

From the table's farthest end, aeons off from the fire and a mile from the last candle, someone said, 'Brothers, in the name of the Most High, we mustn't squabble before strangers.'

So the heads moved again, and one of the hands, pushing forward a candle, produced a voice that demanded, 'Who's that? Is it you, Yaivin? Why are you sitting in the dark?'

At that moment the night wind swept by the door above the sea, out of all the dark there was and in which the island of the badly lighted table was adrift. The wind was like a laugh. It flaunted the candleflames to blue strands and let them recover like drowning things. The dark was so easy to achieve, why not sit in it?

'Speak up, Yaivin. Who has he got with him there? Can you see, Brother Ragis?'

The elderly priest Yaivin, who had concealed himself, perhaps unthinkingly, reached forward and brought the pushed candle nearer. It lit then, for the dim red rat eyes of the priests, his own familial physiognomy, and that of the other. And the other sat by, a face above two slim hands which rested on a bit of blackened bread. The shadow kept him otherwise, making odd variances with his hair, sculpting deep hollows at the cheeks, under the lower lip, and all around the eyes that were pale and animal and watching.

'A travelling godbrother,' said Yaivin. 'He tells me he is known as Eujasius. This I dispute with him. But, well.'

The priests looked at Eujasius.

'A boy,' said Ragis, and he put down his bread. 'Is he? Is he young?'

The one called Eujasius said, 'I'm thirty years. Or more.'

'No, no,' said Yaivin, 'that can't be.'

'I seem younger,' said Eujasius. 'Isn't that true also of your master?'

'Our master? What does he say?'

'Our master is God.'

'No, he speaks of the Christus.'

'Once,' said Eujasius, 'you had a Christus on your altar. He was white as the ice and nailed through by diamonds. There were roses of corundum on his head. But the Church Fathers from the city confiscated him, didn't they? What was Anjelen doing that afternoon?'

At the name, Anjelen's, the old priests moved, were twisted about without leaving their seats, to shapelessness, and reformed like the candles in the wind. It was some inner piece of them, not their bodies, which had writhed.

'Anjelen is Anjelen,' said Eujasius. He raised the burnt bread and broke it. *'Did He not say, This is my Body?'*

Anjelen's priests looked on, and they beheld the scene in which they participated, and were aware of something devilish in the youth who was its pivot, something feminine and reptilian. But there he sat in the centre of the ruin, and the image was on him irresistibly of the Christus at his Final Supper upon earth. The mirror had so distorted for them that anything symmetrical would not have shown m it But Eujasius showed, he bedazzled them.

They were intent upon their own designs, this flotsam of the Church of God, and he intent, of course, upon his, also, yet not maybe to the exclusion of theirs. A union was forming, victim with assailant.

And on the door which no longer shut, leading in from the outer court, there came a blow, harsh and fine, more than sufficient for the silence. It was not a courtesy, not a knocking for admittance. An announcement, rather.

The priests turned gratingly on their silted-up bones.

Through the door came the dwarf, the servant of their master, scuttling like a black crab.

They feared it. It was the Devil's imp. It served God.

Tall, for a dwarf. At first, a millennium ago, it had not had the ability of speech, but the Magister had given it utterance, that it might convey his wishes now and then.

That afternoon when the guard of the Cathedral had ridden into the Christerium, when the letter from the city Administer had been read, when the city Factor had walked with his acolytes the rooms, the halls, the church itself, and given forth words of exorcism and awesome promises, and when the priests had thrown themselves down at the feet of these invaders, when one hundred and ninety-two men in habits of black had whipped themselves before the legate from the city, then, running up to the rooms in the south wall, what had anyone met there but vacancy? Anjelen was not to be come on. And later, in the incoherency of their revenance, when they discovered him again, it was by the emergence of the dwarf. *The Magister requests that you bring him...*

Myopically they glimpsed the disintegration of that hour of their humiliation, that afternoon, the biting slash of the honed sword.

Then they wandered in the forest of stone and webs, until they were old, blinded, forgetful, glutted with the ultimate sin of Dormancy.

Yet, there burned inside the fog a scarlet secret jewel, their rite. The passion.

The dwarf was in the refectory, standing to one side, and after him came a figure that was just the dream a dwarf might fabricate. Tall, straight, slender, and of a metallic darkness in its black habit, its priestly garment that had withstood the centuries of ten years of desuetude, as he himself withstood all time, ageless, like the full-grown tree.

'Magister!'

They got up rushing like boys, their joints cranking.

'Sit,' he said.

One word. The beauty of the voice made of it a thousand cadences. They reheard, over and over, and sat down.

And Anjelen moved towards them, up to the brink of the candlelight, gazing out across it. And the candlelight stretched up to have for itself him.

The forehead was wide and low, and the black hair sprang from it. The eyes and brows were black. The mouth seemed the only feature in his face. His face had no meaning but for the mouth. It was well-shaped, having nothing to it that suggested venality or greed. Yet, it was gluttonous. That was all it was, and all the face was. The gluttony of a drunkard ninety years of age and always at his cups. That young firm mouth, the level teeth. Thirst incarnate.

But the lips parted, and the beautiful voice came from there, music from a swamp.

'On the other hand, you are to stand up before me,' it said. 'Stand then, Mechail Korhlen.'

A kind of motion, a ripple, went along the table. The candles limped and rose. The old priests had no will to be amazed, or even to seek about.

'I said to you, you will stand, Mechail.'

No anger, nothing human in the music of the swamp of the thirsty mouth. But in the black eyes a slight alteration, as if they might for an instant dominate the face.

Yaivin tore himself, a severance of psychic skin, from the

hypnotic of the lips and voice, and looked sideways. *Is that his name? Mechail?*

'Get up – his grace commands you…'

Yaivin began to see what was really there, and this was no one. The boy had disappeared, run on lizard feet unnoticed somewhere, into the hall, or past them all and out of the door.

'Magister, he's gone.'

There was a stifled chorus of outrage from the table, old men ranting in creaks and whispers.

Anjelen said, 'There will be a return. After so great an absence, the visit could hardly be so brief.'

'His name,' said Yaivin, 'your grace, he called himself Eujasius.'

Anjelen's eyes went over Yaivin. Yaivin stared, trying to see, to miss no inch of face or second of response.

Anjelen walked back towards the door and the courtyard. His movements were a little stilted, stiff, as if he did not, often, this antique sot, wander about on solid ground. *'The raven shall live there,'* said Anjelen, *'it shall be a maze. Thorns will come up in the palace, and the walls shall be the stones of emptiness.'* He put his hand upon the dwarf's shoulder. The dwarf looked up at him like a dog of iron. 'Whatever God asks of you is good to do, even if it be to grieve. He will come and tell you' – he meant now the dwarf – 'when to ready yourselves. Ring the bell loudly.'

Ragis wobbled to his feet.

'But he ran away, that one. And now – this one too.'

Anjelen said, 'Prepare the house, and the guest arrives. Crows come from the desert with bread in their beaks, and from the rock bursts the stream of wine.'

Ragis opened his mouth again, and now the dwarf lifted up a hand of admonition. Anjelen went through the door, night into night. Then the dwarf made a mewing sound, and skipped, and turned a cartwheel out over the threshold.

The men had surrounded him as they had their dead, so there could be no sudden flight. They talked to him with the manners of their own Traveller etiquette, and did not ask his name, which he would have given carelessly, the version that the forest left him. They asked what had brought him to them.

'I go with you,' he said. 'I earn my keep. As you see.' For the dwarf, this was a lengthy vocalisation. Once he had begun to utilise speech, he had learned unhesitantly, as with other things. But even so, having got by such a while without them, he was still slack with words. They were tools for everyday or servile matters, not yet the vehicles of concepts, not pretty, or emotive.

The leader of the Travellers asked, 'Where from ye come? Out the church?'

'I shelter here, me,' said the dwarf. 'Bad place. I see your light and come to you.'

They accepted this, for it was reasonable. But the honesty with which it was delivered did not convince. Then again, though, the dwarf might be God-touched. To a simpleton simplicity was not ridiculous. They would have to test him, as they tested most things, biting gold, striking a dog, once, scorning a bride's chastity in a careful song.

'Eat, then,' said the leader, and parted the enclosure of his men to allow the dwarf freedom.

The dwarf ate the cheese and berries a woman brought him, like a small rodent, holding them in his lean man's paws. He did not seem hungry. He had always carried with him a memory of a Traveller girl in his childhood, she who had soothed warm milk to his lips as he lay frozen on the shore of death. But it was only one more memory with the rest. The viciousness before, and after, the jibes, the sticks and stones that helped break and bend the bones of his psyche.

The Travellers watched the dwarf as if he had come to take the place of the godbrother they had watched before. The godbrother was now reckoned lost, like the man who had died to them and whose body was stacked neatly in a cart for burial in other ground.

No further questions were asked. The dwarf rose and went all at once away to the edge of the fires, to a dark spot by a wagon wheel. 'I sleep now,' he said to the man who stood over him.

Then, they watched the dwarf sleep.

He was as still as their dead. He did not make a sound, did not turn. He slept in a ball, like a cat.

'See how he slumbers,' said the leader to his wife's brother.

'I see it.'

'Go, kick him, light. Say to him ye stumbled on him.'

The man crossed over to the dwarf and batted with his boot at the lower leg.

Mechi did not react. Oblivious, he lay clotted in his ball of sleep.

The Traveller looked over at his leader. The leader nodded. The man bent and shook the dwarf by his shoulder. All the camp watched, now.

The dwarf did not wake, did not grunt or protest.

Quickly, the Traveller man seized the dwarf by both shoulders and pulled at him, and Mechi unrolled like a carpet. He was also like a man then, properly grown, but in miniature.

'Leave him,' said the leader.

They dragged the dwarf out from among the fires and put him against the wall. Here they made a circle round him of salt and dropped a cross of twigs on to his chest.

They went on about their preparations for departure, which were prolonged by safeguards.

Mechi had gone back to his master, when called. Which is to say, he had put his other self under the wagon wheel in a pose of sleep and withdrawn his awareness from it. He had been testing the Travellers too. If they slaughtered him, or what stood for him, in their camp, then he would know to avoid them. Although he would have liked to journey in their company, as in the woods of childhood, before Krau and the Korhlens.

Mechi was changing, but it did not bother him. He lived day by day, as he had always had to, as every lesson in the world advised, had he but known it.

For his years at the Christerium, serving Anjelen, and let be by Anjelen (who was less a man than a pillar of wood, and even when he moved about remained so, save in the area of the one obsessive need), in those years the dwarf had been tutored by inference, and taken in schooling through his eyes. The Magister taught Mechi nothing, yet Mechi was privy to much, actually to great wonders, which he merely gazed at. For Anjelen dabbled in alchemy, as if not knowing what he did. These actions would come to be like the abrupt bursting-out of a green leaf on a bare branch, which shrivelled and vanished in half a night. Anjelen's purpose in such sorceries was inexplicable. They were a reflex, perhaps, the hands and mind starting into movement between vast seasons of nullity, But Mechi saw, and knew himself, in an unnamed way, in the chamber of a magician. Magic rubbed off like pollen. And if Anjelen turned on him his black eyes that, gradually, were becoming as superficial as the eyes of a human man, Mechi met the eyes and stared, like a dog at the moon; but the moon was dead.

One dusk in Anjelen's inner room, where the wolf window had mostly cracked to bits whirled away into space, Anjelen was absent, and Mechi had paused to look into the globe of quartz. Three daggers were laid about it, pointing south, west, and north of east. They had been positioned there weeks before, and dust was powdered on them. The globe itself shone, and looking at it, Mechi saw his own reflection. It amused him, for through the medium of the curved crystal, by shifting here and there, he could alter his shape. And in this manner, Mechi refashioned himself in the glass nearly in the shape of a man. Subsequently he would find the chamber empty often, and he would play with the quartz globe. He did not know why he was pleased with the game, or even truly that pleased he was – what standards of pleasure had there been?

But there was a sort of compendium of knowledge in Mechi as in the others of his kind: Jasha, Anillia.

One sunset Mechi saw his shadow on the wall of the ruin, and it was different. He stopped, interested, untheoretically conscious of what had come about. He felt no tearing bitterness at previous possibilities denied him through ignorance. He felt no spur of desire for what he might now make and take and have.

He played with the shadow. He found it would gesture and walk without him. He rendered into this matrix, substance, as they, the others, had done, Anjelen, Anillia, Mechail.

The dwarf created himself almost in his own image. The ectoplasmic projection they had achieved through sorcery, will, madness, dream, Mechi came to as an artist, a pragmatist.

About three years after (three decades of a century of ruination, the spell of the Fall, to the Christerium), Mechi's images bounded and scudded about the walks and courts, and he, his reality, had grown four inches, and his back was mostly straight, and now and then a splinter worked out of it, and he recalled, with no appetite for association, the splinters piercing from Mechail's shoulder, like quills from a porcupine.

Sometimes Mechi, and sometimes Mechi's making, would go to summon the priesthood to its rite of love. The makings, when their use had been served, he let melt back into nothing, but no one saw. They were like water marks drying on the stone. He had got speech by then, which fact spoke too for itself. The business of the priestly rite did not trouble Mechi. The world had never made sense.

It seemed to him though that occasionally he had been made to go about, like a puppet, before he himself began the work of his own volition – but neither did that perturb him. He was a slave. Yet the game itself was appealing, as had been the performance of the tricks the first Travellers had taught to him. The game inaugurated for him himself. (He was also learning not to be a slave.)

He sent himself to the Travellers in the courtyard because their people had once been tolerant of him, useful – if he was yet able to think in this style. But to run away was an idea so alien he gave it no title.

Crouched outside Anjelen's chamber, where Anjelen had sat since Godbrother Ragis had come there with the silver chalice of blood, Mechi had approached the Travellers through his other self. If they were afraid and killed it, so what? He could make another and know to let them be.

But when he had withdrawn from his sleeping surrogate, they only ringed it with salt. And Mechi, as he, in body, attended on the Magister, experienced a weird new excitement, glee, an embryo which might at last harden to malice and joy beyond the capacity of any ordinary hating, laughing man.

Eujasius sat on a hill of stones, once a wall of the Doma, overlooking the night sea. The tide was drawing in, in scarves of blue foam. The moon was rising.

Earlier Eujasius had gone out along the sand like soot, and

explored the limits of the water, encouraging them to come back. There a fish smote up, and Eujasius got hold of it. Till its struggles were finished, he held tight, and then kissed the cold scales up and down.

The fish was all the sea in one flexive drop. On the hill of rubble, Eujasius ate it raw and slow, licking off the silvery blood. He ate everything but the transparent intricate tail and fins, and the tragic head with its black eyes. The perfect skeleton he examined, as if to find the source, what had made it live and spasm, what had gone out of it and left it indifferent to his rending.

Then Eujasius stared along the beach, where the moon-glazed sea was mounting up invisible steps of possession.

The sea. How deep did the staircase drop into the floors of it? What palaces were there, what halls and towers and churches made of bizarre shells, and of the materials which only the ocean could design? And was the forest of basalt there, beyond the skirt of the beach of black sin?

Some other thoughts went through the head of Eujasius, who had bathed in the chill salt sea, and washed there with sand and water his caked, striped hair.

Eujasius thought of a blond man who fought beneath him ripping at his arms until Eujasius broke them. And into the mouth of this enemy Eujasius thrust the hilt of a sword until it had gone through everything into the brain. The crosspiece of the hilt had gouged Krau's cheeks into a lunatic stricture. He had an idiot's grin now, with shattered teeth. The iron pointed out from it like a tongue.

But also, Eujasius thought of the carved chair that had become a thicket, and spread up about the walls and ceiling, and of a white fox which looked out of it, but soon another would come, and then Eujasius must go up to the man in the chamber hung with russet, green and purple, she must part her legs for him and conceive his son. And Kolris Vre Korhlen lay on her asleep, clutching her fast.

And she or he saw the globe of crystal, the brain of Anjelen, and in the crystal the secrets and the learning, facets so bright, like the stars strung over the sea, and as readable.

But also she thought of the path down on to the beach at dawn, and the hot torches against the warmthless sky. The Administress stepped forward and began to read aloud from a prayer book. And there was a ladder up the flank of the platform, and they hurried her, and they tied her, on her back, for the fire…

A light bloomed now on the rock under the Christerium. It swung adeptly down, coming towards the beach without haste or deception.

Not the priests, they would have tottered. This would be Mechi again, sent to search Eujasius out, and Mechi of course would sense where Eujasius was, just as he had done before.

Eujasius rose gracefully, and turning back, approached the lamp.

Beam-lit, the dwarf stood over him. Eujasius cast the skeleton of the fish away.

'Turn a cartwheel,' said Eujasius.

But the dwarf only pointed along the rock. His black eyes were all the dead moon was not. And he looked tall enough now to be the same height as Anjelen, the Magister. Taller.

Chapter Three

After her mother had been inside the hut one quarter of an hour, Jasha had gone to see the horse, taken its rein and led it under the lean-to. She considered Mechail's mare might take against the newcomer, but the two animals moved together for warmth, peacefully, and bowed their heads to the hay on the ground. A limitless soft snow began to fall. From the hut no sound emerged. Jasha waited, and silence pressed in her ears. At last she had crossed the snow and re-entered the hut, quiet as a cat, as if to interrupt them, catch them out.

But nothing had properly altered. Mechail slept where earlier he had elected to, rolled in the blanket on the earth, with a cushion of dried grass extracted from the mattress under his head. He lay on his back, now, his arms across his breast as if thrown there in protection. His breathing was just audible.

Anillia was by the fire, standing up. She was cloaked in black and dressed beneath in a white gown that looked to be banded and embroidered, garments of her own mandate, maybe, off no loom but her will.

Jasha observed them. The sleeping man and the standing women.

The fire cracked and the soft snow sighed.

'He'll wake presently,' said Anillia. 'When he's ready. He knows that I'm here.'

'Shall I go out again and wait, lady?' said Jasha.

She was not humble, and her eyes gleamed, unblinking.

'In the snow? Why?' Anillia turned and glanced into the cauldron.

'Can you conjure more food?' said Jasha. 'If you're a witch, lady.'

'You,' said Anillia, 'were the witch. They wanted to burn you for it.'

Jasha said, 'What did you do with my green dress that I gave you?'

'Gave my poor unclad bones. Your dress ... I forget.'

'A soldier bought me that. And this.'

Anillia said, 'Come and stir the soup.'

Jasha approached her. Anillia's face was like Anjelen's, and there was about her too a ruby darkness, a luminous shadow.

'Dresses. I recall my maids twittered of such things.'

Jasha looked into the cauldron. It was burning dry. And from the ashes the loaf was gone. Perhaps the woman had hidden it?

Jasha said, 'He'll have to go hunting, or trapping. There's nothing here.'

'Do you think he will? Is it probable you'd starve? The witch-fire didn't scorch you up, and the sword only stopped his heart for a few days. For myself, I died and rotted, and came back, and here I am.'

'It's not good to go hungry.'

'Little peasant girl,' said Anillia, 'put away what you were.' And Anillia gazed at her, the same gaze there had been outside. Jasha did not rummage after answers. She did not care how and why Anillia was her mother. But that Anillia was Mechail's, his possession, this Jasha had guessed at once.

Jasha drew aside. Having moved the pot from the fire in a prim housewifely way, she sat down by the hearth.

Then, as predicted, the man woke.

He opened his eyes on Anillia, a figure flowing up out of the dark, sketched in vertical lines by dull firelight, a stem surmounted by a drifting mask of face. Perhaps in turn he could make out her eyes, their blackness. Would he suppose this icon, which revealed no gender, did not lean to him or speak, to be that of Anjelen?

'Who's there?' Mechail said. And then, 'Where's my knife? I'll need it today, won't I?' Then he sat up and flung his right hand round on his left shoulder, the deformed shoulder that had healed itself. He said, 'Ah, no. I remember now. All that's over. What do you want?'

'You know me,' said Anillia. 'Who I am.'

Mechail did not look. He had fixed his eyes on the wall, where the tree-sides pushed through. In tiny gaps there the sprinkling snow was visible, attracting the light from the hearth.

'If I know you, am I dreaming, then?'

'Was it only in dreams you saw me?'

'Yes. And when I was dead, you brought me a drink, wine ... no, it was blood, the blood of the child – the albino girl.'

'That was my dream, I must have sent it you. But I'm here, and you've woken up.'

'I don't believe that. Every day,' he said, looking at the snow in the torn wall, 'I thought of you. I see you now as you were then, gaunt and dying. Your black hair became thin and brittle and there were great strands of white in it. The women used to talk about your hair. I remember when they said you died, and I never believed them. The priest beat me. I cursed God. But you were dead. It didn't matter if I believed or not.'

Jasha sat watching by the cookpot. Excluded, she eyed them, and felt the fine needles of her own hair sewing out of her scalp an inch or so an hour.

'I was called Nilya. The Vre in the Tower made you call me *mother* when you clung to the childish way. My true name's the Crel name Anjelen foisted on me, and which I've made mine, as I've made mine this body whose seed he gave me.'

Mechail regarded the snow falling.

Anillia went forward, two steps, and knelt down at his side. At once, she *became*, for the fire spread across her face, described her throat, her breasts, the three rich thick plaits of oil-black hair. The scent of her, which was young and fragrant, and not quite human, must have been exact in his nostrils. She put her hand on his face, and persuaded it.

'Here I am,' she said. 'The flesh and the life. What do you want?'

'Nothing,' he said. 'What's the use?'

His grey eyes were white from the snow, and Jasha saw them clearly as they fixed on the woman's face.

In Jasha something writhed and chirped, so faintly she took no heed. She stretched out her hands to the fire, and they were full of clean redness. She heard Anillia say, 'You want only rest. I remember how that was, that wanting. To die and so sleep for ever.'

'Yes,' he said. 'But *he*...'

'Anjelen is nothing,' she said. 'We outran him, you and I.'

'He's there before us,' he said. 'I can see him in the future. He claimed me as his son.'

'You are my son,' she said. *Mine.*'

Jasha heard the smooth susurrous, cloth brushing cloth, and the snakelike slipping of long plaits of hair.

She formed strands of firelight between her fingers with the red glow of blood in them. She tilted her head. Her scalp itched from growth. Did the soil itch like this as the grass pushed through?

When she looked over her shoulder, Anillia sat by the wall on the pillow, and Mechail lay against her, his head under her neck, so each face was set near the other, and angled alike, saints' faces on a screen of cloak and hair and dark.

They would not move for some while, or speak, probably.

Jasha said in a sharp-winged little voice: 'Will you have some of the broth?' And tapped the empty cauldron.

They did not reply.

Jasha looked back into the fire. It would last until morning, for it must.

Through the winter night, the girl Jasha closed on herself tightly. As she slept, with her head laid on her knees, her fluent spine bowed and her hands loose, her hair coiled over her and met the ground. The fire gave to it a bronze burnish, such as often it had had in the city, where it was so regularly washed and brushed and combed and caressed. Jasha dreamed briefly that she walked through the city, going to fetch water for her father's hut, at a well near the market. And she came on Anillia and Mechail lying together side by side, covered with leaves. It was summer, however, and their skins had the green glimmer of the foliage that grew from the houses and hovels. Even their lips were green, like moss. Jasha bent to tap them at the temple, the arm. They gave off a drumlike note. As she walked away on her errand, Jasha saw that the fingernails of the hand with which she had struck them had turned to wood.

She roused when there was a wintry first light through all the holes and crevices in the bothy. Sitting up, she peered cautiously at the place where Mechail had lain against their mother, the lady, and there they still were, as if they had not moved. But their eyes were shut as if by mutual consent. They slept a state of unison, but it was remote and pure, there was nothing natural in it. One sleeper in two bodies. They breathed as one and without detection.

Jasha broke a stick out of the wall and dipped it in the fire which, through the will of someone, had persisted without physical help. The stick caught, and Jasha got up and went out of the hut, holding her torch, into the dimness under the trees.

Birches shone like signposts to the stream, where the phantom village had been. There were pines. They seemed to have grown like her hair, swiftly, abundantly, so established and dense and massed with snow.

The stream was frozen, and Jasha got down by it and broke the surface with a slate. Underneath, imprisoned in meandering rafts of ice, big grey fish were lying. It might be they were an illusion, or something magically created. But she had found fish before in this way in the streams of the forest. Jasha took the ice and the ice-fish in the skirt of her habit, and walked back to the hut. Her feet were still bound in strips of homespun stuff Mechail had given her. This would not be enough to save her from the snow, and yet it sufficed. The fish for hunger, the bindings for the cold, were provisions against her own oddity. Only by these methods did she lie to herself, and then not thoroughly. It had been wise in the past to avoid the probings of others.

On her path to the hut, she searched for edible grasses or weeds that might exist inside the bowels of trees. A handful of such savouries she amassed. And going into the room, she threw the ice, fish, weeds into her cauldron, and began to heat them on the fire.

Later she gathered sticks and branches to dry out by the hearth. There was no broom to sweep the floor. The sleepers did not wake. She took snow to the horses for drink.

Jasha plaited her hair. She recalled the long winters with her father, Carg Vrost, and her summer evenings with the irritable soldier Evra Livdis. She watched the fire and saw pictures in it and told herself stories from them, as the women did in the villages. When the fish soup was ready, she took it from the fire and after an interval ate some out of the cauldron, scalding her hand and lips.

She did not like the freshwater taste of these fish. She had liked the salty fish of the sea river in the city.

She turned herself about and stared at the woman and the man, who slept. She thought of flinging pebbles at them or tossing the bubbling soup on them. The vibration of sorcery had begun to come from them; it was not a sound, but it was the only noise they made.

'Will you wake up?' said Jasha. 'Supper's here. I've made you soup, lady. The fire's bright. Come and warm yourself.'

Sometimes she had put wildflowers on the grave-mound that was her mother in the forest. She went out and picked a twig with the snow on it and put it between the fingers of Anillia's left hand. A silver ring had been on one of her hands, but it was not there now. It had dissolved, like the snow on the twig of frozen flowers.

The fire was black, the room crimson. A sunset covered the wood and through the open door, which stood wide, were fire-coals of mountains, and the rose-red snow. And in this heat of colour, the cold burned.

The sleepers had woken, and they were gone. Nothing remained of them but the cushion of grass thrust into a corner.

It seemed to Jasha the woman had put her cool, ringless fingers on Jasha's forehead, as at their meeting.

Jasha went out quickly, and there were no horses in the lean-to. She picked about and found, halfway along a slope, a broad mantle of pink snow pitted by hooves. Then she returned to the hut. Again she provisioned herself with some of the now unhot fish soup. She imagined the cauldron might disappear when she left it. She was glad her hair had grown to warm her.

On her bound feet, she deserted the hut and walked up after the hoof-marks until she lost them among the thicker trees. The crimson was soaking by then into purple twilight. The shades were exotic and extreme, as if to keep her alert. She sought until the light was almost done with her, and then she found the trail again. She sprang along it like a hare.

Despite its effect, the woodland was not yet very old. As the dusk melted out the trees one into another, Jasha sensed slender shoots padding themselves with snow and darkness. Then, after the hues of roses, apples, grapes, the black total of night filled up everything. And as this happened, Jasha heard the syllables of her own name, eerie and bodiless, spinning back to her along the aisles of the wood. It was the woman who called. As if, since Jasha had pursued, she was now bound to go with them. Jasha accepted this. She moved unerringly towards the solitary summons.

They went through the trees, the makeshift invented road pillowing up, giving way, declining, now awkward and now plain. Sometimes, as though to be certain, her own name blew back to her once more. Jasha did not call in response. She had known the blackness of the forest since infancy, and its snows, and the lure of supernatural songs. She was only unsure of how far off they were, the two riders. How long she must travel, to reach them. She did not suspect herself of constancy, or envy, or need, or trust.

They were at the summit of a hill, and in the night without a moon, a vast forest seemed to or did surround them, sinking away, spread in folds towards nothingness, and black mostly, with the glass sheen on it of the snow. On the hilltop one tree, a thin spire, grew towards the sky. The snow had patched it lightly. There were stars upon its boughs, like birds.

The horses they had left below, setting them at liberty to do what they could for themselves. The horses had not seemed real, less so than the forest and the night.

'Why have we come here?'

The black-haired woman said quietly, 'To find the sleep you long for, and that he wished on me. The only rest there is.'

'Anjelen.'

'I know his mind,' she said. 'I know him.'

'Then you're his creature.' Mechail's voice was bored and dull. 'Another hallucination sent to torment me.'

'From the mental rib of Anjelen,' she said, 'I was made. And from my body I made you. And from my mind, at one remove, came Jasha. But also you made Jasha with me – my daughter, and yours. And from your soul, Mechail, the other one. Your dwarf who has your name. But we're all the creatures of Anjelen, or the creatures of what he is. Even he is the creature of that. And the man, that priest formed by others, that inquisitor and magician acting by human rote, losing sight of himself... How much more there will be to lose. I vowed against the man he is, to take away what the man wanted. I shall do so. But that other he is, that other's unavoidable. Its plan is our own. What you long for is what it would have from you, though not what Anjelen, the man, desired. His son upon earth, to walk in his ways. His chastity, his father's ambition – those you and I will ruin. But already, he allows it. What Anjelen truly is hasn't any care for earthly wants. It seeded, and has made its life again, in the image of the maker.'

'Where?' he said.

She smiled, and in the dark any watcher might see her smile like a ripple on night water, might see her smile – but not really her face. She touched her breast, she touched his cheek, then she pointed like a sword towards the single tree of stars.

'There is what we are,' she said. 'The root of our life. The one coffin that will hold us safe.'

The winter snow was on the wood, but then in the east an auburn disc rose like a copper mirror, a moon not of winter, spring, or autumn fall, but the summer moon of blood. The world welcomed the moon. It put off winter like a dew and the snows smoked away. In the life of one minute, the ground was black with the night-black of summer grass, and the flowers wounded it to get out. They rushed on the slopes, around the sinews of the trees, drifts like snow, night born and moon born, white and ash, sable and silver and brass. And the liquid pools were throats that gave out the hymn of frogs. A nightingale sang in an oak of ten thousand leaves. The trees were ancient and ripe with their foliage. The red moon shone on the forest like the sun by night.

The woods girl hid herself in her bush of snow that had become flowers. She breathed their perfume as she crushed them with her body. The bush sweated in the furnace of summer. She thought of a summer wood, and the ice age that had come on it, once, the shattered sugar of frozen roses. But that was then. This was now.

Above, on the hill, the man and the woman had stood before

the narrow mast of the young Tree, and said their words, which she had listened to. The Tree had grown from their words. It was a column now, a pine perhaps, yet clouded at its top, the moon fired it there as if it burned.

And there were brilliants among the trees everywhere, swarming like fireflies, but they swam up the hill, and as they drew closer they lifted higher and grew larger, and she smelled, the girl in the bush of flowers, torches.

The man on the hill stared down at them.

'What is it?' he said. 'These lights.'

The woman said, 'Don't be afraid. It's a memory. The forest has them, as we do. Remember when you were a child and I took your hand? Like that, Mechail.'

'It's death,' he said, but his voice was longing and trembling as if with love.

'Not death. You know, we can't die, not I, not you. Haven't we tried?'

'Then...' he said. And he looked at her, and all of him was only in that look, nowhere else, and he was nothing else. '*Anillia.*'

'Rest,' she said. 'Truth.'

'In the wood,' he said. 'God's in the wood.'

He reached and took her hand, and so they stood, linked by a small connection of flesh, as the torches burned onwards along and up the hill on every side.

They passed her, Jasha, as she waited. There were men and women like wild beasts, children like fawns and kits and the cubs of foxes. The faces were blameless and intent. They were clothed in pelts of things that stank, and in their own foliage of hair. They were a primeval people. They were like the snake before it sheds its skin. She scented their archaism, yet they were *young* as the tree had been that now seemed equally old and unending and unbegun.

Going by, she felt their insubstantial substance, a wind of atoms.

The burning moon lit the hill like the morning of another world.

The crowd was all about them now, the two on the hilltop. Jasha saw that their hands parted. Anillia said, 'My best, my love. Will you trust me?'

'Yes,' he said. 'Do I remember this – if he remembers...?'

'There will be pain,' she said, 'but soon over.'

'It was all pain,' he said. 'Till now.'

Jasha saw them between the figures of the people, or through their bodies – somehow. She never lost sight of them, Mechail, Anillia. But they also changed.

Anillia's hair was loose, played over her. And she was clad in the skin of a doe, and her arms were whorled like those of women in the crowd, with the dark and red juice of berries. There were daisies in a garland on her head. She stood inside the crowd, as if she was one with them, but she shone through them.

Mechail had been drawn against the Tree's trunk. The men had roped him there, his arms uplifted, his ankles bound. One rope ran about his breast like a briar from the wood. He was naked. Jasha knew his body, though it was without any crippling mark. Like ivory now in the gilding moon, the black hair wound at the head and on the loins with shoots of ivy. His face tilted to the shoulder, as when he slept against Anillia in the hut. It was the aspect of the Christus, the arms outflung, the bound legs, the sinking head. It was the god of the wood who died and was reborn for ever and for ever.

And the Tree was a pine that was an oak; the tines of birches fanned out of it, the alders, and near its crown the sweeps of a willow, and near the roots boughs like the apple. It was all trees in one, and vines broke from its bark and entangled it; it was overgrown, and at its peak it had become a pillar of smoky fire.

The crowd murmured antique words that divulged no meaning.

The men were beating Mechail, with bunches of thorns. It made only the slightest noise, that under the chant was scarcely audible. The thorns started on the naked body, curious stitcheries. They formed and met and ran, and others came.

The ropes of briar had been weighted, and dragged on, and the man on the Tree was lifted up off his feet. He was a hanging man, no longer an image of the Christus, yet the shape of the crucifix. He was the shape of the Tree itself, upflung towards heaven.

There were no stars, the moon had devoured them.

The slender seams of blood clothed the body over. They dropped at last on the earth under the Tree.

The Tree was hung with the man, and with a shower of other

tokens which seemed to come visible only as his blood anointed its base. The Tree was as full of bones as there were flowers on the vines. The brain-cases of goats and wolves with creeper growing through their eyes, the skulls of horses polished dark, the colour of walnuts. And where the skulls were not, there were the teeth, the jointed tails and ribs of things, flagged with ribbons, and with the black bubbles of wild grapes poured from them, and honeycomb dripping like molten gold. The Tree was all trees of the forest, it held all sacrifice, life and death and life, each offering past and to come. It was time bent to a ring, turning like a wheel. And the man hung in it. His face was agonised and sleeping, dying awake. Miles above the earth he hung, and bound to the earth. His full weight was on the briary of ropes, and from the pressure of that, and from the stinging blows of the thorns, the adult phallus of his manhood had engorged. It was not innocent. It was the lust of the body under the provoking kiss of death.

One of the men was at Mechail's feet. He cut the veins of the ankles with a sharp stone.

Mechail's eyes had opened. He looked down on the man, scornfully, tenderly, half-amused. It was the face of a prince given valued service by an unknown slave.

The crowd had moved back. They had knelt down. The agony in the Tree excluded them. And as if the moon burned them up, as it had the stars of the sky, they began to go out in drifts.

Only one woman was on the hilltop under the Tree. The woman in the doeskin, who raised her arms and put back her head so her hair brushed along the ground.

To the watcher, the semantics of these things were useless. Reason was only in the power which roared like sound inside a huge bell.

The woman went to the Tree, and bending there, she kissed the bloody feet, and the blood was on her lips like paint, giving an extra feature to her face that had been only two eyes. The sharp stone was on the ground, as the skulls stayed in the tree. She took the stone in her hand, and then she set her feet into the sides of the trunk, and walked up it, like a stair, until she reached the man. She balanced before him, as though the Tree supported her and she had nothing to do with it, did not have to struggle or catch at the boughs.

'Who am I?' she said, looking into the face of a man that, dying, came alive, as once she had done. 'Do you know?'

'Anillia,' he said.

'I was Nilya, when I gave birth to you. She travailed, she held you to her dry breasts. She couldn't give you suck. She couldn't feed you. Nilya gave you nothing but life.' Stretching up, she drew the honed knife of stone steadily across each of his wrists. Fire ran in two streams, along the ivory flesh of both of them, and the skin of the animal discarded itself from her body. Above the left breast, she cut a new flower of blood. 'Now I can feed you. Drink from me.' And she drew his head against her, his mouth against the rose of the wound. As he took this draught, she held him, wrapping his torso with her arms. The stems of their bodies wove, as the vines with the tree, the skulls and bones with the grapes and blossoms and honey. He lifted his head and looked at her wonderingly. She was not his mother. Her body was not Nilya's. She was the earth, and he became the Tree which rooted in her. She had taken him in. Inside her was the core of the world, its soul, and this he touched. The branch of his loins had grown into her. Her arms were fastened about him. As they stirred together, it was the rapacious thrust of animation, the seeking swelling ferment of years amplified to swiftness, passivity now volatile.

The watcher in her bush of distance looked on at something that was a reflection in a mirror. She beheld an act that was to her, to Jasha, a commonplace, the unimportant, foolish, wanton blundering and plundering she knew, that to others was crime and dirtiness, craving, shame and imperfect satisfaction. But in the mirror of the moon, this she witnessed was not what she knew and had learned. Not copulation, not rutting, not even the making of love.

They were three, and they were one. The man, the woman, the tree of life. As the two bodies of flesh rhythmically and quickly beat together, like two white wings against the dark, the Tree encircled them, moved after and with them. They grew together, they grew into the Tree. And the Tree began to make a cry, low in the earth, miles down, where its roots padded like the paws of a giant cat, cracking the soil so the grass itself ran and the flowers there parted.

The earth rumbled, and the limbs of the Tree thrashed in a slow weaving motion, and blood and wine and honey spilled through the boughs, and there were eyes in the skulls that glowed and looked eagerly about. A wind came and tore along the sky. It seemed to blow the moon up into the forest of the Tree, another skull, another honeycomb.

And far away, in the heart of the wood, the listening watcher heard the two white creatures on the Tree crying aloud. They were arched from each other and from their joining, the two wings of a white moth now spread wide to fly. On their faces no features were left, they had become chaos. The sky burst above the moon. White lightning erupted from it and drenched the Tree in a fountain of liquid silver that, like the black wine and the red, the honey gold, sank into the roots of the tree, the caverns of the world.

Out of a strange prudence, Jasha hid her eyes. She curled over the bush and rubbed her face on the soil, to avoid and to receive everything.

No, Jasha. You must see. Look up.

The thing which communicated with her came from the ground, too. It did not employ speech, or her name. Yet she was called by name, she was exhorted.

She could not ignore it, disobey. She sat up, and looked again, and as she did so, warm driven rain began to slant across the hill, easing her perception by its interference.

The Tree had already begun to be different. Much of its bulk had evaporated. The jewellery of flowers and skulls was not to be seen. It was a slender oak mated with a pine... Two white boughs curved upward from the trunk. They were male and female, and their wet black hair flowed in the rain as if beneath the sea. Their faces had come back, not those of Anillia and Mechail, necessarily, but also male and female, and folded together, a kissing of lips, breast upon breast, the limbs mingled. Stillness now as ultimate as the motion before. The moon had moved westward, more yellow than red.

It was the rain of summer's end. It ceased, and the leaves of the tree turned brown and rose, the needles yellowed like the moon, paled as the moon did. All began to drop from the Tree. And the flesh of what clung there, changing from ivory to grey, crisping like the leaves, like sallow petals, fluttered off, feathers, butterflies. The leaves and the flesh fell. The last ghost of a horse's skull depending as if forgotten far above, shook free and tumbled, fading before it met the ground. Only the bones were left of the man and the woman and of the winter Tree.

The Tree was young and slender. It resembled a pine with many broken boughs. Among these breakages, along the lower trunk, it had a formation like that of a skeleton grown into or out of the bark.

Jasha glanced at the sky and saw the winnowing snow. The moon, like a cold opal, had gone down under the horizon. Time had replaced itself and was. The snow and the winter refurnished the shallow wood.

Jasha walked over the snow, thick as several carpets now under her cloth-bound feet.

When she got to the Tree, it was already muffled fast, transmuting into a white mast without shape or meaning.

She circled the Tree, and her footsteps sealed her presence in the snow, and then were covered up, as if she were not there.

All the Tree said to her, the timbre of its power, was *Here. Here*, the Tree said, if in command or assertion of self was not to be known. *Here*.

In the beginning. Blood made the Tree, flesh built the Tree. The Tree had entered flesh, had been flesh. Flesh became again the forest. *Here*.

Jasha struck the trunk with her open hand. It made no sound. Some snow crumbled, and then fresh snow brimmed the place over. Jasha examined her hand, fearful and curious. There was no metamorphosis. Her skin tingled a little, but that was from the cold.

Just then sorcery let her go. And staring around herself, she knew where she was. In the wilderness, in snow and night. She looked at the Tree again, the snow mast that only said *Here*, and that might only be a young pine.

It was mute, like the darkness and the whiteness all about. Jasha had nowhere in the world to go, but she turned and stepped away from the Tree as best she could. As she did so, it seemed to her she had gone like this a million times, out into deathlike emptiness and silence, through the wood.

Where the village had affixed itself, against the side of a long low rocky terrace, the winter had piled up white washing, and from the white snouted hut roofs poked with their smoke holes forcing black into a low stone sky. Every dawn after a snowfall, the villages dug out their door sills and made paths like tunnels down which they sometimes hurried. But there was not much to do abroad in winter. Only to fetch the logs or fill a bucket with icicles from the lintel. They hibernated like the polecat and the toad. But Gedno, who was a hunter, he was out at first light and dusk, to oversee his traps. He was the wolf; and he clambered up the snowbanks cursing and growling to himself, stupidly proud that he did not huddle indoors.

Above, the rock had snapped up through the afternoon snow, and the trees along its crest showed their contours, though they were white. There had been a moment of sunshine that day which might have induced the things of the wood to emerge. In an hour it would be night.

Gedno got up among the trees and went between them whistling his promise to the beasts in his traps, the starved ermines and bitter foxes. But when he came among them, they were vacant, standing ajar under branches and snow with the morsels of food in them hard as obsidian. Disgusted, he blasphemed God. He almost did not bother with the last of the traps, which he had secreted down by the stream. But then, not yearning to return into his prison, Gedno forged on through the pines and slid and scrambled to the water's edge, which was now a snarl of ice.

There had been something in the trap. A brownish matted rag that was once a rat. There was a woman lying in the snow by the trap, holding the rat to her face, sucking its blood, that ran down her chin and from her wrists and scarred the whiteness so it smouldered. Gedno stopped and stared at her. Where she had come from, God knew, and God had no care. Her hair was a fearful bush. She wore a dark sack that had wound round her, giving her the form of a serpent with breasts. What urged itself on him was that she had no proper protection from the cold, her hands bare and her bare feet sticking out from the snow, yet she was alive, glubbing the blood out of the rat that was like a shred now. And he felt hatred for her, taking from his trap. She meant nothing, only that hatred. But hatred was novel after the winter's tedium.

'You bitch,' he said, and he went and got hold of her, pulling at her. Her head swung. Her eyes were a peculiar shade of blue or grey, half shut and perhaps sightless. She did not pay any attention to him, though at the briskness of his grip she had dropped his supper. He peered at it. The meat was intact. He grabbed it into the pouch at his belt and hauled her up. 'Where are you from?' It was rare to see an unknown face, let alone a female face.

'Traveller folk, are you? Slung you out for your sluttishness maybe. I'll teach you to tamper with Gedno's traps.'

Her bare feet had gone under the surface of the snow. He looked at her hands. They should have been frostbitten, but possibly she had not come far.

'Where are your men?' he said. He checked the rock and the trees spreading over it. The sky was muffled, anyone might be lurking. 'Some trick, eh?'

The woman did not speak. She had not wiped the blood off her chin, and it set black in the cold.

Gedno's senses were keen, he inventoried the country again. No one, surely, was there.

He must accept her. That was what the priests taught, when you saw one. Venerate God and treat all men with love and reckon yourself a piece of dung.

'Bitch,' said Gedno. He began to propel her through the gathering twilight, in which she seemed moment by moment odder and more hateful. While in his pouch the drained rat was light as something invented.

When they came down the street, no one was about, and the frozen tunnellings were already rigid. Tonight the world would freeze altogether, a Hell of ice. She was lucky, this trull, he had found her.

He thrust open the hut door, and got her in.

Like the others, Gedno's hut was a room of wood, with one window covered by a shutter. It was lit by the fire, and by a wick in fat that grizzled and smelled in an old clay lamp on a shelf. So, it was a room dyed like blood after the darkness and white outside, and in it were a wife and two brats and a goat, who glared in alarm and distrust, all their eyes the same, red and round, slotted with blind reluctance.

The girl was not blind, no, for she glided her head about, looking back at them. She seemed drowsy. She did not seem to know them for a man and woman, children, even the goat she studied an instant, as if she had never seen such a thing.

'What?' said Gedno's wife.

'Be quiet,' he said.

'But what's she?'

'On the hill in the snow,' he said. 'Now sew up your lip. Put this in the stew.' And he tossed the rat to her.

She caught it, well used to such amendments to their diet, thankful to get it, not aware what was wrong with it. She put it on the wooden table and fetched a knife from the shelf by the lamp.

The children, crawling on the floor, gazed at their father, uncomprehending as always his acts. They did not like the snow-girl. They went into a corner, where they kept their toys, a stone, a patch of fur, and there they eyed her now and then, warily. The goat picked a route to her straw in the opposite corner.

The man thrust his prize up to the fire.

'Now you can skive all winter,' he said. 'She'll help with your tasks. In the spring I can trade her, sell her. She's strong.' He got a bladder of ale from behind the door.

The wife began to skin the rat.

'There's no blood,' she whined.

Gedno ignored her. He drank from the ale-bladder, and bore it over to the girl. 'Would you fancy a taste? Good ale. She gets none.'

The girl looked at him, her eyes had focused now.

'Give it to me,' said the girl.

Gedno jumped. By some obscure logic he had believed she could not speak.

'Saucy sow,' he said. He hit her without weight across the cheek.

Her head went sideways at the blow, recoiled. He thought of a snake, as before. But then she lowered her eyes. Her hair was bunched with blizzards of bits, twigs and slimes, the refuse of the forest.

His wife watched.

'Get on with your work,' he said.

He pushed the ale-bladder at the girl's mouth, which was smooth and whole above the trail of blood, unlike the mouths of harsh winter.

'Who are you, then?' he said.

'Jasha.'

'Jassi,' he said. 'Who are your kin?'

'In the snow,' she said. Her eyes were like the frozen stream. 'I forgot, there.'

'Then you're my slave. Maybe you'll remember someone who wants you. Who'll pay me for you, eh?'

She shook her head. Her terrible hair was long, though some of it seemed to have been torn out in her travels. 'No one. My da,' she said, 'he died.'

'Ah. Well. Gedno's your daddy now.'

That spring, Gedno killed his wife. It happened on the village street.

The winter had been long and unkind, but so it always was. Spurts of community violence were often the result of such closeting together, barricaded by snow, breathing the air out of each other's mouths. Yet there had been no village murder for thirteen years, which for some was a lifetime. (Murders there had been farther afield, for that was occasionally their business.)

Gedno had gained a slave during the winter. One day when there was a thaw that brought the snow crashing from the roofs and made the street into a stream, this slave was observed paddling to the well. She was unusual. Her hair was brown and separated into three wide plaits that hung to her knees, her eyes were devilish, fishlike. And her complexion baffled them also, since she was tanned, there at the hub of winter.

Gedno had stridden out of his house to see them stare.

Finally he shouted, 'Tell them who you are, girl.'

And the girl said, 'Gedno's slave.'

Then, over their ale, he described to the men his find. One or two muttered that he must share, his good chance should benefit the village. Gedno disagreed with his fists, and it was decided that she was his, and the profit he might get from her his too.

The village subsisted in the normal manner, sowing and reaping, hunting, and bartering with other hutments along the valley below the wood. But the village also had for a trade robbery of any worthwhile sort.

In the summer there were persons who travelled the wood up and down between far off, unknown cities, or there were strays, and sometimes there might be mounted a raid on an alien village beyond the valley. They took whatever they could, were not particular. Silver coins, for which seldom was there much use, nicer wine barrels, corn in sacks, a horse, a knife. Failing all else they would accept the clothes off backs, and sometimes they had had women, now long amalgamated into the female drudge hierarchy of the huts.

But it transpired Gedno's wife did not like the slave he had found. She resented the slave. It was not, of course in her contract to resent anything, and when the green tendrils began to worm out of the slush and unwary birds sat in the trees by the well for handy stoning, she came out on the street in her apron, crying and squalling. Gedno had been to the slaughtering of a pig. He was splashed with blood and full of ale. He walked from the butchering hut and positioned himself, watching her. But she only raised her voice. 'You plug her!' cried Gedno's wife.

'Well? She's the slave, isn't she?'

'In front of your sons, in the bed...'

'Swallow your row. Or do I make you?'

Then she howled.

Gedno lumbered over the street and landed a blow on her ear. He noticed that at the impact her eyes comically crossed, and this made him giggle. Some of the other men had come out to see. They all saw Gedno's wife thump into the mud and lie there. After a minute he kicked her, to remind her to get up. But she would not, and when he lifted her head by the hair, her eyes slipped over as if she were interested in the ground. She made a snoring noise and matter came out of her nose. That was all she would do, and soon enough Gedno was aware his aggravation with her was wasted.

The other men were uneasy at first. One even remonstrated, but Gedno said, 'She was a nag.' They could hardly deny it, they had seen.

After this, the slave, Jassi, tended Gedno and his two boys, and the goat.

His sons were partly afraid of Jassi, and they blamed her for the loss of their mother. They called her Snake. They devised silly, nasty pitfalls for her, putting grit in the curds, letting the fire go out, spilling the water she fetched. The elder boy crept up to her as she stirred Gedno's soup. 'Want you go.' And when Jassi did not answer – she never spoke to them – 'Make you die.' When this was said, Jassi turned her evil eyes on him. He shrank and shrivelled in her gaze. Later, he wrenched at her viciously, and coming around, she struck him with the big spoon she had been working in the soup. 'Tell da,' he said. 'He beat you.' But Jassi said nothing, and neither did the child. Gedno was liable to lash out at them all. The slave had not been misled into thinking she was the only victim. Besides, she warmed the man's bed – the mound of grasses against the wall where the goat was not allowed. Gedno had got up on her and grunted throughout the winter, initially shoving her to the bed from her allotted place by the hearth. (Those times the wife had lain beside them, pushed against the wall of the house. As well she was gone. It gave him more room.)

As the summer came, the village went about its habits. The fields were ploughed, and the women scattered the seed. The goats went to graze. The men, most of them, took up their thieving. Whole days and nights they were gone. (The slave lay on the bed of grass and the children said banes at her until they slept – these did not take, she was hale and tough.) When the men came back they feasted on the best the village had, and drank. Gedno would come into his house. He would drop on Jassi like a collapsing sodden hog: often he could not finish.

The slave's brown skin faded to cream, contrastingly as the summer heightened and the village's arms and faces burned.

A man said to Gedno, 'You should watch her. Something's bad there.'

'Want her?' said Gedno. 'You must want.'

He did not sell her, barter her, slough her.

By the time the summer waned and the dark night of winter threatened them again, some of them spoke of her as Gedno's wife, it was a politeness. They had nothing to do with her. Nor she with them.

During the second winter, she dreamed of the Tree.

It was neither as she had beheld it in reality, or in the vision, the memory or prophecy of what it symbolised. In the dream it was taller and stronger, it had more boughs, and perhaps it had already an immature architecture of several trees, the pine, the oak, the cedar. It was cased in snow, and between the branches long strands of luminous ice portrayed the true formation of the Tree, or dissembled.

Nothing moved. No wind blew. A zircon sun smelted the sky, and did not rise or sink.

Around the Tree, twining it, was a dragon, scale-made of the ice, its crystals, scintillant, and motionless like the rest. The long head lay along an upper limb. It was remarkably distinct, could be mistaken for nothing else. The Serpent. In its eyes, a faint sourceless glimmer. It held the Tree, guarding it or bracing it, or containing it, what it was to become.

Jasha woke from this dream, and thought the soldier, Evra Livdis, was lying on her, but it was this other one, this Gedno. She submitted, guiding his hands when he tumbled. The dream was like music. (A woman had sung, in a market, under a window.) As the man rammed her body, Jasha floated on the plank of the dream. The two children no longer watched and abhorred. They had given up. Just as Jasha had always known, acceptance was everything, it meant survival. When Gedno slumped, before his weight had even left her, she returned into dreamless oblivion. Her days were busy. She required her sleep.

For ten years, Jasha existed in Gedno's robber village. It was enough like an earlier existence, the years in the village to which Carg Vrost had dispatched her. She came to such a life now with foreknowledge, yet even that did not make it difficult to bear, for Jasha. What else could there be?

That she had lived through her lost wandering in the snow wood, until the moment of discovering the trap with the dead rodent in it, still warm and lush with blood, when she had bitten and drunk, not thinking, those events had never been examined, and the ten years of slavery were not. To the passage of time she was mostly immune, going only from day to day. She was not demeaned, nor demoralised. Her morality was not like that.

Nor was she disconcerted by the signatures of time. She noted the ageing of everything, the crankiness of the huts, the height and girth of trees, how animals gave birth and thinned and died, how the sons of Gedno imperceptibly reformed into cloddish men of about sixteen. For all her treatment, under which the other women bowed and limped and were gnawed away, grey-headed, creased like autumn leaves, Jasha grew no less. She did not change. As for ageing in herself, who expects that? Old age, even when anticipated, surprises, seems unrelated, stuck on or in, like pins. Jasha did not age.

The village overlooked it too. They had always reckoned her peculiar, and to stay peculiar was in a way her conformity. There was some white in her hair, where Gedno had sometimes bashed her across the temples – they accepted that as a substitute.

The younger son evinced signals of preparing to rape Jasha, and for this, thoughtlessly, she readied herself. The elder threw his shoes at her but taking care to miss.

Gedno was large and beer-soaked, and left his hunter's work to his heirs, although they all went raiding and robbing. Some nights she was alone.

She would lie on her back and watch the firelight on the tilted hut roof.

All she had nostalgia for was the sea. The sea had been the forest, yet so unlike. She wondered where it was, for none of them spoke of it, though once, twice, she had heard a rumour of the building, the Christerium, awkward hissings of corruption and the punishment of those who preyed on ordinary men, fat priests, sorcery going under the auspice of knightly ritual. But the phraseology they employed, even in rumour, was obstructive. They knew virtually nothing, and invented illogically. And Jasha inclined not to have any attention for it, although sometimes she found she had listened closely, as if she meant to bear the tale away for the man Mechail, or her mother, the woman Nilya. But they were dead. They were not hers.

The sea lived. She visualised it. There was a window in a dream from which she saw it come and go, and the dawn meadowed on the water and the black blooms of night.

The morning the priest came into the village, most of the men were heavily asleep. They had been jaunting in the wood and met a wagon taking provisions somewhere; all these arrived at the village. Then there had been a massive junketing. Even some of the women got drunk. Of all things that might follow, an itinerant priest, bearing his beads, and a few pages of the Book, footsore and hopeful of hospitality, was the last thing they had looked for.

Jasha was at the well. The priest came down the track that in summer was baked out plainly as a city road. He nodded to Jasha a big brindled head. 'Give me some water, girl.' So Jasha took him the pot with the water, and he drank straight from it, from its cracked rim, where all their lips had been. Then he glanced Jasha over. And something struck her. In the second year, she had been given the dead wife's clothes, which did not fit yet abstractedly grew to her shape. Under the grass bed lay the priestly habit in which she had journeyed. How if she had been wearing that? 'Where's your husband?' said the priest to Jasha, irked at the sparseness of his welcome. 'Where are the women?'

'Asleep,' she said. And then, 'Do you come from the Christerium?'

Perhaps it was only that the decade of interval, offering nothing, had left her concentration in the past, where the Christerium still reared, important and indelible. Whatever the immediate reason, the priest flinched away and marked himself over in a pushing manner, with the cross of the Christus.

'What can you know of that? Hold your tongue, girl.' Jasha said no more. The priest glared at her and said, 'Don't you know better than to jabber of vice? That place – full of wicked men who worked against the Lord God, using Father Church as their shield – dealt with, shovelled in the ground, and may the Devil have them.' Then, 'Take me to your house.'

'Not mine,' said Jasha, with some fastidiousness. 'I'm Gedno's slave.'

'Slave? What business has this peasant with slaves? What goes on here? Asleep at noon – the Evil One's been busy.'

And then again, as they walked towards Gedno's hut, he said, 'Demons and vampires nest in the ruins. Unsafe when the wholesome sun is down.' And he hit her in the back. 'What can he be thinking of, your master, letting you hear of it?'

Jasha indicated the hut door, which in summer stood wide, emitting Gedno's guttural drunkard's snores, and those of the younger son – the elder was courting a girl and abed elsewhere in a haystack.

'Is it a pigsty?' shouted the priest. He fetched the table leg a brawny kick. 'Up! Sloth's a sin. Yes, a sin. Woe betide the fool who sleeps, for how shall the trumpet wake him on the Final Day?'

Gedno and his younger son opened their eyes. They had thick heads, and Gedno a thick gut, but their ears performed very well.

'What's this?' said Gedno. 'Who dares to come in and kick my table?'

He and his son sat up, each on his wall, and eyed the priest cautiously, unlovingly.

'I am God's,' said the priest. 'If he prompts me to kick, I kick.'

'Maybe,' said Gedno, 'the Devil will prompt me to kick back.'

The priest's face flamed as Gedno's did in drink. 'On your feet, you swine. Up! Up! Do you see me, who I am? I stand for my Lord, the Christus. Sinners all. I shall have labours here.'

He was intrepid, belligerent, and these qualities they unwittingly respected. They got to their feet and presently came to breathe their beer-stinking kisses on his crucifix.

As he had said, he had labours there. He dug out the erring flock from their stupor and brought them to the trees by the well. Here he preached Damnation to them and they, loathing and writhing, sick and drunk, must stay to heed, for such was the might of what he was sprung from, the Church Paternal, of which this roving bully in filthy darned robe, filth ingrained in his neck and fingers, warts on his cheeks, yet remained a representative. He bore upon him, and he knew it well, the seal of Heaven. What might he not give – all the horror of Hell, the limbo of spiritual exile, misery everlasting. And if they did not entirely believe in him, or in his waxen god (so like the dolls the women put in the trees at holy days and harvest), they could not bring themselves to risk it.

She heard them mutter how they would like to spit him, throw him down a hole. She watched as they kneeled and reverberated their confessions. And when she, with the other women, was sent flying for ale and breads, dishes of butter, a cold roast starling, apples, Gedno caught her arm. 'Hide the loot, do you hear?' She did not ask where. 'In the cupboard,' he groaned, 'back of the bed...' And in the hut she stowed the pair of lumpy bundles, which the priest had not seen, or wanted to see. For it must be true, also, he would have a code whereby to deal with villages of this sort.

After he had eaten and drunk, the priest visited each hut. Here he saw nothing ethically amiss, but he ranted, in his dirt, about floors unswept, the pots unscoured.

'Here's a slave,' he said, daggering his thumb at Jasha, 'keeps better house.'

He returned to Gedno's mansion at evening.

And there Gedno sat faultlessly with his two sons at the fire, where the supper kettle bubbled. And Jasha was tying up the two latest goats that she had brought in from pasture.

'What are you doing, owning a woman?'

'She's my wife,' said Gedno.

The priest lifted his brows. 'She said she was your slave.'

'Oh, once, godbrother. But then I saw fit to wed her.'

'Under some tree. Do you want the service now?'

Gedno scowled.

Jasha turned from the goats. 'No,' she said.

Gedno rolled about with an oath. It took the elder son to laugh. The priest mashed his brows down. 'Are you a pagan, girl? Or what are you?'

Jasha, called Jassi, stood in Gedno's hut, in her dead woman's apron, her three long brown plaits, her green eyes that measured the floor. 'I won't marry him,' she said. 'He's nothing to me. Tell him to let me go.'

'How did he come by you?'

'I found the bitch,' cried Gedno. 'I took her in from the snow. She'd have died if not.'

The priest, who had made them dance to God's tune, would not force the music for worldly matters. Man had governance over woman.

'You owe this man your life, and gratitude,' he said to Jasha. 'What are you, a shrew?'

The elder son said with a flourish, spitting in the fire, 'She's a fey from the wood. You should burn her, godbrother.'

'And you swill out your mouth with brine and vinegar,' said the priest. 'You must learn to keep quiet where you know nothing.' Then he beckoned Jasha. She crossed the room skirting Gedno, who fumed like the fire. 'What do you say to it?' he said.

'I say,' said Jasha, 'I'll turn into a white hare at moonrise and get up into the forest.'

The priest struck her in the face.

'You've no religion. I can't save you.' He stared at her weird eyes, but they looked away over his shoulder. 'Like Eve, you're for the land below. He's earned you.'

And he went out and left them. They heard his coarse voice speaking aloud a prayer and he passed his beads through his grimy hands, not looking back, shaking the dust off his heart upon them all.

There passed a piece of time then, in the hut, without much movement, noiseless. Outside sounds came from the other huts, the dusk filmed the sky and the valley. Where the priest had gone (boldly, unwisely, despite his earlier tirade, as if night were only another kind of day), the spirits of darkness gathered.

After the silence, the elder son spoke first.

'What will you do, eh, Da? What good is she, the sow? She's barren too. Beat the hide off her. I would if she were mine.'

'She isn't yours,' said Gedno. His voice was deep down in his belly with the soured ale. 'Get out, the two of you, take yourselves off.'

They got up, and as the elder one went by Jasha, he tweaked her plaits and grinned.

'Shut my door,' said Gedno, 'you rotten bloody bitch.'

Jasha, his slave Jassi, shut the door.

Jasha turned by herself, and then Jasha, and more than Jasha, stood looking at him, but he did not see, and maybe as yet she did not completely know it, either.

'What do I do to you,' said Gedno, 'to teach you manners? A white hare, is it? You'll be a skinned hare when I've done with you.'

He started to hoist himself, and stopped.

His slave was coming forward from the door, out of the shadow, and the fire shone on her lizard's face, attentive and serene, and her tongue flickered between her parted lips; she held her right hand towards him. In the unnatural light, it might have been made of smooth-planed wood. A wooden hand that could not move its fingers yet was alive with purpose.

Gedno reached and seized the hand, to check it, and he cried out wildly. For the hand was icy or scalding, it scorched him.

'Look in the cookpot,' said Jasha. Her voice was only cool and mild. Her eyes were black in thin rings of silver. Her tongue darted. 'Look in there, Gedno.'

Gedno tried to struggle, to get up and grasp her, but instead he lowered himself and hung over the kettle, so the steam of the vegetables seared his cheeks.

'What do you see?' asked Jasha.

'Bitch,' said Gedno. And then foolishly, 'Let go.' Through the steam he saw in the soup a black snake that swam. As it squirmed through its bath, its scales glinted and pulsed. He was afraid. His eyes had boiled dry and he longed to close them.

'Gedno,' said Jasha, 'put your head into the pot.'

Outside, it was the younger son who had idled near his father's house. His sexual intriguement with Jasha had been enhanced by notions of violence done her. Perhaps he wanted to hear her scream. Instead he suddenly made out a crazy muffled howling and rattling, the crashing of something metallic. It seemed his father was thrashing the slave with the food kettle, moaning and choking as he did so. While she, oddly, did not even squeak. Then the man's vocality ceased, there were a few thumps, a nothingness.

The younger son grimaced at the darkness. He tried to make it join him in complicity. He wished his brother was there, had not slunk off to his slut again.

In a short while the younger son swaggered to the door. 'Da? What are you at?' And, having no answer, 'I'll come in now. Will you let me? Yes?'

When he came in through the door, the hut was very dark, for mostly the fire had gone out. Something had fallen or spilled and put it out – there was an odour of boiling, wrong and unpleasant, and of charred wet cloth. Gedno's younger son went forward, and tripped over his father's legs, which were sticking out in the mode they had when he collapsed drunk on the bed. They were not so unusual, these drunken legs, but his father's torso in the fire was what the son contacted next, and his father's shoulders that ended at the rim of the soup kettle, where flooded squashed vegetables, peeled ribbons of skin, drowned hair.

The boy screamed as he had thought Jassi would. And the scream, raising his head, let him see someone standing across the fireplace. This someone was not Jassi. It was a man, surely. Tall and dangerous.

One of the goats bleated a gentle inquiry.

'There, now,' said Jassi kindly, to the goat.

'You,' said Gedno's younger son. 'What have you been doing?'

He pulled himself up from his father's corpse and went over the burnt tunic and splashed wet flesh and the sticks and soup to take Jassi by the throat.

Jassi slewed away. Her hard left hand blazed into his jaw, and as he staggered, she stabbed him in the heart, exactly, with the skinning knife from the shelf. They were male blows, set with the precision of one who had been trained to fight, he almost realised as he died.

'What now?' said Jasha's cool Anillia voice. She watched through the dark a moment Gedno and his youngest son lying on the fire which they had, between them, totally suppressed. It was with a quirky lightness that she discarded them, and all of this, this hutment, this life, the ten years. Need she have endured even one of them? Could she not, long since, have released herself? But it was as if the seed she had taken with her from their tree had asked her latency, the opaque soil wherein to germinate. She was with child of them. They had not possessed her. It was she who had possessed them.

She remained on her feet in the dark by the corpses, not noticing especially, looking in at what she now was.

She was the fox that had received the dual soul of a man and a woman. She had always understood how to run upon four feet, now also she might walk on two. She might bite and bark, she might speak and sing.

It was magic and a mystery. It was the ultimate passage of a psychic atom, the ribs of her makers, and she had fastened herself about it and closed it over with her body and her mind.

If she glimpsed now she had ever been incomplete, spare, it was for the reason she might be filled.

They had gone back into the wood. But the library of their brains, their mortal dreams, were hers. She was what they had been, but more.

Mechail, Anillia. And beyond them, the other, the Angel, the root and the destroyer, she beheld him, too.

Jasha stretched herself, waking from her ten-year sleep.

Going to the bed, she took out the tattered priest's habit Mechail had given her. She put off her other borrowings and inserted herself into the pelt of God. This amused her, and phrases of Mechail's sarcasm, Anillia's contempt, skimmed her awareness.

She knew where she would go. She knew what she wanted. She was lawless as they had not been, no, not even Anjelen. Sing and speak and bite.

As soon as she was ready, she opened the hut door and stepped out.

The elder brother and a brace of his cronies were on the street, and in the other doorways lights glowed. A tableau of normalcy and so of threat.

'Who's there?' said the elder brother.

They stared, the four or five robber men, and saw a priest as unlike the visitor of the morning as was imaginable.

Despite towering, immutable evidence to the contrary, they began to recognise Jassi, the slave Gedno had been beating – for they had heard a scream.

'What are you at now? Get in, you, and see to supper.'

'Supper's seen to,' said Jasha. She smiled.

She started to walk right by them. They gawped and did nothing. 'Get hold of her,' snapped the elder son, unknowingly sole lord of the hut and the two goats.

'But – it's a priest – I can't go laying my hands on a...'

'It's the slave, Christus send you to fry.'

One of them grabbed Jasha.

She turned her head and spat directly at his eyes. The man floundered back cursing, 'Poisoned me – blinded me...'

It took Gedno's elder, now only, son to rush at Jasha, grip her arms. In the chequered light of the neighbouring doorways, at which here and there a man or two had appeared, Jasha was shown to her attacker. Her gaze was grey like steel. It was black, ink on adamant. And it was green like the sea, of which he had been told by his mother at the dawn of his days, before the mould of slobbishness and witless cruelty had clamped him in its vice.

'A white hare,' said Jasha. 'Look there. It's away.'

And he looked and saw, and afterwards two of the others also claimed they did, a white slight springing thing sewing up the street and off over the slope towards the rock and the forest.

He must have released what he held. They said Jassi vanished. Vanished from their sight into the air and the darkness. And that by then was possible, for she had now all the lessons, the making and dispersal of flesh streamered out by will from the soul, the deception of enemies, the grandeur and inconsequence of the magician melded with the fox.

Chapter Four

Three of them went with him. It was as if he had them on a leash. But they stared. The one who called himself Eujasius, the Angel of the Bread of the Body of the Redeemer, he must feel that rheumy concentration, just as he heard their desiccated bones crackle on every step, at every turning. They had met him in an alley of the Christerium, where the dwarf conducted him. Then the dwarf retreated somewhere. Eujasius and the three priests paced on, one leading but always looking back, the others behind.

The chamber where they arrived burrowed in a jumbled block of leaning cells, close under the tower of the church.

'You see that? You will wash yourself.'

There was tub with hot water. (Where from? Their wells were sewers, their cistern a swamp. Could it be they took water from the women's well of the Doma?)

Eujasius, who had bathed in the cold sea, offered no discouraging remark. He said, 'Go out, then.'

'You must wash, you must be clean.'

'Why?' asked Eujasius, innocently.

The priests exchanged their gazes. The one called Ragis said, fussily, 'To be included in our ceremony. For the honour of God.'

They withdrew, and left Eujasius to the bath.

He shut the door to the cell and hung the habit up over it. Eujasius dipped into the bath, comparing its curdled warmth to the freeze and play of the ocean. They had left him another robe to put on. It was white, or once it had been.

When the bath was over, and Eujasius dressed in this garment, he opened the door again. The unlit corridor ran, unoccupied, to the court outside, only the candle they had left in the cell dripping and flicking at it. Across the corridor's end, over the arch of more transparent black that was night sky, night walls, something went. It was low, a skinny humped back, an eared head hanging. Eujasius caught the whiff of its smell of redness, darkness, and the milky wink of its eyes.

Then, disembodied, the one called Ragis quavered: 'Are you there? Are you ready?'

Eujasius came along the corridor with the candle and met Ragis in the yard. Shadows crouched, breathing. Over stonework and mounds of ivy, shaggy like the beast which had gone by, the seaward tower flew towards Heaven. By night, the broken top was lost in stars. A bell rang unevenly, with a dolorous, halting clank.

'What's that?' said Eujasius.

'The summons.'

'To what?'

'To the feet of God.'

'Wolves,' said Eujasius, 'pad about your ruin.'

'Oh yes,' said Ragis. 'Yes.'

'Mangey wolves, with invalids' eyes. Is that all that's left to you?'

Ragis averted himself, his whole body. He flapped Eujasius on. The other two were no longer in attendance. All the shadows swayed.

They negotiated the yard, a shattered area, squeezed through a compressed tunnel wolf-haired with creeper, smelling of wolf. They came out on the paved court where the slabs had lifted out like graves. There was light. A torch exploded its fire over the fantastic ivy doorway, ripped at the slivers of tinted glass above, the untidy nests of birds. Some gulls had been displaced by the bell. They yawed about the tower, and they too caught the torch flame under their wings, and were bits of fire, demons...

There were wolves in the church, all over the Christerium. Under the faltering of the bell, the screek of the gulls, their shufflings, their panting, ebbed and flowed. A phantom slanted up a roof, among the twisted weathervanes, another flashed between two windows its pupils, the razor leanness of its back. In the tower they crustily inhaled. They were old, stinking, loping on taut chalky legs, cracked claws fumbling. But he let them run, as always. It was their reward, their proof. That Ragis had not been granted the privilege might be the sign of his master's displeasure, or an oversight. There would be oversights, now.

'Walk along by the wall. There's a little door left ajar. Go on, and stay yourself there. You must remain, you understand?' Ragis was blossoming strangely on excitement. He no longer distrusted Eujasius or doubted Eujasius must be part of what was to come.

'Very well.'

'There'll be lights. You'll see. And the Magister will be with us. You must keep still. Whatever you witness or hear. Until he calls you.'

Eujasius said, 'How many have you brought here, to your God-hovel, for Anjelen?'

'Oh, very many,' said Ragis. He was not thinking or reasoning. He craned forward, at the same moment pushing Eujasius away with one hand towards the wall.

Eujasius moved off along the tower and found the door amid the litter piled against its base. Inside was pitch darkness, but he smelled the Christerium church, what it was, what it had been. Laid finely on the musty excrement of gulls, the rot of timber, damp stones, weather, were the hues of incense bright as dust from the stars. Eujasius waited, and nocturnal vision was bestowed on him, on his feline female eyes, rendering up for him his own boy-girl body in its sheath of lacking white, the male body the priests had given him, that even Anjelen had given him with the name *Mechail*. Eujasius had cut his hair with a knife in the mountains, before the Travellers met him. Now, in the dark, Eujasius began to let his hair grow. He guided it under the neck of the robe, suggested it hid there, as it went on, trickling down his back, the male back the priests had given. Striped Anillia hair. *Anillia*, Anjelen might have said, sensing this latest nuance.

Did Anjelen perceive? What did he learn? Nothing. *I read him*, thought Eujasius, Angel of Bread, *what he is*. It was a void. Mindless. Only the craving shone in it, like the ruby in the lacquer cross. And that drew near, floating down through the layers of the building.

The candles lit in the church. The magician's alchemy brushed them into being with the beauty of a glamour. But Eujasius, who knew, knew this was only the glamour of practice, almost an aberration. Anjelen was what had revealed itself in the dining hall. *That.*

Nevertheless, the church tower had changed, now it had been entered into the light.

The floor had lustre under its dullness, water under scum. The adornments of the gulls were a mosaic, like secret forms that might be solved. The great altar was draped, and the faded material, like a flower, shone white from within. But there was no gold or gems on it, whose riches were gone, like the great crucifix, and magic did not fake them. Instead there stood now on the altar top a silver cup in a garland of ivy.

Then the brethren came, the Knights of God.

There were thirty of them. They were clad in mail, helmed, with visors lowered. The cobwebs of cloaks trailed behind them, and torn, yellowed plumes. They walked with the firm sure tread of ghosts, forgetting they were dead. The mail was blistered, it was rusty, in spots it had dropped away. And it hung on them, too large for their shrunken frames. Yet they fired like fevers. As they creaked forward, to make a circle under the altar, the helms gave to their faces a fearsomely unsuitable and horrific arrogance. They were the cadavers at the feast, crying *Behold our splendour* while the worms gnawed in their bellies.

Outside the light, their creation, Eujasius, regarded them. Others there had been, bemused, terrified, but Eujasius watched, thinking of Anjelen and his black-haired warriors, their swords rainbowed from the windows, the loaves of bread prancing from the basket. A gull shrieked in derision high above.

And Anjelen was on the stair above the altar, descending, as once before, in the rainbow time.

He was not dressed as a Knight. He had on his body, which did not physically alter, the same black habit he had worn in the refectory.

Eujasius nodded. The memory of Mechail provided the thought, *He doesn't bother with it any longer. The ritual, its trappings, bore him. He only wants his drink. But they cherish all he puts aside, the old wolves. What can he give them? What will he spare them from his high table?*

Anjelen spoke.

'We are here for our faith.'

They lifted their heads, every one of them, and one third of each face was tarnished metal, and the rest the triumph of age, motivated by avidity. They hungered. Their old lips and parchment-covered jaws begged. They were dogs of famine.

Anjelen had reached the altar. 'The wine,' he said.

There was no music in his voice. It was the voice of a man. He did not exert himself.

And the withered flowerheads of his greed hung around the centre of his indifference.

And around that, the ruin.

Anjelen's own brain supplied for the brain of Eujasius, like a book, the illusions and wizardry of all times past. There had been forests woven with serpents, budded with beasts. Roses grew from the broken vase of blood. There the melody was, the wings, the power, and the glory. But there was only this, now. And Anjelen turned his head, looking at the gloom beyond the candlelight, where Eujasius stood waiting.

With no particular elegance, in fact quickly, peremptorily, Anjelen beckoned.

And like all the others of the past, as if afraid, mesmerised, staring only into the eyes of Anjelen that were the eyes of a man, Eujasius moved towards the circle under the altar.

The circle parted, to let him go through.

Anjelen intoned swiftly, 'They hung Him on a tree. In the sight of the world. Do this, He said.'

Eujasius had reached Anjelen. He saw that Anjelen was pulling from a wristlet in his sleeve a sharp pale knife.

Eujasius put back his head and looked up into the face of Anjelen. He looked with Anillia's look, and Mechail's. And even that, Anjelen could not discern as he bent forward to force and to have. He had taken this one for Mechail even, and now forgot all that, like all the forgetting. For he was in the summer drought of thirst.

'Drink,' said Eujasius, 'for here is the wine.'

His hand darted out and ripped the knife from Anjelen's fingers.

He leapt away, blithely, and jumped up on the altar, where he struck aside the cup with his foot. It swirled along the cloth in a blur of lights and poured to the floor with a kitchen sound of pots and pans. Eujasius snatched up the ivy garland. He swung it upon his head.

The priestly Knights groped after him with their eyes and hands, not moving otherwise. And Anjelen was still, all but his mouth, where the lips contorted, lengthened, strove, without opening.

'I'm the wine,' said Eujasius. He laughed out loud.

With the knife of the sacrifice he tore down the robe they had given him, all the way from neck to thigh, and shrugged it off. And there he was, not in the body they had given him before the robe, but in the body of a woman. Jasha's body. Slim and apple-breasted, the hips slenderly rounded, the groin a bird-brown silk, weaponless and clandestine. Her hair rushed free, the wave of it, down to her ankles, carnival striped. Her eyes were the green grapes that made the white wine, having no savour of blood.

'Eujasius,' she said, 'or Eujasia.'

She stepped about the altar, parading herself.

The old Knights began to caw and wail. They smothered up their visored eyes. They turned; they went to their crunching knees. They prayed.

'Woman's blood,' said Jasha. '*Forbidden.*'

Mounted on the altar, she glanced sidelong at the fallen angel, to see what he would do.

He was a graven image. Even his mouth had ceased to work.

'I told you,' she said. 'Whatever you want, I'll take it from you. You shan't have it. I mock your bloody god,' she said.

Anjelen moved away from the altar. He went to one of the old Knights. It was Ragis, moaning and beating at his breast. Anjelen got hold of him, raised him like a bundle of branches. Ragis glared into the mask of his lord, and like a wolf Ragis howled, between terror and exaltation. Anjelen, no longer having the knife, sank his fingers into the priest's throat, where the mail had given way, and tore it out, crudely, to its strings and cords, as if clawing through to find the source of water. The blood vomited up in a scarlet veil that flared across the pool of the light and tossed on the faded wall a shower of colour.

Anjelen was drinking. In the stone clearing, by night, a wolf on its hind limbs and clad in black, sucking out the life of an ancient child.

And when he let go of Ragis – no longer Ragis, a few remnants of iron, cloth and skin – there came another, pawing at him. Another of the priest Knights had crawled to Anjelen, pleading.

Now Anjelen made a noise. It was the wolf's growl. And hauling up this other one, he bit into the throat, spitting and tearing, while the blood sprayed, glittering through the light, gilding, moistening, making flowers.

The rest of them began to limp towards him, holding up their old men's hands. They wanted. He gave. What other terminus for their service...? wWhere else could they go to, whom else could they seek? Heaven and Hell were here. They stretched their throats like herons for his talons and his fangs.

Everywhere there was blood. The marvellous red of it was like the panoply of former days. On the altar the drape had a crimson device. How white the drapery looked now beneath this red.

When he was done with them, he threw them aside, the bodies. Their fragile bones sometimes broke at the meeting with the tiles, and so everything was contorted.

There was the smell of salt over the incense. The sea was high, and a wind blew against the Christerium. The waves rushed like the blood, and all sounds were lost in the ocean as one year the tower itself might be, drawn under for ever.

Jasha was sitting on the altar. A jewel of blood starred her left breast, some others were on her arms and feet. The ritual was finished, and the order with it. Thirty carcasses were on the floor. The gulls did not cry. Anjelen lay at the limit of the light, with the last of his priesthood crushed under him. And then Anjelen separated from the flaccid lolling thing, he too lolled back and the dark embraced him.

Jasha slipped off the altar. Naked but for her gown of hair, she walked between these drained wine-skins, picking daintily over the floor, until she came to Anjelen where he lay on his back.

He was bloody. More than this. He was bloated, swollen. His very skin looked red, as if it must crack on redness, although it was white in the dark, and his half shut eyes bulged, sightlessly. His mouth, under the mess of his debauch, was couth and firm. It was not thirsty anymore.

Jasha lowered herself to the ground. She laid aside the silver knife, which she had kept, and put out her hands, well-versed, and neat in what she did. Sliding away the habit of the priest, she found the core of the body which, after all, might only have been made of wood. But what was there was flesh, Jun's flesh. In the black male hair, the snake of Eden was hard, and lifted up to its own instinctive eyeless life by the tumult of the engorging blood. To Jasha, this was no different to the penis of any man. Jasha knew quite well what to do with it. She bowed over him, the Angel of Death, and put her woods girl's mouth around him.

Anjelen did, could do, nothing. The Tree had grown into his brain. The crystal was closed by leaves. And his belly was full of the Wine of the Sacrifice. His purpose was ended. Anillia... Mechail... Jasha had sprung from him, three in one. No matter humanity's false notions of him, he had become himself his grave.

But Jasha's mouth went on about its business, the satin goad of her tongue. She licked and lipped at the final mortal part, and it answered.

A shudder spasmed through the bloated felled thing beneath her, and into her throat washed out the other drink of life, its salt, the sea of beginnings.

A wave broke against the glassless window. It was a compounded invisibleness that crashed over and sang on the tower. The gulls rose like a second spume. Here was the future, the drinking of the land by the sea, of the world by God.

Jasha kneeled above the angel.

'And that too I took,' she said. *'Your chastity.'*

But his eyes were only slits of white, no black in them. As Anillia and Mechail had gifted her through the Tree in the snow, so from this she had swallowed up the fountainhead.

He and she were wetted by the sea wave. It had cleaned the blood on the walls and moved the knife a short distance from her hand. Jasha reclaimed it. Without a word or cry, flinging up her arm, she plunged the blade into the gut of Anjelen, forced and drew back. His body gaped, a velvet chasm of blood, and there the rib bones were, like the spine of a large fish. Jasha saw, in the little candlelight the wave had not drowned, that every rib was encircled, ridged and ringed. She put in her hands, concisely, and snapped out one of them, fashioned like carved white jet, a wonder. She extracted from him the rib; she held the rib. Then with both hands she hammered it home into his heart.

There was the faint ticking of waters on the walls. Later the skipping of mice and swoop of gulls. Nothing else. Huge silences built from the floor.

On Anjelen's body the gulls did not squander their efforts. He was obdurate, and cold. In the darkness, and the other occult dark which was his own, he had the shape of a narrow tomb, and out of this the ringed rib protruded like a sword. He did not bleed. His blood had stayed in him, seeming to lapidify. Death, for what he was, must be solely passage. He must transmute, as any god in any story. In the night, before all candles were extinguished, it seemed that Anjelen was changing into stone. But who was left to see?

And in the autumn dawn where the green ocean met the wetly flaming sun, Jasha walked along the beach under the rock.

She was like a sea thing, maned with weed. Her feet were not cut by the sharp defences of the sand. She watched the water, remembering the fire which had closed over her head, cooked her, eaten her hair, let her go. The fire had been hot to freezing. How icy was the sea.

Behind her, the ruin had become the rock. The tower was an eccentric fretted cliff. The blackness of the sand was only the soot of shelled creatures which had died there.

Jasha thought of a myth of the coast which might come to be. A village by the water's edge, constructed of wrecked ships: the fisherman returning with his tale; how squinting over from his boat, he saw into the ocean, and a woman was there under the sea, a woman in a smoke of hair, walking in a forest with leaves of marble and coal. One day she must rise from the depths, with the winged wave at her back. Angel of Storms.

Jasha entered the water. It was as cold as it had been when she had bathed there. To the eye it was a surging floor, but the way led down. Jasha followed the way. The cold shocked at her groin, her waist, her breasts, her hair spread out on the tide. Was the forest so green? The cold of the water grew slowly warm.

The Tree had made men. They made themselves over into magicians, or went to ground, became the Tree again. But she was a rogue sapling. The mutant plant.

She lowered her head and was gone under the surface and the sunlight, into the water greener than the wood, warmer than the fire.

echailus

Book Five

Chapter One

Because she had been flung from a great height, Veksa, the miller's daughter, had remained through her accruing years an object of marvel. She was a cipher both for the improbable favour of fortune, and the smiting of fate. Her resolute and double-jointed cunning had fastened on this. Without knowing exactly what she did, she had dramatised herself, to make herself more into the proper image. Her wheaten hair went stark white yet kept its abundance. Her body, which would have run to fat in the comfort of her Vre's Tower at Korhlen, restrained on the leaner diet of the village, had an unsightly magnificence, tempting still to some, repugnant to others. Though almost fifty years of age, she had kept her teeth; her eyesight and hearing were keen. Her skill with herbs was respected and occasionally feared. Women who had insulted her at first, learned to keep to their own counsel (how she doctored their stomachs they were never sure, maybe their own nervousness saw to it – only when they had begged her forgiveness, when she had pardoned them, did the sickness and cramps dispel). For her own father, he did not much care about Veksa's crash. She had managed to bring away with her from Korhlen all her own and certain extra valuables, which amply repaid anything the dad might reckon he donated at her marriage. They had heard the Vre died four months after Veksa was cast off. That was God's judgement on him, they said in the village, loudly, so Veksa might catch the words. Now, she kept house for her father, but then the old man had a pair of servant girls, she need lift no more than a finger or two, and give her orders in the voice of one accustomed to obedience.

Once a year, in the spring, Veksa would go mad for three or four days and nights. These insanities surrounded the anniversary of her son's death. He had been a wonderful man, her boy Krau, blond, brawny and handsome. The Vre's elder son, a weakling and cripple, naturally envious, had plotted to harm Krau, until Krau had had to kill the monster to preserve himself. Thereafter Kolris Vre

Korhlen had had Krau murdered almost under the eye of his mother, before tossing her out into the forest. Yes, God's judgement indeed was on the Vre. And she, as she had said, was glad to be done with that Tower of villainy and blood. But her boy, her lovely Krau, she had only to think of him for enormous tears, fat from grazing in fields of hurt, to sluice down her face, which too was fat, and red and lax, from the beer she liked to drink. The yearly climax of her drama the village attended on with relish. They would listen to Veksa screaming and weeping in the miller's house. They would see her go out into the wood, there – as they knew – to brand evil on the souls of the men of Korhlen. Women who had beheld Veksa at her antics in the oak grove, where sometimes even now a bride might hang a string of coins or berries, saw her rocking a ghost baby in her arms, saw her pierce small lumps of tallow, having two legs, two arms and a penis, with pins whose heads were Korhlen amber.

As for the Korhlen Tower itself, she knew nothing of it, save what the now-and-then traveller might tell or invent. There had been fighting among the Raven kindred, for Kolris had left no heir, stipulated none. The enemy neighbour Esnias had paid some visits, too, and the Owl Tower. But these foragers were apparently beaten off.

Sometimes, when she had fed her dad his evening herbal, in which she mixed a little of this and that, to stay him in a sociable docile mood, Veksa would go into her tiny chamber and put on herself her jewels. There was the necklace of beaten gold her father had given her, stamped with the Korhlen Raven. There were bangles and earrings, the rings and combs and pins, the girdle of golden links, whose tying cords had had to be lengthened. In these she appeared for herself in her copper mirror. And she would say, twisting up her thick hair, sunny in her metal glass, 'Not so bad, my girl. He would have had luck to have kept you, rot him.' Even her red face in the copper looked only peachy. She had had men since Korhlen, better between sheets than he. She would raise her beer cup, drink, remember the one thing she had truly been robbed of. And the slick fat tears would ooze from her eyes. It was the mother felt the anguish. Her lad, her Krau... And then, perhaps, she would recall Mechail, malignly, speculatively. Was Mechail in Hell? As her hatred of him had gone on, perhaps he too continued, tortured and burning in the Pit. But if Mechail had gone to the Devil, then possibly Krau also had descended, as must she. And Veksa would kiss her amulets and offer a few redemptory prayers on holy days even to the Christus. She must live long in order to expiate her faults, for she was not certain she could give them over quite yet.

The forest was black and bannered with tawny lace the colour of the copper mirror: Autumn. As the sun came up, Veksa was dreaming that Krau stood in her room. He was in his crimson tunic, and the sunrise combed his hair, and he was grinning merrily, but only half his face was on.

Veksa woke in fright. She recognised an invitation from the dead. Though he was her son, she did not wish to go with him, not to that…

She prepared herself for life, dressing herself and putting round her neck the golden necklace, which none of the villagers would ever dare to snatch from her. She plaited her hair up on her head and put the amber pins into the plait.

At her breakfast she called for beer.

'You like your cup,' said her father, who liked his.

'There, Da. I'm drinking your health.'

Outside, in the fenced yard, she sent the thinner serving girl on an errand, and took the arm of the other, who was sometimes, in various acts, her accomplice. 'Go over to Nine Toes' house. Get a dove from his cot.'

'How if he says no, mistress?'

'Tell him, I say yes,' said Veksa. A quarter of an hour later, the girl was back with a cindery dove in a wicker casket. Veksa hid this in her apron, showing she had something but not what.

The grove of oaks lay half a mile beyond the village, out in the tawny-flushing wood, where the darkness of the pines surged like a wall. The sun was there. It was a bright morning, even under the trees.

Veksa entered the grove and going near the oak tree where the offerings were hung, she spoke words, ancient phrases almost nonsensical, that her aunt had taught her. Veksa did not know all their meaning, but she knew their intention. Then, she opened the cage and drew out the dove in her big hands. Used to human touch, the dove was quiet, and Veksa said to it, 'All's well,' as she walked straight at the tree, intending to smash the bird's neck directly on the trunk, before slicing with her sewing knife to let out the blood.

Six paces from the oak she heard the warning of the wood, the fanfare of lifting finches, scraping leaves, that evidenced some onslaught.

Veksa paused, clasping the dove. It was too late to hasten away, she would do best to stay, dumb and immobile. What came?

Through the cloister of oaks, against the black tapestry of pine trees, eight men rode through the forest in front of her. Their mounts were nourished and burnished, motes of sun broke on stirrups, the decorations of reins, and here and there on a jewel, for they were smart enough, the riders, in the forest way. A few black-brown dogs loped with the horses. Veksa felt the strangest thing, as if she had been whirled back in time. It was like the day Kolris had ridden into the village with his men and dogs, out hunting, seeing her suddenly, and the unrealised look on his face that said to her: *Take hold, your chance is here.* But she had been bereft of her chance. And the rider at the head of his men, he was not Kolris, for he was young and slender, clad in black and red like the wood. Then he wheeled his horse abruptly, swung round at her. She caught a scarlet arrow from a gem on his breast, and saw the embroidery worked at his shoulder, rust, green and purple, the Raven. An enormous bitch dog followed his horse, and as he drew rein, the dog leaned in on him, against his boot. And then Veksa saw his face in the clear sunlight.

Her mouth sagged and her hands undid themselves on the dove, which, instinctual at last, fluttered up and was gone among the beams of the wood.

The young man with the Korhlen badge grinned at Veksa, just as Krau had done. But his face was entire. That did not help. It would have been more suitable if he too had been the death's head.

Veksa said some more of her words, a forest spell.

'That won't bring you any assistance,' he said, 'old lady.'

She felt the bite of that, even in her extremity. Who, till now, had called her old?

'You're undead,' she screeched. 'Get away!'

'Listen to her,' said the man to his companions.

They were young nobles of the Tower. They laughed and spat, and the dogs grunted. 'My lord's wife,' said the man, 'is it you?'

'No, no,' she said, 'no.'

'You foul fat witch,' he said, 'shall we ride you down? For a deer you'd hardly be swift, you'd give us very little sport.'

Veksa toppled to her knees. She knelt there with the gold necklace on her throat, and the amber pins in her white hair. She was sobbing, but this time not for her son Krau.

'Mechail,' she said, 'I was never an unfriend to you.'

'You lying trollop,' he said. He did not grin anymore. His face was chill and priestly, as she remembered. He was all her memory, lean and strong and tall, black-haired like rage. An animal face, cat and wolf. The eyes were black now; they must have altered in the grave. She recalled their craziness, the flame that came and went, never going out. And the hunched shoulder, she remembered that, but it was mended, remoulded in Hell, and now he was flawless. 'I don't thank you, lady,' he said, 'for your nice wishes. Where's your son?'

Veksa groaned and covered her face. Under her breast a forge of fire had her heart on its anvil.

'Mechail Korhlen,' she said.

He had dismounted. He stood over her.

'I am Mechailus,' he said. 'I sit at dinner in the Raven Tower, and I sleep in the bed of Kolris. I have what I was bred to have. What Krau would have liked, but Krau's not got it, has he? They threw his bones out for me in the wood, so anything might take its pick that might find a use for them. The crows carried them off.'

Veksa did not cry any longer. She struggled to breathe and to listen.

Mechailus said, 'Only think, if you'd been a mother to me. Only think, if you'd been sweet and loving. Now Mechail would escort you back to his Tower, make of you a lady, perhaps succumb to your wiles, if you had any charms left, but you don't, old lady. And anyway, you were never kind.'

Veksa felt some squeezing obstruction give in her body. Streams of loosened pain ran down her arms, and up into her throat. She knew, like the warning of the wood, the forecast of death. She had no spirit left. She bared her face and looked at him. He was not Mechail. He was what Mechail had never been. And his eyes were black like some other's she had seen... So funny. So terrible.

'Veksa,' said Mechailus. His voice was melodious, winning. 'Come here to me, my darling.'

She stared, and the bitch dog came forward and leant now on his thigh gazing up at him, and he stroked her fierce head, to and fro.

He had given the dog her name.

Veksa's skull, under the weight of age and amber, sank down on her breast.

She heard them ride off, and the dogs running gladly.

She could not make her body get up to go to the village, and so she fell down on her side in the grove. She lay there feeling the life tick out of her like drips of water. She was stiff as a board. She could not move her hands or feet. She thought of rocking Krau in her arms. Had that been, or was it to come? She hoped it was to come.

Chapter Two

In the spring, the cathedral of the forest, green as an apple, candled with lights. Emerald on the pines. The grass, the moss, the fern. Where men had shorn the trees to make their tiny bivouacs of fields and huts, churches, villages, and Towers, how would it go in the end? Which would have which? For the forest ate the earth. Or would men eat it?

The question posed itself as he slept, but he woke, and the question was not.

The servant, Boroi, was thumping at the door. When he entered, he carried the usual things, the water and razor, the wine and bread,

Mechailus said, 'You're my clock, now. Give that here.'

The servant, who had come back out of the wood early in the spring before, no longer wore the torque of slavery. His brown face was a blank, but to Mechailus everything was discernible.

'Come on, then, shave me.'

As Boroi's razor smoothed his jaw, Mechailus sat in the Vre's chair of oak banded with brass. The western window was still dusk and Boroi performed his work by the shine of a candle, that in turn lit the masculine treasures of the room. The rings in their box, the cups of greenish glass. Light ribbed the purple raven on the bed curtains. When Boroi wiped his face, Mechailus took back the wine and sipped it.

As he dressed himself, Mechailus watched his reflection in the glass mirror.

I know who I am. No need to tell me.

The servant watched him too.

'What?'

'My lord's knife.'

'Yes, here it is. Ready for its day.'

Mechailus was also ready. He wore crimson, tunic, breeches, even the boots a treacled red. On his chest the crucifix centred its four black tines, and in them the crimson ruby, at one with him.

He broke the bread in his hands and gave a piece to Boroi. 'You finish the wine.'

Outside, the dawn was down in the yard with his men, waiting. The slaves of the house were also there, and inside the wall of the Women's Garden, the girls were already about in the orchard, gathering blooms for garlands, their voices wild and vernal, flowers come alive.

Mechailus looked around him. There were thirty men of the garrison and their captain, the nobles of the Tower, all mounted up. On foot, the plump priest, toying with his ash wood beads.

They brought Mechailus his horse, the sable gelding.

Mechailus went up into the saddle with the agility of the acrobat he had been, and still sometimes would be, to make them laugh or make them scare. Mounted, he seemed to fill his body with his spirit. He was alive as other men were not. Then he rapped the gelding lightly, and it started off, through the wide yard gates and on to the bad old road, dry from a week of rainlessness.

The soldiers, some of the slaves and servants of the house, fell in behind Mechailus, their lord. Behind these came the Tower court, the uncouth nobles in tan and purple. The priest walked along, telling his beads.

The fields sprawled under the sky, the forest rose over them, the rim of the bowl. There were no slaves on the fields today.

The feud with Esnias was over. The Korhlen clan had recently scorched out their valour and their quarrel. But they had raided the Owl Tower ten days before.

They turned on to the mill track. The mill was idle, its sails set.

Above the mill the track thinned and disguised itself among blue flowers, and then came in under the trees. Ahead, was visible the clearing, and the grove of birches, filigreed with slim green.

There in the core of the birch grove was the black stone. Mechailus sat his horse, regarding it. Father and mother. God and self.

Mechailus nodded to the stone, ignoring at first the man tied there.

The priest chanted; his beads clicked. If you heeded, you heard nothing Christian. They were the words of the wood. The priest knew them off by heart as he knew the Intercession, the forgiveness of sins. He believed that God was in the stone, as God was in the forest. Mechailus, who liked his tame priest, and went once a year to Khish and made liking to the priesthood there in the church, turned his wolf eyes inward at his own smiling. He knew where God was. He spun from the horse, which stood like a rock when he bade it do so.

The victim, trussed to the stone, had been assured of freedom and got drunk. Now he slumped, conscious of nothing, except dreaming maybe of his return to his Tower. (The black stone leaned, holding him close. *Mother and father.*) He was young, naked, only a blue bruise on his cheek to reveal how he had been made sure of.

Mechailus waited, as the soldiers, his pigs of nobles, the slaves with faces creaseless as new paper, formed up around the grove, which, with two years, had expanded itself to receive them.

The naked man was clean, bathed, shaven.

Mechailus approached him. He lifted the black lacquer cross on its silver chain and pressed its ruby lightly to the alien's lips. 'Your transgressions are forgiven you. Forget tomorrow. We thank you for your gift to this earth.' The knife was in his right hand. 'There is no Hell,' said Mechailus Vre Korhlen. He drove the knife into the man's body, braced for the resistance of flesh and muscle, and removed himself from the jetting blaze of blood, the hue of his garments. The man did not wake, only his brows twitched, relaxed, his head slipped sideways. He was dead. The mystery of the carcass, its mechanical astonishment laid wide, the steam of the blood that had showered the stone and the eternal ground, at these the assembly gazed in stillness, permitting them their honour. Then the shout was raised.

'Give me the cup.'

They brought it to the Vre, the captain and the priest, the nobleman whose daughter, likely, Korhlen would marry, come summer. The cup was of gold, with garnets, made in Khish for festivals.

Mechailus filled the cup from the life blood. He drank from the brim, gold and red. Then the slave came and poured in the blessed red wine. Mixed, the chalice went to the priest, to the captain, to the noble. And then the slave bore it to them all, the circle of the acolytes, and they drank of the Blood of the Life, of the Wine of the Sacrament.

Mechailus said to his priest, 'It was rich, this year. The crops will be sturdy.'

'Yes,' said the priest. 'This one was sound, God love him.'

One of the soldiers came and drew the knife out of the corpse. He cleaned it on a cloth and gave it back to the Vre.

'Are we absolved, godbrother?' said Mechailus.

The priest said, 'I absolve you, and all here.'

The sun was growing into the clearing in a silver branch. The black stone sparkled.

Mechailus called to his gelding, which stepped across to him and stayed waiting until he mounted.

They had known from the start, the Travellers, that the Dwarf was possessed, bewitched, something to be avoided, but – since they had not managed to avoid him – one to be treated with, bargains not war. For in with them he was. They had left him sleeping like the dead in their salt ring; riding through the night amid their landslip wagons, they found him again, trotting after them. This time he was in the actual flesh, and though they did not comprehend that, they gaged it. His knack in pursuit spoke volumes concerning his vitality, physical and otherwise. He had selected them as companions. They complied. Theirs was a stoic and experienced race.

He gave no trouble on the journey. In fact, he was a shining addition at the markets and roadsides where they made camp. He juggled goblets and daggers, became a human cartwheel, and presently acquired the craft of guessing what men had in their belts or up their sleeves. How he did this, without a mate to tip him off, they could not be certain. But then, perhaps he was a real magician, a shape-changer toiling back into his proper form. For he was never a day the same, so they noted. He shot up like a forward child, he lengthened and expanded. Inside a month his body fitted his head. And then everything realigned itself, like a sheet that was straightened. In the second month, when they moved away from the river through the late-harvesting grainlands, the tall dwarf was a tall vigorous man, well-proportioned and at the peak of his youth.

They would be able to tell of all this in tales in years to be; he would pass in among their legends and become one with them. But for now he was their liability. They were careful of him, to be fair and to be aloof. They gave him his share of their takings, the food and drink. Though he made no hint of anything towards their women, they drove them off from him. For it was a fact, the women were intrigued by Mechi, who had sprung down to them from the ruin by the sea.

He himself, offering no thought and few words, seemed only interested in the earth, the country through which they travelled. The city they had skirted he had stared at, turning in the saddle of the pony they lent him, looking at the uphill towers, the heavy steel coil of the river with its ships. And in the villages and ramshackle towns he would go off roving, a man now, nothing to be picked on, and come back just before sunrise, always amused at something, perhaps only the same thing; the ways of the world.

They did not try to slough Mechi. Occasionally they believed he would leave them. When he did not, they were philosophical. Of all the frightfulness, the worst had been that, though he had grown to man-shape and height before their eyes, they had not been able, at any moment or hour, to lay hold of it – for this was the subtle development of the plant in the sun. Yet it grew so fast that in a week they might glance back and measure it against its former self, and startle. They had to offer it, over and over, fresh clothes. If he had stretched like a bowstring in their view, they would have feared him more and shunned him less. This had been as if he tried to fool them with the unconscionable.

Winter began to finger the journey. One early morning two of the young Traveller men, savage with drink from a dubious tavern of the stubbled plain, stole up on Mechi in the lemon twilight. The younger rowdy had convinced himself that his betrothed cast her sight on the man-dwarf, to which attraction the man-dwarf had wheedled her through some hedgerow sorcery.

They meant, so they reckoned, to pin the wretch, cut his throat, haul the body away for the winter foxes, and then bother with what type it was, dwarf or man.

As they were leaning in, Mechi opened his eyes, black and lucid, youthful as something unimaginably ancient.

'And who is here?' said Mechi, who had begun to speak too in another way, placing words differently, so now and then they caught the voice of the trained alchemical priest he must have been.

'Clamp him!' snarled the would-be cutthroat.

The other grabbed and Mechi struck him a blow in the neck that sent him flying. Then Mechi looked at the knife and said, 'Stick it in. I'll die. Bury me. The others will see you and say, *Tut, ye shouldn't have done that.*' The cutthroat tensed for the killing swipe, and Mechi said, 'In a day or so I'll come up from the earth. I'll follow you. I'll bash your knife in through your mouth, through the soft of it, into your brain.' And then he punched hard in the boy's gut and pushed him off to bring up his noisy drink in a bush of frost.

But that was the winter day on which Mechi left the Travellers to their travelling.

He went with nearly nothing: the latest shirt and jacket and breeches, a scatter of coins he had earned, a withered apple plucked from a tree at the wayside. The pony, he left; and they soon found it was fractious with other riders.

Mechi walked over the plains, which were blasted now like the outlands of the punishing afterlife, under a white dizzied sky. It was cold, and Mechi had only cloth wrappings on his feet, which wore and came off. He had become bearded among the Travellers, where before a beard had never grown on him. He knew nothing in his formed brain of the Tree, which was all the trees, which sent out and reclaimed its life. He knew nothing of where they had gone, Mechail, Anillia, Jasha, Anjelen. But again, again, in the deepest chamber of thought, he did know, knew it all. Mechail had wrought Mechi through the semen and the ovum of the man and woman in the wood, through the psychic thrust of anger, pain and puzzlement. Now Mechail had ceased to be Mechail. At long last, Mechi might flow up to fill the empty shadow. All Mechail had denied in himself, that was Mechi. But now Mechail denied nothing. It was a saint's name, and Mechi put it on in its fullness, pleased by it, for he had every capacity for pleasure Mechail had put away. Mechi-Mechailus welcomed his uniqueness as the prisoner runs from his cell. He greeted the world like a ripe fruit. He was ready. For he had had to wait in chains.

When the dark began to rise from the plain, a coral hill in the sky was the sun going down, and Mechailus looked over his shoulder, and the Traveller girl was following him still. She was walking as he did, but her boots were stalwart, and she was strong. He had first heeded her at noon, when he sat a while on a stream bank observing the lethargic fish under the reeds. She was about two miles behind him.

She came close, as if they had been lovers, as close as that.

Then she stood there, looking at him. Mechailus in turn looked down from his young man's height and watched as she took out her knife and made with it a narrow slot of blood in her left wrist, among the bracelets of weasel-bone and painted husks.

'For me?' said Mechailus.

He raised her wrist and gently sucked out the blood from the wound. It was a pleasure, like everything else, a great pleasure, like eating or drinking, striding, riding, sleeping, sneezing, making water, having a fantasy of sex. No lesser pleasure of the flesh, and no more.

When he finished, he said, to her dreamy eyes, which heard on their own: 'You scratched yourself on a bramble, did you? Tear your skirt and bind it up tightly. Don't tell your kin, you know what they'll do. Put away your knife now.'

And when she had complied with these orders, he drew out from under his shirt the cross he had stolen from Anjelen, or that the Mechail in Mechi the dwarf had caused him to steal. He held it for the girl to see.

'What do you make of that?'

'A black moth,' said the girl, 'with its belly full of blood.'

'You're clever,' said Mechailus. 'What shall we do now?'

Then she put both her arms round his neck, the bracelets and bandage, the warm skin, the tindery inrush of long hair.

They lay in the bushes on the black leaves. He had her several times. She was the first woman he had had, ever.

In the morning he kissed her and sent her away, and she cried a little, but off she went. It was most ordinary. And the plain was the same scoured desolation, and the sky even whiter.

Mechailus overwintered on the plains, in two villages, and at a deserted inn. He behaved like a man and was treated like one, with suspicion and fellowship. Nothing of moment occurred, though to him everything was of moment, equally, from the village girl he was supposed to have got with child, and had not, to the beryl buds that shone around the inn's edges, the spring.

He knew everything there was to do, but he had never done any of it, and brought novelty and enjoyment to the mundane matters and the gross. When he got to Khish, he worshipped God and the Christus in the church, bought boots, a barber's razor, a knife, a sword that – never having done so – he understood exactly how to ply. He hired soldiers for his bodyguard and won a black gelding in a wine shop where someone had said five cups and a lighted torch could not be juggled.

The six men he took with him into the forest were enchanted by Mechailus, the novelty and enjoyment. They sensed in him an aspect of themselves that living had trampled over, they copied him, and it poked up its head. They believed his story, too, or taught themselves to believe it – that he was the heir to a Tower, an exiled wanderer, cheated by a stepbrother while the stepmother poisoned the lord.

Armed with this, they reached Korhlen.

The Tower had gone on with its functions, for the slaves had been made to see to that. But otherwise it had changed hands eight, nine times, as this or that one butchered and bundled himself to the crest of the heap. There had been no priest would stay there in five years, few tithes paid, and the church at Khish, having sent messages of disapproval, had heard out Mechailus in a small stone room and seemed not adverse to his tale, either.

But those were the tales. The truth would seem more curious. It would need tales to mask it over.

It had happened, the game of exchanges had come round to Gaj, the steward's son. He had grown corpulent, balded. But of the several who had known Mechail the crack-shouldered heir, he was the only one left of those who had stood by at the hour of Mechail's murder in the wood.

If ever it had been, the evening Cup Hall of the Korhlens was now a cave of beasts. Females, but for the slave women, had been excluded altogether. The men gathered to their fire, the long tables and the high table crossing them, the dogs slinking about among spillages. There were brawls and bouts of insane drunkenness, girls raped across benches; the walls smeared and the raftered Raven banner itself had been torn, draggled, as if they had had to make sure it showed how they slipped.

And that night there were even some Esnias at Gaj's board, for where the tithes had not gone to the Church they had wended to the neighbours, who would be in before too long, if nothing else was done.

Mechailus rode out of the forest with his six soldiers when the sky was violet and the dew was down. The poor road was there for them, with the muddle of village below, the inn, the Tower and its buildings, where the lights were blaring. The slave-tended mill revolved its sails. As they came closer, five dogs, gone wild from the Korhlen hunting packs, bounded over the track, baying, thin as strings.

'Omens, sir,' said one of the soldiers. 'So flee your foes.'

Mechailus laughed. 'They won't get so far.'

In the village, half abandoned, unkempt, the few lamps blinked, and spies looked out. The inn gate was off, and a goat sat in the gloom with Devil eyes.

At the Tower, the courtyard doors were secured but unguarded.

'Who can climb?' said Mechailus.

'What, up there, sir?'

'It was climbed once. The heir climbed it, to escape.'

And standing up on the gelding, which let him do anything, Mechailus gripped the beam, rose like fluid, and was gone over the top.

The soldiers exclaimed. Leaving two with the horses, four followed their lord's example, not so wieldy, but thorough enough to take them too up and down into the yard.

No one was out, all were in. Between the stone ravens, that had been hacked and spoiled, up the stair, the entry was open. Mechailus, ahead of his men, walked into the Hall.

For a while not one of them noticed. They were intent on the habitual loudness, liquor, the programme of the bear-cave.

Thus Mechailus hung over them like a sword, and in his brain maybe were the recollections of the one whose place he took, and those also of what he had been, many powerful impressions of powerlessness. If that was the case, he did not mind them. Most of all, he had the look of Anjelen, but an Anjelen alive, with the humour still there under his lips, although he was a wolf, a priest, a drinker of blood and night.

Then, someone did see. It was Gaj.

He choked and dropped his cup of wine, and clumsily jumped up. Through the torch-blear and the candles, he saw precisely who had come in. And as if there had been nothing in between, no years, no happenings, Gaj beheld Mechail Korhlen, who had risen from the dead, come back again for a taste more of revenge.

Between them, Gaj dampening his drawers, and Mechailus, an exquisite simplicity of arrival, the Cup Hall was jogged into awareness in wedges and dots. There were plenty now who could identify Mechail. How not, when he looked faithfully as he had done more than a decade ago, save for his straight shoulders, the curve to his mouth, the eyes the nearest might see were much blacker than black. Such items enhanced the reproduction, did not devalue it.

And most of the Hall knew the ghost story of Mechail. Dark nights it had even unnerved some of them. Even where they would not believe it, the weight of it had charge of them.

Mechailus went up the Hall then, between the silent tables, by the hearth where the house dogs cringed, fawned, wagged their tails, flattened themselves.

He went to the high table where once Mechail's father had sat, with Krau, and the blonde woman Veksa. And the four Khishan soldiers, who knew their job, stayed two at the door, and put two along after him, with hands on swords, courteously looking everywhere.

Mechailus came to Gaj.

'I...' said Gaj.

'You?' asked Mechailus and struck him between the eyes with his fist. Gaj leapt over backwards. He was dead; that was that.

And Mechailus sprang up on the table among the trenchers, cups, while the men there slewed away, trying for knives, snorting like hogs surprised.

'Here I am,' said Mechailus. 'One of you, name me.'

Silence.

A man fiddled with steel at Mechailus' back. Acrobat, trained fighter, the new prince of the Tower whipped round in a sort of jig. The bright Khishan sword cleavered through a neck and blood hit the rafter, splattered the banner as if it deserved it. The head skidded away like a child's ball. It was easy to kill men. One found it so.

Mechailus balanced on the table, bright red sword, friendly darkness.

'Come on, name me. Shall I offer a reward?'

The slaves were there, male and female, poised stilly, an absolute of acceptance. *They* knew, *they* named, but all without action or words.

Then a man shouted.

'Mechail!'

'Yes,' said the one on the table. 'Mechail, son of Kolris Vre Korhlen. If you know me, take me. Get on your knees."

His voice had an authority that must have come from tutoring in the church schools southerly. Oh yes. On your knees, it said, and on their knees they generally went, and where they did not, the four soldiers glanced, and it was thought better of, kneeling.

'You've made wreckage of my father's Hall, his hold, everything,' said Mechailus, enjoying, not harsh. 'For the Esnias here, they may leave. Take my greeting to the Esnias Tower. We'll return your visit.'

The Esnias men got up and hurried out, cheered to be alive.

'Now,' said Mechailus Vre Korhlen, 'where's dinner?'

It was during this dinner, so structured and momentous, that one thing happened that Mechailus received in another way. While the soldiers fenced him, taking precautions, and the Hall of men strove to emit duty, trapped as they were in a fable, an old thin dog, limping, came in at the door, and crept along between the tables and the servers, the ones who flung things at it, glad of release, the other dogs who snarled. The dog was not wild, it had not hunted in the wood. Its muzzle was grey, and it came to the high table, shivering, its dull eyes sure. The dog knew Mechailus, as the others knew Mechail. Oddly now it approached from the table's left, the bitch's side. It had made a bizarre partnership in the buildings of the Tower, and so survived. It knew Mechi, who had starved in the kennel with it. It knew Mechi even now.

Mechailus leant over the table and lifted the dog and brought her up on the table's top. His current nobles, who had not yet fallen under his magic (as they would; in six months he would be able to spell them to his will, even to the assailment of Esnias), reacted with disgust. Then shuttered it prudently.

But Mechail put the meat in his mouth, and so offered it to the bitch dog.

'Here's my lady,' said Mechailus, when she had eaten to his lips and he let go.

He smoothed her gently as she ate.

Later, as he lay in the chamber of the Vre, with two soldiers unneeded at his door, the bitch dog lay among the furs, spine to spine with him, for he had sent the woman away after their dalliance that the dog might slumber easily.

'Mechi,' said the fawn-haired girl, 'will you still call me to you, when you're wedded?'

'Of course,' said the young man in the bed. 'Provided you and she are amicable with each other.'

'But you'll make me go now. Will you make her go?'

'And provided you ask no questions about each other.'

When the girl had gone, the dog approached from the hearth. She had grown strong and young; her eyes were clear. She outstripped the other dogs of Korhlen. She could kill any of them she wanted. Mechailus stroked her jaws, her forehead. 'Now rest. Tonight you must be with me for Korhlen's Feast of the Sacrifice.' The bitch dog mounted the bed and lay with her dark head upon her malt-brown paws. She had watched as he drank the blood of the fawn-haired girl. In the room was the scent of it, with the burning cones on the hearth, the spangle of spring.

'Veksa,' said Mechailus to the dog, really to joke, and slept.

A scene engraved in ruby, the Korhlen Cup Hall. The torches red, the flush-red walls, the rafters like cinnabar.

Once, in the winter, their Vre had come to the centre of the Hall and juggled scarlet apples for them, but the apples melted – they were made of blood. Once he juggled with a globe of quartz that burst, and out ran the green sea.

Now he sat at the high table and led the feast. His pigs and bears were crowned with flowers and ivy. The women returned in all their trinkets and half the roses of the earth. They would get very drunk tonight, and they would come to him, up to the high table, and offer their wrists with tiny and concise cuts, and he would sip from them. The Hall was not as it had ever been, yet noisier maybe than ever before, and looking at it from a distance, where the light shone out, who could not tell by its redness, something.

And beyond the gardens, in the women's apartments, the glow and sound were muted, like a far red star, that sometimes growled or sang.

'The dog never comes now,' said Chirda. 'Do you remember the dog we fed?'

'She was blind nearly. Once I looked for her,' said Charina. 'I think he has her.'

'*He.*'

In the spring darkness without the moon, they sat together on their bed, two small elderly children, with long white fragile hair, and blossom breasts lying on their skeletal bodies like lilies on rope.

'I'm cold,' said Chirda. 'Cold, cold.' She snivelled, forgot to, plucked up a rag from the bed, petted it.

They had met the dog on the grass by the willow tree. They had been afraid, and Chi had waved her arms, but the dog came to them on its belly, seeming to take them for its sisters. They found she was a bitch dog. She trailed them to their cavern of room, and sniffed the moulting civet, and put her head on their knees.

Sometimes, even then, a slave would bring them scraps of food. They nibbled them, not having any appetite, and once Puss (Chirda), had snapped at the slave girl with her teeth and drawn a fleck of blood, and had that. They gave most of their paltry meals to the dog, and at night they lay beside her, and Puss hugged her and had dreams, sighing *Mamma*.

Then he came, and the dog left them. He never came to them, though sometimes at first, sensing him, they had gone on to their balcony and looked for him.

'Is he on the walk?'

'Will he be kind to us?'

They confused him with Krau, and their moistureless old bodies, prematurely aged to those of skinny hags, palpitated with green shades of lust, but this fell from them like petals.

'Do you remember,' said Puss, 'when Mamma would take us into the wood?'

They sat and stared into the crystal of false memory: Mamma had never taken them anywhere. But, in the quartz of illusion, she altered. She grew succulent and dear.

'Shall we go in the wood,' said Puss wistfully, a little crone girl.

Chi got up. 'We shall need a torch, to see.'

They went down from the galleried apartment, past the willow, and along the garden walk. There were lights in plenty now, since the massacre of the Esnias, the burgeoning of the Raven. The garrison guard were on the walls, but drunken. Korhlen was sorcerous. Odd things were said of its Vre. Who would outface jeopardy and try for it, even on the feast night of the sacrifice?

Near the doors, in the yard, a lit torch lay on the paving. Someone might have put it out for their convenience. Chi took it up. Seeing them, one of the soldiers mocked and bowed. 'Off on an outing, ladies? Go careful now.'

They went out through the open square of the doors and strayed along the track, and the soldiers watched them go, attaching no significance, not concerned as to who or what they might be, for they were also merely women.

Anjelen made them, via semen and ovum of man and woman, and the psychic thrust of will. Choked Catra's daughters.

It was a bleak night for spring. By the path the flowers hid their heads, the grass was sleeved with frost.

'Cold,' said Puss. 'It was never cold when we were with Mamma.'

But even in the false memory, Mamma was not with them. They were alone in the forest, up beyond the house, the mill, the grove, into the night.

'In the wood,' said Chi, 'who is this coming?'

'Who is it?' said Puss anxiously.

'He has a black horse. On his shield is a rose. His cloak is bones. Mind the thorns.'

Puss minded them, though none were there.

The forest was enormous, as was the night, and they were one. The towers of the trees resolved in sky and there the stars were dashed, unfinished and not near enough. The frigid grasses splintered, and through the aisles creatures fluttered on winged feet.

'I'm cold,' said Puss.

'The wood's cold,' said Chi. 'Nasty, uncharitable.' She looked about and wondered where they had thrown the remains of Krau, a deed done in some parallel life. On her wrist was a straight pink scar; it had stayed with her, like her sister. Raising the torch, of which she had sole command, she saw the cold black needles of a pine, like claws to rake her eyes, and put the fire into them.

'Look!' cried Puss. All her attention was garnered.

The pine tree was blossoming with gold, so bright, so beautiful. A gust went up its tower into the roof of night. Perhaps the stars would burn better for it.

'Will Mamma come?' asked Puss.

Chi shook her head. She thought of Catra with the worm in her throat, dying on the floor. She pushed her torch into a thicket, and golden vines curled up and away. The dark was glinting with fireflies now. Sparks arced and dazzled.

Puss clapped her hands.

The wood was on fire.

The two albino crone girls stood at its heart, on the pyre, watching. The tinsel vapour of Chi's garment caught alight. As Chi moved to see it, she smiled at last, a very little, and fed her own dress into the circling feeding flowers. 'Pretty,' said Puss. Her white hair was saffron, Chi's hair was silver-red. Such loveliness. The wood began to race with flight and terror. The pine trunks burst like bonfires and the sky howled. 'It's warm,' said Puss. 'It's warm.'

About the Author

Tanith Lee (1947-2015) was born in London. Because her parents were professional dancers (ballroom, Latin American) and had to live where the work was, she attended a number of truly terrible schools, and didn't learn to read – she was also dyslectic – until almost age 8. And then only because her father taught her. This opened the world of books to her, and by 9 she was writing. After much better education at a grammar school, she went on to work in a library. This was followed by various other jobs – shop assistant, waitress, clerk – plus a year at art college when she was 25-26. In 1974, her career as a writer was launched, when DAW Books of America, under the leadership of Donald A. Wollheim, bought and published *The Birthgrave*, and thereafter 26 of her novels and collections.

Tanith was presented with a Lifetime Achievement Award in 2013, at World Fantasycon in Brighton. During her lifetime, she also received the World Horror Convention Grand Master Award, as well as the August Derleth Award and the World Fantasy Award for short fiction (twice).

In 1992, she married the writer-artist-photographer John Kaiine, her partner since 1987. They lived on the Sussex Weald, near the sea, in a house full of books and plants, and never without feline companions. She died at home in May 2015, after a long illness, continuing to work until a couple of weeks before her death.

Throughout her life, Tanith wrote around 100 books, and over 300 short stories. 4 of her radio plays were broadcast by the BBC; she also wrote 2 episodes (*Sarcophagus* and *Sand*) for the TV series *Blake's 7*. Her stories were read regularly on Radio 4 Extra. She was an inspiration to a generation of writers and her work was enormously influential within genre fiction – as it continues to be. She wrote in many styles, within and across many genres, including Horror, SF and Fantasy, Historical, Detective, Contemporary-Psychological, Children and Young Adult. Her preoccupation, though, was always people.

Books by Tanith Lee

Series

The Birthgrave Trilogy (The Birthgrave; Vazkor, son of Vazkor
[published as Shadowfire in the UK], Quest for the White Witch)
The Blood Opera Sequence (Dark Dance; Personal Darkness; Darkness, I)
The Flat Earth Opus (Night's Master; Death's Master; Delusion's
Master; Delirium's Mistress; Night's Sorceries)
The Lionwolf Trilogy (Cast a Bright Shadow; Here in Cold Hell;
No Flame But Mine)
The Paradys Quartet (The Book of the Damned; The Book of the Beast;
The Book of the Dead; The Book of the Mad)
The Venus Quartet (Faces Under Water; Saint Fire; A Bed of Earth;
Venus Preserved)
The Vis Trilogy (The Storm Lord; Anackire; The White Serpent)
The FOUR-Bee Series (Don't Bite the Sun; Drinking Sapphire Wine)
The S.I.L.V.E.R. Series (Silver Metal Lover; Metallic Love)

Novels and Novellas

34
The Blood of Roses
Companions on the Road
Days of Grass
Death of the Day
Electric Forest
Elephantasm
Eva Fairdeath
The Gods Are Thirsty
Kill the Dead
Heart-Beast
A Heroine of the World
Louisa the Poisoner
Lycanthia
Madame Two Swords
Mortal Suns
Reigning Cats and Dogs
Sabella
Sung in Shadow
Vivia
Volkhavaar
When the Lights Go Out
White as Snow

The Winter Players

Young Adult and Children's Fiction
Animal Castle (picture book)
The Castle of Dark
The Claidi Journals (Law of the Wolf Tower; Wolf Star Rise,
Queen of the Wolves, Wolf Wing)
The Dragon Hoard
East of Midnight
The Piratica Novels (Piratica 1; Piratica 2; Piratica 3)
Prince on a White Horse
Princess Hynchatti and Other Surprises
Shon the Taken
The Unicorn Trilogy (Black Unicorn; Gold Unicorn; Red Unicorn)
The Voyage of the Bassett: Islands in the Sky

Story Collections
Blood 20
Cold Grey Stones
Colder Greyer Stones
Cyrion
Dancing in the Fire
Disturbed by Her Song
Dreams of Dark and Light
Fatal Women
Forests of the Night
The Gorgon
Hunting the Shadows
Nightshades
Phantasya
Red as Blood – Tales from the Sisters Grimmer
Redder Than Blood
Sounds and Furies
Tamastara, or the Indian Nights
Space is Just a Starry Night
Tempting the Gods
Unsilent Night
Women as Demons

Tanith Lee Titles Published by Immanion Press

This anthology is a tribute to Tanith Lee, comprising short stories written shortly after her death by some of her writer friends to whom Tanith was a profound influence and inspiration: Storm Constantine, Cecilia Dart-Thornton, Vera Nazarian, Sarah Singleton, Kari Sperring, Sam Stone, Freda Warrington and Liz Williams. With an introduction by Tanith's husband, the artist John Kaiine. Illustrated throughout by the contributors and with photographs from Tanith Lee's personal collection.

IMMANION PRESS

Purveyors of Speculative Fiction

A Wolf at the Door by Tanith Lee

Includes 13 tales, most of which appeared only in magazines or rare anthologies. 'A wolf at the door' implies hidden threat – until the door is open, we don't really know what's out there. And now the beast is upon you, scratching at the wood, its hot breath steaming on the step. Will you survive the encounter? Perhaps, once the door is opened, what you might have thought to be a threat turns out to be something else entirely. But of course, it can also be a werewolf…
ISBN 978-1-912815-04-3, £11.99, $15.99 pbk

Breathe, My Shadow by Storm Constantine

A standalone Wraeththu Mythos novel. Seladris believes he carries a curse making him a danger to any who know him. Now a new job brings him to Ferelithia, the town known as the Pearl of Almagabra. But Ferelithia conceals a dark past, which is leaking into the present. In the strange old house, Inglefey, Seladris tries to deal with hauntings of his own and his new environment, until fate leads him to the cottage on the shore where the shaman Meladriel works his magic. Has Seladris been drawn to Ferelithia to help Meladriel repel a malevolent present or is he simply part of the evil that now threatens the town?
ISBN: 978-1-912815-06-7 £13.99, $17.99 pbk

The Lord of the Looking Glass by Fiona McGavin

The author has an extraordinary talent for taking genre tropes and turning them around into something completely new, playing deftly with topsy-turvy relationships between supernatural creatures and people of the real world. 'Post Garden Centre Blues' reveals an unusual relationship between taker and taken in a twist of the changeling myth. 'A Tale from the End of the World' takes the reader into her developing mythos of a post-apocalyptic world, which is bizarre, Gothic and steampunk all at once. Following in the tradition of exemplary short story writers like Tanith Lee and Liz Williams, Fiona has a vivid style of writing that brings intriguing new visions to fantasy, horror and science fiction. ISBN: 978-1-907737-99-2, £11.99, $17.50 pbk

www.immanion-press.com
info@immanion-press.com

www.ingramcontent.com/pod-product-compliance
Lightning Source LLC
Chambersburg PA
CBHW020946260626
47169CB00006B/1847